THE
FIRST
SISTER

BOOK ONE OF THE FIRST SISTER TRILOGY

THE FIRST SISTER

A NOVEL

LINDEN A. LEWIS

SKYBOUND BOOKS / GALLERY BOOKS

NEW YORK   LONDON   TORONTO   SYDNEY   NEW DELHI

Skybound Books / Gallery Books
1230 Avenue of the Americas
New York, NY 10020

First Skybound Books / Gallery Books trade paperback edition February 2021

Skybound is a registered trademark owned by Skybound, LLC.

GALLERY BOOKS and colophon are trademarks of Simon & Schuster, Inc.

For information about special discounts for bulk purchases, please contact Simon & Schuster Special Sales at 1-866-506-1949 or business@simonandschuster.com.

The Simon & Schuster Speakers Bureau can bring authors to your live event. For more information or to book an event, contact the Simon & Schuster Speakers Bureau at 1-866-248-3049 or visit our website at www.simonspeakers.com.

Interior design by Michelle Marchese

Manufactured in the United States of America

10   9   8   7   6   5   4   3   2   1

Library of Congress Cataloging-in-Publication Data has been applied for.

ISBN 978-1-9821-2699-5
ISBN 978-1-9821-2700-8 (pbk)
ISBN 978-1-9821-2701-5 (ebook)

To Pablo, the Rapier to my Dagger

CHAPTER 1

[14] The men came unto Sister Marian and demanded of her the truth that belonged to her Captain. [15] But Sister Marian was a woman of the Goddess and refused them. [16] She said unto them, "By betraying my Captain, I betray myself." [17] And she took the knife with which she prepared the supper for her Captain and cut out her tongue, so that no man might compel her to speak.

The Canon, Works 3:14–17

The new fool captain arrives in two hours, so I sort my belongings and pack them into a small bag. Even with all of them together, I have plenty of room. Ringer offered me one of the military trunks that all Gean soldiers keep locked at the ends of their cots, but I refused him because there is nothing I can take that does not technically belong to the battleship ACS *Juno*, my gray uniforms included. My shoulder bag carries only three sets of underclothes and one pair of boots, but I hold tight to it regardless; just because these items are nothing important does not mean I will leave them behind for the next person who claims my title. What's mine is mine, even if the room no longer will be. Today I am leaving this ship, and I refuse to come back.

Will I miss it? It's not the bed, wide enough for two, or the immense size of the suite, nearly three times larger than the rooms the other Sisters share, that will carve this space into my mind; it's the presence of memories here, haunting me like ghosts. I remember lying sprawled beneath the livecam screen, watching the stars streak past. The way the sheets brushed against my cheek, soft as silk, when I pressed my face into the pillows. How I would wake in the night and feel steady, recognizing even the shadows in the corners, instead of lost in an unfamiliar land.

I shouldn't miss it, though. Soon I will have a whole house full of beautiful rooms like this one.

To think, I will own a *house*. Me, who has never owned anything substantial in her entire life. I shouldn't care that Second Sister will move into this room when I leave, this place as close to a home as I have ever had; I will have so much more than her that I won't even think of her again when I settle on Mars with Captain Deluca. *With Arturo*, I correct myself.

I wave my hand at the room as if to erase it from my mind, and let my eyes blur to take in the shapes instead of the actual furnishings. The spherical screen like a port window with its live view of the stars, the dresser and its three drawers, the sturdy square bed—all become vague hazes of colors instead of solid objects. I step into the hallway with my head held high and let the door slide closed behind me. I do not look back.

Since the *Juno* is an *Athena*-class warship of Icarii make, seized a year ago in battle, the hallways are wide enough for two men to pass by without breaking stride. The oblong ship, black as space, is both stealthy and comfortable. My first ship assignment had been a small Gean pleasure liner, cylinder-shaped and constantly spinning to create gravity, and even as thin as I was, I had to shift sideways to walk down certain corridors. I never understood how the broad-shouldered soldiers made do, men like Ringer, who stands solid in his navy-blue Gean uniform at end of the hallway, waiting to see me off.

"First Sister." Ringer bows his head to me, ever the faithful parishioner. His piousness is eclipsed only by the kindness in his silver eyes. If we were alone, he might pull me against his wide, muscular chest and hold me tightly, but that would be all he would do. His hands would not wander, his eyes would not burn with lust, unlike so many of his fellow soldiers'. "Are you ready?"

I put on the mask of happiness tinged with concern, a slight furrow of the brows mixed with a tentative smile. As a Little Sister at the Temple of Mars atop the glorious heights of Olympus Mons, I always pleased my Aunt Delilah with my animated expressions, with the way I imparted a mix of feelings with a simple adjustment of eye and mouth. She impressed what an exceedingly important skill communicating in subtle glances was for Sisters to learn. A necessity, once your voice has been taken.

"I know you'll miss us here—and we'll miss you—but you'll adjust to your new life." Ringer's thin lips pull taut in a smile, but the rest of his expression remains static. His face is that of Mars stone, sharp and deeply pitted, an unfinished sculpture of a warrior at rest. "You deserve what happiness Captain Deluca can give you."

My smile fades. I offer a solemn nod. I will soon be free of the Sisterhood's politics—no more jealous Sisters, no more controlling Aunties—but I must not look too eager.

Another reason I maintain a steady friendship with Ringer: he intuits what I want to express. I wish to look like I will miss the *Juno*, like Arturo is taking me away from duty and home, instead of appearing excited and ready to abandon my post, and that is what Ringer sees. He may be one of the few from this ship I will think of fondly on Mars.

"Do you need an escort?"

I shake my head and clutch my bag to my chest. Ringer has been good to me on the *Juno*. In thanks, I hold out my hand, and Ringer, a head taller than me, kneels. I press my palm to his forehead between his blond hair and thick dark brows and close my eyes as if praying, offering him one last blessing. But the words running through my head are those that Arturo whispered to me, a description of my new house. *A home in the gravity-controlled dunes with a little patio in the sun where you can grow pansies and honeysuckle . . .*

"Thank you, First Sister," he whispers.

My fingertips slide from his forehead to his cheek and trail down his stubbled chin. He watches my hand retreat to join the other gripping my bag. When Ringer stands, he offers me a traditional Gean salute, his right fist clenched over his chest, his arm parallel to the ground. The salute is meant for those higher ranking, usually officers, and while the Sisterhood is exempt from military hierarchy, his gesture is an honor. I am unaccustomed to being saluted, and pride swells within me.

I make sure to keep my smile bright as I part from Ringer and back into the elevator. Just as the door is closing, an arm snakes into the gap, and the door reopens fully lest it crush the slender limb. Second Sister steps inside, and Third Sister trails close behind, both dressed in the same gray as me, only without the white captain's armband pinned about their right biceps. They smile like I do, but I can see through their expressions; the rest of the cosmos might be blind to our true meanings, but we Sisters know each other well.

Aunt Marshae comes floating after, prim face pinched into a smile that does not quite reach her eyes. I do my best not to let my frustration show; I had hoped to escape the *Juno* without facing her, cowardly as it might be. Our Aunties are charged with the task of speaking on behalf of the Sisterhood, and while Aunt Marshae has trained Little Sisters to hone their expressions, she rarely masters her own. But another reason for her sour look flowers in my mind.

She wants me to see her displeasure.

"You look lovely today, First Sister." My Auntie sniffs pointedly. The door closes after her, trapping me in the circular elevator with the three of them. I am deeply aware of each sharp pair of eyes turned in my direction.

I tuck my bag beneath my arm and tangle my fingers in my skirt, purposefully keeping my hands still. Aunt Marshae straightens her uniform, the same gray as mine but more covering, with a scarf about her neck and a hemline that falls to the floor. "Perhaps leaving the *Juno* and its believers thrills you?"

I quickly put on the mask of hurt. Furrowed brows and a trembling lip. I'd cry if I could. *Of course not,* my face says. *I would never want to leave my Sisters.* At least, I hope it does, but my Auntie laughs.

"Your face does credit to your training," she mutters, but she finally looks away from me. "If you girls have anything to say to First Sister, now is the time."

Second Sister's milky white fingers tuck inky black hair behind her ears in order to give her hands something to do while she considers what to say. I expect her to rebuke me or express her thankfulness at my leaving; Second Sister was Captain Deluca's favorite companion on their previous ship, but as soon as we all moved to the *Juno*, Arturo promoted me over her. I suspect I will never be forgiven for that. But instead of the expected hatred, her hands move with grace and poise. Her smile is genuine, reflected in her amber eyes. *Much luck in your future,* she signs in the hand language reserved for the Sisterhood by law.

I'm so surprised by her gesture it takes me a moment to respond. *Thank you,* I sign at last.

This is our sole method of communication, we Sisters, for we are not allowed to write and we cannot speak.

Third Sister shoulders the smaller Second Sister aside on her way to me. If Second Sister has held a grudge against me, Third Sister outright hates me. She glares at me, her lip curled, fury radiating out of her green eyes. Her vibrant red hair looks like fire as she whips it over her shoulder. Her hands flash at me. *Get out and good riddance,* she says, ending with an offensive gesture that even the soldiers would understand. She flattens her hand like a blade and slaps it on her sternum, as if cutting her heart in two.

I straighten to my full height and look down on her. She is almost as tall as I am, but I have long been favored for my slender legs and golden hair, and I remain defiant even in the face of her anger. Second Sister seizes Third Sister's biceps and digs her fingers into the soft flesh there, stopping the red-haired girl from doing anything more than signing. Aunt Marshae says nothing.

Long ago, when I was not a ranked Sister, just a girl first assigned to the small pleasure liner, Third Sister might have cornered me in the bunks where there were no cameras. She could have had others hold my limbs so that she could pull my hair or strike my body with the flat of her hand, avoiding my face and trying not to leave bruises.

But that is the way of being a Sister, and all of us have both endured these attacks and led them.

For now, I am lucky, and I have been so for a long time. With my excellent physical features, I became a ranked Sister quickly, and the Mother herself rewarded me with my posting on the *Juno*. From the moment I met Arturo, I received his favor, and he rewarded me with private quarters and the captain's armband, allowing only him to call on me for anything more than confession. Third Sister has never been able to lay a hand on me. She is as powerless now as she has been since I was promoted above her.

"Walk with the Goddess in this new season of your life." Aunt Marshae's words are but an empty platitude from the Canon, the book that guides the Sisterhood. She also favored me until Arturo asked for me as a lifelong companion in his retirement. Since his request, she has made it clear that she had higher hopes for me. *Your success is my success, niece,* she used to say. Now she says little other than to shame me.

I will bloom in Her Garden as She commands, I sign in answer to Aunt Marshae, but my Auntie simply scoffs, clearly believing I am not blooming as I should be. *Farewell,* I sign to the others.

As soon as the elevator reaches the docking bay, we trail out—me first, as befits my rank, followed by amber-eyed Second Sister and red-haired Third Sister, whose bitterness somehow hasn't put her at a disadvantage in life. Aunt Marshae comes last, herding the other two girls in the opposite direction from me.

I shouldn't have expected heartfelt goodbyes from anyone on this ship, particularly when a large part of my reason for accepting Arturo's offer was to escape people like them. On Mars, I'll only have to care for and impress Arturo; how much easier it will be when I don't have to worry after my fellow Sisters and Auntie too. My stomach unclenches as I enter the docking bay and cast my eyes about the various ships moored there. Which one will I be taking away from the *Juno*?

The side of the hangar gapes, openmouthed, and beyond it the swallowing black of space and the light of a thousand burning stars. It looks like a window to the cosmos, a thick pane of faintly glowing glass between the outer vastness and the *Juno*'s interior, but it's actually advanced Icarii tech that allows ships to launch and dock at will while keeping oxygen inside. The shield is created by the hermium engine, technology built with a substance specific to Mercury. Hermium is so influential to Icarii designs that it's also the basis for the *Juno*'s gravity generators and power system. Most Geans will never experience technology like this in their lifetimes.

If only the Icarii would share their hermium. Doing so could save all of our planets. But the Icarii have forgotten their origins now that they live lavishly on Mercury and Venus, abandoning their humanity just as they abandoned Earth and Mars. We Geans remember; we have a long memory, and the Sisterhood's is longer than that. We have been here since the beginning of it all.

We were the ones who worked on Earth against the pollution that tore apart the planet. We were the advisers to captains from the very first mission to colonize Mars. We preached against the excess of machinery, rightly predicting the Synthetic rebellion against humanity. And now we watch over both Earth and Mars as half of the Gean government, providing homes for the homeless, jobs for the jobless, and health centers for the sick. We exist to ensure no one repeats the mistakes of our past. As a species, we simply cannot afford another Dead Century War.

The ships moored in the docking bay vary in size from small cruisers, two-man craft used for errands, to military carriers that drop infantry planetside, a mix of Gean-made and those seized from the Icarii. I don't see Arturo anywhere, but the bay is full of workers, as usual, men and women in jumpsuits unloading crates of rations, mechanics working under metal panels or on the humped backs of various craft. A group is gathered on the far side of the bay. Since Arturo was the *Juno*'s captain for its first year of service under the navy-and-gold Gean flag, he is sure to be in the middle of that crowd, receiving praise and saying his goodbyes. He's had a home here on the *Juno*, one that I've helped to provide with my loyalty and love.

It is an odd sensation when no one looks at me as I approach; I am accustomed to attracting attention as if I were shouting aloud. But then, all at once, faces turn to me and blanch.

I keep my expression neutral. Unease ripples through the crowd as more people turn to me, as their voices quiet to murmurs, as someone points at me but says something only to their companion.

A fist tightens in my chest, holding my heart captive. Why is everyone acting like this? Where is Arturo?

The crowd steps back from me at my approach, creating a bubble around me, a liminal space they cannot—or will not—touch. The jovial chatter dims and dies, and only whispers remain. Eyes look anywhere but at me: at their formal uniforms, at the surrounding shuttles, at the glasses of sparkling water filled with strawberries as red as my lips from the hydroponic gardens.

But where is Arturo?

I look at the clock: 0900 hours, the time of his disembarkation. Yet I don't see him or any members of his family come to retrieve him.

"You must be the First Sister," a smoky voice says. Some girl in Gean uniform steps forward; it's hard to tell her age, but I doubt she's even a handful of years older than my twenty. As soon as she speaks, the crowd takes it as encouragement to resume their celebrations, chatter picking up as if, thank the Mother, someone put an end to the First Sister's hysteria.

I clutch my bag tightly to keep my hands from shaking. I have eyes only for this soldier, her hair shaved on the sides but long on top, fluffed up like some greenboy's. If I look anywhere other than her, I may wither, so I harden my face.

"Captain Deluca wanted me to personally offer his thanks for your year of service on the *Juno*," she says, her voice low and heady. She places a hand on my shoulder and guides me to her side, turning my back to the crowd. She doesn't want anyone else to hear what she has to say. Or, more likely, she doesn't want anyone to see my naked reaction to her words.

She leads me deeper into the docking bay, back toward the elevator, ushering me away from where I should be. Where I *need* to be.

Where is Arturo?!

I cannot ignore my panic any longer. I ground myself and stop walking. She halts as well when she realizes I no longer intend to follow. "Do you know who I am?" she asks.

I shake my head. Perhaps because she was part of the celebration, her uniform is disheveled, her jacket unbuttoned, revealing a white tank top beneath. I cannot see her command rank. Besides, I don't care. I shouldn't be answering to anyone other than Arturo.

He *promised* me.

"I'm Saito Ren." As soon as she says her name, I realize that I *do* know who she is. She's the new captain of the *Juno*.

She's Arturo's replacement.

And if she's already here, if she's part of his farewell party, then he really is—

I spin back to the docking bay and look for his ship through the crowd of people. Where is it? Where is he? How could he—

He promised me.

Captain Saito seizes my shoulder and turns me toward her, quick and effortless. "I'm sorry you missed him. He wanted to say his farewells, but he didn't want to miss his flight."

But it was supposed to be at 0900 hours! That's the time now! That's the time he told me, and yet he's already gone . . .

He left me.

The truth sinks bone-deep and leaves me shaking. The fist holding my heart squeezes until it pops. All of his promises whispered between white sheets meant nothing. The house he described is gone, the two bedrooms and the patio I could fill with flowers and the latest gadgets, the home he would visit twice a month when he could get away from his wife and children.

Did that house even exist? Why would he promise to take me with him and then abandon me as he left? Why would he promise me my freedom from the intricacies of the Sisterhood only to leave me in their clutches?

Certainly this is a mistake. He didn't mean to leave me. Surely he'll send for me when he gets settled, and this Captain Saito just hasn't given me that part of his message yet.

I look at her, but . . .

"Should I call a medic?" Captain Saito's voice is stern, almost disapproving. I realize how unsteady I must seem, and I quickly school my face into blankness. I press a hand to my stomach and count my breaths. Even if my heart races, I cannot outwardly show how utterly destroyed I am. How terrified I am.

Because if Arturo really left me—*And he did*, a little voice whispers—then I am stuck here as First Sister with a new captain who may promote someone more favored to my position. I am not free, and I am not safe. And if I cannot keep my position as First Sister?

I press my hand to the white captain's band on my arm and remember Third Sister's hateful gesture in the elevator. Back to the bunks, back to the beatings.

I need to leave—I need to return to my room and reassess before someone sees me so undone—

Aunt Marshae appears at our sides before I can extract myself from the conversation with Captain Saito. Goddess wither it, now I must deal with her as well.

"I just heard the news," she says, and this time her smile radiates through her entirety—her lips, her eyes, even the roots of her sculpted auburn hair, hard as an Ironskin helmet. "What a blessing that you will continue to work alongside us, First Sister." I clench my fists to hide their trembling as her deft hands strip the white band from my arm. "Though this belongs to you, Captain Saito, until you see fit to distribute it."

"I suppose so." Captain Saito takes the armband and rubs her thumb over the coarse fabric.

I look at my bare arm, and . . . I am as good as naked now.

I am again property of the soldiers. My *body* is their property.

"Aunt Marshae, I'd like to see all the highly ranked Sisters, and even some of your best unranked girls, in my quarters later. First Sister, will you come by?" Captain Saito calls my attention back to the docking bay. She makes it sound like a suggestion.

But it's an order. With a captain, it's always an order.

My Auntie nods encouragement, and I mimic her though my eyes burn. I want to retreat to a hidden room and cry—wordlessly.

"Then I will see you soon," Captain Saito says. "If you'll excuse me, I have a schedule I must keep." She marches away without a second glance. I try to swallow, but my throat is too dry.

"May you bloom in Her Garden as She commands," Aunt Marshae says in a sick parody of my earlier words. Second Sister and Third Sister start across the docking bay to join us, and I break away at their approach. I do not want them to see how shattered I am. I do not want to read their gloating words on their hands.

I start my long walk back to my quarters, my few belongings in the small bag clutched tightly to my chest. This is not the way a First

Sister should act, but for the life of me, I cannot do anything other than run away like a fool.

At least I reach the elevator before the tears come. I try to blink them away, but then the intercom overhead clicks on in warning and Captain Saito's voice fills the small space with me. Haunting me, even here.

"As of 0900 hours this morning, you are no longer under the command of Captain Arturo Deluca."

The tears roll down my cheeks in thick tracks.

"I am Captain Saito Ren, and I am honored to be taking this journey alongside such a brave and diverse crew on the most advanced battleship in the Gean fleet. You are the pride of Earth and Mars, and together, we will more than fulfill our duty to protect Ceres and keep our newly claimed territory clear of Icarii ships."

My nose runs. I do what Aunt Delilah told me never to do and rub my face; in this moment, it does not matter that I'm breaking the sensitive capillaries in my skin.

"I have one simple goal: to serve the Gean worlds."

The elevator doors open, and I thank the Goddess that the hallway is empty except for a single Cousin with a broom. She turns her wrinkled face from me. The hard laborers of the Sisterhood and the only sect that accepts men, the Cousins are nothing more than servants—and a reminder of what happens to a Sister when she is no longer beautiful or wanted.

Is that what will become of me now that Arturo has left me behind?

"I will fight without mercy to keep the Gean people from perishing as our planets wither."

Finally, *finally*, I come to my quarters and open the door with shaking hands.

"I will not allow for any distractions that interfere with our future."

My knees give out beneath me before I can even reach the bed.

"This is no longer Captain Deluca's ship. This is my ship. And you will find it a different place than before. A changed place."

There is nowhere I can go that Captain Saito cannot follow. There is nowhere to hide that she might not snatch from me and award to someone else. I had thought I was safe with Arturo, but now I know: I am not safe anywhere.

"I expect absolute dedication and hard work. There will be no handouts here, no special treatment for anyone on board."

I reach for my armband—only to remember Aunt Marshae has already taken it away. *No special treatment,* Captain Saito says. Not like Arturo and his playful eyes and wandering hands. At least I knew what he wanted. I could protect myself with that knowledge.

"Now all of you get to your stations," she says over the intercom, and I think of my little chapel and its accompanying bed.

"Earth endures," Captain Saito begins, and I hear other voices lift to join her in response, "Mars conquers."

I drop my face into my hands and let the silent sobs break me apart at last.

CHAPTER 2

Like Icarus, our forefathers flew close to the sun. But unlike our mythological predecessor, the scientists aboard the *Icarus* who seeded Mercury and, eventually, Venus, were aware of their mortality and the necessity of a future protected by those who understood peace. It was peace that split us from Earth and Mars, and it is peace that will guide us on our path through the stars.

First Icarii president Pablo val Cárcel,
address to the Venus Parliament

In the split second that Talon's arm twists, his mercurial blade lengthens, and I hunch so that even with his extra distance, he cannot stab me in the stomach. He curses as his feet hit the ground. My movement has changed the diameter of battle, and he'll have to recalculate the angle if he wants to pin me.

Students hate mathematics, but it's integral to everything, even battle. *Especially* battle.

"You're swinging wildly," I tell him. "Your anger will get the better of you unless you do away with it."

I hold my arm at a ninety-degree angle from my core, my blade's point thrust at Talon's face. This is the math of it: My arm is longer than his. My blade has more reach. There is a line between us, and the circle that eclipses that line is the diameter of battle. If he can shift that diameter in his favor, getting inside my long reach, he can win. Or so he thinks.

Then again, I have a decade more of experience than him.

I see him calm, his face blanking as his neural implant washes away his feelings. When I was a student like him, our old professor would hold my wrist in this very stance and provoke my opponents with taunts. *Sol Lucius is the top of the class, which makes you, what? Space trash!* I used my implant to erase any bitterness at his throwing my inferior name around, while my opponent would seethe. Math, like war, should be performed with a cool head.

I'll give Talon this: he's the best in his year. Throughout the week I've been training with his class as a mentor, he's the only one who has come close to hitting me. But so far, the only things that have cut me are Talon's geneassisted yellow eyes with irises that narrow like a cat's.

"Again," Talon says, a demand more than a question, and his mercurial blade ripples into silvery liquid, shortens, and hardens into his preferred form, a short sword that suits his growing limbs. In time, his blade will become standard length, but the benefit of a mercurial blade is that it can change with the flow of battle. Sometimes short'll do it.

"You don't have to ask, Talon, you can just attack." Even after months of alternating classes, I'm still not used to being someone's teacher and receiving an instructor's respect, but I've been out of Icarii military rotation for so long that I'm itching to do something—anything—and that includes dueling with kids.

"Yes, sir. I mean . . . Lito." My name is so soft, like he fears to say it aloud. I don't know why. I'm no hero that kids look up to.

Not anymore. Not since Ceres.

He jumpjets forward, shortening the diameter. He wants, like so many others, to get inside my arm's reach, and he hopes to do that by being quicker than me. It's a solid plan, but in the same way that my arm length allows me to strike more easily, my leg length allows me to step and shift the geometry back in my favor.

I see what he's doing and do the same—only successfully. My mercurial blade never changes form as I slide sideways on the balls of my feet and press the thick of my blade near the hilt against the tip of his. Even without my superior strength, leverage says I win.

Talon curses again, face going red with frustration; if I actually were a professor, I'd write him up for the loss of temper, especially after I already commanded him to watch it. But I'm not a professor, and I'm far more concerned with his foolishness than his bucking command. He grabs the base of his blade with his *hand* and twists it more like a wrench than a sword.

"Talon!" I snap.

His blade pivots around mine and liquefies as it prepares to lengthen—right toward me.

The scar between my shoulder and chest wakes and burns like a wildfire.

His blade is already forming, crawling toward my skin, and my instincts kick in like a primal scream in my gut—

Shift shoulder. Swing blade beneath his arm. Gut him.

For a moment, he is an Ironskin soldier on Ceres, and my arm is dripping blood—

But as my muscles twitch in response with the impulse to kill, I realize—*he's a damn kid, not an enemy.* Through the haze of adrenaline pumping in my veins, I kick the jumpjets in the heels of my boots to life and bound away.

Mierda.

He's breathing hard when he lands. I realize I am too.

Thousand gods. Did I almost kill a kid?

Worse: Why is the memory of Ceres haunting me now?

I force my implant to erase my anxiety, to slow the racing of my heart. I refuse to let Talon take even a peek at the shadow that war has left on me, at the machine it has made of me. I want to curse at him for being such an idiot, or praise him for coming so close to hitting me. Instead, I settle for instructing. "Talon, what's the first rule of engagement?"

I send a thought command to my mercurial blade from my neural implant; the metal turns liquid and seeps back into the hilt. When the metal disappears, the blade's gentle glow does too. I place the hilt on my belt as I meet Talon back in the middle of the sparring courtyard. It's only now, as I take in the world around us, that I realize every uniformed kid in Talon's class—and some in the classes above at the oblong windows—is staring wide-eyed and pale.

"Don't lose control," Talon recites, looking at his gloved hand that touched the blade. The fabric is burned through, the skin beneath a bright pink and bubbled with blisters.

"And what did you do?" I ask, straightening my spine.

His face is burning with humiliation when he responds, "Lost control."

"It was a good strategy if this was a life-or-death situation," I admit. "But this was not that. Now go see the medic."

Talon tosses his wounded hand aside without care for his injury. "I don't want to miss practice because of a damn doctor's visit."

I snort. I was like him at this age, begging for another fight even if I got my ass handed to me. It was the only way to get better.

No, a little part of me whispers. *At his age, you were already kicking ass with Hiro at your side.* And because of the strength that Hiro and I possessed as a pair, I was pulled into the grinding gears of military life, assigned to the dangerous planetoid Ceres, and battling Geans before I even turned nineteen, making me a legend at the Academy and causing boys like Talon to look up to me.

With the scar on my shoulder still aching and memories of Hiro too fresh to ignore, teaching is the last thing I want to do. "We'll continue training tomorrow," I tell him. "Now get to the damn medic."

Talon's a Rapier like me. A Righthand. His Lefthand, his Dagger, lurks nearby, and as soon as I dismiss Talon, the girl rushes toward him like a well-aimed shot. "Let me see," Key says in a tone that clearly brooks no room for disagreement, her dark brown hands grasping for Talon's.

Talon sighs and offers his Lefthand his literal left hand. "I'm all right, Key," Talon whispers, but when their eyes meet, something passes between them in the silence.

This scene has played out time and again in this cobbled courtyard. How many times have teachers watched in wry amusement, surrounded by a blur of faces, at the connection between a partnered pair?

Even now, do Key and Talon speak without words? I remember the comforting feeling of Hiro on the other side of my neural implant, the two pieces of tech inserted in our brains programmed to link our thoughts and feelings. It wasn't telepathy, or anything so invasive; it was something soft and soothing. The warm acknowledgment of an inside joke. A communion. A bond.

At last, Talon's shoulders slump, and Key leads the way to the double doors that open into the school's hallowed hallways. She's clearly won whatever invisible battle waged between them—most likely convincing the stubborn Talon that he should listen to his elder and see a medic. It's only as I watch them walking shoulder to shoulder that I realize how badly I miss my former partner. How long it's been since I last saw them. How home isn't home without Hiro.

"Lito val Lucius!"

My name rings over the courtyard, sending a wave of silence after it. The class turns toward me, even Talon and Key, who pause midstride. They watch me like they did during the duels, as if my name is a challenger's call.

"Lito val Lucius?" A uniformed man strides into the courtyard, the wooden door surrounded by old stone falling closed behind him.

"It's sol Lucius, actually," I tell him, fighting the sinking feeling of my old friend inferiority.

To the class, I order loudly, "Get moving!" They shuffle twenty pairs of identical black boots into the looming Icarus Prime Military

Academy, some groaning at the order. So much for having a teacher's respect . . .

Even if this man is wearing military blacks, he's not here to duel me. As much as the Academy prioritizes dueling in its curriculum, duels don't just spontaneously occur. Especially once you've been assigned, as I have been.

And when you've been assigned a chump job like this, training various groups of kids as the months scrape by . . . you only have so much pride left.

Better than nothing, I remind myself. I could be rotting in the basement still. I repress a shudder at the thought of that dark and cold place, and my shoulder throbs.

"Lito sol Lucius," the man says, correcting himself. He hands me a summons paper when he reaches me. His hair is the downy white of feathers, obviously geneassisted. The soldiers of Venus—*especially* those in Special Forces—trick themselves out as flamboyantly as they can—eyes, skin, hair—all to better stand out when wearing the plain, slim-cut military blacks. He's a Dagger, I note from the pips on his shoulder.

The last time I saw my Dagger, Hiro's hair had been rose red, a bright flower above a bloodstained bandage around their forehead, half their face the purple of a sick bruise. I try to imagine what color it is now before I remember that, since Hiro is on assignment, it's likely a natural shade to help them blend in. Brown or black, something they wouldn't like at all.

"Thank you." I salute with two fingers to my temple. The Dagger salutes in return and heads back for the Academy proper, letting his eyes linger on the courtyard in remembrance. He too hears the ghosts of duels long ago, remembers training with his Rapier before he was assigned his place.

Once I'm alone in the courtyard, I open the summons, marked with Command's blazing phoenix symbol. It's from my commander, which I expected, but it doesn't say anything close to what I'd imagine a summons from him to say. Four simple words, and within them a multitude of possible meanings:

Get here. New assignment.

I TAKE THE bullet train downtown, watching the Academy's melted-wax spirals retreat into the distance. Its ancient, bonelike architecture is soon swallowed by the clustered gemstone skyscrapers of the floating city Cytherea. The sky is an autumnal tree, hung in reds and golds as the dome above simulates the sun's descent to nighttime.

This city and its hermium-powered shell were created after scientists perfected the building technique on Mercury's Spero. Hung as carefully as a cocoon on a leaf, Cytherea floats in what our scientists call the "sweet spot" of Venus's atmosphere, a place with the perfect pressure and temperature for human life. Cytherean air filters turn Venus's carbon dioxide into oxygen for breathing, and the basic genemodding we receive as children helps us with the variations in gravity. The domed cities are a marvel of science and proof that a government led by scientists works for the betterment of all mankind.

Not that there aren't drawbacks to Cytherea, of course. They just won't be found here on the uppermost layer.

Because of the evening hour, the train is packed with commuters, those who either can't afford a podcar or don't want one. Since the majority of those involved in science, industry, and commerce reside on Mercury, these travelers are probably low-level government employees or manual workers in Cytherea's vast entertainment industry. There are definitely no factory workers on board. No one whose name bears my inferior title, *sol.*

I watch fingers dancing in the air as passengers engage with the images on their com-contact lenses, watching the news or reading the latest studies; kids in various school uniforms, absorbed in biobooks or sleek compads in order to finish their homework; and, oddly, a couple of Asters in sand-colored, bandage-like wraps that cover them from head to boot, save for the green goggles they wear over their eyes.

The scar on my shoulder aches—it was an Aster who shot me on Ceres, I recall all too vividly, before pushing those thoughts and the pain away. Why is my past so determined to haunt me today?

The Asters are . . . other. Humanoid, but not human. They have two arms and two legs, but they are tall and thin, stretched out with odd proportions. Few make Icarii planets their home. The gravity, the light, the pressure on Mercury and Venus—these are all things that Asters grew beyond with the help of those first ancient gene-assists on Earth who made them the perfect spacefarers but had no idea of the mutations their modifications would allow to take root. Centuries later, the Asters are their own people, living and working and breeding in the asteroid belt, deformed compared to the humans they used to be.

The Asters have a range of skin colors, but all of them are as translucent as long-dead bodies, like walking bruises in blue and purple and gray. Their hair is white, devoid of color like bleached bones, and beneath their goggles, their eyes are swallowing black and soulless. Their wraps keep sunlight from burning their sensitive skin, while their goggles allow them to see in our bright lights. But as secretive as they are, it's no wonder the majority of people find them unnerving, even if the rumor that they carry disease is completely false.

Still, they usually live apart from humans. On Spero, they stick to the Under, a series of stone tunnels burrowed into the surface of Mercury, but here on Cytherea, they live on the lowest levels, where the pressure is higher, or even on the surface of Venus, where they oversee mining efforts. It's rare they're this far up, mixed with normal humans, and the unease in the air is palpable. A mother keeps her energetic child from venturing to their side of the car. Others clutch their bags to their chests protectively. Many eye the Asters with suspicion, while a group of teens glare with open hatred. Only once the toddler starts to cry do the teens lose their tempers.

"Ey, bruv!" A boy with a geneassisted white eye and the bright, choppy clothing favored on the higher levels of Cytherea calls out. "Cockroaches, I'm talking at you! What're a couple of bugs doing off the surface?" When the Asters don't answer, he leans across the aisle toward them. "Can't you see you're making people uncomfortable? You're scaring children."

The Asters do their best to ignore him, leaning as far into their seats as they can. I doubt they speak any of our human languages, but they understand the boy's expression and body language clearly enough.

His daring seems to catch and inflame the others in his group. A girl with pink hair sings an off-key song about catching rats. A skinny kid with some sort of metal implant above his right eyebrow turns to me. "Bruv in black come down from his Spire to shit among the rest of us and don't do a thing to protect the people from the real problems. That right, bruv?"

A few others look up at me expectantly. Even the Asters' green goggles turn in my direction as if expecting me to intervene. But I'm not in the peacekeeping division, I'm a duelist, and patrolling trains isn't even close to my job description.

"Fucking useless." The kid spits at my feet.

As much as I want to mess up his geneassisted face, I calm myself with my implant and let my eyes wander to the windows and catch on the overflowing plants on apartment balconies, greens interspersed with a thousand jewel tones. Kids like him and his friends want to feel big, and any reaction I give them will just fuel them.

The Asters leave at the very next station, their heads bowed to avoid hitting the ceiling with their great height, their spindly limbs tucked tightly to their sides. The remaining passengers pointedly avert their eyes but immediately relax when they're gone, slouching into their chairs, chatting with the person next to them, smiling at things other than their screens. The kids who'd hassled them slap shoulders, celebrating a job well done, and return to their inside jokes. The entire incident is forgotten.

I don't feel bad for the Asters. I grew up in the lower levels of Cytherea, side by side with several of them, but I pulled myself out. I got *my family* out. I used my talents playing gladius, earned the Val Roux Scholarship to the Academy, and secured a future for my little sister so that she can involve herself wherever she wants in the entertainment industry—cinema, theater, music. My name, sol Lucius, is proof of where I belong, yet here I am, having climbed the ladder of success one painful rung at a time.

The bullet train reaches Cytherea's central terminal, Einstein Station, and I shoulder my way through my fellow passengers to disembark. In the very center of the station, a statue of two men stretches toward the ceiling, three meters tall and made of clear quartz. One man places wings of copper and gold on the other's back. This statue and the numerous others like it throughout Cytherea depict Daedalus placing his grand invention on his son's shoulders and serves as a reminder in two parts.

The first reminds us what our ancestors faced. During the Dead Century War, they left Mars for uninhabited, unexplored, and dangerous Mercury on the science vessel *Icarus*. But instead of perishing in fire, they flew to the planet closest to the sun, survived, and flourished.

The second reminder is this: while technological advancements can carry humankind to impossible heights, power must be exercised responsibly. After all, people tend to forget that Daedalus's wings for his son did work; it was Icarus who used them incorrectly.

Despite the overwhelming crowd in the station, I stand apart. Black isn't a popular color among fashionable Icarii, and my uniform carves a space for me in the press of people. A peacekeeper, an officer of the law also clad in black but in a different cut, respectfully nods to me at the exit of the station. As I descend the stairs toward Cytherea's main thoroughfare, Newton Street, the city overwhelms me.

Cytherea is a wild and sprawling youth. Where other cities breathe sighs of relief, Cytherea sings of its glory. Mercury's domed city, Spero, was created in a time of necessity, but Venus was seeded out of prosperity; every corner is full of substantial sights and sounds that assault me as I walk by—pulsing music from floating speakers that zip through the air like insects, Paragon influencers in the newest fashions lounging on the trendiest furniture as if they're selling nothing at all, holograms of celebrities encouraging everyone to come to their newest interactive play. Everyone who's anyone has a building on Newton Street, from vid studios to the president of the Icarii. Even the military.

The Spire is an obelisk of a building as black as our uniforms that stretches into the domed sky. It houses the Command division that provides orders to all branches of the military. Surrounded by other buildings in pearl white and shimmering opal, neon-bright advertisements pasted on street-level windows, the Spire stands out in its restraint. The building is bare of ornament other than one bold word that flashes red in the three most-used languages, English, Spanish, and Chinese. *ENLIST. ALÍSTATE.* 參加軍隊, the Spire reads.

But everyone knows the truth behind the Spire's command: those who don't attend the Academy won't be duelists of the Special Forces, one of the elite Icarii soldiers. Instead they'll be low-ranking infantry, their neural implants programmed to answer to their commanders en masse. In the Academy the duelists joked they were like worker bees, unable to make decisions without their queen. Dad just called them cannon fodder. I went to primary school on the lowest level of Cytherea with a few kids who were so desperate for credits, they joined up to pay their debts, and I'd quickly lost track of them. They'd ship out on a vessel bound for the Gean space around Earth or Mars, and they'd disappear into the stars, never to be heard from again.

When I reach my destination, a scanner confirms my neural implant at the Spire's gate, and an infantryman in a formal black-and-silver uniform salutes me as I enter. The grounds in front of the building have well-maintained green bushes but no flowers, another thing that separates the Spire from the lively surrounding buildings that overflow with vines and blossoms. Still, we do our part toward air purification, even if our hedges are plain.

While the exterior is imposing, the interior is similar to what you'd find inside any other of the skyscrapers downtown: clean, white hallways blink with interactive maps on the floors, and people stroll through the lobby on their way to their assignments. But that's where the similarities end. The workers here are soldiers, duelists, and commanders. There are no animated images acting as advertisements on the walls, as would be common in other buildings, and there are no desks or secretaries; to even get this far, you have to belong.

"I've been summoned by High Commander Beron val Bellator," I say aloud.

The intelligence in charge of the lobby reads my neural implant, checks scheduling, and opens a gold-trimmed elevator door in less than a second. It's not quite AI; it doesn't approach the Marian Threshold—not after the Dead Century War, when the Synthetics left the inner planets because of Gean abuses—but it's smart enough, following yes/no protocols with ease. Beneath my feet, a red arrow points toward the elevator. "Please proceed, Lito sol Lucius," a genderless voice replies.

I enter the elevator, and my stomach pitches at the descent. While the Command division holds offices on the top floors of the Spire, Beron prefers to assign missions below. But the dark, plantless basement and its incessant pressure can drive someone stir-crazy even with the sunlamps and fresh air pumped through the vents that line the hallways.

I remind myself I won't be stuck here this time, that this visit is only temporary. I suck in a deep breath and let it out slowly, picturing the ocean to calm the nervousness that tightens my chest. There's something about Earth's seas, something I've only seen in vids, that soothes me. The rhythmic lapping of the waves, the sound of the water . . .

"Refreshment while you wait?" the intelligence in the elevator asks, pulling me from my attempt at meditation. But before I even have a chance to refuse, I arrive at my destination and the doors part.

The basement levels are a nondescript gray, long tunnels of concrete and sharp turns. Only Beron, a slender man of average height with close-shorn brown hair and cutting blue eyes, serves to differentiate the space.

"Lito," Beron rasps, standing poised with a thin black compad tucked beneath his arm, the red phoenix with wings displayed pinned on his chest and the crossed rapier and dagger pips on his shoulder denoting his rank in Command. I have a hard time believing that he wasn't waiting for me. The harsh lighting from above deepens the soft scarring of his face, something he had his geneassist leave when he rewound some years. I suspect Beron is in his eighties, since his neural implant has been removed, but I can't know for sure, since he looks not a day over forty.

"High Commander." I salute him with two fingers. "You summoned me?"

"I did. I have a new assignment for you. Follow me." He turns before I have a chance to drop my salute.

I trail him down the identical corridors, unsure how he navigates this place where everything looks the same, or why he even wants to. The building regulates the temperature so that it matches the lobby, yet I can *feel* the change in the air. The basement seeps into my skin and permeates my lungs in such a way that I just know that I'm in the lower levels. Underground and trapped, just like I was as a kid. Just like I was after Ceres.

Beron opens an unnumbered red door seemingly at random and motions for me to enter ahead of him. Did he choose this room on impulse, or is there something here we need? I aim to sit in one of the two chairs when I realize that it's already occupied. Coming here was clearly part of his plan, then. With nowhere else to sit, I remain standing as Beron takes the chair on the opposite side of the metal desk.

"This is Ofiera fon Bain," Beron says, motioning to the sitting woman without even looking at her. *Fon*, indicating she comes from a lineage of government workers and politickers. It doesn't matter what her family does now; the title remains. All of the titles, from the lofty scientist *val* to the lowly maintenance worker *sol*, can be traced back to the first Icarii who left Mars during the Dead Century War. The three letters were a code that our ancestors used to denote their jobs aboard the *Icarus*, and while the titles don't restrict our movement through Cytherean society, the prejudice remains.

I fear in my core why he's introducing me to another deulist when I am currently partnerless, and my stomach twists into a horrid shape when she stands. I command my neural implant to neutralize my nervousness so that I can objectively measure this Ofiera fon Bain.

She is slender with willowy limbs, good for fighting, and of average height for a woman of her age and build. From her musculature, I determine she would be quick in combat. The crossed dagger and rapier pips on her shoulder denote that she's also Special Forces Command. Strangest of all, she's plain. If she's ever seen a geneassist, I can't find their work. Her eyes are hazel, one slightly darker than the other, her hair a chestnut brown. But normal. Someone you would absolutely look past in a crowd even if she has pretty features, like well-formed lips and dark brows that keep her face in a perpetually serious scowl.

"Ofiera fon Bain," I say, and salute.

She salutes in return. "Lito sol Lucius." Her eyes flick over me once, as if she's unimpressed with what she sees; or perhaps she has already sized me up and finds me lacking. Maybe it's that *sol* in my name. That feeling assaults me again: *I don't belong here.* Her eyes dart away as if she would prefer to look anywhere else.

I straighten. I've *earned* this. I *do* belong here. How much more must I do before I prove it?

"Good, then." Beron reads something from his black compad. "As you know, Lito, after the Fall of Ceres, the Geans have much to celebrate. They're currently planning something to honor the Mother, whom they credit with the idea that wrested Ceres from us."

Beron's eyes come up to meet mine, hard and full of anger. As if it's personally *my* fault that Ceres fell. And since I was there on the ground with Hiro, he does blame me . . . at least partially. Me and every other duelist who was surprised by the Gean coup, who lost a battle that could turn the tide of the entire war.

Hell, I don't know that he's wrong to blame us. The weight of that loss has dragged me down every day for the past year.

Because we lost Ceres, Hiro was sent on assignment away from me, punishment enough, and I was confined to the lower levels of the Spire for six months until Beron let me out to teach kids . . .

For a moment, I remember waking in the cold, stale air of the basement, my shoulder aching and bandaged, reaching out for Hiro with my neural implant, and finding nothing but silence. The fear that Hiro was dead overwhelmed me so quickly that I couldn't send it away, and I screamed and screamed, flailing against the vast ocean of fear like a drowning man, until nurses came to sedate me. The next time I woke, it was only Beron's explaining to me that Hiro was alive and on assignment that calmed me enough to allow the doctor to patch the wound I had reopened.

But that emptiness has remained with me, and the fear still clings to me like a shadow.

It rises now, burning like bile in my throat, and I command my neural implant to do away with it. Save it for another day. I can't use that emotion here, now, just as I can't openly miss Hiro when the man who took them away from me is sitting across the table with a smug look on his face. I'm lucky Beron isn't one of the commanders who utilizes an implant to sense what his inferiors are feeling. I'm sure he'd notice the wavering emotions rising and falling within me like the tide.

But Ofiera—is she watching for that?

"We have several operations already in place regarding the Mother's Celebration." Beron drops his gaze to his compad. The faint wrinkles of his forehead smooth as his judgment dissipates. "We want you on the ground for one of them."

"On Ceres?" I'm sure the surprise filters into my tone. "We lost Ceres only a year ago."

"Do you have a problem returning there?" Beron asks, his words a loaded weapon.

"Of course not," I respond quickly. "But without Hiro—"

"Yes, about them. Unfortunately . . ." Beron's lips thin as he considers his words. "Hiro has been compromised."

Compromised.

What is that supposed to mean? My hands shake at my sides. There's no way Hiro could be—they can't be—

"Hiro was assigned some months ago to return to Ceres alongside Ofiera." Beron rubs his eyes with thumb and forefinger. When he pulls his hand away, the bags beneath his eyes look deeper. "But Ofiera reports they've gone completely dark."

So they're not . . . ? I still can't ask.

"Off book is Hiro's style," I manage in a weak voice.

"Not this time, Lito." He motions to the compad on his desk as if I could read the file he references. "This time, I'm afraid Hiro has defected."

A shudder runs down my spine. Hiro had only been reassigned to spy on Ceres as punishment for the Fall. *Beron* had assigned them there, and now Beron wants me back on the ground for the Mother's Celebration—and what else? My mind races.

"You assigned them to Ceres as a spy for us, and then—"

"They disappeared. Stopped working with Ofiera. I think you get the picture." Beron flattens both hands on the desk. "We fear the Geans may have turned them."

Somehow this is worse than Beron telling me that Hiro is dead. Because if Hiro betrayed us to the Geans, then they're as good as dead. There won't be a single place in Icarii space where they will be safe, even if their father is Souji val Akira, CEO of Val Akira Labs and one of the richest, most powerful men in the system.

"And Ofiera fon Bain?" I ask.

Ofiera squares her shoulders at her name.

"Your new Dagger," Beron says.

My eyes shoot to Ofiera and land on the crossed rapier and dagger on her shoulder. There were always rumors that some in Command could act as either Rapier or Dagger despite the years of training each position required. Most of us at the Academy waved it off as the talk of the drunk or braggarts. But if Ofiera was Hiro's Rapier and she'll now be acting as my Dagger . . . it's absolutely true.

But despite discovering the answer to this old mystery, all I can focus on is this: What does her presence mean? Why would Beron assign someone so highly skilled to accompany me on this mission?

What kind of mission *is* this?

"What's our assignment?" I ask, forcing my words through numb lips.

"Two parts. First, finish Hiro val Akira's assignment: assassinate the Mother."

Thousand gods, is that what Hiro had been assigned—hunting down and killing the religious leader who commands half of the Gean government? And right after what happened to us on Ceres?

Beron dips his chin but keeps his eyes on me. Watching, waiting to see what I will do. "You will be given a full debrief regarding this mission, should you accept."

But I don't do anything because I fear, in the deepest pit of my stomach, that the worst is yet to come. "And the second objective?" I prompt.

Thick brows furrow as Beron meets my gaze. "Find Hiro val Akira." Even Ofiera turns to look at me when Beron speaks. "Kill them."

My shoulder throbs. "*Kill*—not capture?" I ask, ignoring my scar until it stops aching. "Certainly Hiro deserves a trial, a chance to explain their reasoning—"

"Those are your orders, Lito." Beron's voice is harsh, his anger rising to the surface as his face reddens. "Are you unable to follow them, sol Lucius?"

The emotions swarm me, one after another. Blinding anger, deep sorrow, claws of agony. My mercurial blade hums on my hip, itching to be released. There is only animal instinct, only the urge to fight and kill as I've been trained. But as these feelings come, I wish them away, banish them, as I place one gloved hand into the other and bend my fingers backward. I want to feel that pain, disappear into that hole, not drown in the tide of unwanted emotions that cloud my judgment.

The pain brings clarity. I cannot lash out here. These are my people. This is my assignment. This is who I am, Lito sol Lucius, a soldier of the Icarii before all else. And I will not falter, I will not fail and doom myself and my family back to short, shallow lives.

I focus on the physical for three more seconds. Five. I stand a whole fifteen seconds in silence before I release my own hand and leave myself a clean slate. The emotions are gone, the sorrow and sting of betrayal banished, the anger and anxiety quieted. My blade is hushed. My head is blank. Even the burn of my fingers lightens until the soreness is nothing more than a dull pang. My scars are silent.

"I accept this assignment, Commander," I say at last, the binding words that grant my assent. And even as I say it, I wonder if this is my punishment, just as assigning my former partner to spy on Ceres after the Fall was Hiro's. Because now I will return to the place where it all shattered, where I almost died, where we lost a battle that could lose us a war, without Hiro at my side.

And this time, my blade will be wielded to kill them.

What have you done now, Hiro?

PLAY:

▶ 01

---◇———◈———◇---

Fucking gods, I've started this recording over a hundred times now. I'm never going to figure out what I want to say before I say it. You'll just have to deal with the shitty, rambling quality of it. It should answer your questions.

At least, I hope it will.

That's the only reason I'm bothering with all this. I know how dangerous it is to leave any trail connecting us now that we're no longer Rapier and Dagger. I know Beron will be watching you like you're compromised and your every sneeze is a sign to a Gean agent.

But I also know you, Lito.

I know how you sleep on your back with your arm thrown over your eyes so no one can tell if you're awake or asleep. I know you hate when people see through the perfectly cultivated persona you wear like a uniform. I know you chase not just the first layer of truth but also the *why* behind it with a single-minded focus that you'd never let anyone, least of all yourself, admit to.

And you . . .

[A deep breath in. A heavy, rattling breath out.]

You at least deserve the truth. The unaltered, full version of it. The *why* of it.

So I'll make this easy for you.

I'm guilty.

There. Easy, right?

And I know what you're thinking: I *can't* be guilty of everything they say I am, because so much of it is conflicting.

But I am guilty. Maybe not of everything, but of some things.

This doesn't help you, does it? It doesn't help me either. Saying it aloud doesn't lighten the load on my shoulders. But isn't that what confessions are supposed to do?

Maybe this isn't a confession. It's certainly not meant to ask for forgiveness. It's not meant for anyone other than you. And I don't care what the Icarii think of me—what my father or Beron thinks of me.

So please. Just listen, Lito.

Let me try to explain everything.

CHAPTER 3

The Sisterhood in its entirety, from the lowliest Cousin to the highest and holy Mother, serves on behalf of the needs of others. From the Aunts who dedicate their lives to speaking laws into existence to the Sisters who give of the very voice from their throats, all is done in supplication to the Goddess.

Warlord Vaughn at the Ascension of Mother Isabel III

Nothing has changed in my personal quarters. The floor is waxed to a shine; the sheets are tucked tightly into the corners beneath the mattress; the livecam screen shimmers with the starlight beyond. Yet everything feels different.

It is mine, just as I left it an hour ago, but there is a spirit of wrongness in the air of the room; I am the ghost who haunts it.

When I finally find my strength, I drop the bag of underclothes onto the mattress. It would take no time at all to unpack, but I cannot bring myself to do it. Do Captain Saito and Aunt Marshae expect me in the chapel today? I remember the captain's words, commanding everyone to work. *There will be no handouts here.*

But no . . . I have no strength of will to perform any duty expected of me today.

Where am I to go from here? Perhaps it is like Aunt Marshae says, and this is the Goddess's punishment for being so willing to abandon my life among the stars. I had hopes of being anchored to one captain. Naively thought of myself like Sister Marian, the first Mother, and her lover in the Canon. But now that Arturo has abandoned me, I am unmoored, a Sister with no captain at all.

I'm sorry, I pray, hoping the Goddess will listen when she has turned a deaf ear to my prayers for so long. *If you wish for me to stay on the* Juno, *then that is where I will take root.* I gather each and every wish to leave the Sisterhood, place it in a box deep inside me, and lock it away with my other childish dreams: for a family, for a trade, for a life of my own choosing.

Your will be done, I tell Her.

I focus on the new: Saito Ren is the captain. I do not want to lose my rank as First Sister. I must regain the white armband, symbol of the captain's claim, so that the entire crew does not expect services from me.

Goddess, I do not want to be forced to warm hundreds of beds. *Please don't take this rank from me*, I pray in desperation. But I know, even as I ask, that the Goddess does not bargain; I cannot say "Let me do Thy will, but only if it is as First Sister."

No, for that I must work . . .

I give myself another minute to cry before I wipe the tears away. After a quick look in the mirror, I pinch my cheeks to give my blanched skin spots of rosy color. I dressed well in the pale gray sheath of a Sister when I prepared for my supposed departure; it will suit me when I visit the captain.

I must make up for my behavior this morning. I need Captain Saito to think that I am happy here on the *Juno*, that I am ready to serve her as I served Arturo. I must be careful with every glance and twitch of my lips. If I am careless, she will see through me for sure, and I will be demoted before I can even try to remedy the situation.

But how much am I willing to commit to her? I gave Arturo everything, believing him to be my way out. But all my giving, all my support and long nights spent at his side, were for nothing. He spat on my dedication and left me behind. Cast me aside when he was done using me. Will Captain Saito do the same?

It feels as if the Goddess Herself answers me: *Does it even matter?*

No. Even if Captain Saito gave me the captain's armband and I kept it for a mere year, it would be better than living without, an open target of any soldier's desire.

I have but one choice: I must do anything I can to keep my place and impress Saito Ren.

"PLEASE, TAKE A seat." Saito Ren motions to a chair across from her expensive, real wooden desk. The seat is not quite as plush as the one she sits in, but all who visit the captain must know their place.

I smooth my skirt beneath me as I settle, doing my best to ignore the rest of the captain's quarters. The room is a blank canvas compared to when Arturo inhabited it, devoid of all personal touches, a screaming testament to his departure. I remain as the sole evidence of his lie.

There is no concept of night in space, but the *Juno* runs on a clock synchronized with Earth and Mars, and Captain Saito is clearly off duty, her navy Gean uniform fully unbuttoned so I can take in small details of her—the rise of her breasts, the sharp carvings of her collarbones, the faint scarring toward her left shoulder. She's handsome for a woman, her jaw square and eyebrows thick in an unfeminine way that somehow suits her. But her lips are soft and smile freely, and her black eyes shimmer in the overhead lights with a hint of mischief.

She's young for a ranked soldier; there is an insipid hopefulness in her gaze that has yet to be sucked dry by age and experience. But she's *very* young for a captain. She must have done something brave to receive this honored posting. If we Sisters were not tucked away on starships, hidden away from the rest of the cosmos, I'm sure I would know of her exploits already.

I'm considering how to ingratiate myself to her when Captain Saito steeples her fingers, and my eyes flutter to her hands.

One hand is flesh-colored, the other the stark white of tech.

So she *lost* something to become captain of the *Juno*. I hadn't even noticed the prosthetic earlier that day because of my distress over Arturo.

"How are you faring, First Sister?" Captain Saito gestures at me with her flesh-and-blood hand. I tear my eyes away from the robotic one and meet her gaze. "You seemed quite distressed earlier today. I worried over you."

Words. All words. Captain Saito's tone is dispassionate, uninterested. Her eyes roll over her desk instead of me. I doubt she gave me another thought after this morning.

I show her my best smile and look up at her through my lashes, like a shy young girl. Perhaps she will forgive my rudeness this morning, or forget it completely, if I make a good impression on her now.

"I want to meet with as many of the Sisters on the *Juno* as I can," Captain Saito says, looking at a slim compad. Most likely Aunt Marshae has already provided her with a list of eligible Sisters, their current ranks, and pictures of them. "I'd like to learn more about you before I make any decisions." She finally meets my gaze. "What are your goals here on the *Juno*?"

I smile to keep from grimacing and let my eyes wander to the wall behind her as if considering the question. I want to prove my usefulness to her. If I can't, I could be not only on my way back to the cramped living conditions the other Sisters have but right off the *Juno*. I could be sent to another starship, one of Gean make with poor artificial gravity, and start as the lowest Sister, where I would know no one and have no allies. And at twenty, in my prime years for working my way up the ranks, I cannot start over.

But Captain Saito is a soldier, and soldiers are all the same; they ask us questions as if they really care about the answers, then talk big about helping us poor, hopeless Sisters, promising they'll give us whatever we want so that we will pray to the Goddess on their behalf. And at night, they press hot kisses to our thighs and pray to us instead. They don't care a single credit for what we really want.

Because what *I* want is not to have to do this.

I slip from my chair and lean my hip against the desk. It is the exact same desk that Arturo used, bare of a single personal item, and I know exactly how to slide onto the slick surface and pivot so that I turn and find myself face-to-face with Captain Saito, my legs on either side of her chair. When I take her in, she's straight-backed and stiff.

"Stop that," she protests, voice barely above a whisper.

My deft hands reach for and release the first three buttons of my dress, baring my neck, my collarbones, my breasts. I'm reaching for the next button when Captain Saito slams a fist on the desk.

"Stop that, I said!"

I freeze in shock. My heart pounds, a frantic caged bird. My breath rattles through my lips.

What scares me most is not Captain Saito's outburst but her refusal of me. I am still young and fit, my hair the gold that soldiers love. But if she does not want me . . . if I cannot make myself useful to her . . .

Maybe she does not favor women. Perhaps she has requested one of the male Cousins to warm her bed, while she looks to a Sister only for confession. Or maybe it's something more. There are many women who do not just avoid us but hate us, who believe we lure their husbands to our beds during deployment.

But they would never say so aloud; to admonish the Sisterhood is to denounce the Mother herself. And no one, not even Warlord Vaughn, would denounce the Mother, our mortal link to the Goddess, She who weaves the threads of the cosmos together.

"I'm sorry," Captain Saito says, sounding anything but. "I didn't mean to scare you." She runs a hand through her hair and leaves it standing awkwardly atop her head. She is too old for the unkempt, boyish look, and it makes me hate her because I am normal and natural and she is some patched-together soldier girl too big for her captain's seat, yet *she* refuses *me*.

I button my dress back to my neck and cross my arms over my breasts. My eyes burn.

"I don't want you to do any of . . . that." Captain Saito stands and backs away from the desk. From *me*. She stands awkwardly in the middle of the room, and I cannot help but look for everything that is missing—pictures on the walls of Arturo's family, awards on the dusty shelves, various antique gunpowder weapons in the glass display case. Even the sheets on the bed have changed to a rumpled, wine-colored fabric. It takes all of my willpower not to cry.

"That's what I was trying to say," Captain Saito mutters. Captains shouldn't mumble, but she does. "I don't want you Sisters to do anything you don't want to do."

It is hard having a conversation with someone who refuses to see the obvious: even the captain can't give a free pass on all of our duties just because they don't take advantage of their station. The captain's armband is a captain's claim; it is given only to the First Sister to let the crew know that she is not free to be chosen among them. But anyone without the armband?

We end up on our knees.

"Can I ask you something personal?" Captain Saito returns and leans her own hip against the side of the desk, crossing her arms in mirror image of me. It reminds me just how closed off I must look to her, so I straighten myself and press my arms to my sides, pushing my chest out and my chin up. I imagine my Auntie smiling with praise. "Did you choose to become a Sister?"

Every Aunt within the Sisterhood not only chooses that life but pays an exorbitant sum to be there. But those who choose to become Sisters are exceedingly few. Only the poorest and sickest would exchange their voices for food and shelter and health care. And even then, that's rare. Most of us are sold into it by our parents, like Second Sister, or gifted from a Sisterhood-funded orphanage, like me.

I shake my head to indicate that I did not choose this. What I cannot say is that I don't understand those who *would* choose this life. Yes, perhaps it offers more food than begging on the streets, better accommodation than a back-alley brothel, more sights than living in one house beneath a polluted, smog-filled sky on Mars or Earth, but as soon as we are named a Sister, we slip into a long, long sleep and wake up with our words taken from us.

I touch my throat. There's no scar there, because of course they would never make us ugly in the process. But how could we keep our captains' secrets if we could repeat them?

Captain Saito turns her back on me. "You're dismissed," she says as she gazes at the livecam screen in her room, so big it takes up an entire wall. It offers a prime view of black undercurrents mixing with heated starlight crashing in the Goddess's galactic ocean.

I want to protest, to find some reason to be of use to her to ensure I will not lose my rank, not be sent from the *Juno*—but I can think of nothing that she would want from me, so I turn away from her. I miss Arturo, and the certainty I felt at his side, as the door slides closed between us and I consider returning to my private room. But it will stay *my* room. I am determined not to lose my rank.

"FIRST SISTER, PLEASE come in." Aunt Marshae's eyes twinkle with joy, alongside another emotion I can't quite name. Something akin to gloating. I half expect her to choke on her words, so stuffed is she with the glee that I have once again been relegated to her care. "Sit down."

The door closes behind me. I sit.

"You're not the only Sister to visit me today." My Auntie does not join me in the reception area but instead looks over the packed bookcase behind me, forcing me to turn in my chair to face her. "Could you possibly guess what for?"

My hands, clenched in my lap, unfold as I prepare to sign. *The new captain*, I reply.

"Indeed," she says, fingers fluttering over gilded spines. "They asked for her dossier. Just as you will, I'm sure. But why should I provide it to any of you when you could just as easily seek out the captain to learn of her past yourselves?"

You have helped me before, and I am one of the Mother's chosen, I sign. And her help would save me valuable time in getting to know Saito Ren. If I knew Captain Saito's past intimately, I could provide her with better care, and with better care, I could become her favorite companion. I would be safe as First Sister.

"I did," she says, and lets the unsaid threat hang there: *I don't have to help you again.*

I want to keep my position, I sign. I need not point out that she provided me with Arturo's dossier upon my arrival on the *Juno*; she seems to remember that all too well.

"But if you become Captain Saito's favorite, what will stop you from leaving with her when she goes, just as you tried to with Captain Deluca?" My Auntie withdraws a book from the shelf and reads the title. Finding it unsatisfactory, with a little frown she places it back among the others.

There is little I can offer her other than the truth. *I have given up on obvious lies from captains,* I sign.

She smiles again, and I finally realize what that other emotion is lurking in her eyes: triumph. Like a predator who has successfully cornered its prey, she boasts at her victory over me, reveling in my defeat. I have come to her because she is my only hope, and she knows that, knows that she can use it to her advantage.

Your success is my success, Auntie, I sign to her. *What do you want of me?*

She could just as easily send me away, punish me for accepting Arturo's offer. She could choose Second Sister or even Third and give her the dossier, allowing them to grow closer to Captain Saito and eventually replace me. But instead she leaves the bookcase and gathers a file from her desk. "Not what *I* want, my dear niece," she says, tossing the folder into my lap. I keep my expression neutral as my hand caresses the navy plastic, opening to the first waxy page.

As soon as I see the name on it, my heart drops. The dossier starts with a letter from someone whom I never expected to offer me an assignment.

High Sister of the Geans, Sovereign of the Goddess, Matriarch of the Earthblooded, Her Holiness, Sanctus Mater. One of the two leaders of all Geans, alongside Warlord Vaughn.

The Mother herself.

I remember her hand on my cheek a year ago, her choice to send me to the *Juno*, a blessing that has made me a target of many Sisters' jealousies. Many Aunts whispered that I was a favorite of hers. Still, why in the Goddess's cosmos would the Mother *personally* contact me?

The letter is brief.

Dear First Sister of the Juno,

It is with great joy that I send this missive, for a favorable opportunity to serve the Sisterhood has presented itself. Provide for Saito Ren with your talents and keep close to her, as is your duty. But on this occasion, you must also entrust your Auntie with anything remarkable about Captain Saito.

I am praying for you and your endeavors. May the Goddess watch over you on your path of service.

Mother Isabel III

Behind the letter are pages and pages on Captain Saito's history, her full dossier. My breath catches in my throat. My eyes flick over the letter again and again, not quite believing what I've read. We Sisters are not supposed to tell our charges' secrets to *anyone*, not even our Aunties, yet that is exactly what the Mother has asked of me.

Is this an answer to my prayer? Has the Goddess withered one branch only to bless another into flowering?

"Will you do as your Mother bids you?" Aunt Marshae asks, her hands squeezing the back of an empty chair until her knuckles turn white. "I feel it necessary to say that if you are caught, it will be you who takes the blame, not the Sisterhood."

Now the bare, cold offer presents itself. They want me to be a spy. If I do as I am commanded, I will receive Captain Saito's dossier, a sure way to keep my position; but in return, I will be expected to break the rules of the Sisterhood, becoming some sort of holy operative. Yet the Sisterhood is the body asking this of me, and if I don't do as the Mother wills, I know Aunt Marshae will simply find another girl who is more pliable. The letter is addressed to the *First Sister of the* Juno; that could be anyone if I am demoted.

No. I must keep my rank. I must impress Saito Ren. This is certainly a step deeper into the politics of the Sisterhood, but it is still the best way to survive on the *Juno.*

Perhaps the Goddess does bargain after all.

As the Mother commands, the Goddess wills, and I obey, I sign. If I was so willing to give myself to one captain for the rest of my life in order to change things, I should accept the benefits this assignment offers me. Perhaps the Mother will personally reward me at the end of it. Yet my stomach twists at the wrongness of it, at the way I am supposed to go against all I have been trained to do since childhood.

"The dossier is yours, then," Aunt Marshae says, her grip loosening until her fingers bloom pink.

Thank you, I sign, and gather the file beneath my arm. I want to be done with this strange interaction with its blasted bargain. But as I retreat from the room, one question burns in my mind: What does the Mother want with Saito Ren?

PLAY:

⏵ 02

◇—·—◇◇◇—·—◇

The first time I ever saw you, Lito, I loved you. You were some
skinny boy who looked more like a mistreated dog: scrawny, hungry, ready to bite if anyone got close to your snarling mouth.

With one look, I sized you up. You weren't like the rest of our class
at the Academy. The glimpses of your wrists between your gloves
and sleeves said your uniform was secondhand, but your boots, polished to a shine despite the worn soles, told me you were proud to
be there.

All of it together? It screamed your truth. You shouldn't have been
able to afford tuition, yet here you were. Determined. Rebellious. A fighter.

And there was something in the brutal way you stood, with your
shoulders hunched forward and your dark eyes like black holes meant
to swallow stars, that said you'd keep fighting anyone who made the
mistake of underestimating you.

You would have to, if you were from a worker-class family. I didn't
even need to know your name to recognize you weren't from my level
of Cytherea.

You glared at me like I was the source of all your problems. Maybe in some way I was. But everyone looked at me like that.

All of our classmates hated me. I know they did. How could they not? I was Hiro val Akira, and my father had either worked with their parents or donated to their causes. I could trace my lineage directly back to Murakawa Akira on the *Icarus*. My family built the worlds that theirs worked to maintain.

Here's something I bet you didn't know: I didn't plan on going to the Academy that morning. I wasn't late because I thought it would make a joke out of the instructors or my fellow students, or whatever everyone else said later. I was going to run away.

I know, I know. Stupid plan. Where could I run that my father's long arms couldn't reach? I was val Akira, and all the benefits of having that name came with just as many disadvantages. There was nowhere in this universe I could disappear. I couldn't even visit a geneassist and change everything about me without my new genetic makeup being reported via a Val Akira Labs computer and stored on a Val Akira Labs server. Hell, the majority of geneassists were using Val Akira Labs techniques, leaving copyrighted markers in my very DNA. Proof that my father owned me through and through.

So after standing at the train station, looking at the line that would take me to the Academy and the one that would take me away from it, I made a decision. I'd go to the Academy. I'd do as my father asked. But I'd do it my way. I wouldn't try for high enough scores to go into Command like my eldest brother, Shinya, and I wouldn't be a Rapier or a leader. I'd be a Dagger. A Lefthand. The perfect tool of subterfuge, a sinister liar through and through.

Then I saw you, and it was like everything fell into place.

I was late. I wasn't in uniform. My hair *certainly* wasn't regulation. So we had to run—all of us—because group punishment is a staple of military life. But as we were running, you in your used boots and me in my flexglass platforms, we kept pace with each other. No matter how hard I pushed myself—and for once in my life, I found myself actually *trying*—you dogged my heels. We were meters ahead of everyone else. We were a world unto ourselves. And I knew, right then, that you were exactly what I needed.

Throughout the rest of the day, I shadowed you. Instructors paired us in all our classes, in math, languages, and philosophy. I sat with you at lunch. I even bribed a girl bunked next to you to move her shit to another location so I could sleep above you.

And when a snarky voice asked into the dark, "Hey, Hiro, are you a boy or a girl?" I remember your answering scoff.

Maybe the asker had made fun of you earlier in the day. Or maybe you didn't know her at all, and simply wanted to fight everyone around you. I could hear your heavy exhalation, and the whisper that followed: "Hey, Barker, are you an asshole or a bastard?"

I laughed. Really, truly laughed, until everyone else fell silent, and the room echoed with my voice.

"I am what I am. Neither. Both. Who cares?"

I was me. Finally, I was who I wanted to be. You never cared about anything beyond what I could do as your Dagger.

And that made you my perfect Rapier.

CHAPTER 4

It was the discovery of hermium on the surface of Mercury that gave the scientists of the *Icarus* their first breakthrough. With its extraordinary ability to withstand extremely high temperatures and conduct energy with almost no transfer loss, hermium became the key to unlocking the mysteries not just of energy production and harnessing but ultimately of living in previously uninhabitable places.

From Cytherean History *by Rebecca val Kuang*

The first time I met Hiro, I hated them. Now I feel lost without them. I can't imagine spilling their blood, even though that is exactly what's expected of me.

"You can't go, Lito," Lucinia says, calling me back to here. To now. We sit side by side, eyes pointed upward so that we don't have to see each other's expressions as I tell her about my new mission. Her face would be hurt. Mine would be detached. And we can't stand to see each other that way.

So we keep our gazes up. The dome has fluffy white clouds drifting by, but they're programmed, so if you watch for hours, you'll see certain shapes repeat themselves. Funny how so few people notice this, but Luce pointed it out to me when we were children only visiting the uppermost layer of Cytherea. Now I can't see anything but the patterns.

"I have to," I tell her. I fight the urge to say more: *Hiro would understand. Hiro would come after me if our fates were reversed.* "I already accepted."

"¿Qué cojones?" I know she's angry when she slips into Dad's Spanish. "Dale al coco, Lito." Slang for what she really wants to say: *Use your head.*

But I don't want to spend time thinking. I can't, because I don't want the overwhelming sorrow and guilt and anger to come back. I neutralize them with my implant before they can take root and spread.

"You're not even considering how this ends, are you?" she asks. As much as I try to hide my feelings from her, she reads them as easily as words on a page. I've always thought the Thousand Gods Below the Sun—all the gods humanity brought with them to the stars, more for cultural community than lawful divinity—meant for my sister, two years my junior, to be the elder one. "You're not *saving* Hiro. They're not in trouble. They're not out there waiting for you. They made their choice, and unless you do what you've been ordered to do—"

She cuts off. I don't think she can say it. She drains the rest of her Verdad coffee, a black brew that all the Paragon influencers are drinking these days, just to give herself time to stew at me.

"They'll send someone to kill me," I finish for her.

Her frustration obvious in her sharp movements, Lucinia crumples her coffee cup in her hand, triggering a chain reaction that causes the papery material to disintegrate. After it breaks down into soil, she sprinkles it onto the grass behind us and claps her hands together. But she says nothing more.

I offer her my milk tea, barely touched.

Her nose wrinkles. "No thanks," she mutters. "You like it too sweet."

"Since when do you not like sugar?"

"Bitter is a flavor too, dear brother." She carelessly flings herself into the grass, numerous necklaces and charms tinkling as she settles.

This place, our hill, sits in the middle of a beautiful park surrounded by crystalline buildings, peaceful—and, more importantly, sheltered from others. We can speak freely here.

There was nothing like this where we grew up, layers below in our old neighborhood, Faraday Square, and we meet here as often as we can. It's our reminder that we made it, that I became a duelist and she followed in my wake as an artist, sharing my salary so that she could follow her dreams. If I let my eyes focus on her and the trees surrounding us, I can pretend my mission doesn't exist, that we are happy, at least for a little while.

"I've gotta do it, Luce."

"I know it's your assignment, but don't pretend you don't see this for what it really is."

"Of course I do. This is Beron's punishment for what happened on Ceres." A burn mission. If I succeed, the Icarii win. If I fail . . . well, the Icarii lose nothing but a disgraced soldier. But I don't dare to examine my feelings too closely regarding the mission itself. It's complicated and messy when I know I have to do as I've been commanded. My feelings about Hiro are irrelevant: there's no other option.

"I'm a duelist, Luce. This is what I was trained for. This is my purpose."

She rolls her eyes but doesn't reply to that thread of conversation. "Have you even told Mamá and Papá you're leaving?"

I look at her beside me, but she keeps her eyes on the sky. I take in the strong profile of her face, so much like mine with her olive skin and prominent hawkish nose, remnants of our father's Spanish and our mother's Italian heritage, things she could have had gene-assisted away but didn't. Neither of us have strayed too far from natural, though her purple hair frames cheeks shimmering with glittering freckles.

"No."

"Do you expect me to always be the one to tell them when you're gone?" She sounds more disappointed than annoyed, and somehow that makes it worse. "They ask me a thousand questions about you, and you leave me to try to answer when I don't even know where you are or what you're doing."

"I don't know why you bother to talk to them." I know the words are a mistake as soon as they're out of my mouth.

She bolts upright, eyes widening like our mother's do when she's furious. For a moment, childhood fear awakens alongside the instinct to either freeze or run. But Luce is not our mother; she wouldn't raise her hand against anyone. "Oh, so you can accept Hiro betraying all of the Icarii—selling *you* out—but you can't forgive your parents, who are *trying* to be better, for what happened when we were children?"

And the truth is that, no, I cannot. Whenever I try, I remember bruises the color of Luce's hair mottling her wrists. I remember the sting of my mother's hands and the anger pulsing in my veins before I could will that emotion away. I remember wishing that my father would step in and stop her, only to be disappointed time and again. And I remember that helpless feeling, more than anything, that we would never escape them. Maybe I could forgive their treatment of me, but not of Luce. Never Luce.

I don't care that they've suddenly decided to become better people. They can't make up for what they did to her.

"What if you leave and something happens to them while you're gone?" Luce asks. "What if something happens to *you*?"

I grasp for words that will please her, calm her—but she must realize from the look on my face that I don't care. The neural implant is doing its work, filtering out useless emotion. Her lip trembles. Her eyes well up.

"You care more about the person they forced on you than your own flesh and blood?" she asks, and for a moment, I wonder if she's talking about our parents or *herself*. She snatches her bag and throws it over her shoulder. The strap tangles in her many necklaces, and they jingle as she shoves herself to her feet.

"Luce, don't go—" I reach for her hand, but she snatches it away.

"Congratulations, Lito. You're everything the Icarii want you to be."

My guts twist with something hot like anger and shame that I shove away. I don't know what to feel as she marches away, not even bothering to brush off the grass that clings to her. Sorrow? Guilt? This could be the last time I see her.

She holds her head high. Her shoulders are squared. Do I want this to be the last image I keep of her?

I want to call after her, but I don't.

She won't listen anyway.

But I know I'll succeed in this mission and come back. I have to. So much of her success is based on mine. And I love her more than anyone else in the cosmos. Even Hiro. Even myself. And I'm willing to do whatever I can, even hunt my former partner down, if only I can take care of Lucinia.

Because without me? No one else will.

CHAPTER 5

Those Sisters who grow too old and frail to continue the Goddess's work among the stars still remain part of the Sisterhood. Becoming Cousins, those who perform physical labors, they rejoin the Order of their training and prepare a new generation of Sisters for service. But of those who break the laws given by the Agora, the seven Aunts who speak on behalf of their Orders? Those who communicate outside of the Sisterhood are stripped of rank and given to the Agora for punishment. The Canon makes it quite clear what that punishment will be.

Aunt Edith, Order of Cassiopeia

The call for all crew members to assemble in the docking bay comes far too early the next morning, especially since I was up late reading Captain Saito's dossier. I splash water on my face in an attempt to freshen my appearance, but dark circles have already bloomed on the sensitive, pale skin beneath my eyes. There is little to do about the fact that I look exhausted.

But it was worth it, I reassure myself. I finished Captain Saito's entire file and even memorized the most important details about her family and work history. Now I understand her at her most basic level, and I won't have to rely on confession to know the sins of her past.

I exit my room, and soldiers brush against me as they pass, carried by the powerful current of a river. I follow after them, a small silver fish darting through the stream in my ashen dress. The few who notice me bid me a good morning and bow their heads to me, but most stomp ahead with thinly veiled concern on their faces, ignoring all in their path. It isn't every morning that we are called to assembly, and everything about the packed hallway feels strange, from the quiet clapping of boots against the metal floor to the stiflingly hot air around us.

Perhaps Captain Saito wants to give one of her inspiring speeches in person, one that prepares us for whatever changes she promised will take place now that Arturo is gone. I hope that is all. But as the men walk side by side with me, their faces blanched of lively color, I wonder . . . and I worry.

"Good morning." Ringer's gruff voice rumbles from all six and a half feet of him. He shortens his steps to walk alongside me, shuffling lazily.

I flash him a smile and lean into his presence so that our arms brush each other as they sway at our sides. Ringer has always been a shield to me, and if I am to stay on the *Juno* by necessity, then I will continue to rely on him as a safe harbor in the storm of his fellow soldiers.

"I'm both sad and joyful to see you still among us, First Sister," he says. "I know you cared for Captain Deluca."

Did I, or was it simply a role I played so well that even Arturo believed it? I suppose he didn't believe it wholly. He still left me behind.

"I'm selfishly glad for myself," Ringer says. "You are faithful to us, and we could have no one better interceding with the Goddess on our behalf."

My smile brightens without my forcing it; I am fond of Ringer and the way he believes the best of me. He sees me as I hope others do.

I wish I could ask Ringer what he thinks of Captain Saito, or draw the conversation toward this meeting. As a soldier, he would most likely know the reason for the assembly.

But as we come to the elevator, he halts and drops his voice to a whisper. "I'm going to stay at your side today." I feel his hand hovering just above my lower back, not daring to touch me, but lingering in a protective gesture nonetheless. "I don't want you to be afraid of what is to come."

All the air leaves me in one breath. His words confirm my deepest worries.

I shuffle alongside the soldiers as we crowd into the elevator. My stomach churns when I see Third Sister through the closing doors. She stands alone. She catches my gaze, and in her expression I read a warning. For once, no rank separates us; fear turns the world into *us* against *them.*

What are we walking into?

It's only as I ride the elevator down that I realize why the hallways feel so strange: the *Juno* isn't moving.

When we reach our destination, I am smiling and pleasant, happy to be in attendance, just as I should be. A Sister, and nothing more. Only Ringer takes notice of me as we walk together into the docking bay.

The bay is not so different today than it was yesterday when I met Captain Saito, only now there is no jolly festivity in the air, no celebration. Everyone in the room has drawn in a single, bated breath, and holds on to it with dismay.

Captain Saito stands above the packed soldiers on a platform in the middle of the bay. Aunt Marshae lingers to the side, hands primly folded in front of her. Her expression reveals nothing.

To the left of the platform my fellow Sisters are clustered, a flock of gray birds in their fluttering dresses. I do not join them, but instead walk to the right side with Ringer. Since the Mother assigned me to the *Juno* as a reward, I have been an outsider; I do not fit in with those girls any more than they care for me. But what is most shocking is that when Third Sister arrives, she comes to stand with me.

A strange feeling emerges, a tightness in my stomach . . . I can't fight the concern that something is off. That someone is missing.

I cast my eyes around the room, searching, trying to remember who or what I have forgotten, when I hear Captain Saito say, "That's enough of them."

People continue to enter the room, but a hush has fallen. Even whispers are snuffed out. All eyes turn toward Captain Saito, three golden stars blazing on her uniform, no trace of the young, slouching captain that I saw in her private quarters.

"Good morning," Captain Saito says. She doesn't use the intercom, but she doesn't need to; her smoky voice carries. "I'm sure you know who I am by now." Many soldiers salute without prompting. Already Captain Saito has developed a camaraderie among them with her preceding reputation and war stories. "For those few who have somehow missed my announcement, I am the new captain of the ACS *Juno*, Saito Ren. You will refer to me as Captain Saito. Is this clear?"

This time the salutes ripple around the room, hundreds of fists pressed to hearts. My hands shake at my sides. Ringer holds me steady.

"I hate that this is happening so early in my captaincy, but—well, even as a new captain, I cannot allow my limits to be tested." Captain Saito's tone is not as threatening as her words. Many stare at her in confusion, even as a cold sweat breaks out over my forehead. I feel I balance on the edge of a cliff. What is she about to do? Dismiss all of the Sisters? I eye Aunt Marshae, but she gives nothing away with her dour face.

"We have, unfortunately, discovered a spy on board." Crew members gasp, *actually* gasp, like in my vid sims. Captain Saito draws her hands behind her back and straightens her spine as she speaks. She is young, but Mother help me, I cannot believe I ever thought she was an easy mark. Her black eyes sharpen into daggers ready to kill with a look.

"Some call me the Hero of Ceres," she announces, speaking words that I read in her file, words I hoped to use against her. "I am the one who led the coup that resulted in the capture of the new Gean home, in the Icarii defeat. I lost my limbs to this fight." She holds up her white prosthetic hand for all to see. "The left side of my body—gone. But do not think this makes me weak." She clenches that hand into a fist. "I faced the demons of war. I emerged victorious. And I will not tolerate even a *hint* of treason on my ship."

Goddess, oh Goddess. I look at my Auntie, who looks at me, her gaze softening as she meets my eyes. My knees give out beneath me, and I clutch Ringer for aid. He holds me up, his hands burning through my dress. "First Sister," he mutters in a tone better suited to a child.

"Bring the traitor up here." Captain Saito motions to someone offstage.

I fear for a moment that they will come for me, that somehow, impossibly, Captain Saito has discovered I am to spy on her for the Mother. But no one grabs me. No one's face even turns in my direction, and instead all watch as two soldiers march onto the stage with Second Sister held between them.

Second Sister, her black hair a tangle about her pretty face. Her cheeks pink and puffy, blotchy with tears. Her amber eyes ringed in purple shadows.

Third Sister makes a pained noise low in her throat. No, not a noise—it can't be a noise—just some sort of exhalation against her shock.

"Observe," Captain Saito says, "the Icarii spy."

I release a shuddering breath. My traitor's heart swells with relief. Captain Saito does not yet know about my assignment, then.

The two soldiers position Second Sister in the middle of the stage and release her. She does not move. Though she hunches into herself, she does not even try to escape. She's surrounded by soldiers with railguns on their backs. She knows her fate.

"Though she was once a respected member of this crew, Second Sister was caught trying to smuggle information to a third party later identified as Icarii sympathizers," Captain Saito says, and Third Sister presses her hand to her mouth, stifling a soundless cry. Our fellow Sisters' eyes shine with tears like stars.

Was she? I wonder, and try to catch my Auntie's attention. *Is it true?* I furrow my brows, but Aunt Marshae dips her chin to hide her expression. Her words echo in my head. *I feel it necessary to say that if you are caught, it will be you who takes the blame, not the Sisterhood.*

A tear slips down my cheek, as cold as my heart.

Second Sister was the kindest of the Sisters to me. I remember her words in the elevator when we believed I was leaving with Arturo. *Much luck in your future.* She had wished the best for me, regardless of what I had stolen from her.

"Second Sister, you are no longer a member of the *Juno*." Captain Saito's voice finally takes on the sinister quality I have been listening for. Her tone matches the anger of her words. Second Sister's face silently contorts into another round of tears, but Captain Saito ignores her, as if it is all theatrics.

Everything about our captain shouts a warning: *Do not fuck with Saito Ren.*

"Is there anything you would like to add, Aunt Marshae?" Captain Saito gestures to our Auntie with her prosthetic hand.

Aunt Marshae looks every bit the authority she is as she stares down Second Sister. Her sculpted auburn hair curling at her chin; her ironed gray dress, its scarf sweeping elegantly around her shoulders; her eyes, tearful but not overly so—all speak to a woman who cares for us Sisters, but also one who has hardened her heart to do what must be done. "I mourn what has happened beneath my very gaze, sorrowful that a girl could be so swayed as to court the enemy." But there, her expression falters; the edges of her lips lift ever so slightly into a smirk, her eyes hardening like gemstones, and I feel, for but a moment, I have glimpsed the true face of my Auntie. "But the rules are clear. Strip her."

Second Sister's legs give out, but two soldiers pull her upright, holding the weight of her body between them as Ringer does mine. Then they grab her dress and pull, and the thin silk parts, the sound of ripping filling the air as they bare her for all the *Juno* to see.

I do not look away. I cannot, for this shameful fate could also be mine.

The soldiers release her, each holding a portion of her tattered dress, but Second Sister does not fall again. She does not hide herself behind her hands. She cries, but she also lets them look. Lets them see her as she is before the Goddess, without adornment. Men shake their heads in scorn, judging the body they so happily prayed to not a day ago. But she keeps her shoulders squared, even if the rapid rise and fall of her breasts reveals how scared she is.

Captain Saito doesn't give the order. It's Aunt Marshae who waves the soldiers forward. They snatch Second Sister's arms hard enough to leave bruises and half lead, half drag her—she tries to walk with them, stumbling to keep up—not toward the exit of the docking bay, but to the deep-blue hermium shield, the shimmering wall that protects us from the vacuum of space.

Goddess, they're going to do it here. Now. In front of all of us. My breathing comes quicker, and I press a hand to my diaphragm. I count my inhales, as if I can control the terror this way.

"'For those who sow betrayal shall reap death.'" Aunt Marshae quotes the Canon from memory. But she does not cite the second half of the verse from the book of Works: *But those who confess in the name of the Goddess shall be forgiven.* She ignores that part.

There will be no forgiveness today.

The soldiers throw Second Sister against the hermium shield, and she lands with her hands pressed against it, instinctively catching herself on the energy wall made up of microscopic bots. Their programming specifies what they allow to pass through their barrier, though now, glowing dark blue, the wall is solid. But Second Sister only has time to turn her face toward us—red, tear-streaked, defiant—before one of the soldiers presses a button and the shield lightens, signaling that every-thing but essential gases like oxygen can pass through the wall.

Second Sister straightens. As the soldiers step toward her, she knows what they mean to do. Instead, she looks to her Sisters and raises her arms like wings. As if to take flight. She opens her mouth, but of course, no sound comes. Instead, she makes a hand gesture that only we Sisters would understand.

Trapped, she signs. *Trapped.*

"Seize her—" Aunt Marshae starts.

With her face twisted in a silent scream, Second Sister jumps.

She breaks through the barrier like it is thin ice over cold water, slipping into the black void beyond.

My mind fills with a detailed awareness of what is happening to her now, all remembered from the mundane safety demonstrations on every ship I've served on. Instead of counting my breaths, I count her seconds.

One, two, three . . .

She exhales immediately. At least her lungs will not burst, but it is a hollow comfort when it will give her only a few more seconds to live.

Four, five, six . . .

Her mouth is caught in a scream, her blue eyes wide with horror, and the moisture on them boils in the deep freeze.

Seven, eight, nine . . .

Her skin swells and blooms with bruises as the liquid inside evaporates.

Ten, eleven, twelve . . .

Her body violently jerks with convulsions, her hair floating around her like spilled ink.

Thirteen, fourteen, fifteen . . .

She stops moving. Hangs limp in the lack of atmosphere.

But she's not dead. Not yet. No, she's just blacked out.

Now she will turn blue with a lack of oxygen and her blood will boil, though she won't be awake to feel it. But I wonder, is that more merciful?

Her body follows its initial motion, floating farther and farther away from the ship. The *Juno* has stopped so that we can all witness this, and Second Sister keeps going, nothing to halt her. All hopes of saving her disappear as I make it to two minutes.

One hundred and nineteen, one hundred and twenty . . .

She's gone.

"Enough," Captain Saito says. Do I imagine the pain in her tone? She never looks at Second Sister, growing smaller by the second, as the soldiers solidify the hermium barrier. "You're dismissed." She waves us away, though some soldiers linger.

"Earth endures, Mars conquers," a few intone. Captain Saito does not join them.

Many turn on their heels and leave, thankful to escape this horror. If only we Sisters could dismiss our nightmares that easily.

"First Sister, let's go," Ringer says, but I pull away from him and stay with my other Sisters. At some point, he must leave; when I reach for him again, I do not find him, but I also know he must follow the order to return to work.

But I cannot move.

I watch until Second Sister is gone, until I can no longer pick her out amidst the other space debris.

When I finally tear my gaze away from the barrier, I find Aunt Marshae on the dais. Her eyes, as hard as diamonds, slice into my skin. Without words, I hear her speak, her lips curled into that whisper of a smirk that I saw when she wore her true face. *Do not become her,* she says.

PLAY:

⏵03

◇—◆—◇◆◇—◆—◇

I know you don't get it, why I hate my father. I mean, I've seen your home life, and I know your past. Your parents are *openly* dysfunctional, which is totally different from a family who has scripted dinnertime conversations. Yes, the val Akira family has built worlds. But how many bodies have they stepped over to make them?

Do you remember that one year for our annual leave we went to my house instead of yours?

[Laughing.]

First of all, did it ever occur to you how weird it was we spent our breaks together? Other Rapiers and Daggers would go home separately, spend the week with their families, and return, most of them relieved that they wouldn't have to pretend to like Mama's new vat-grown whale recipe or listen to Daddy's shitty work accomplishments as if they mattered anymore. But we never split, not once during our six years in the Academy.

The military paired off kids, creating a unit where one could rat out the other for disloyalty or whatever, but with us, something stuck. They had created some facsimile of family that was stronger than blood, because, despite our differences, we were kindred. We both understood what it was to grow up before we ever should have had to.

Isn't that what growing up means, learning to be disappointed by your parents? You've said it is accepting them as human, but that's the same damn thing, Lito. Seeing your parents as humans instead of the perfect, loving caretakers of your childhood is accepting disappointment and learning to live with it.

Childhood is a lie. The end.

[A heavy sigh.]

I'm sure you don't like that thought.

Anyway, one year we went to see my family instead of yours. I think this was the year before Luce moved into her own apartment, or maybe it was the year after, I don't know. I just remember the way we all crowded around the low table in my family's private dining room, legs tucked beneath us on tatami mats.

For the majority of the meal, I felt like I was practically glowing. After years of being apart from my family, the visit was going so well. I know I had annoyed you the week before, prepping you endlessly for this, and I was happy you remembered everything. You'd removed your shoes at the door. You'd bowed properly, arms held at your sides. You'd even brought a gift for my father, though now I can't remember what it was. But everything changed when you pointed out the empty place at the table, set as if we were waiting for just one more guest.

Did you see it then, I wonder, when my father's mask slipped—the rage of the monster you woke when you destroyed his carefully preserved facade?

Guilt swarmed me until I feared I would cry. I should have warned you about that empty spot, should have coached you to ignore it. But how could I tell you about it, when we had lived a lie for so many years that I had forgotten what it was to look truth in the eye?

"I'm s-sorry," you stammered, sensing my distress through the implant, but my father, mask back in place, smiled at you.

"It's for my wife," he said, gesturing to the spot at the table, "when she joins us."

You must have wondered, after everything I had told you about my mother not being part of our lives, why my father said that. Why he acted this way. My mother's place was set as if we were just waiting for her to arrive home late from work. Like she'd come trotting in, slipping off her shoes and tossing her designer bag somewhere she'd inevitably forget it. You couldn't know it, but her spot was always set like that, despite there being not one single picture of her throughout the sprawling multilevel townhome.

But you said nothing more, and neither did he. Then the meal continued, as if you'd never pointed it out at all.

When we left, I remember you telling me that my father wasn't how you'd imagined him. A CEO, a scientist, a man who collects Earthen-Japanese artifacts and enjoys the sitar-heavy classical music from Mars. You wouldn't expect that man to also find enjoyment in heavy weights and a protein-rich diet. He's powerfully built, my father, handsome, with wide shoulders and a lightly lined face and dark hair that has a single streak of white above his forehead, as if even age is afraid to mark him.

Does he use geneassists to keep himself youthful? Probably. Can you see the evidence of that on his face? Not one bit. Not like my mother, who changed herself so much and so often that Jun once started crying because she mistook Mother for a new lover of Father's, some imposter he had brought home.

But the reason my father isn't how you'd imagine him is because he's the greatest storyteller there is.

When we were children, Father used to tell us stories of foxes that his father had been told by his father, and on and on and on, all the way back to an ancestor who probably wasn't even remotely interested in science. Some of the stories we can trace from Mars to Earth and that bow-shaped island called 日本, or Japan, but some of them my father made up himself, as if he stands alongside those ancestors and believes his words are as worthy as theirs.

I loved the trickster stories, the way his face lit up as he told them with a smirk that I tried hard to imitate. Jun also loved the stories where the foxes got the better of people, especially proud warriors. Maybe that's why I was always closest to her. Shinya liked the stories of fox spirits that acted as guardians. Fitting, given that he immediately went to the Academy and tested into the Command division like a good first son should.

Hanako, despite being the youngest, liked all the stories that mentioned a wide variety of foxes. Sometimes they were white, sometimes they were black; sometimes they had nine tails, and those were the most powerful of all. She would listen with her lips pursed like she would be able to solve why there were so many types, like she was trying to codify millennia worth of spirits. I liked watching her almost as much as watching my father when it was story time.

Asuka, a romantic despite her scientist heart, liked the stories of shape-shifting foxes who would turn into beautiful women and marry unsuspecting men. But I hated those stories.

Every time my mother left and we feared she was gone for good, never to return, those were the stories Father would tell. The fox women in the stories would have a soft, round mouth like our mother, or large black eyes like our mother, or a smile that revealed long canines, just like our mother's did.

Maybe my siblings didn't see what our father was trying to say with those stories. Or perhaps they did, and they hated her just like Father did.

But I knew our mother wasn't a fox in disguise. She was just a woman—a tired, selfish woman who was all too human. I could understand those flaws, at least.

In truth, the one who had the most cutting eyes, the most dangerous mouth, was the storyteller. Our father.

Sometimes I would dream my siblings and I were sitting at our family's low table, and on one side was our mother, pale as a ghost, and on the other side was a fox with a wide mouth. "Come and serve me dinner," he would call to us, and I would watch as first Shinya and then Asuka crawled onto his plate and offered themselves up. Then he would turn to me, the thirdborn middle child adrift between my elder siblings and the two I had cared for as babies, and ask the same of me.

Jun was at my back, pushing me forward, Hanako behind her in one of her best dresses. "Hurry, hurry," they whispered as one. "You don't want to upset him."

But I wouldn't. I couldn't. Even if I wanted to go, I found the legs of the table had grown too high, like stately trees, or that I had somehow lost all the strength in my limbs and was stuck in place.

Then the fox would take off his mask and would become my father again. "Always late, Hiro," he would say, and I would fill with such a shame that I would wake in my bed trembling.

That's how I know. My mother was never the fox-wife of stories. If anything, there was a fox lurking in my father, wearing his face.

He's always been a skilled storyteller. But that's the thing about my father. He's so skilled at telling stories that no one but me, it seems, has realized that his entire life is a story.

The man looks like a chaste and loyal husband, but he's had his string of affairs. He acts like he hates politics, but he's got all of Cytherea's politicians in his pocket. He joins ethics boards and discussions on patient consent, but he experiments on Asters who don't truly understand the consent forms.

And the worst truth of all, the one I think none of my four siblings wishes to hear: our mother is never coming back.

She can't.

No matter how far I dug into the val Akira computers, I couldn't find her. Father followed her for three years after she left, and then . . .

[A shaky exhalation.]

Gone. Disappeared.

Now, I'm not a detective or a hacker or anything like that. I can only extrapolate from the data my father collected. And to me, it seemed like Mother had moved on, found a nice life with some man and his children, and then stopped existing. No more health records to indicate she went to the doctor. No more drawing her annual salary. No more occasional featured picture of her as a Paragon influencer on the Cytherean streets. Nothing.

I guess I can see why Father did whatever it was he did. Why did Mother choose that other man's family over ours when she had five kids and a hardworking husband at home? Maybe he just forced her to wear a new face and go by a new name and get a new citizenship number, something to help him avoid the shame of a woman who didn't want him or their kids. Or maybe she left for Gean space, somehow took refuge on Mars, and hid away in a land where my father couldn't touch her.

But I don't think so.

My father doesn't have it in him to be that forgiving.

Our mother was gone, and we would never dress her in a white kimono, light incense for her, or place her picture in the family altar. Instead, we would stare at her empty place at the table, never offering her spirit a scrap of food.

And that empty place at the table my father sets for my mother? Now I know the reason it exists.

It's not to remember her. It's not because he misses her.

It's a warning to his children.

One I didn't heed until it was too late.

CHAPTER 6

The human psyche is no longer an unknowable, impenetrable labyrinth; we have pried open its doors. With aid of the neural implant, we're closer than we've ever been to the truth of consciousness. Under its lens, cognitive processes have been laid bare for us to objectively measure.

This is truly the Promethean fire: No longer will we be limited by subjectivity, blind emotion, or mental illness. Now, for the first time in history, humanity has broken free from the chains of its mind. The past of dissonance between the subjective and the objective is over. Now is the time for certainty and harmony, an era for collective logic.

Souji val Akira, CEO of Val Akira Labs

❖

"Syncing in three, two . . ." Beron val Bellator points to me when the countdown ends, but I don't need him to. I *feel* the connection snapping taut between Ofiera fon Bain and me. My new Dagger. My Lefthand. We're bonded now.

After having my neural implant tied to Hiro's for so long, being untethered to anyone was a bit like drifting in space. But having Ofiera here in Hiro's place isn't much better. I grew up with Hiro. I was used to them. And as much as I can feel Ofiera radiating confidence in our upcoming mission, her emotions aren't the ones I want.

I force myself to calm. Lean into my implant. Stop fighting it. It whispers: *Ofiera fon Bain is safe. Ofiera fon Bain is trustworthy. Ofiera fon Bain will help you accomplish your mission. Because you* have *to.*

"Now," Beron says, sliding his compad toward Ofiera and me so we can see the screen, "this is the most updated layout of the Val Nelson Mining station on the mid-atmosphere level that we have. We've spotted several notable faces on that level with historical ties to Dire of the Belt."

I grimace. Dire has a criminal record longer than both my legs combined. He's one of the outlaws who lives in the asteroid belt, a known thief, smuggler, and anarchist who spouts anti-Icarii views. Anti-Gean too, if I'm being fair.

"Latest intel shows that Dire's men load the ships with contraband here in this hangar." Beron points to a square building at the back of a cluster of four. "And here"—he points to another building set apart by thick lines half a kilometer away—"is the space elevator where you'll enter the mid-atmo platform. As you can see, there are other mining operations surrounding Val Nelson's. You'll need to infiltrate their hangar specifically without being noticed by competition, Val Nelson's own employees, or Dire's men."

"Val Nelson has offices on the bottom level of Cytherea as well?" I ask.

Beron nods. "For clerical duties and suiting up."

I nod. While the space elevator is pressurized, the mid-atmo platform isn't. "Then we need those suits." I wish we had blueprints of the offices as well; I wonder if we could pull them before our mission.

Ofiera nods her agreement. "Wearing Val Nelson suits, we could enter like employees."

"The smugglers will realize you're not one of them quick enough if you're poking around the out-of-bounds hangar." Beron rubs a finger over his upper lip. "It would be best if you could do this without being seen at all. Just get in, plant the micro-EMPs, steal a grasshopper, and get out."

"And the Val Akira Labs tech that we find on the grasshopper?"

"That's part of the beauty of this plan," Beron says, and when he grins, he looks like a much younger man. I wonder if he misses combat now that he's stuck with a desk job. I know I would. "You'll take the grasshopper on the same route to Ceres that the smugglers use, and whatever's on board can be used as part of your cover story when pretending you're an outlaw."

Beron's right: the plan makes a great deal of sense. Since the Icarii government does not wish to *officially* interfere with the Mother's Celebration, Ofiera and I will need to make it look like we're independent operators. That means stealing an unaligned ship, like a *GR9079*-class Aster rig, nicknamed a grasshopper, to make us look like we're at home in the belt. As a bonus, we'll also cripple Dire's smuggling operation that's been going on under our noses for months, and any way we can cut down on the outlaws in the belt is a huge benefit.

The belt and the spheres beyond it are dangerous places. When combatant AIs in Earth and Mars' Dead Century War reached consensus, they abandoned their creators and disappeared on a fleet of ships for the harsh planets beyond the asteroid belt, leaving behind one warning: do not follow.

If humanity takes even one step beyond the belt, the Synthetics will destroy us. We're effectively locked into the inner planets because of Earth and Mars, whose treaty came only when they realized they could no longer afford to fight each other. Now, as the combined power of the Geans, they wage war against us, wanting the tech we created in peacetime for their own.

But Dire and people like him are every bit as dangerous as the Geans, even if they don't have the same level of tech or the numbers that we do. While the Asters live within the asteroid belt on planetoids and other rocks, the outlaws routinely operate close to Jupiter in gray space and spit in the face of the Synthetic ultimatum, tempting retribution against all humanity.

"Make it look like a rival gang hit." Beron shifts in his chair, his shoulders squaring as he leans toward us. "There are to be no witnesses. Is that clear?"

I add that to the growing list of restrictions. No military blacks, no government-issued HEL guns, no mercurial blades. Also no shields. What a pain in the ass, and we haven't even started yet. "Yes, sir," I say, and Ofiera echoes.

My finger traces the edge of Beron's compad. "Do you think we could get a map of Val Nelson's offices on the lowest level of Cytherea?" I ask at the same time I hear my name.

"Lito sol Lucius." An officer in formal black and silver steps into the plain basement room. "You have a visitor."

"Who?"

"Lucinia sol Lucius."

My heart speeds at her name, but I return to base level with a nudge to my implant. I turn to Beron. "High Commander?" As much as I want to, I can't very well storm out of the room with him right here.

Beron levels a frustrated glance in my direction, but it's Ofiera's encouragement that I focus on. "We're not scheduled to go dark for another two hours," Ofiera says, more to Beron than to me. "Let him say his goodbyes."

Beron huffs but waves at me. "Go. I'll see about the blueprints." I slip through the door with the quick movements of a duelist. "You are due back here in fifteen!" he calls after me.

The officer leads me through the labyrinthine concrete hallways to the elevator. I don't pay him much mind, too focused on the news of my sister. What is she doing here past midnight? "Lobby," I tell the intelligence in the elevator, and we rocket upward.

It's only three seconds later that the officer speaks. "Nervous?"

"What?" I shouldn't be surprised—most people hate silence, find it awkward—but his question confuses me.

"Sorry." He gestures to my boots. "You were tapping your foot. Here I thought duelists didn't feel anything."

I say nothing—I don't owe him an explanation—but of course we feel things. Right now I feel excitement at seeing my sister, anxiety at how we last left things, worry that something terrible has happened to her and that's why she's come to the Spire.

I'm saved from the awkward conversation when the elevator reaches the lobby, and I exit before the officer. He'll return to his duties—thankless though they may be—and I'll find Luce.

It's not difficult. She's the only one dressed in pink and holosilver. Her shoulders relax as soon as she sees me striding across the lobby toward her, and my mind doubles its frantic activity. *What's happened what's wrong are you okay—*

I force it away.

"Luce," I say calmly.

"Lito," she says, less calm.

"I'm surprised you recognize me." On Beron's orders, the gene-assist burned away all that made me who I am, leaving behind someone I don't recognize. My lank black hair has none of its characteristic blue shine. My skin, usually clear, now has a spattering of lines at the corners of my lips and eyes. My nose, always big, now seems to dominate the entirety of my face. I look exhausted. Defeated. Old, despite my twenty-two years.

Luce furrows her dark brows. "Oh, Lito, I'll always recognize you." She reaches out and takes my hand. "Even now it's like seeing your face through water."

"Poetic." It's just like her to turn a bad situation into an artistic statement. I can't help but smile.

"See? That's the Lito I know."

I clear my throat. Focus. "Why'd you come?" I ask instead of all the questions that plague me.

She licks her lips and tangles her hand in her many necklaces, a ring on every finger clinking against gemstones and charms. Her eyes dart around the room, checking her surroundings. For some reason, she's nervous.

"Something came for you—to my house." She produces a small box from her pocket and shoves it into my hand. It fits in my palm and looks like something that holds jewelry. But when I open it, I don't know what to make of what lies within.

It's old tech, something our parents used in their youth. About as big and thick as my thumbnail. Glittery and pink, a model Luce would buy. I take the little slip of metal from the box and turn it over as if that will reveal its secrets, but I know it won't. It's a playback device. I'll have to put it on the bone behind my ear to hear what it has to say.

"I started listening to it, but stopped as soon as I heard who was on the recording."

"Who?"

But Luce doesn't answer. She looks around the lobby again. She's being careful because she knows they're watching us. *Listening* to us.

"The property manager says it wasn't delivered by a drone. It just showed up in front of my door. Someone must have hand-delivered it." She speaks quickly. "But management says no one was allowed in other than the tenants. Turn it over."

I turn the box over in my palm—and almost drop it.

9tails, it reads.

I don't say their name. Luce doesn't either.

We both know who this is from. The one who told us stories of shape-shifting foxes, and the nine-tailed fox, the most powerful of them all.

I started listening to it, but stopped as soon as I heard who was on the recording, Luce said.

Hiro has sent me a message after all this time. And right when I'm set on a mission to hunt them down.

With one hand, I palm the playback device, pretend to return it to the box, and hand the empty box to Luce. Loudly, just in case someone is spying on us, I say, "I'm about to leave, so I can't take this." But Luce's keen eyes followed my hands, and now she releases a shaky breath, as if the device's disappearance is enough to satisfy her.

"How long do you have?" she asks.

"Little less than two hours now." The device feels like a fire in my pocket. I want to listen to it immediately, but I can't. Not here, not now. And Luce . . . she looks so distraught, I can't stand it.

"Oh . . ." Her lips press into a little pout.

"Luce . . ."

She throws herself into my arms and squeezes me tightly. I hug her back, her head tucked beneath my chin, her hair smelling sweet like coconut. Her fingers bunch in my clothes as she clings to me.

I don't even need my implant to calm me now. This is as it should be. This is how it was in our childhood. Us against the world.

"Tienes que volver a casa, Lito," Luce says through her tears. *You have to return home.*

"Voy a volver," I tell her. *I'll come back.*

When she pulls back, her eyes are glassy.

"Luce." I grab her shoulders and hold her steady. "I will. I promise." I press a kiss to her forehead, and she places her hand over my thumping heart.

We stand like this for a few seconds more until Luce breaks our contact. Then, with a sniff, she wipes her cheeks, smiles at me, and leaves the Spire.

I lift my hand to wave at her in case she looks back.

She doesn't.

OFIERA FON BAIN and I take the bullet train from the top level of Cytherea to the bottom, hiding in plain sight, just another couple of plant workers on their way to the factory. We carry twin sets of gear for this mission in slender backpacks, except I have one tiny thing that she doesn't: mine secretly holds the playback device from Hiro.

When we reach the last stop, we disembark with the other tired-looking workers and head for the building that manages Val Nelson Mining. Outside the train station, the streets are cramped and in disrepair. No podcars zip past, as no one can afford them. Everyone walks, heads down and shoulders slouched in exhaustion. A caustic and sour stench lingers in the air, a mix of odors from the meat-growing vats and recycling plants across this level.

There's such a slight shift in atmosphere and air quality that visitors might never notice, especially if they're focused on the dirt and the stench. But I lived here, once upon a time, and I can feel the difference like an invisible hand on my skin. The pressure down here is heavier, the air filters older and poorly patched.

Home, a part of me says, but I refuse to call this place that. Home is *not* where I was born.

We didn't have time to requisition a set of blueprints for the facility on this level, so when we reach Val Nelson's, Ofiera and I stop outside the gates, and she bends down to tighten the straps of her work boots—an excuse for us to pause and stake out the location. I spot the massive single-story metal structure that houses the space elevator climber in the middle of not just Val Nelson's but all the Cytherean mining management companies. But we need suits first, so I simply point it out to Ofiera, then watch to get a feel for the comings and goings of the miners, all of which are Asters in wraps and goggles going out of their way to avoid us. I don't see any humans, but part of the reason we planned this for so early in the morning is that only humans who pulled the shit shift will be on duty, which means less people to see us.

Let's go. I nudge Ofiera through the implant, and we make our way into the station through an unlocked side door I saw several Asters use.

Inside the warehouse, Asters dart out of our way, sure that we're managers come to judge their progress or measure their output, but no one stops us as we look around, pretending to take notes. Finally, we come upon two sets of locker rooms. The Asters trail into one, while the other must be for humans. I poke my head around the corner, spot pressure suits with a hermium-generated barrier to fight radiation, and let Ofiera know through the implant that we've found the right place at last.

Most of the suit stalls are empty—I wonder if more managers are on duty than we thought—but one man in the middle of dressing turns to us as we enter. Not recognizing us, he draws his thick brows down, turning his expression into a scowl. "Hey, you can't be in here!"

"Don't worry, just a moment," I tell him, reaching into my pocket. I see him go for a weapon at his hip out of the corner of my eye. "Let me show you my clearance." With my implant, I nudge Ofiera to take care of him, and, like a ghost, she slips behind him and seizes one of his arms, twisting it behind his back.

"Agh!" He gasps in pain and bows forward, and I seize his head between my hands and sharply twist. I feel a pop and hear a crack, and the man slips from Ofiera's hands to the ground, dead.

No witnesses.

Since there's only one remaining suit hanging, one of us will have to use his. "Yours or mine?" I ask, pointing to the man at our feet.

"Yours," she says, and grabs the smaller hanging suit.

We dress quickly in the pressure suits, baggy and silver and not at all like our body-conforming military blacks. Only the gloves fit, and the helmets are bulky and don't move with our heads when we look around. At least they'll keep us from being identified, but it's a trial to move in them, and a downright struggle to fit the man's corpse in an empty locker. With that done, we take a moment to check our suits one last time.

My suit has *sol Nast* written on the breast. Ofiera's has *val Farah.*

No one looks twice at us as we exit the locker room and join the queue to ride the space elevator. When our turn comes, we join Asters in mining suits in the spherical climber on their way down the tether. The gangly Asters are much more relaxed here than on the higher levels of Cytherea. While they're wearing protective suits for mining on the surface of Venus, they've removed the bandage-like wraps they usually wear on their faces. Between their long white hair tied into Aster-fashioned plaits and their green-glass goggles, I catch glimpses of skin, thin as silk, spider-webbing veins giving them a blue or purple tint.

It takes forever—almost five minutes—to reach the mid-atmo station twenty-four kilometers down, and I have to use my implant several times to erase my impatience. Ofiera, on the other hand, is a steady source of serenity, as if nothing fazes her. I try to probe for her true emotions through our connection, but like a door slamming in my face, she shuts me out and glares in my direction. Fine, let her keep her feelings secret.

Since this is just a quick stop between Cytherea and the surface, the Asters remain on board while Ofiera and I exit. The station has no hermium force field, so I can see the Venusian atmosphere as it is, heavy metallic rain in thick clouds of yellow. Our pressure suits keep us safe, but I have to force myself to focus on our mission instead of the atmospheric threat around us.

We pass miners and managers in the uniforms of other companies, but as we approach the four Val Nelson warehouses, I feel Ofiera urge me away from her. I send back confusion. Then I see a man coming toward me, and Ofiera darts between an Aster *TR4494*-class termite ship that is used for mining metal on the surface and a *DG3561*-class dragonfly ship used for water transportation.

"Nast, bruv!" the man calls.

I wonder if he's an employee of Val Nelson's or one of Dire's smugglers, working undercover. His suit reads *sol Joshua*, so I make my voice as gruff as I can—like that of the man I subdued for this suit—and reply with his surname. "Joshua!"

"You're scheduled for the surface later today, Nast. What the fuck are you doing here?"

My mind races. If I say I'm ill, I'll be expected to return to Cytherea, but I have to come up with an excuse.

"Upstairs wants to see you," I say quickly. "Told me I could hold down the fort here while you head back up. Something about a family emergency."

I can't see his face through the helmet, but I can read his body language. At first he is wary, his hands up in a defensive stance, but as soon as I mention his family, he becomes panicked, rubbing his gloves together.

"Shit," he says. "Fuck."

"Go," I tell him, pointing to the space elevator.

"You got no more news than that?"

I shake my head before realizing he can't see it. "Sorry, bruv."

"Well, fuck you too." Joshua rushes to the elevator, and I slip between two Aster crafts to get away from him in case he looks back.

Where are you, Ofiera? I search for her with my implant. Unfortunately, it's not a perfect science. I can feel her somewhere around here, but it's hard to pinpoint exact locations in so much chaos. I stick to the mission and head toward the rearmost hangar, where the smugglers have set up shop.

I enter through an airlock corridor, thankful the suit seems to do the job of triggering the doors. Then I spot the small black dot of a camera and lift my hand in a little wave, greeting the airlock operator. Even if they weren't expecting sol Nast until later, sol Joshua's disappearance will raise questions that I can easily excuse as his replacement during an emergency. But . . . that's the first camera I spotted. How many other cameras are there that are too small for me to see?

The door opens, and the dimly lit main hangar stretches before me, a thousand square meters of stacked cargo, hover forklifts, and even a crane large enough to move lightweight ships. In the center, the five grasshoppers wait. Built for quick trips through space and usually well-provisioned, one of these will be perfect for our mission. I can sense Ofiera closer; she must already be inside. Is she planting the micro-EMPs to fry them as we leave? Probably not. How would she do it in these cumbersome suits?

Remembering the layout from the blueprints, I follow the perimeter of the hangar and look for the locker room. Exactly where I expect it, I find a sign designating the way to unisex restrooms, including changing stations, but before I can head down the hallway toward them, wobbling in the puffy suit, a hand snakes out of a walk-in supply closet and jerks me inside.

I take a blind swing at my attacker, but in this thing, a punch will be like being hit by an angry marshmallow.

"Easy there, kiddo," Ofiera hisses, and I have never been more grateful to hear her voice. "Pressure and air are regulated in this hangar. Whatever Dire is smuggling must need it."

I remove my helmet and breathe deeply. Never thought I'd be thankful for low-level air, but it's worlds better than being inside the stifling suit. Ofiera helps me along, tugging the legs over my boots. When I'm finally free, she tosses the suit on top of the one she abandoned amidst metal racks full of cardboard boxes. "Masks on," she says, pulling a black balaclava-and-goggles set from her backpack. She slides it on and becomes faceless. I do the same.

"They're watching us," I tell her. "I spotted a camera on the way in."

"They saw two employees enter," she says. "If we're quick, we can grab what we need and leave before they wonder where we wandered off to."

"Clearly a closet to have an affair," I joke.

Ofiera snorts.

"I'll find the keycode to the grasshopper we're taking, and you plant the micro-EMPs," I say, but Ofiera shakes her head, surprising me. I'm the Rapier; I should be calling the shots.

I'd almost forgotten she was Command.

"Other way around. Hangar is darker, and you're bigger and slower than me."

"Gee, thanks, my self-confidence is skyrocketing," I say, but she doesn't laugh. *Hiro would have*, I think before I tear that thought up and throw it away. I can't keep thinking of Hiro and what they would or wouldn't do.

Ofiera is not Hiro. She's an efficient and capable operative, but I can't call her my partner the same way I did Hiro. And I fear her rank will prevent us from becoming anything more than fellow soldiers with a common cause, because—with her in Command—we will never be equals. Hopefully that doesn't keep us from succeeding in our mission.

"See you at the grasshopper in ten." Ofiera slips from the closet without another word, and I wait thirty seconds before exiting after her.

She was right about one thing: the hangar is darker than the well-lit corridors and office areas, a few of which I can see through dirty, smudged windows. I wonder if the windows and lighting are so the managers can watch the employees in the offices, or so the employees can't see what the smugglers are doing in the hangar. Plausible deniability and all that.

I keep low and rush into the shadow of the first grasshopper. After sticking the micro-EMP to the hull, I check my surroundings and the path I'll take to the second. It's clear.

I'm starting toward the craft when an Aster appears from around the corner. Quickly I press my back to the grasshopper, hoping they don't notice me. Asters can see in almost total darkness; my dark clothes won't help me blend in and hide from them. Nervousness prickles my skin, but I calm myself with my implant so that my heart rate doesn't increase. Meandering, the Aster passes by without looking in my direction.

I take five seconds to regulate my breathing, then rush into the shadow of the second grasshopper. I repeat the process until each but the last craft has a micro-EMP on it. I don't see anyone else, and wait for Ofiera close to the airlock doors. Once she brings the keycode, we can leave.

But as the minutes trickle by and ten becomes fifteen, impatience gets the better of me. She should have been here by now. Has she been held up by something? If someone had discovered her, wouldn't I have heard the alarms? Wouldn't the hangar be swarming with smugglers?

I chew on my cheek and consider my options. I could go after her but risk missing her. Or I could sit here until I'm caught. As fifteen minutes becomes sixteen . . . seventeen . . . I decide to go after her.

Once again I move swiftly from shadow to shadow, but this time I head for the crates and packages littering the hangar. Slipping through the tight corridors between stacks, I keep my eyes out for any labeled Val Akira Labs, but don't spot any. I briefly wonder what tech the smugglers are taking before realizing it doesn't matter. I have a partner to find.

I'm not thrilled to pass back into the well-lit hallways of the management area, but I don't have much choice. I pull my knife from its sheath on my boot and hold it before me, moving slowly so that I don't come upon anyone unprepared.

No witnesses, Beron said. I'll make sure of that.

A door flies open in the hallway, and I take three large steps forward to slip behind it. An Aster and a plainly dressed man with long hair exit. The human holds a cup of steaming liquid.

"There's just no good food to miss, you know?"

The Aster replies in his own language, and the human laughs.

"You said it, not me!"

I wait until their voices disappear down the hallway before continuing.

It's by chance that I spot Ofiera. She's taken off her mask and stands with her back to the door, thumbing through a folder of biopapers. With the way the room lies in disarray, things piled on the desk and on top of filing cabinets, it's no wonder it's taken her so long to find the grasshopper's passcode.

Then I spot him.

An Aster walks up behind her, slowly and warily. She straightens and holds up something from the desk, a single slip of biopaper, as the Aster comes to her side.

Ofiera! I shout over the implant. *Watch out!*

My knife is out. The door is open before the Aster even moves. He starts to turn, but I jump and pull him into a headlock, my knife pressed to his throat.

Ofiera spins, her attention going to me instead of the Aster. "Don't!" she says, and in that moment, I hesitate. It's just a second, but it's enough.

The Aster reaches into his pocket.

"No!" I yell, and slice my knife across his throat.

But it's too late.

Alarms flare to life. Warning lights strobe in the corner of the room. The Aster's blood slicks my hands, the same red as the lights. And now everyone knows there are intruders.

CHAPTER 7

Ranking among the Sisters may seem a complicated matter to outsiders. The top three Sisters on a vessel are ranked as First Sister, Second Sister, and Third Sister. If a First Sister becomes too old for her duties or joins her captain in their retirement, Second Sister becomes First Sister, and Third Sister becomes Second Sister. Unranked Sisters succeed based on popularity, and may be promoted to one of the ranked positions by the vessel's captain at any time.

From Inside the Sisterhood *by Dr. Merel Jäger*

"I did it, Sister, I didn't want to do it, but I did, because my commander ordered me to, and I had to follow orders, didn't I?"

The boy—older than I was when I was first assigned to the pleasure liner and yet a boy nonetheless—kneels at my feet and clutches the skirt of my ashen dress in his trembling fingers. His downturned face is pink with frustration, and my knees are damp with a spattering of his tears. But I do not cry with him. I am merely a conduit; I listen so that the burden may pass from him, so that he may continue to fight without guilt.

"Ceres was such a mess, and they were all looking at me as I took the knife in my hand, all of them, eyes wide, waiting for me—even the corpse, it was like all of a sudden, his eyes were looking right at me, and I knew he was dead, but he was looking at me, and I didn't have a choice, I had to dig the knife in the back of his neck anyway, and I tried to turn his face away, but he was stiff because he was dead—I kept thinking that over and over, 'He's dead! He's dead!'—and even when I turned the body over, it was like he was still looking at me, begging me not to do it. But I had to, you know, I had to because I was ordered to, so I did it, I dug that little metal thing out of his neck, out of the back of his head, that Icarii thing they use, that brain implant, and I put it in my officer's hand, all bloody with these chunks of skin and brain clinging to it, and—"

Jones gasps, and finally, as his words fail and become shuddering sobs, I press my hand to his chin and angle his face so that his eyes meet mine. His eyes are the most beautiful blue, not like a gene-assist's idea of beauty, but natural, like an Earthen summer day from vid sims, and it makes the tears look like a flood. But then all at once, I remember the amber-eyed girl jumping through the airlock barrier, and my heart races.

"I've been dreaming of him. He's still watching me, Sister. Watching as I desecrate his corpse."

I cup his cheeks in my hands and force myself to smile through my fear, though I'm not really smiling at him.

I have found that the secret of smiling even if you don't feel like it is to focus on something else instead of where you're looking. I imagine my harbored daydreams of living on solid, gravity-controlled land with a house and a little garden of my own, grown for the glory of the Goddess in peaceful quietude. That always makes me smile true, so when Jones looks at me, he sees love and thinks it's for him.

"I know the Icarii put their bodies out to space or burn them up, but all I could think about was my mama crying if she didn't have a body to bury back on Earth. They've made me weak, these dreams," Jones says, voice shaking, a broken little boy. "Goddess forgive me."

I wipe away his tears with my thumbs on each cheek, then stroke one hand over his soft, shaven head. I nod at him, because he is forgiven. The Goddess knows, and the Goddess forgives, and the Goddess offers not just second chances but a thousand of them. I am proof of that.

"Thank you, Sister, thank you." He stands from my knees and straightens; the weight on his shoulders is lifted. He's twice my size when not crumpled on the floor, and he takes a few moments to compose his face, red from crying, to something hard and unbending. In moments he is a warrior again. A killer, prepared to do his duty.

Then his eyes fall to my arm and flick away. I know what he sees—or doesn't see. In the protracted space before he moves toward me, fear settles in my belly like a cold, hard stone. With no captain's mark, I am free to him.

And he wants me. Oh Goddess, he wants me.

His dry lips press against mine, and his hand cups the back of my head, guiding me from my seat to stand in front of him. His opposite hand falls to the button at my neck and works with fumbling efficiency. The dress falls open over my collarbones, my skin prickles in the cold ship air, and I sink down, down, down, withdrawing into my center as I did before Arturo, when I was unclaimed and did this every day for hours.

Smile and act, smile and act, smile and act. But it is a hollow game played with puppets, and the memory of my Auntie pulls at my strings.

Be what they want. Be what they need. Be everything for them, so that they will leave your chambers without sadness, without guilt, without lust. No distractions while they're on duty.

Mother, no.

I push Jones away. I am shocked by my own actions.

His face is a study in confusion, his eyes boiling with a heat I do not want. "Are you . . ." He trails off, and I know I must either find an excuse or pull him under even deeper than he was before so that he forgets my actions, because my actions are those of a traitor to the Sisterhood.

Second Sister's punishment flashes in my mind, and I fight a shudder. I won't be her. I pat my arm, the place where the captain's mark should rest. An excuse. A sad, pitiful excuse that I am not sure Jones will buy.

For a moment, he doesn't seem to. His brows pull down as his eyes rove over my dress and settle on my face. "But you don't have the armband . . ." He's not sure if he's willing to challenge what I've indicated. Internally, he debates whether he is bold enough to take me regardless and perhaps offend his new captain.

I pat my arm again more insistently.

Caution wins against lust. Jones steps back and straightens his uniform. "I'm sorry, First Sister," he says, "I didn't know Captain Saito had claimed you already."

I shrug a slender shoulder as if to say, *I have not yet gathered my armband . . .*

Jones flashes me a sympathetic smile. But. . . the way he stares, the rut forming between his brows, suggests he knows something more.

He knows I'm lying.

"One thing . . ." He shuffles from one foot to the other, conscientiously choosing his words. "Be careful with her. I used to know Ren. Captain Saito, I mean. She's not been the same since Ceres."

I nod as if I will keep it in mind while I lead him to the door. First the Mother asks me to keep watch on Captain Saito, and now Jones warns me that she is not the same person she used to be. I think deeply on her dossier, wondering what is missing from the file.

"I will come again," he says, bowing his head to me at the door. A promise. A threat.

If I don't have the armband next time . . . I don't want to imagine it. There is only so long I can get away with this lie.

The door slides closed behind Jones, and I collapse into the single chair in the center of the room. Holoflame candles flicker across the soft walls of the chapel, casting shadows that dance without any heat. I look to the ceiling and focus on the soft folds of white cloth pinned there, part of the canopy that stretches to the four corners of the room and trails down the walls like flowing water.

On the back wall beneath a screen with a livecam view of the stars is a bed big enough for two. My small prison.

I close my eyes and take deep breaths to calm the fury of my heart. I am playing a dangerous game by lying to soldiers to save myself trouble. If even one word reaches Aunt Marshae, I will be harshly punished for my disobedience.

But I cannot give in to that despair now . . . I must take one step at a time. I press a hand to my forehead to fight the coming headache.

The door slides open, and I jolt upright. I did not permit anyone entry, and immediately my features arrange themselves into lowered brows, pinched lips, curled nose—*anger*.

But it's just Second Sister.

The *new* Second Sister, who was Third Sister until . . . until the amber-eyed girl was stripped and cast out of the *Juno*. A Sister no longer. A *person* no longer.

They've made me weak, these dreams, Jones said, and I understand all too well. The amber-eyed girl watches me in my nightmares.

The woman who stands before me with her freckled cheeks and red hair does not look any better for her new position. *She is Second Sister.* I must commit it to memory. A beautiful girl with ebony skin and narrow shoulders was promoted to Third Sister by Captain Saito from among the unranked girls. I will learn to pair her face to her title easily enough; we are all accustomed to change this way. It's a hazard of our profession. Of being nameless.

What? I sign to her.

Second Sister points to my arm and smirks. *Nothing still?*

I frown. Does she know I turned Jones away? Of course not. How could she? My fear is getting the better of me.

I had hoped after what happened to the amber-eyed girl, we might try at friendship. But the way Second Sister tips up her chin so that she looks down her nose at me washes that hope away.

It will be mine, she signs.

My frown deepens. I point to the door, my meaning clear. *Get out.*

I wonder for a moment if Aunt Marshae gave Second Sister the same dossier she gave me, the same assignment. *I feel it necessary to say that if you are caught, it will be you who takes the blame, not the Sisterhood.*

You do not deserve the armband, she signs. *Someone so willing to abandon the* Juno *and the soldiers who need her should never be First Sister.* Her hands still for a moment, but I can see from the burning in her eyes that she is not finished. *I do not believe you hold any love for the Goddess in your heart. You are a fraud.*

My lips twist into a grimace, and I point again at the door and sign, *Leave.*

She does. And for a naked moment, I am free to shake and curl into myself. To collapse, like a dying star. Sobs come, silent but strong.

I wish I could wallow in self-pity, but I am allowed no privacy. No respite with which to explode into stardust. I force myself to straighten as another steps in uninvited. I didn't even hear the door, I was so lost in myself. I wipe away my tears in an attempt to look presentable and turn to my visitor . . .

But it's Ringer.

Just Ringer.

I do not ask him to leave, but I also do not smile. Immediately he can see there is something wrong with me, that I am not as put together as I would like to be. Perhaps he even sees through my mask to the upset beneath. He crosses the room in two strides of his long legs and wraps me in his arms.

Unlike being enveloped in Jones's embrace, this feels safe.

Ringer has never—would never—treat me the way Jones has. The way other soldiers have. Even when he had every right, he never took advantage of me. Though that's not what it is, really. It's *not* taking advantage of us Sisters when it's our duty . . . right?

"Astrid," Ringer says, so softly I wonder if I imagined it. I stiffen against his chest, but he does not move. I press my hand to his shoulder and push him away; he removes himself without fuss.

"Astrid is . . . like you, I think." Ringer's silver eyes do not meet mine. This is something he does not wish to talk about. A confession? "Or perhaps . . . it is more accurate to say that you are like her."

I cock my head and press my fingers to his jawline. I push away the thought of Jones and his threats, Second Sister's words, Aunt Marshae's true face.

"The two of you could be . . . you could've been sisters." He sniffs, but I say nothing. I do not think he means sisters in the sense of the Sisterhood. And like so many others in my chapel, he stands and forgets what he was saying moments ago.

If that was a confession, I do not know what to make of it.

I grasp the hem of his navy jacket. *Stay.* I wish I could ask him with my words. The longer he stays here with me, the less time I'll have with someone else and their wandering hands. *Please, Ringer.*

But he does not read me this time. Cannot, because his eyes seek the wall behind me, the screen with the view of the stars.

"Captain Saito wants to see you."

My stomach sinks as I remember the coldness in her gaze as she declared the amber-eyed girl a traitor. As Aunt Marshae stripped her.

Do not fuck with Saito Ren. She's not the same since Ceres.

I stand, and my legs shake beneath me. Ringer does not reach out to comfort me.

Does the captain know? Am I to meet with her only for my treachery as a spy to be revealed? Was that what Second Sister meant by tormenting me? But there is nothing I can do after Ringer has passed on her orders. I am summoned, and I fight the trembling of my entire being as I leave the chapel at his side.

PLAY:
▶04

———◇◆◆◇———

I know it's wishful thinking that I can do what I've done and still say my goodbyes. Hell, this whole recording might never reach you, Lito. I know that. It might be lost on its way to you, or you might trash it without understanding what it is. But I can't stop talking. I suppose I'm saying everything that I need to say before . . . well, before I face what's coming.

If I had the time, I'd send one to each of my siblings. But I don't have that time, so I suppose I'll simply say what I wish I could tell them. Who knows? If the universe conspires to bring this message to you, maybe my words will somehow reach them.

So here we go . . .

[A long, sorrowful sigh.]

Shinya: You are the biggest asshole I've ever met in my entire life. You're so much like Father, but you haven't figured out how to rein in your temper yet, and that makes you almost worse. *Almost.* Still, I can't deny that you *have* taken good care of us all. I get why you're so strict, since you suffered Father and Mother's storms from the very beginning, and . . . to be honest, Oniisan, I wish we got along better. I wish we had at least tried to find some common ground between us, because I don't think you're all that bad deep down. I actually look up to you, because of how strong you are. Keep using that strength for the family.

Asuka: Do you remember the three months we only slept under the kotatsu? Or when we wrote out prayers and slipped them inside the jewel of the white fox statue Father told us not to touch? Everyone always said that you babied me, but you were exactly what I needed as an older sibling, Oneesan. I hope you never stop using others' assumptions to your benefit. When they see *quiet* and *demure* and *feminine*, they overlook that you're the smartest person in the room, and that underestimation has made you as sharp as a mercurial blade. Don't be afraid to cut like a blade does. It's not your name that has gotten you ahead; it's your brain. Don't let Father's accomplishments overshadow yours. You're every bit his equal.

Jun: Please forgive me if you've changed your gender marker in the time I've been gone. I've been referring to you based on how I last saw you. I want you to know I'm proud of you, Jun-chan, even when you think I'm mad at you for giving in to Father's whims. I think you're amazing, and every little centimeter you take for yourself is a victory. Make sure you celebrate them.

Hanako: You're coming to the age where you'll soon choose what you want to do with your life. I wouldn't be surprised if you followed Father's and Asuka's steps into the lab, but also know that you can do whatever you put your mind to. You don't have to give up your love of fashion and interior design, or even hide it. Be who you are unapologetically, Hana-chan.

And to all of you: Though Father may remove every picture of me from the house, please do not forget me as I was. Though he may leave an empty seat for me at the table . . . please do not believe I left you by choice.

CHAPTER 8

Why should we live under the philosopher kings of the Icarii or the two-pronged tyranny of the Geans? Both are self-serving. Both care only for those who echo their chosen societal virtues. And both allow people to sicken, suffer, and die because they are not considered "productive." Let them call me an outlaw. Let them call me an anarchist. The truth is that they fear the freedom and equality we have in the belt.

Dire of the Belt

The dead Aster slips through my arms. He hits the floor with a thud.

Ofiera screams at me through the implant until my head aches with her assault. Fury and anguish crash about in my brain as she mourns. "He was just a boy!" she cries.

I don't want to confirm her words—don't want to look—but I do. She's right. He's younger than us, too young to be working a smuggling operation like this.

But we don't have time to feel for our enemies. I erase it with my implant.

"Ofiera, those aren't fire alarms—"

"I know," she snaps, and I don't miss the anger in her tone, hard and full of fire. "He was helping me."

"Helping—" I swallow a curse. "He set off the alarms because of us."

"You held a knife to his throat."

I growl in frustration, but say nothing; we can fight later. The longer we stand here, the more chances they have to block us in. "Do we have what we need to leave?"

At first Ofiera doesn't move, just stares at the body of the Aster boy. Then, slowly, she holds up the slip of biopaper. On it is information about the five grasshoppers, including their manifests and keycodes.

"The one we're taking is farthest from the door." I spot its keycode and memorize it. "Let's go."

I pick up her mask from the desk and shove it into her empty hand. She pockets the biopaper of codes and pulls the balaclava over her face.

"Get your knife out. Are you ready?"

"Don't kill the Asters," she says, grabbing another page from the desk instead of withdrawing her knife. She holds it up for me to see, but I ignore it. "They're innocent bystanders. They just work as miners for Val Nelson. They're not the ones who stole the tech from Val Akira Labs, and they're not part of the smuggling operation."

Is that what she was doing—looking for proof of who was on Dire's payroll and who wasn't? She risked our lives—*my* life—for *this*?

I want to shake her, yell at her, curse at her stupidity, but we need to leave. *Now.* "No witnesses" is all I say before I open the door and storm into the hallway. Ofiera can follow or get herself killed—whatever she wants; I have the keycode, and I'm leaving.

The hallway is empty until we reach the break room where I saw the human and Aster chatting. Now there are men and women with weapons rushing about, looking for the source of the alarm. I feel Ofiera at my back through the implant and don't hesitate: I rush the group, my knife taking the first man I reach in the chest. He screams, drawing others' attention toward me.

"Intruder!" a woman yells, pointing her railgun at me. Her cry is cut off a moment later by Ofiera's blade plunging through her neck.

Weapons come up. Ofiera and I sync, our implants humming, warning each other, nudging each other onward. They may have superior numbers and firepower, but we stick close to them and fight as one, rendering their advantages useless.

A man fires, and for a moment I'm back on Ceres—*gunshot, fire in my shoulder, blood like rain*—before I'm moving, sliding on my knees across the slick flooring, knife slashing across the Achilles tendon of the shooter's foot. The throbbing scar on my shoulder dulls.

Ofiera moves like a dancer, her weapon an extension of her arm. Only one attacker is foolish enough to take a shot at her—and the railgun's metal bullet misses her completely and clips his companion's arm. She kicks him in the chest, fighting for space, and spins into another, slicing through his hamstring. She is a winged predator, the knife her talons, riding a bitter wind of death.

I fight without regard for my opponent. It doesn't matter whether they are human or Aster, whether they are armed or not. *No witnesses* echoes in my head along with the command to make it look like a rival hit.

When we reach the end of the hallway, I cast a quick glance back. Seven bodies lie behind us, those few who are alive bleeding out and groaning in agony. Ofiera and I are covered in blood, but none of it is our own; through the implant, I can tell she's unharmed.

"Run to the farthest grasshopper and get it started," I tell her. She's got the keycode; she'll be able to open it. "I'll keep the smugglers occupied until it's ready to launch." I retrieve one of the fallen mercs' railguns from the ground. It's slick with his blood, but as I suspected, the fingerprint lock has been disabled, allowing anyone to use the weapon.

Ofiera nods, though I don't miss the pained look that shoots across her face. I try to sense what she's feeling through the implant but come away with a vague wash of guilt. I push back encouragement, but she's already running across the hangar, oblivious to me.

A group of men spots her and opens fire, but she's fast, slipping around the grasshoppers and using their bulk for protection. "Hey!" I yell, and the majority turn toward me. The railgun is unfamiliar in my hands when I'm accustomed to the pistol-sized, laser-firing HEL guns, but I brace the body against my shoulder and pull the trigger, laying down suppressive fire, peppering the crates and forcing the men to duck for cover.

I retreat into my core. The fight becomes me.

Most fire wildly without looking, railguns held far from them, shots missing completely, but a few peek around the crates to take aim. I shoot at each face I spot while backing toward the grasshopper and getting far enough away that they'd have to be top marksmen to hit me.

"Don't let them get away!" a man screams, pointing toward the grasshopper. He's wearing the silver suit of a manager, and I recognize his voice: sol Joshua. A group of Asters at his back rush toward us, weaponless but ready to maim and kill to protect their smuggling operation.

I pop off a few warning shots at their feet, hitting one in the leg, before the gun clicks without firing. Out of ammunition. I toss it aside.

My fingers itch for my mercurial blade as the group approaches, but all I have at hand is my knife. I fish a small black device from my backpack and activate the micro-EMPs on the other grasshoppers. Like miniature explosions, the devices spark and hiss, and one Aster, passing close by, screams and falls to the ground.

Ofiera's voice finally comes over the grasshopper's intercom. "Ready!"

I jump into the grasshopper's airlock and slap the button to close the outer door. An Aster, faster than the others, grabs at me, and for a moment, I think he's going to lose his hand. At the last moment, he jerks back to keep from being crunched between two thick slabs of metal.

The mechanics hiss as the airlock cycles. The inside of the grasshopper stabilizes, the oxygen generators kicking in. I rip off my mask and call down the hallways, "Go, Ofiera! Launch!" Asters slam into the grasshopper, pounding with their fists, staring at me through the airlock window.

"Get to a chair!" she calls back.

While Aster rigs are built with the same layout as Icarii ships, I'm surprised to see all the retrofits on this one; they must have been added for whatever Dire and the outlaws were smuggling. I take the ladder up from the hold and run down the hallway, hoping the command area is located in the center like it is on Icarii ships and that I'm going in the right direction. I stumble into a wall as the ship bucks, a metallic crunch screeching around me—we must have rammed straight through the hangar wall to get out.

"Lito, in here!" Ofiera calls, and I hurry toward her voice. The hermium-powered force field will keep the grasshopper's acceleration from grinding me to a pulp, but that won't matter much if I slam my head against the wall hard enough to kill me.

My body grows heavier as the ship ascends. Instead of taking the grasshopper down to the surface, as so many do from the mid-atmo station, we go up, and I struggle as I finally reach a chair and dump my body into it. I don't even have time to fasten my belt; I simply grab hold and cling for the life of me.

Both Ofiera and I are plastered into our chairs as the grasshopper activates its rockets. I watch the monitors as we leave the station and pass into the gaseous sky, oily clouds of gold and orange swirling like thick paint around us. I catch a brief glimpse of the wind kites tethered above Cytherea, collectors that turn Venus's powerful currents into energy, before losing track of them. The grasshopper shakes so violently that I fear for a moment we may break apart until, at last, we emerge into darkness. The ship slows as black space swallows the world around us. Little pinpricks of starlight reappear on our screens as the ship evens out and settles into cruising speed.

It takes me a full ten seconds to catch my breath and slow my heart rate. I peel my fingers from the safety belt and reassure myself that I am, indeed, alive.

"We've cleared planetary gravity," Ofiera says, and in her tone is something like wonder.

"I hate to say it, but that was the easy part," I tell her.

Her face is so serious, it's like she didn't hear me. "The Asters . . . Did you . . ." She trails off, and I imagine her using the implant to calm herself down. She pulls the biopaper she risked our lives for from her pocket. The one that lists who in Val Nelson Mining knew about the smuggling and took a cut. "Never mind. I'll set up communication with Beron, send this to him."

But if she's expecting Beron to care about some Asters, she's deeply fooling herself.

Ofiera unbuckles from her chair and pushes herself toward the control panel. Her hair floats after her like the tail of a shooting star. "There are lots of retrofits on this ship. Did you notice?"

"Yeah, they must be smuggling something big."

"There's even a hermium-powered gravity generator. I'm going to turn it on, okay?"

"Sure."

"Want to float a bit beforehand? It's relaxing." When she looks up, her eyes don't meet mine, instead looking past me to—

Oh.

Already, one of my arms has begun lifting itself without my consent. Gravity is funny that way; if you're not paying attention to your limbs, they go off without you. I pull the arm back to my torso. "No thanks. I like things where they belong."

Her fingers dance over the control panel, and within five seconds, I hear the hum of the hermium engine working. Two seconds later, gravity jerks me down into my chair. Ofiera lands on her feet like a cat.

"I'll set up communication with Command," Ofiera says, and I excuse myself from the deck.

After taking a quick look around the ship, locating a simple but well-stocked galley and a habitation suite with four mattresses bunked into the wall, I head down the ladder to the hold. With all the effort put into this operation, curiosity gets the better of me. What tech were they smuggling that could possibly justify the retrofits on this grasshopper?

I break into a thick plastic crate with a pry bar. Sure enough, the metal box inside is labeled VAL AKIRA LABS, but when I push it open, cool air wafts out to meet me. I pull a vial, carefully and expertly packed, from its shelving and inspect the clear liquid within. At first I'm not sure what I'm looking at, but then I notice the minuscule writing on the glass.

It's medicine.

I put the vial back and close the metal case. One after another, I open the crates and the Val Akira Labs coolers. It's just medicine. All of it. For a range of diseases that affect both humans and Asters.

Maybe Dire and the outlaws are stealing it to sell. Or maybe they're nabbing it to make drugs with.

But somehow, as I close the last crate of medicine to combat bone density loss, doubt begins to creep in.

Maybe the people in the belt just need the medicine for themselves.

CHAPTER 9

[23] Ye who bond yourselves as Sisters, uphold the following virtues: Thou shalt remain silent. Thou shalt not divulge, through sign or written word, what has been told in confidence. And thou shalt serve as a mirror of the Goddess, so that those who go to war may serve without a shadowed heart.

The Canon, Judgments 16:23

Ringer and I walk in subdued silence, and by the time I reach Captain Saito's door, my heart is firmly lodged in my throat. Even if I had the ability to speak, I couldn't in this moment. Is this how the amber-eyed girl who used to be Second Sister felt as she approached the dais? Did she know what awaited her? Probably no more than I do.

I press a hand to my belly and give myself a moment to let the stress show on my face. Turned away from Ringer so he cannot see, I allow the anguish to overwhelm me, and mourn for what might happen. Will Captain Saito be cold but firm in her words? Will she call for soldiers, perhaps even Ringer, and have me arrested? Will she have me stripped in front of the crew tomorrow morning for all to see me as I am, a traitor to the Geans? Will she throw me through the hermium barrier into the cold embrace of space until I turn blue and my blood boils?

I run my hand over my face. The moment is over. I fix my lips into a smile and straighten my back. I am a Sister, a holy vessel for the Goddess's light, chosen by the Mother. I am beautiful. I am confident. I am not walking toward my undoing.

I knock on the door.

"I'll leave you here," Ringer says. With the worry in his deep voice, I doubt he will go far. I do not turn to face him; I cannot, if I want my strength to be unwavering.

I remember the words he whispered in the chapel and the name he told me. *Astrid*. Someone who could be my sister, he said. I do not know what he meant by it. If I ever have the chance to speak with Ringer again, I will try to find out. It is the small thread of hope to which I cling.

The door slides open, and Captain Saito's black eyes swallow me like the darkness between stars. I do not know the hour, but from her attire, I assume it is sometime late in the ship's cycle. She's dressed down in training clothes, navy pants and a matching tank with the Gean military insignia on the breast. She clutches the ends of a towel around her neck. One arm flesh, the other the cold white of prosthetic tech.

"First Sister," she says, sounding somewhat taken off guard. "Would you like to come in?"

A kind formality. Yet if she were going to interrogate me or arrest me, would she not be in uniform? And why does she sound surprised to see me? Or is this a way to put me at ease, hoping I drop my guard? I follow her into the room.

"Sit," Captain Saito says, gesturing to the chair on the opposite side of her desk. "I was just about to shower, but it can wait."

I don't sit. Instead I gesture to her private lavatory, palm out, an offering. She could take it as either an invitation to bathe while I wait, or an offer that I accompany her into the shower.

She ignores me. "Sit," she says again.

I sit, as commanded. She perches on the edge of her desk, glancing at the chair. I wonder if she remembers our last interaction in this room, on this desk, and is avoiding a repeat.

"I considered visiting you in the chapel," she says, taking the end of her towel and dabbing her forehead. "But I haven't gotten around to it."

I straighten in my chair and lean forward. If she wants to confess, she can do so here in her chambers. I hope beyond reason that this is why she has called for me, that she remains ignorant of my actions regarding her file. I remember the Mother's command to me, Aunt Marshae's expectant face, even Jones's warning of caution.

"Trouble is I'm not terribly interested in a one-sided conversation." She shrugs her mechanical shoulder.

I fight my frown. I had begun to think that perhaps she had taken a vow of celibacy, like Ringer. It would explain why she refused me, and why I've heard no rumor about her calling any other Sisters, or even male Cousins, to her bed. And though celibacy isn't terribly commonplace, I can think of no other reason to avoid us. Even if she didn't like women, she could unburden herself with talk like some of the other female soldiers do, allowing us to stroke their hair and listen as the guilt melts away.

But with her admission, now I'm not so sure. I cock my head and lean toward her, the picture of an interested party.

Captain Saito pulls the towel from around her neck and places it on the desktop. "What I mean is that I'd prefer to get to know you."

Even though I have practiced for years to control my face, I cannot keep my eyebrows from arching up my forehead in surprise. When she smiles, only one side of her mouth curls upward. "I think that's the first honest reaction I've gotten out of you," she says.

I flush, because she's right.

"And that's the second," she says, laughing.

I smile as well, a true expression I do not need to fake. Her relaxed state puts me at ease: I cannot imagine her calling for soldiers now, arresting me after asking to know me better. I banish my worries to the corner of my mind; for now, I must focus solely on the assignment I've been given.

She clasps her hands together in front of her, white metal meeting tawny skin. She is elegant in the way a sculpture would be. I can picture her eight feet tall, towering in one of Mars's sparse parks. But instead of being cast in bronze, she would be formed of curling driftwood mixed with geometric iron and black onyx jewels for her dark, dark eyes. *The Hero of Ceres*, the plaque beneath would read.

She watches me with her usual expression, eyes sparkling with mischief and lips prone to smiling. She looks like she alone knows the most important secret in the universe. "You're interested in my arm," she says. Her words are not a question, and I fear that lying at this point will halt all conversation, so I nod. If she admires the truth, then the truth is what I will give her.

"You're the first who doesn't pretend to ignore it completely. Here," she says, and holds out her prosthetic arm. I have not had the chance to truly admire it out of fear that I might offend. Now I allow myself to. The prosthetic matches her flesh arm in length and thickness, the rounded shoulder tapering and then rising to a toned biceps. Her forearm is slender, leading to a feminine wrist that flares into a rather masculine hand with stubby fingers.

It is odd that she has not chosen to paint the surface the same color as her skin, to try to naturalize her appearance as so many others would. Unlike the Icarii and their addiction to geneassists, part of our worship of the Goddess is reverence for nature and all things natural, including our physical bodies. Yet because she has chosen to leave it bare and white, it makes a bold statement.

What that statement is, however, I have yet to discover.

"You can touch it, if you wish," Captain Saito says, holding very still, as if any movement might startle me.

I reach toward her prosthetic hand and let my fingers brush against the seam of her wrist. I trace the line up her forearm to her elbow joint, and jump when she moves her arm so that the fluid mechanics flawlessly shift beneath the exterior white metal. "It's okay," she whispers, and I find myself standing from my chair, my hand exploring farther, up past her elbow and over the rise of her musculature to her shoulder.

I want to tell her it is beautiful, that in another life I wanted to become an engineer's apprentice, that I might have worked on prosthetics just like this one. But I cannot tell her anything at all.

I touch the scarred, puckered skin where the prosthetic meets her body, and she trembles. I jerk my hand away.

"Sorry. That's always a strange feeling." She knocks against her prosthetic shoulder with a knuckle of her flesh hand. "The nerve endings are damaged there."

I touch her prosthetic again, then slap my opposite arm. I make an exaggerated face of pain, and then mime slapping her prosthetic.

"You're asking me a question." Her face lights up in that moment.

Her excitement encourages me. I pretend to slap her arm again, then slap my own and twist my features as if feeling pain. I point to her face.

"Oh! You want to know if I can feel with the prosthetic?"

I nod excitedly. I've had years of play-acting this way, but it doesn't always guarantee that the other person will understand me.

"No," she says, and I do not miss the hint of sorrow in her voice. "No, the left side of my body is . . . well, sometimes I still feel it, but not in the way you would imagine."

My eyes drop to her feet. Below the hem of her pants, I can see her left leg is the same stark white as her arm.

"I cannot feel your touch any more than I can feel a refreshing breeze or the heat of a hot bath." She holds her prosthetic hand in front of her face and stares at it, almost longingly . . . I touch her arm—her flesh-and-blood arm—and she starts.

She can feel my touch now, yet . . . Ren is unaccustomed to it. Scared of it.

She looks away from me as my hand returns to her prosthetic shoulder. Calms considerably. She does not mind my touch, so long as she can pretend it isn't there.

Then she speaks words I never thought I'd hear. "I wish this war were not necessary..."

My grip involuntarily tightens on her arm in shock at her words, and I'm glad it is her prosthetic so that she cannot feel it. She treads on a cliff's edge. A captain in her position cannot be soft, cannot even be *seen* as soft, toward the enemy. She could lose her commission for that.

Could this be what the Mother wished to learn about Ren?

I place my hand into hers. Her fingers brush my wrist. There's no softness, no humanity, in her touch. The prosthetic is cold. After a moment, it warms from me, leaching my heat. We stay this way for several quiet minutes, the captain holding my hand but unable to feel it.

Then she breaks away from me so quickly, standing from the desk, that I am left breathless. There one minute and gone the next. I can see the warrior in her movement, even if her prosthetic leg gives her a slight limp; she is fast and efficient.

"Here." She digs into a drawer of her desk and lets several things fall to the tabletop. One I know intimately—the armband of the captain's favor. White for a noncombatant, the armband is delicately stitched with a golden oak leaf, symbol of the Sisterhood, and three stars denoting the rank of captain. My heart speeds at its appearance, excitement and fear mingling into one complex drive to reclaim it.

"Take it," Ren encourages, and I tentatively reach for it, "but if you take one item, you must take them all."

My hand snaps back to my chest.

Sitting alongside the armband are a notepad full of paper and a black cylindrical tube, something I recognize as a pen.

"There's so much in your face... I want to know what you're thinking. I want to know *you*."

She doesn't stop me as I reach for the armband and push it aside. The pad of paper is no bigger than my hand and bears the image of a small black bird in the corner. A designer's mark from one of the factories where they recycle refuse and 3D-print plastics into waxy biopaper.

I remember her words. *I'm not terribly interested in a one-sided conversation.* I point to the pad of paper and then to myself.

"Yes, I want you to use it. I want you to write to me so I can get to know you. So *we* can get to know *each other.*"

I snap my teeth together to keep my jaw from falling slack. My heart races until my head feels light. This is more than just forbidden; it's treason! The Sisterhood has declared it a crime to write, yet that is exactly what Ren asks of me. But she also offers me a gift in return: the captain's protection. I fear, deep in my core, that this is some sort of test.

Would Aunt Marshae want to know about this request? Or is there something even more extreme about Ren? Certainly what she has told me is not enough to warrant the Mother's involvement; no, whatever I am meant to learn, I will have to glean in future sessions. And for there to be additional meetings between us, I will have to write with her.

I step back from the desk. Ren's face shifts in the slightest way. Is that disappointment I see?

"Think about it," she says. "I'd love to speak with you further."

I try to swallow, but there is a lump in my throat. I need to seek out Aunt Marshae.

"Have a pleasant evening," Ren says as I leave.

I FIND AUNT Marshae in an agitated state, pacing close circles around the sitting area of her room. Her long, polished nails scratch faint rows into the sleeves of her dress. She does not even greet me. "Jones says you refused him today."

My hands, held before me, slowly curl into fists. What I had been about to tell her concerning Ren is adrift amidst the roaring sea of her anger.

"What do you have to say for yourself?" She stops in front of me, and I fear she may slap me or seize me, digging those white-tipped nails into the soft flesh of my arms. "You claimed to be Captain Saito's with no armband as proof."

I will have it soon, I tell her, though my hands fumble over the signs weakly.

"Soon?" Her hand comes toward me, and I step away. "No, niece. I've helped you before, but this is too much."

I am close, I say, remembering Ren's offer. If I had taken it, I would already be wearing the armband.

She reaches for me again, and I back into the wall. She's pinned me. "I lied on your behalf to a soldier. The crew's trust in me is at stake because of your selfish choices." She grabs my forearm. Her nails are thorns of pain.

She confirmed I was claimed to Jones? I try to focus on my Auntie's blue eyes instead of how she pinches me hard enough to draw blood.

"You have one cycle to get that armband, or I will tell Jones the truth and you will be punished."

I press my lips into a thin line. Would she really demote me if I am poised perfectly to be her spy? But then I remember Second Sister's bragging. She must have received the same assignment I did if Aunt Marshae is not concerned about doing away with me.

But I won't lose my position as First Sister that easily.

I pull my arms from her grip so I can sign. I can already feel the bruises blooming where she grabbed me. *I will get the armband*, I tell her. *I was coming to tell you—*

"You had better," she interrupts. "I don't want to explain to the Mother that a stupid lie to a soldier is what kept you from doing your duty."

It's so easy for her to speak over me when she has words, and all I have are my hands and their symbols. I let the frustration show on my face as I lift my hands again. *I just met with Ren*, I sign forcefully. *She has agreed to give me the armband if I write with her.*

At the sign for *write*, my Auntie snaps upright. Anger gives way to hunger in her gaze. "She asked you to . . ."

Write, I sign again as confirmation that she has not misunderstood me.

She grabs my shoulders. I jolt at her touch, but she does not dig her nails into me this time. "Oh, niece," she says, and her tone is all praise and kindness. Her entire bearing changes in seconds. "You have done well. What a good girl you are!"

Is this what you wanted? I ask, though I should ask if it's what *the Mother* wanted, as this was her assignment.

"You're on the right path indeed." Aunt Marshae's hand comes to my face, and she strokes my cheek gently. Her hand is cold and sweaty at the same time. "Accept her offer and write with her. Use it to grow closer to her, and bring me proof."

I almost don't dare to ask. *Proof of what?*

"That Captain Saito is a traitor, of course."

My heartbeat speeds at that word and echoes it with each thump. *Traitor, traitor, traitor.* The same brand that the amber-eyed girl wore as she was thrown from the *Juno.*

But writing is . . . My hands fall before I finish.

"Is what?"

My fingers fumble as I make the sign. *Forbidden.*

Her red mouth splits into something like a smile. "It's only forbidden if I say it's forbidden," she says, low and heady.

I back away from Aunt Marshae and nod as if I understand. She offers me a few more scraps of praise, but my ears ring so loudly, all I can focus on is that one word: *Traitor, traitor, traitor . . .*

I leave her chambers even more confused than when I entered. And I know, with a shaking certainty, that dancing between Ren and Aunt Marshae is a dangerous game.

IF I ACCEPT Ren's offer and she is sincere, we will write together and I will be given the armband, a mark that keeps me safe from the rest of the crew and beyond their use. But that is only if she is telling the truth.

She could be testing me. As soon as I accept the paper and pen, she could inform everyone that I have committed treason against the Sisterhood. Did the amber-eyed girl who was thrown from the *Juno* receive this same offer? Her bruised skin and open, gasping mouth haunt me even in my waking hours.

Do not fuck with Saito Ren.

But if I do accept, I will be writing with Ren only to spy on her. If she discovers my mission, how much worse will my fate be? I could be beaten, tortured, before I am stripped and discarded in front of the crew. I hold no illusions that my Auntie would save me; she would feed me piece by piece into the maw of a great machine if only to save herself.

I feel it necessary to say that if you are caught, it will be you who takes the blame, not the Sisterhood.

I could disobey Aunt Marshae's direct order. Ignore the Mother and her Goddess-withered mission. But that will ensure that I never get the armband and lose the Mother's favor. I will go back to my chapel, knowing that Aunt Marshae will whisper poisoned words to Ren, ensuring she picks another First Sister over me. A First Sister willing to spy for the Mother. I will go back to the dorms on the lower decks and act in service to every soldier who comes to visit me.

I remember Jones pawing at my dress and press my hand to my mouth.

So which way do I turn? Do I take this chance with Ren, praying she does not immediately brand me a traitor to the Sisterhood?

Traitor, traitor, traitor.

Or do I deny Ren's request and remain loyal to the Sisterhood, allowing Aunt Marshae to choose someone else better suited to the task?

It's only forbidden if I say it's forbidden.

None of this feels as it should, and deciding what to do is like choosing between death of the body and death of the soul.

All I can do is pray as I walk. *Goddess, shine Your light upon me now in the darkness. Guide my roots as they grow. Let me see Your will and know it is Yours.*

I find myself in front of Ren's door. I have only to knock. Only to accept. Who do I trust more, Aunt Marshae, whom I have known for years, or Ren, whom I just met?

Goddess of Earth and Sky, is this why You kept me on the Juno? I pray.

I brush my hands over my forearms, tender with bruises from Aunt Marshae's nails. I recall the hunger in her eyes, the way she watched me like I was bait for her prey.

But I also remember Ren. The shock in her face as I touched her with kindness. The excitement in her voice when she realized I was asking her about her prosthetic.

It hits me then. The captain is unbelievably lonely.

I knock on her door.

She answers quickly. Her hair is wet from a shower, plastered to her forehead, and her cheeks are flushed from heat. "You're back," she says, and her lips hold the ghost of a smile. It is strange to recognize hope in someone who is accustomed to commanding and expecting pure obedience.

I enter the suite and wait until the door closes behind me before I nod at the desk. The armband, along with the paper and pen, has been put away. No one outside of the Sisterhood knows our sign language, so I make a gesture with my hand as if I am writing with an invisible pen.

"You want to . . . ?" Ren doesn't finish. With the speed of an eager lover, she crosses the room to her desk and withdraws the three items from the top drawer. In a few paces, she is back at the doorway.

At their appearance, I do not hesitate. I snatch up the pen and paper. My hands are shaking too wildly to write anything in this moment. But Ren's are steady as she picks up the white armband and wraps it around my biceps, pinning it in its proper place.

"I'll expect your first letter soon," she whispers, and I press the pad of paper to my heart like a shield. With a little bow of my head, I turn to leave. It's only as the door closes between us that I notice Saito Ren's mischievous smile and the spark of danger that dances across her eyes.

PLAY:
▶05

◇—◆◇◆—◇

I was sitting on the edge of your bunk, our legs almost touching, the rest of the room humming with the whispers of our fellow students. No one wanted to speak too loudly. We were all afraid of this imposed, enchanted quiet.

"I didn't think it would hurt so much," you said. Your hand kept going to the back of your neck and the bandage there before you forced it away, dropping one hand into the other to pick at your cuticles until your fingers bled.

I think I said something like "That's the part they don't tell you about." I don't know why I said it. Our instructors had told us what to expect from the surgery and the best ways to encourage healing afterward. But I was still raw at the idea of having a piece of Val Akira Labs tech in me, especially one that interacted so closely with my brain.

I worried that my father might have found a way to look into our minds, to read our memories like the pages of a book, to calculate our futures from all the thoughts and plans we made in secret. I should have known better. He didn't care enough about me to do that, even if he could.

I knew we'd be paired as Rapier and Dagger, but it wasn't until our second year at the Academy that our instructors made the match official. And as a reward, they shaved our heads, took a needle the length of my hand, slipped it between C1 and C2, and pushed something the size of a grain of rice into our spines.

Our neural implants.

Strangely, it wasn't the implantation that hurt. It was the after-effects as our entire bodies synced with the devices. It was the buzz that stretched between us, programmed by our professors. It was the way I couldn't sleep because of dreams that didn't belong to me. I was used to dreaming about foxes, not screaming cyclones that forced me and my siblings beneath a blanket in a cold, dark closet.

It was our . . . becoming. The two of us forming a chrysalis that would break into a singular, monstrous being.

"You know, outside of the military, adults have these things put in so they don't have to be all depressed anymore," I told you. I thought maybe it would help to know we weren't the only ones who had to get used to this. If others could survive it, we could too. We'd lived through things that would have broken normal people. "And if we weren't duelists, we'd be programmed to respond as a unit, the whole group of us, so it would be even harder to adjust."

I could see by the blood draining from your face that I wasn't helping.

"We can use them to control our emotions, is what I'm saying. We could learn to use it so that like, I don't know, we always feel like we just won the lottery and came at the same time."

I laughed at my own joke, trying to get you laughing too, but you didn't.

"What if the pain never goes away?" you whispered. "What if I wash out of the Academy? Some people do, when they can't handle the sync."

Or because their bodies wouldn't accept the implant. Or even because of neural degradation. You didn't say either of those possibilities aloud, but I could practically hear them in the rapid flow of your thoughts.

"You mean, what if you have terrible headaches or start hallucinating? What if your behavior changes, and you become someone else? What if we bleed into each other until we don't know where I begin and you end?"

I shouldn't have pushed you. I just wanted you to see how ridiculous it sounded. Instead, you picked at your fingers faster, blood welling up in little ruby drops.

"What if my parents and Luce don't even recognize me anymore?" Your words came softly, a gasp as your breathing quickened. "What if I can't handle it and they send me home? I can't go back to the bottom levels. I won't be able to provide for my family. I'll be in pain, unable to work."

I grabbed your hands, stilling them at last, your blood running into my palms, and a shock ran through us both. Neither of us was used to it then, but we would be in the future, that lyrical hum of a Rapier's and Dagger's neural implants singing together.

On your end of the bond, I could feel your mounting anxiety, sharp and staggering. I pushed calm comfort to you, letting you feel what I was feeling. "I'll make sure you stay you, okay? And you make sure that I stay me."

You didn't answer at first. Then, softly, you said my name. "Hiro."

I squeezed your hand so hard it would hurt. You stopped shaking. "Lito, I'm not changing. No one can change me. Believe me, my father has tried. I'm not going to let anyone change you either."

Do you remember what you said then, as you closed your eyes and let your anxiety fade away, as the room swayed around us but we held each other up?

"If we lose ourselves," you said, "at least we'll lose ourselves together."

CHAPTER 10

Common side effects include upset stomach, dry mouth, and drowsiness. In some patients, more serious side effects may occur. Neural degradation is characterized by hallucinations, mood swings, and marked change of behavior. Talk to your doctor if you believe you are at risk for ND.

From a neural implant ad

The grasshopper is small, and there's nowhere I can go that I can't feel Ofiera. Even in my bunk, my fingers rubbing the smooth metal of the playback device Hiro sent me, I can feel her swarm of emotions—guilt, worry, and anger—until a headache forms behind my eyes.

I remember the pain from my neural implant syncing with Hiro's, but it was nothing like this. At least with Hiro, they were by my side, curled into the same Academy bunk as me, and we found comfort with each other; there's no chance of that with Ofiera, when we're more likely to butt heads.

But I have other things to focus on. Ever since Luce gave me the playback device, I've wanted to hear what Hiro has to tell me. Perhaps part of my hesitation now is fear.

I'm afraid that I'll put the device behind my ear and hear nothing.

Maybe Luce was mistaken, and it wasn't from Hiro. Or worse, I'll hear Hiro, but they'll admit to something I don't want to hear. That they really are a traitor. And I know that Ofiera can't read any thoughts that I don't send to her, but could she figure out what I'm up to based on my erratic emotions? I can't promise I'll be calm listening to the device.

I suck in a deep breath and let it out slowly. Fear is just another face of shadow. I must step into the dark to see its true shape.

Despite my headache, I place the device behind my ear, directly on the bone, and tap it to start its recording.

"Fucking gods, I've started this recording over a hundred times now—"

I jerk the device off so violently that it tumbles from my bunk to the ground.

Fucking gods. It *is* Hiro.

My heart races frantically. I lean on my implant to calm myself so Ofiera won't sense something amiss. Somehow Hiro's voice makes everything real—the Fall of Ceres, Beron's assignment, the Mother's assassination.

I'll have to kill them. If I find them, I'll have to *kill* my partner.

I don't want to listen after all. I don't want to hear the truth. But curiosity drags me back to the device anyway.

I *have* to know what Hiro says. I *have* to know the truth.

I place the device behind my ear again.

"Fucking gods, I've started this recording over a hundred times now. I'm never going to figure out what I want to say before I say it. You'll just have to deal with the shitty, rambling quality of it. At least it will answer your questions."

THE FIRST TIME I met Hiro, I hated them. The whole class did. The morning of our first assembly at Icarus Prime Military Academy, we were to arrive in the dueling courtyard at 0600 hours properly dressed in uniform, the pleat in our charcoal pants perfectly pressed, our jackets buttoned, and our hair either trimmed short or bound in a bun or topknot.

But Hiro was different. Hiro arrived at 0612 with their shoulder-length hair vibrant pink on top and black on the bottom and an outfit closer to a Paragon influencer's than a student's. Between the floral leggings and the yellow sinvaca leather jacket, I didn't know what to make of them.

"Father says hello," Hiro said to our teacher, interrupting the welcome lecture. They dropped a designer bag at the feet of a student in the assembled two rows, almost as if they expected him to play servant and pick it up. That bag, which likely cost more than my family's flat on the lower levels of Cytherea, fell sideways into the dirt.

The instructor sputtered, trailing off the topic of Icarii glory and the responsibility we had as children of the elite. I had been filling in the gaps with my own narrative because I had earned a scholarship—the Val Roux, the highest honor the Academy offered; my parents certainly weren't powerful, and they couldn't afford to send me here. But Hiro . . . from their custom-made clothes alone, I could tell their family was wealthy.

I expected our teacher to yell until his face turned red. Coming to the Academy, I had been prepared for anger and raised voices, something I had heard went hand in hand with military life. That wouldn't have scared me—I was all too accustomed to cursing and slammed doors in my own home. What scared me was when the instructor went silent, his eyes going icy and his lips tugging down into the smallest frown of distaste. He rolled his head on his shoulders until his neck popped.

"Run," he said, his voice barely above a whisper but with all the sharpness of a mercurial blade. "All of you. Laps around the courtyard. Start running, and don't stop until I say so."

I have to give it to Hiro. Even though they were wearing these clear high-heeled shoes that gave them an extra seven centimeters of height, they led the group. It was like they knew their appearance would get us all in trouble and, by doing so, would show us all who was meant to be the top of the class. Their rebellion was also a calculated move to assert their dominance, the clever jerk.

But I was long-limbed even then, though skinny as a rail, and I had spent years before playing gladius, the sports version of dueling, on the lower levels of Cytherea where the recycled air was thick and the pressure heavy. I wasn't about to let some rich kid show me up when they had been breathing pure filtered air from the moment they were born. Sure, my fellow students may have actually been from the best families across Mercury and Venus, but I wasn't, so I had a chip on my shoulder and way too much to prove. Hiro had simply walked into the school like they belonged, while I had fought for my place here, never allowing myself to truly embrace childhood but instead throwing myself into a sport I wasn't sure would pay off. This was what I wanted, and Hiro wasn't going to take it from me.

Once the instructor had watched us run ten kilometers, he let us pause for water. I came in second, then threw up my breakfast in the corner of the courtyard. Hiro laughed at us all.

"I'm Hiro val Akira, bruv." Everyone knew that name—even me. Hiro's family legacy stretched back as far as the pacifist scientists who left Mars during the Dead Century War to seed Mercury. Their father was the CEO of Val Akira Labs; some even credited a val Akira ancestor as the discoverer of hermium, the element that powered all our tech. "Don't even try to beat me!"

I think I would have kept hating Hiro if we hadn't been partnered throughout the rest of the day as the top two in our class. Every time anyone said something to me about not belonging, about my second-hand uniform, Hiro threatened them with physical violence, and if that didn't work, with having the val Akira family destroy theirs. After Hiro's stunt that morning, everyone believed them. At that point, I wasn't even sure whether Hiro liked me or they just wanted to fight with everyone else. But I appreciated it nonetheless.

I'm not sure when I started to think of them as a friend. I'm even less sure when I began to think of them as my family. But I do know, as I listen to Hiro's voice on the recording device, that I miss them with a pain so tangible, I feel infected with it. My love for Hiro has grown until it has tainted my head, my heart, even my very bones, and now I'll have to cut those feelings out like a cancer.

The first time I ever saw you, Lito, I loved you.
I listen to their words again and again.
The first time I ever saw you, Lito, I loved you.

THE LIGHTS ARE off. The ship is dark. I haunt the command deck, because I don't want to sleep. To dream. To put my trust in my subconscious.

It doesn't trust me back.

Go to sleep, I sing.

"No," I tell myself.

Go to sleep, I beg.

I am a traitor to myself.

The stars are bright on our screens because we are close to them. I wish they looked like this all the time.

Would that I could live on a ship, even one this small. Two people in a place big enough for one. One day . . . perhaps.

"Go to sleep," I say aloud. My voice echoes.

"At least try," I whisper.

My eyes are heavy. My body is numb. I lost control of myself hours ago. The first time neural implants adjust to each other is the hardest. Or perhaps it's not the implants adjusting, but the people.

I force myself down the hallway and look at the two branching directions. One, to the hab quarters. The other, to the hold.

The door is open. The beds are calling. I step into the little room and look . . .

At Lito. At myself.

Wait.

Who am I?

MY MIND SPLINTERS with a headache, and I shove myself upright in bed. My heart races—I was just looking at myself, standing there—

Where Ofiera stands.

"Ofiera, what the fuck—" My voice doesn't sound like I expect it to. Why the hell doesn't my voice sound like I expect it to?

Even in the dark I see that her eyes are glazed. Her hands twitch at her sides.

Shit. She's having some sort of episode. "Ofiera!" I jump out of bed, heedless of my undressed state, and seize her shoulders. I shake her, and her head lolls on her shoulders. "Ofiera, snap out of it!"

My heartbeat asks a singular question: *Who am I? Who am I? Who am I?*

I saw myself through her eyes—I was *her*, looking at *me*.

Her neural implant is reaching, seizing onto mine, twisting my mind toward its own demise. This shouldn't be happening, neural implants aren't meant to pull a mind into another's body, not without risking the sanity of every party involved—

She has neural degradation. Thousand gods, she has ND and I'm stuck on a suicide mission with her and she can't even control herself—

Red clouds my eye. I grip my shoulder over the gunshot wound. The sky is gray with smoke. Ceres—

No. It's the bleed. She is bleeding into me, and I into her, my memories surging up like a tidal wave in a tsunami. Does she see them too?

The scar on my shoulder roars in agony. A knife slices into my temple. The pain is cutting something out of me—or pushing something into me—

I scream.

There's no one to hear me.

"OH-FEAAAAAAAAAR-UHHHHH."

Someone calls to me. Where are they? Who are they?

It's a girl's voice. Not scared, but playful.

"Oh-feaaaaaaaaar-uhhhhh."

I step over the body on the floor. I must follow the voice. Not far from the hab suites. Just around the corner.

"Oh-feaaaaaaaaar-uhhhhh."

It comes from a glowing doorway. A gate to faerie. Like stories I know from my childhood.

Tinkling laughter fills the air.

Oh. It's *my* voice. *I'm* laughing.

I press a hand over my mouth. Fight the giggles. I cannot scare them away now.

I step close to the glow and see . . . a thousand little fairies, small points of light. They sing and dance and throw their hands out to me.

Join me! Join me!

I want to. I reach out to touch them and—glass. A mirror lies in the way. But on the other side of the looking glass . . .

If I look just past myself, I . . . Wait, who am I?

A girl. Brown hair. Luminous hazel eyes. But I am not me . . .

Little lost creature, who are you?

MY EYES SNAP open. I'm on the floor.

Who am I? Who am I? Who am I?

"Shut up!" My voice is deep. That seems right.

My mind feels like a fragmented stone, half sharp amethyst points that is me and half . . . Ofiera's, I suppose, faceted squares of crystallized bismuth.

I push myself upright and place a hand on each side of my head, which pounds in time with my heartbeat. With the way I fell, I'll be lucky if all I end up with is bruising. Was any of that real? Too real, I fear.

And Ofiera . . . I look down the hallway. Where did she go?

The bathroom? What was that light, those fairies, that mirror?

"Ofiera . . ." My voice, crackling, sounds like the voice in my memory. Or not my memory, but Ofiera's head. Her memory? *Oh-feaaaaaaaaar-uhhhhh.*

The bleed has me so confused I can't think straight. I was listening to Hiro's recordings, and then . . . then I woke up, and saw myself—no, I saw *Ofiera.* Thousand gods, what's happening?

In the quiet with my eyes closed, I use my neural implant to call out to hers and . . . and I think I know where she went.

I come to my feet so quickly my head spins with dizziness and my stomach pitches with nausea. But it doesn't matter—I run down the hallway to the ladder and climb down. How did Ofiera manage this feat as deep as she was in her hallucination? "Ofiera!" I cry, to no avail. I bound from the ladder and run through the crates in the hold and—

Freeze.

She's in the airlock chamber. The interior door is open, and her palms are pressed flat against the reinforced window on the exterior door. She's faced away from me, but I can see the reflection of her expression, mesmerized. By what she sees or by the light? By the—thousand gods—by the fairies that are stars?

"Ofiera, come away from there," I say.

She doesn't seem to hear me. Her hand slinks toward the button on her right, the button that will vent the airlock. But the interior door is open, and neither of us is wearing a suit.

"It's *space*, Ofiera!"

Not to her. To her, it's a fairy garden. I know because I saw it too.

I dart forward as her fingers grasp the button. I snatch her wrist and jerk her hand away.

My entire body becomes stiff as stone. I cannot even breathe.

Red clouds my eye. I grip my shoulder over the gunshot wound—

No, don't fall now. Focus. Concentrate.

"Don't *ever* touch me," Ofiera snaps.

She can talk—

Her heated eyes rove over my face, but I cannot turn to look at her. My entire body . . . frozen stiff.

"Don't you dare!" Ofiera yells.

She is . . . herself again?

The edges of my vision go black. I can't breathe . . .

"Release me," she commands, and I do. Each finger unfurls from her wrist, my back snaps straight, and I salute like I am in lineup. Like I am one of the cannon-fodder drones, those unfortunate Icarii infantrymen, and my queen bee commander is demanding the unwavering loyalty of my mind and body.

She's Command, I remind myself. A Rapier *and* a Dagger. And this is what she's truly capable of.

She looks me up and down as the tunnel of my vision narrows.

Gods, Ofiera . . . what have you done to me?

I am screaming in my own mind.

What will break first—her will over my body, or me?

It's dark. Ofiera says something else, but I can't hear her. I'm slipping under.

If Ofiera is big enough to fill my body and her own, where will I go?

My name is Lito sol Lucius . . . I don't look like him anymore, but I am him. I am . . .

Who am I, in this light?

A shock runs up my spine. I think it's odd that my knees ache so much, and then I realize I am gasping in glorious cool air. I'm breathing again, and it is as sweet as water on a hot day. Sweeter even. I fell to the ground, to my knees—I collapsed—

"Lito? Lito! Gods!"

Ofiera taps my face with the flat of her hand, her arm around my shoulders to hold me steady.

"Ofiera . . . ?" My voice cracks.

"Lito!" She throws both arms around my neck. Hugs me. Holds my head against her chest and strokes my hair like a mother would.

"Ofiera . . ." She smells sweet like coconut. Or is that a memory of Luce?

"I'm so sorry, Lito," she says, and tears hit my cheeks—not mine . . . hers. "I'm so sorry . . ."

I close my eyes and let the nothingness wash over me. The only person I am in this moment is myself.

CHAPTER 11

Earth is a cold and harsh planet, but not so severe as her children, the moons known as Selene and Diana. It was common for my family to lose members when raiding the dead satellites and ships in Earth's exosphere for supplies. But more common than that was for us to lose children to sickness and deformity.

From Outside Earth's Moons *by Magnus Starikov*

Worry makes a nest in my belly, keeping me from both food and sleep. I need to write Ren, and I need to do it soon. But I have thought that for two whole weeks, and have yet to feel brave enough to put pen to paper.

I while hours away in the chapel, waiting for Ren to call me back to her room. She never does, which intensifies my anxiety instead of subduing it. Ringer visits me each day for confession, more to check on me than to unburden himself. I am not surprised to find him waiting for me today outside the chapel after confession hours are over. It's like he senses when I need his comfort.

"In certain lights, you look exactly like Astrid," he says.

That name again. I have yet to discover who Astrid is, but now that Ringer has brought it up, I change tactics. I furrow my brows and cock my head, placing one hand upon his biceps. Though my worry still gnaws at me, my curiosity takes hold.

"Would you walk with me, First Sister?" Ringer asks, and I nod assent. He leads the way, and I soon fall into step beside him, each one of his steps equal to two of mine.

"Do you ever miss your home?" After a moment, he corrects himself. "Do you even have a home to miss?"

I shake my head and pat the wall as we pass by to indicate that the *Juno* is my home. As much of a home as I have ever had, anyway.

"I miss mine," he says, undeterred. "The longships tethered to the mountainous gray rocks, the brown and white of Earth on the horizon each morning, my family—from my siblings to my cousins—all under one roof, bigger than most Martian families."

I raise my brows to show my curiosity. Though it is considered a social faux pas for those of us born on Mars to separate ourselves from those born on Earth, Ringer seems to take it a step further, separating himself from Geans entirely.

"I grew up on Máni. Though I suppose you would call it Selene."

I let him read the shock on my face. Selene is the barely habitable moon of Earth, orbiting alongside its smaller twin, Diana. The moons are home to families from the coldest lands on Earth, places like the Russian Federation and the Ice-lands, and the people who live there do so in the gray area of Gean laws, surviving by repurposing the rubbish left in Earth's atmosphere and raiding the odd lost traveler. From what little I know, they also have little to no connection to the Sisterhood.

"I'm sure you've met many of us without knowing," he says. "It's shameful to leave our families, so those of us who do also leave our birth names behind. My name is Hringar Grimson. 'Ringer' came later."

We have stopped walking without my noticing. Ringer glances about the hallway, finds it suitably empty, and continues. "You may think that living on Máni or Skadi—that is the true name of what you would call Diana—is a terrible fate, substituting one ship's interior for another, even our homes made of grounded ships. But that's not so. It's quite beautiful, and there's nothing like sharing a longship with your kin."

I find that I'm smiling despite myself. Family, at least, sounds nice.

"We even have temples made of many-roomed ships, places in which we may make offerings to the gods."

I had truly believed Ringer a devout follower of the Goddess. Is that not so? Has he his own gods, or does he hold to none at all?

"Though none of the gods are greater than Freyja, our goddess of war and fertility. She gives in times of raiding and through cultivation of the soil. Were I to further describe her to you, you would find that she has much in common with the Goddess of the Sisterhood. I believe they are one and the same, or were when all humanity lived on Earth. Though I'm sure others don't share my view."

I wonder how Ringer sees me, then. A handmaiden of his Freyja? Is that why he is so kind to me? But as I begin to wonder, he continues.

"One day, a visiting ship arrived on Máni, a captain and his best soldiers come to feast with my father in his longship. He brought a woman in gray with him, and she did not say a word."

A Sister. My heart sinks into my stomach.

"The day they were set to leave, they asked for Astrid, my sister. She took this as a sign from Freyja, honored to be chosen to fight, and readied herself for war. But it became clear she would not be on the battlefront. No, the woman in gray wanted her to join her order. Astrid didn't want this, but the captain offered my father whatever he would ask in return for her: ship parts, food, clothing, anything that would make our hard lives easier. My father considered, but Astrid did not. She took a knife—"

My hands began to tremble.

"And cut her face like so." He runs his hand down the length of his face from forehead to chin on both sides. "She did not even hesitate. She said she would go to war or not at all. When my father saw what she had done, he wept, but the captain and the woman in gray did not want her any longer, not for the Sisterhood and not for war. I gave thanks to Freyja for Astrid's quick thinking.

"But of course, that was not an answer they could bear. It was my fate, instead, that was resigned to the stars. Freyja chose me to go to war, and I joined the captain and his crew so that Astrid might choose her life, even if that life was scarred."

He wipes a thumb across my cheek, catching a tear. I didn't even know I was crying . . .

"So you see, little sister, whenever I see one of you in gray, I think of Astrid."

Astrid and her freedom . . . The Sister could have taken her anyway, sent her to surgery to have her face fixed. But what I cannot say, what I know to be true, is that they deemed her unworthy for her rebelliousness. Why take a girl who would rather maim herself than be a Sister?

But her story shames me. I would not mar my own face. I had never thought to. And my hesitation with Ren . . .

I press my forehead to Ringer's wide chest. This brave man sacrificed his home, his family, his life, so that his sister might live. And yet, instead of blaming Freyja, he continues to worship her under a different name and treats the Sisters as his own blood. He is a brave child in a world too cold for him. *Thank you.* I cannot say it, but I want to.

He pats my head like he would his own sister's, like he would Astrid's, and a true smile comes to my lips. I must return to my room and write.

I WAS TEN years old when the orphanage that had cared for me throughout my youth gave me to the Sisters. By then I knew how to read and write, and spent the majority of my time in the small common room perched beside the one-shelf library filled with out-of-date volumes on art, history, and engineering. I cared more for those brittle pages and the musty smell of old books than I did my fellow orphans. I spoke little. Had I known what was to come, I like to believe that I would have filled my days with talking, or at least with reading my books aloud. But I was quiet and shy and kept to myself.

Matron Thorne, an old woman with flyaway graying hair and soft jowls hung from a bony, thin body, saw me despite my shyness. She knew I was intelligent and did her best to help me learn, providing me with new reading material whenever she found a cheap manual for trade or allowing me to help her with the maintenance on her simple hand prosthetic. But the orphanage brought in little revenue, and medicine to combat Mars's low gravity was expensive, so I was forced to read and reread the same passages until I could quote them.

Strange that I have forgotten so much of who I am, and yet I have not forgotten those books.

There was no chance of going to university when I had no parentage. I considered volunteering in the military, but Matron Thorne stopped my talk, showing me the stump beneath her prosthetic. "Foot soldiers are easily forgotten," she said. "You are better than that."

Another option was to find myself a trade, and this was the plan of which I was most hopeful. The majority of Martians worked in industry, the factories and their thick gray gases as old as terraforming itself. There were many workshops I could apprentice myself to, and Matron Thorne even knew someone at a mill that made small metal parts for Gean crafts. But it would not come to be.

The older I grew, the more beautiful I became. I knew this because it was commented upon by all around me: fellow orphans who either vied for my attention or vilified me; strangers we met on errands in town; even Matron Thorne herself. I did not understand beauty, but I did not mind it, for what child ever turns away attention when she has been given so little throughout her life?

One night Matron Thorne told me someone was coming to see me. In my excitement, I believed that my beauty, that strange but tangible thing, had finally drawn a loving couple to adopt me. I groomed myself as well as I could, brushing my hair until it shone like liquid gold. I put on my best dress, two inches too short but cornflower blue like my eyes. I packed my few belongings—a box of matches, an ad I'd found of a beautiful woman selling health care policies, and an assortment of ribbons I'd pocketed one day at market—into my pillowcase and set it aside for later. Certainly my parents would have a suitcase for me filled with new clothes and shoes—shiny shoes that fit my feet, with little golden buckles, like those I envied on other children.

But the only person who came to visit was a silent woman in somber gray. She did not speak and did not stay long. She gripped me by my shoulders and turned me around and around until I felt dizzy, and then departed. She did not even smile.

I cried that night, believing I had failed some test, that my beauty was not enough. I should have cried because I had passed, though I did not know that at the time. The next day the Sisters sent another woman in gray who did not speak to gather me, and Matron Thorne pulled me aside and told me to do as they instructed me. If I did, I could have a good life with many beautiful things.

At the time, I believed Matron Thorne wanted the best for me. Now I think she wanted one less mouth to feed. I am sure the Sisters donated to her orphanage handsomely in return for me, and that she pocketed some of the proceeds for herself. Though perhaps that is what this world has made of me, and she did nothing of the sort. Perhaps she treated the other children to more medicine and clothes and books. If only I could believe such niceties existed for those like me.

Living with the Sisters was nothing like living at the orphanage. The Temple of Mars had reclaimed Icarii tech that formed a barrier around its grounds, generated gravity, and controlled oxygen flow, and I was thrilled that I no longer had to take the disgusting medication that kept us healthy in Mars's low gravity. I was never allowed to play in the Temple, but outside my window I could watch the bustling space elevator atop Olympus Mons, more beautiful than I could have ever imagined anything man-made. Like the trunk of an ivory tree, the elevator stretched toward the heavens and held the red sky of Mars in its formidable branches.

I was assigned to the Order of Andromeda—not surprising, since out of the seven Orders, Andromeda is charged with the care and education of children. Aunt Delilah, who was as dark and stern as a winter storm, became my mentor, and I traveled everywhere at her side as her Little Sister. She was so clever I wanted her to love me, and while she could speak, she taught me to communicate with gestures and facial expressions, minute changes of my body. I learned how to sit still as a statue and present myself as cultured. I learned how to care for my skin and to enhance my eyes and lips with cosmetics.

If I or any of the other Little Sisters spoke aloud, we were slapped. If we spoke again, we were whipped with a cane. If still we continued to make noise, even a whimper from our beatings, we were locked away in what I can only call the quiet room, which allowed no sound in or out, for a whole day without food or water. I learned quickly to hold my tongue. Quicker than many.

When I turned twelve years old, I woke to find my sheets covered in blood. I cried then, so sure was I that I had done something horrible. I did not fear for myself, never once considered that I was the source of the blood despite the pain in my stomach, but wondered whom I had harmed or killed. Finally my dreams of violence had come to fruition, and I had become a monster.

My Auntie heard me crying and came to see what was the matter. She did not speak, but in the lines of her ecstatic face, I saw that she was pleased. She held me to her chest and hugged me, then slapped me across the face for making noise.

That night I was given an adult's portion of food at the dinner table. Fellow Little Sisters looked on in jealousy, and I preened at my Auntie's side. They even allowed me a glass of wine, which made my tummy feel twisted like a knot and my head clouded with sweat that would not come out. The ordeal made me sleepy. So sleepy that I fell asleep right at the table.

They had drugged me. Though perhaps that should not be surprising with all else they did to me. For when I woke a Sister, my head throbbed like I had been struck by a grown man's fist, and when I cried, I no longer needed to control the sobs, for no sound came.

I was silent. My voice was gone.

And with it, the name I had always known.

Somehow, at twelve years old, I had been forced to forget my name.

I was sent away then to my first assignment, a pleasure liner that brought soldiers home from deployment, with a dozen other Sisters who attended to passengers. And that was when I used all I had been taught, the taking of confession, the act of forgiveness, and, when I grew older, the comfort of the body. Yet I clung, ever so tightly, to the secret part of me. I wanted a home. I wanted a family. I wanted to be anything other than what I was.

This is what I write to Ren.

WHEN I FINISH, I stop in front of the captain's quarters and knock. I have never been more scared in my life than when the door opens and I see Ren on the other side. She leads me deeper into her room, and I shake as I pull the letter, written in a childish scrawl, from my pocket.

She paces as she reads, her eyes darting over the numerous pages the size of her hand. She could call for soldiers at any moment now. She has the confirmation that I am a traitor to the Sisterhood.

But beneath my fear is something more, something I hesitate to name: excitement. For someone outside the Sisterhood to have heard my words and responded to my inner thoughts . . . I press a hand to the desk to keep myself from tipping over. I feel faint.

"You should sit." Ren guides me to a chair, helps me settle as my head spins. I press my cool hand to my forehead.

"You're okay," Ren says. "You're safe here." But I don't feel safe anywhere.

When the vertigo ebbs, I find I'm across the desk from Ren, and she's sitting in the smaller of the two chairs. Which means . . . I'm sitting in the captain's chair. *Her* chair.

She looks at me, unmoving. She doesn't call for soldiers. Doesn't name me a traitor. Just . . . meets my eyes.

"I'd love to talk with you now, if you feel up to it," Ren says.

It is hard for me to rationalize the two sides of Ren I have seen. The hardened warrior who punished Second Sister for stepping out of line stands in direct opposition to the lonely captain who asks me to write her and promises me safety.

It takes all my strength just to nod.

She flutters the papers before setting them between us. "I'm sorry you had to face this. You were just a child, and it was unfair of them."

Her words make me feel like a fist is tightening around my heart, so I wave my hand through the air as if brushing the past away, like what happened doesn't even matter. But it does matter, and it chills me to my core that she *knows* about it now.

She can see something is bothering me, but she seems unsure as to what. "Why don't you ask me questions? Whatever you're curious about."

I can't help but smile, at least a little. The fact that she's offering me her story in response to mine makes our exchange feel more equal, like a true conversation. Perhaps that is the point.

A thrill runs through me as I withdraw the tools of my betrayal from my dress pocket. As the pen hovers over the paper, I realize how pathetic I must be, some sad-eyed girl with a sorrowful tale that half the cosmos shares. I harden my expression and let the ink flow without hesitation.

I start simply. *Where were you born?* I write.

I offer the page to her when I finish, and she takes it with her flesh hand. She reads it with a quick flick of her eyes. "I was actually born off-world. In a ship." She chuckles. "So I'm not from anywhere, I guess. Or maybe I'm from space itself, and that's why I'm so comfortable here."

But I recall her dossier saying something different.

I heard you were born on Mars, I write. I think twice before I hand it to her.

Half her mouth curls upward, and she musses her own hair. If I didn't know any better, I'd say she was nervous too. "Listening to rumors about me?" I start to apologize, but she forces a laugh. "Don't worry, I'm not upset. Just know that no one truly knows *everything* about me."

Perhaps not even her dossier, I begin to fear.

"As for where I was born, they don't issue you a birth certificate until you come planetside. As soon as the ship landed, Mars claimed me as a newborn citizen."

Oh. I hadn't known that. I smile as Ren picks up another pen from her desk and taps it against her lip. "Do you have any friends here on the *Juno*?"

I try not to frown as I look at the blank page beneath my hands. Perhaps she expects me to name a few Sisters, but instead all I write is Ringer's name.

"Ringer?" Ren asks, eyebrow quirked high.

Hringar Grimson, I write on another page.

She reads it but shakes her head. "I haven't met him. Right now I'm still learning the names of my subordinates, so I can't say I have any friends yet . . ." I quirk my lips at the idea of a captain trying to make *friends*.

What did you want to be when you were a child? I write. Safe territory.

Ren's gracious enough not to point out any spelling mistakes I make or my terrible handwriting. "I only ever wanted to go into the military."

Why? I ask with a raised eyebrow and cocked head.

"Why did I only consider the military?" Ren asks, looking at me to ensure she understood my question. I nod encouragement. "Well . . ."

She looks embarrassed with the way her eyes flick around the room, unable to settle on any one thing. "At first it was only because my father wanted me to. Then . . . I felt that a good warrior could change things. Could change *everything*. And I want this war to end, for everyone involved."

I'm not sure how to answer that, so I place my hands flat on the desk. This is an unmarked section of the map, dangerous to speak of.

But also . . . perhaps this is what Aunt Marshae wants me to pursue.

You aim for peace? I write.

"Just think how much we could achieve during peacetime with the Geans and Icarii working together." Ren's eyes float from me to the screen showing the stars beyond. "During the Dead Century War, Earth and Mars fought for one hundred years without progress. One hundred *years*, and nothing to show for it, nothing but senseless slaughter."

I want to disagree with her, but I don't know enough history to do so. The Dead Century War was fought because Earth continued to demand resources from its child, Mars, while they were both suffering. Unable to help Earth any longer, Mars went to war. And afterward, when the war stopped because the Synthetics abandoned their makers on both sides, there was no choice but for the two planets to enter into a reluctant treaty and become the Geans. While the Dead Century War had raged, the Icarii built paradise and then refused to share it with the rest of the galaxy.

Her eyes burn as they turn on me, like two coals in a near-dead hearth. "Think of all we could do if we dedicated ourselves to peace. Is there anything you dislike about the Sisterhood you would want to change?"

I think of the amber-eyed girl thrown out of the *Juno*.

There is so much I want to change. Too much for me to fit on one sheet of paper. I could write and write and run out of sheets. I could start writing and never stop. I settle for an affirmative nod.

"Wouldn't you like to change it?"

Her words set off warnings in my head, but I find my hand moving before my mind catches up. *How?* I consider crumpling the page, throwing it away, but Ren has always shown preference to my honesty, so . . . I hand her the page.

"By changing the minds of the leaders in charge, or by replacing them with people who aim for peace. Warlord Vaughn is old but refuses to name a successor or retire, and the Mother wants to expand this war now that we have the Icarii tech from Ceres. She will start by expanding the Sisterhood."

I don't ask how Ren knows this. I simply swallow hard at that thought. More Sisters means more girls who will lose their families, who will have their voices silenced, who will lose their control over their bodies to the will of the Sisterhood. A tremor runs through my hand, and I clench it into a fist.

"It might be worth considering where your future lies in the Sisterhood."

I fight a shudder at how close Ren's words come to my Auntie's. Why should it matter what I want for my future? If I had a choice, it would be apart from the politics of the Sisterhood, not entrenched in it. I can worship the Goddess in my works by dedicating myself to a single captain and growing a garden of my own; I don't need to be Her conduit.

"Let's talk about something else." As quickly as she approached the subject of the Sisterhood, Ren abandons it. Perhaps she has sensed how far she has pushed me and how confused I am by her words. "Why don't you ask me another question?"

But I am overwhelmed, and the only questions I have are too pointed and sharp, like daggers made of words.

You'll make enemies if you talk this way. Why do you care about peace that much? I write.

But then I realize, she already *has* made enemies. Enemies like Aunt Marshae and the Mother, who assigned me to spy on her.

I rip the page from the notepad and make to throw it away, but Ren halts me. "Hey, I said you can ask me anything. Or tell me anything. Hell, call me an asshole for all I care."

My emotions run high, and, spurred on by Ren's boldness, I write down another question. *Why did you do that to Second Sister?* I stop and scribble out *Second Sister*. Instead I write, *the amber-eyed girl who used to be Second Sister.*

When Ren takes the page from me, her face falls. "Aunt Marshae . . ." Her flesh hand digs into the arm of the chair where she sits. "She brought me proof that Second Sister was a traitor."

Traitor, traitor, traitor, my heart beats.

"She told me it was my duty as captain to take care of her according to the Canon. So I did as she asked. Perhaps it's a shitty excuse, but I couldn't think of a way to get out of it."

A test. Even Saito Ren had to face a test of the Sisterhood. And if she had refused, Aunt Marshae and the Mother would have had their proof she was a traitor. They wouldn't have needed to enlist my help. But Ren passed, so here I am . . .

What if Aunt Marshae made up the evidence against the amber-eyed girl? The question comes so suddenly, my heart jumps into my throat. How much of a fool am I to even consider that? Perhaps not all is as I thought within the Sisterhood, but even Aunt Marshae would never kill a high-ranking Sister as a test for someone else. Would she?

I take the crumpled-up paper from my lap and spread it flat. *Why do you care about peace that much?* it reads across wrinkles. This time I hand it to Ren, not with anger, but with curiosity.

She hesitates as she speaks. "It sort of . . . came to me, after Ceres. I was dying, and . . . I suppose it makes you reconsider things." She closes her eyes, but I can see the continued movement beneath her lids.

"A quicksilver blade split me through the Ironskin." So an Icarii warrior did this to her, perhaps two, since they fight in pairs. Her eyes flutter around the room, looking for something or someone, but she is not here; she is back on Ceres. "I should have died. I wanted to die."

Her voice cracks when she speaks. I remember Jones's words vividly. *She's not the same after Ceres.* Is this what he meant?

I stand from the captain's chair at last. Walk around the desk until I come to her side. Slowly, so slowly, I take her hand—her flesh hand against mine, tawny against pink.

She doesn't jerk away.

"I didn't die, so . . . they sent me here. Away from the front lines, because I could no longer pilot an Ironskin. Away from the war. To a battleship, where I will hold a comfortable position with a desk and a soft chair. Where the last person to die will be me, because I will send soldiers to die instead . . ." She snorts.

My grip tightens on her hand, and I find myself frowning without forcing myself to. Her words have angered me. Of *course* she's not the same after Ceres, not after losing her limbs and facing battle after battle. Who is anyone to judge her for that?

"Don't give me that look," she says.

But I keep my sneer, and her pain melts away until she is at peace. Finally, I smile; I have done my job well to help the captain in a moment of agony.

"I enjoyed talking with you, First Sister," she says, looking up into my eyes through her thick lashes.

Heat rises to my cheeks, and I have to separate from her in order to take my paper and pen. My hand misses hers when she's gone . . . and I find that surprising.

I enjoyed talking with you, Captain Saito, I write.

"Ren," she says, wearing one of her happy smiles. "Just Ren."

PLAY:
▶ 06

———◇——◆◇◆——◇———

Ceres. The place where it all began. The place where we ended.

I only wanted to keep you safe, Lito. That's all I cared about. So when the bomb went off at Command headquarters and the rain of Gean ships began, I wanted nothing to do with the city. I wanted to find a port and get us off that damned rock, leave it for the Asters and Geans to squabble over. But you . . . I should have known you'd refuse to leave with any of our fellow duelists in trouble.

Lito, the perfect soldier. The warrior. The shot-calling Rapier. Decisive and hard. That's what you want people to believe, isn't it? Because you're scared, more than anything else, that if you falter even one step, you'll wind up back on the bottom of Cytherea with no one to care for your family. A ladder is hard to climb but easy to fall down, right?

Even as we fought our way back into the city, the sky overhead a gray smudge, the dust from bombarded buildings and gunfire clouding out the dome above, you were focused more on your objective than our survival. No, it wasn't your objective—it was the mission that Command had given you. *Protect Ceres.* The Fall went against that order, and you were willing to die in defense of it.

The city crumbled around us, the Geans swarming like ants in their black Ironskin armor, picking their way through the abandoned streets. When I finally saw that you were bleeding, we were standing deep in a cobblestone alleyway, listening to the song of gunshots and screams. At our feet was a carpet of the dead—Icarii infantry in black and silver, Geans in navy, citizens in vibrant clothes dyed dark with blood, even an Aster in their goggles.

"Let me see your forehead," I demanded.

"How could this happen?" you whispered, staring at the body at your feet as if hypnotized. She was a young woman who looked nothing like Luce, but I knew that's who you saw when you looked at her.

"They want the water here. They need it for their shit planets." I couldn't say the rest: I had known something was coming to Ceres. I had been warned. But I never knew it would be something like *this*.

Instead, I tugged on your neural implant, forced you to look at me. "Let me patch that gash."

You bowed your head so I could reach the wound. A chunk of metal the size of my thumbnail stuck out of your forehead like a horn. "Shrapnel." I grabbed tools from my belt of pouches. "Do you want to sit down?"

You shook your head no.

"I'll catch you if you fall." I took a thick set of tweezers and placed the grips on either side of the shrapnel. "Deaden the pain, Lito." You groaned as I yanked the metal out with a sharp pop, evidence you hadn't done what I told you to. "Damn it, Lito." I covered the wound with pelospray and waited as the synthetic skin stopped the bleeding.

"I'm fine," you said, but I only halfway believed you.

"If your shield is down, we have more trouble than your dumbass fascination with feeling pain." I put my tools away as you wiped leftover blood from your eye.

"I dropped the shield when shifting my blade. I wasn't focused. It won't happen again."

"It had better not." I threaded my fingers into my hair, not even bothering to hide my nervousness. "What's the plan, Lito? Why are we returning to a city that's obviously lost, running straight into the shit?"

You shifted from one foot to the other. I expected you to spout off some propaganda bullshit about duty and honor, but instead, you shook your head. "I thought we could find other survivors."

But since the bombing had knocked out the comms, the only fellow soldiers we had come across were dead. "It'd be best for us to get off this rock," I said.

"And do what?" you asked halfheartedly. Perhaps you'd already had this debate with yourself. "Retreat and let the Geans have Ceres?"

"Better than being dead and still losing this place."

"We can't just leave," you said.

So I snapped at you, "I don't care if I have to march you to the nearest shuttle myself. This is over. It was over before we even got back to the city. There's nothing we can do."

"We can keep trying to find others . . . We can . . ." Your hesitation was all I needed.

"It's *over*, Lito. It's done." I grabbed your shoulders and squeezed as hard as I could. I should have deferred to you as my Rapier, but this was a moment for subterfuge, and I was your perfect Dagger. "Don't make me explain to Luce that you died on Ceres."

Your eyes widened. You sucked in a breath. You knew I was using her to manipulate you, but you allowed it, because I was also right. "Okay. We head for the nearest launch station. But if we find anyone along the way, we help them."

I felt your determination on the other side of the implant, so I smirked like a fox for show. "And kill any Geans in our path. That's our duty, after all."

We knew there was no point in heading for the main docks. By now, all the escape ships would have either launched or been destroyed. So instead of going deeper into the city, we retreated the way we'd come, returning to the outskirts in hopes of finding a military emergency launch station that wasn't controlled by the Geans.

Even though the ships there were small and not meant for long-term space travel, if we could get off-world, we had a chance at hailing another Icarii vessel. With just the two of us, we'd have enough air for a full day, a bit more if we took turns sleeping. After that . . . we'd face death by asphyxiation in the uncaring void of space.

I could feel you worrying over this as we ran. "Stop chasing your tail," I told you, but it was something I needed to hear too. Do you know what I was telling myself then? *My fault*, I kept thinking. *I knew something would happen, and I did nothing. It's my fault.* But what I said was: "Worry isn't going to suit you here on Ceres. Get rid of it and focus."

But the calm stretching between our implants didn't last. "If the launch station has already been seized, we go back to our speeder, head to a depot, and hole up," you said. We'd only make it two days max at one of the Icarii depots, but I didn't point out the fault with your plan; we both needed the slim hope of survival.

My fault, I thought as we ran. *My fault* as I guided you with a light touch to your neural implant, like a hand on your back. *My fault* as I lurked behind, close enough to bridge the gap if a fight erupted, but far enough back to act as a spotter and protect your rear.

When we reached the edge of the city, the dense urban sprawl opened to a small, ragged park, the bushes fuzzy in disarray and the trees half the green of summer and half the bare of winter. This close to the dome wall, the array was pixelated and strange, the sky effect immobile, chunks of clouds glitching and disappearing.

I caught up with you where you ducked behind a tree. "Station is just around there," I said, nodding to the bunker entrance where it was hidden in a small grove of trees near the dome's edge. Since this was an emergency evac point not listed on any manifests, only the Icarii military would know about it. At least, if it hadn't been compromised. "Are you ready?" I asked.

"Always," you said.

We rushed forward, side by side, keeping low. As we approached the bunker, we saw how bad our luck was. The Geans had already taken the evac point. One of their smaller ships blocked the hangar doors.

I felt your shock on the other side of the implant, and I knew it wasn't because of the Geans. It was something else, something much worse. I quickly surveyed the area: two Geans in navy uniforms, a fidgeting Aster, and—there they were—a row of four bodies, all in military blacks. Duelists. Dead Rapier and Dagger pairs . . .

Where there were dead duelists, an Ironskin wasn't far. As we waited, one appeared from behind the shuttle.

I know the Geans revere the natural body, but an Ironskin—I could never see anything but a monster in its design. Hulking and black, like a two-meter god clad in thick chitin, the Ironskin marched with sure, heavy steps. It was humanoid in the same way a flayed man was human: the exterior swelled with carved musculature, the smoothness broken by protruding bone spikes. The helmet was sleek and black, so dark it obscured the face within, but the pilot—because of course there was a person inside that thing—could see from the ring of burning gold projected in a halo around the head.

The Ironskins were the Geans' answer to us. We duelists were elegant, fast, able to flow like water with the tide of battle—but the Ironskins were power, patience, a mountain set in its ways. During the Battle of the Belt, I had seen an Ironskin reach into a soldier's back and rip out his spine as if it had been plucking fruit from a tree.

And there was something different about this one. It was more slender than the others I'd seen before, but I wasn't sure whether that meant it was a newer model or a smaller pilot. There was too much I just didn't know.

I was scared, Lito. For the first time, I was really scared.

"Plan, Lito," I demanded.

"You take the Gean on the left, I'll take the other. Then we'll focus on the Ironskin." You didn't mention the Aster.

"Not the Ironskin first?" I asked.

"It'll take too long to dig through the metal when the soldiers have railguns."

"Lito." The fear roared inside me. Could you hear it in my voice? Feel it from my implant? "Is your shield down or not?"

"It's not."

I couldn't tell if you were lying. Maybe even you didn't know if your shield was down.

I reached for the hilt on my belt regardless. "On the count of three, then," I said, and together we counted beneath our breath.

"Three!"

We both darted from the bushes. With a thought from my neural implant, the liquid metal seeped up from the hilt and glowed in standard formation. I slid the blade through the soldier's back, right through the heart, before checking to see you had done the same.

The Aster screamed in surprise and stumbled toward the evac station. I hoped he'd grab a shuttle and get the hell out of here. I didn't want to kill him.

Then the speakers in the Ironskin crackled as its pilot spoke, its voice amplified to be heard through the thick armor. I'd always had an ear for languages, but this one seemed foreign and strange to me. Then I realized why—they weren't words. The Ironskin was laughing. The fear came back, stronger than before.

"ヘムロックはどこですか?" the Ironskin asked, and a chill ran down my spine at the name. It was a name I never wanted to hear again after this day.

I wondered if your Japanese was good enough to know what the Ironskin said, but then it switched to English, as if that was the reason we hadn't answered them. "Where is Hemlock? Did he talk?" The voice echoed with the speakers, making the slow Gean accent even stranger. "How did you find me?"

"We just want to leave," I snapped, "and you're in our way."

Again the Ironskin laughed the cold, soft laughter that sounded like stones striking.

"Then leave," the Ironskin said, holding out an arm toward the hangar as if in invitation. Instead, it called attention to the four duelists in the dirt, dead.

That was when I noticed the scraps of black fabric tied onto the Ironskin armor, fluttering with its movement. Five, ten, a dozen, something like over twenty—

Strips of military black. Pieces of duelist uniforms. Trophies of the dead.

How many had this Ironskin killed?

I felt your resolve harden to kill this Gean bastard through the neural link, and I mirrored that feeling. You would never run from an opponent who had met your gaze, and I knew there was no way we would get off Ceres without killing it.

The Ironskin whooshed, like air blowing through a narrow corridor. A sigh, I realized a moment later. "So be it," it said. It straightened its arm at its side, and from the underside of the wrist, a panel opened up and emitted a blue-white glow. Out snaked a crackling, electrified whip that coiled onto the ground, two meters in length. Like the trained duelists we were, we both shifted so that we were outside its reach.

You darted in first for the Ironskin's right side, straight toward the electrified weapon. But the whip rushed up to meet you, and you were forced to break off your attack and use your jumpjets to sling yourself out of harm's way.

The whip missed you by centimeters, and I didn't see your shield ripple once. Out of battery, or had your suit been damaged?

I slipped behind the Ironskin and curved my blade like a scythe. As the arm holding the whip started its downward arc with all the power of the Ironskin behind it, I wrapped my blade around the thickened wrist and transformed the glowing metal into a sharp loop, holding the arm in place so that it could not complete its trajectory.

The Ironskin stopped, its movements sharp and precise. Faster than I had thought possible for the bulky armor. Perhaps this slender model *was* new to the Geans. I could hear the hum of its golden halo, and though there was no way to tell what it was looking at, I could *feel* its eyes on me.

That's when I saw it.

I called for you through the implant, pulling your attention to the area where the arm met the shoulder. A seam had been cut open, probably by an unlucky bastard who had faced this Ironskin already today but hadn't survived the encounter.

You transformed your blade into a thin point to slide into the gap—a rapier, like your namesake—and jumped for the open seam. I smirked, believing we had it. But before the blade could make contact, the Ironskin toppled backward, falling like a puppet whose strings had snapped.

I screamed. The spikes on the rear of the helmet bludgeoned my face, the points of its spine scraped against my torso. Its weight was twice or three times mine, and I fell beneath it, my shield heating and rippling to keep the spikes from piercing my skin and drawing blood.

But I could no longer hold the Ironskin in place. It flicked its whip after you, and though you tried to turn your momentum into a flip, the whip lashed across your leg.

You bounded away, the whip cracking against the ground. As the weight of the armor shifted, I slipped from beneath it and rolled away. I could feel my shield flickering, overclocked and running low. The Ironskin used small boosters to set itself back on its feet, and as we all shifted back into battle formation, I finally saw your leg.

Your pant leg was torn, as was your skin. Your calf bled from a cut from the side of your knee to your ankle.

Your shield was completely gone.

"Commander Saito!" someone cried.

A shot rang out around us. You didn't move. Yet from one moment to the next, a wound appeared between your shoulder and chest, blood spraying like red rain.

"Lito!" I screamed, out loud and through the implant.

The Aster wasn't a stone's throw away from you, his long-fingered, shaking hand clutching one of the Gean soldiers' railguns.

I should have killed him. That's all I could think as you stared at him, eyes wide in pure shock. You didn't know—how could you have known—that the Geans and Asters had joined forces. *My fault, my fault, my fault . . .*

The Aster raised the weapon again. I jumped without thinking, my blade in standard formation, and sliced through his neck. His body and the railgun fell at my feet. His head spun clear of the shuttle into the woods on the other side.

I hadn't wanted to kill him, but I had, and I should have done it as soon as I laid eyes on him.

Behind me, you collapsed.

"A shame," the Ironskin pilot, Commander Saito, said. Though the Ironskin had no need to turn its head to look at me, it did so, as if to make a point. "I had hoped the two of you would be more of a challenge."

I had only a few moments to decide what I would do. Attack the Ironskin alone and leave you to bleed out? Try to help you, only to expose my back to the attacker?

Honestly . . . it was never a choice. I reached to the many pouches on my belt.

I only wanted you to live, Lito.

I threw my blade at the Ironskin, forcing it to dodge, and jumpjetted to your side. With the last of the pelospray, I closed your wound.

It was four seconds at most, but that was all the time I was given before the Ironskin was on me. I felt its spiked hand brushing through my hair like a lover's, something too soft, before it seized my neck and jerked me away from you.

I thought I would be afraid as the fist tightened on my neck, as my vision blackened at the edges, as punches from the opposite spiked fist rained down on my face and body and my shield gave out.

But I wasn't scared at all. I was . . . I wouldn't say calm, but I was at peace.

I would die before you. And maybe . . . maybe you would survive, and all would be right in the world.

I'm not sure which broke first—the delicate bones of my face or my ribs. But when I finally saw you stand, your left arm hanging limply at your side, it was through eyes swollen to slits.

Run, Lito, I tried to say—not with my mouth, because I couldn't with the fist crushing my larynx—but through the implant.

Your answer was anger, raw and violent. You screamed a wordless warrior's cry and, despite your limp and dead arm, launched yourself onto the Ironskin's back. The spikes cut through you, pinning you like a butterfly to a board, and the Ironskin frantically moved to dislodge you but couldn't. You were tethered by your skin, bound by your blood.

The Ironskin released me, reaching for you. You battered its armor with your sword, face lit by its glow, again and again striking where shoulder met arm, where the seam had been broken by another duelist, where the armor was already damaged.

I pushed myself up from the ground, from where I had buckled at its feet. I threw myself on it too, wrapping my arms around the helmet and clinging with all the strength I had left. My life was inconsequential in that moment.

Then the Ironskin's shield went out and your blade slipped through the joint like a knife through thin paper, and I fell from its shoulders with its helmet clutched to my chest. A shocked face stared back at me in disbelief.

I wish I'd known then what her face would come to mean to me, but at that time, there was no warning. It just was.

She had a pointed chin and the apples of her cheeks were round and red and her soft lips twisted into an unpleasant shape. Unable to see us both at the same time without her helmet, her gaze bounced between us as blood poured down her side. Her arm lay limp on the ground, curved like a question mark.

"Commander Saito." My throat strained to form the words. "I had hoped you would be more of a challenge."

Snarling at my words, she reached for the railgun at her side. But you were behind her, waiting and ready.

Your blade went through the place where hip met leg, and the gunshot went wide, blasting into the air. With the mournful cry of a fatally wounded animal, she collapsed beside her limbs.

"Stay down," you growled.

I tried to push the pain away, but my implant couldn't tackle it all. There was too much of it. But I was alive. If the pain had any use, it was the proof of that.

"Quicksilver bastard!" Saito cried, her breath hitching with sobs. "I feel it—oh Goddess, I feel it all!"

You stumbled toward me. I held out a red hand.

"Who are you?" she screamed. Cried out, because she couldn't keep the pain inside as she died. "I am Saito Ren! I am the one who has taken Ceres! Give me a warrior's death! Give me your name!"

Your hand found mine, and our implants sang together, a calming hum that was so familiar, I felt we were somewhere far away and long ago, just children playing at being duelists.

"Tell me!" Saito demanded. "Tell me who you are!"

You couldn't pick me up, not with your left arm unresponsive, but you wouldn't leave me there. You slid your right arm around my chest and, with every tug a struggle, pulled me toward the waiting shuttle.

"Please!" she begged. Tears streamed down her cheeks, and so I gave her what she asked for, her dying wish.

"Lito sol Lucius!" I said through the agony, my voice loud and true.

She stopped struggling. She savored the name. And then she fell into the silence that precedes death.

CHAPTER 12

The Icarii as a people are a quilt, a patchwork of cultures, languages, and histories from Earthen societies by way of Mars. For those who are religious, sprawling temples of many rooms are dedicated to the Thousand Gods Below the Sun, kept by priests educated in a variety of historical services and freely available for everyone to worship as they please. There is no place more exemplary of this pluralism than Ceres.

From A Brief History of Ceres *by Toliver val Berquist*

For two weeks on the grasshopper, I live alone with my aching scar, my memories, and Hiro's voice. Some things Ofiera dragged from the depths of my mind. Others Hiro imagined into existence. And others still I have not thought about since those six months in the dark basement of the Spire while I healed from the Fall.

Hiro says they are guilty.

It should make my mission that much simpler, but all of their answers leave me with more burning questions.

I know what Beron would say. His voice is the voice of Command. *You are a duelist. You have your mission. You must complete it.*

I imagine Luce on the level where we grew up, the air filters flagging, the caustic stench of the meat vats overwhelming. Her annual salary alone wouldn't pay for her art degree, and our parents would never help her in that regard. Their money is theirs, and ours is also theirs. She would have no choice but to work in a factory. Who else would hire an art school dropout? Lucinia sol Lucius, back where her name says she should be.

In my dreams, I see Luce turning old and gray, withering as she ages. She begs for me, cries my name, but even though I stand beside her, she cannot see me. When I try to speak to her, my mouth is so full of blood, I can't form words. I wake when she is a withered husk, riddled with diseases she couldn't afford to fight.

The nightmares force me to remember why I'm doing this: I have to kill Hiro so that I can protect Luce.

Ofiera and I don't slip into each other's minds again. Whatever that had been, whether it was ND or Ofiera trying to read my thoughts and going too deep, our neural implants have adjusted and regard each other with strained curiosity and no more.

I wish I could believe it was simply our way of getting accustomed to each other, something I never had to do with Hiro, since we had grown up together. But secretly I worry it's something else. Something worse.

Ofiera knocks on my door, soft and tentative.

I pause the recording of Hiro's voice, the soundtrack of my long days and longer nights. "Yeah?"

"We're landing, Lito," she says, and then she's gone. She doesn't linger. She doesn't try to see me face-to-face. We find comfort in speaking nothing about the incident.

Landing on Ceres is the first time Ofiera and I have been in the same room together since that night. I strap myself into a chair on the command deck as her slender fingers dance across the control panel, turning off the hidden hermium engine and releasing us from gravity's pull. The grasshopper jitters beneath us, straining against its retrofits.

It's hard to believe I'm returning to Ceres. That I'm rocketing toward the place that tore Hiro and me apart a year ago. That almost killed me. That would have, if I hadn't been able to drag us all, bleeding out, onto the nearby shuttle . . .

I tighten my grip over the armrests, digging my fingernails into the soft padding. *Here and now*, I coach myself. Not the past. Not the future. We're only here and only now.

"They hailed us?" I ask.

"Yes." Ofiera's voice is soft and slight. I had almost forgotten its cadence.

No, that's not true. I had forgotten how she sounds when she speaks out loud, not how her voice sounds in my head.

"Our credentials held up, then." Since Asters also work with the Geans, the grasshopper is a make and model that won't draw attention, and we can spoof a code for an unallied trader with Icarii tech. The real test will be down on Ceres, where security will be thick due to the Mother's Celebration. Our background checks will be more stringent than our ship's, and since they already scanned us and found two life-forms aboard, they know they'll be able to arrest or shoot us if our IDs are bad.

Ceres has no atmosphere, just a hermium-powered dome like Cytherea, so entry is straightforward; the ship's intelligence has been slowing us down for the past few hours to make this landing, and it guides us now. We approach Ceres at the edge of the dome and pilot our ship to the docks where they'll either allow or deny us entry. *Or kill you*, a dark voice whispers in my mind as my shoulder aches. It sounds like Hiro's.

Shut up, I tell them, then feel stupid for doing so. I use my implant to clear my emotions. I need to be steady for what's coming.

After the grasshopper rattles to rest at its designated dock, the ship hisses as its interior pressure releases. Air from the dome filters in, far fresher than the recycled air Ofiera and I have been breathing for two weeks. At least Ceres was in perigee to Venus and we didn't have to spend *more* time together.

I suck in a deep breath as the comms sound. "Prepárense para ser abordados," a Gean agent says, then repeats herself in both Chinese and English, the three most-used languages in the galaxy. "准备登机. Prepare to be boarded."

It's odd knowing that the Geans are using the tech we left behind. Whatever they find, they keep. Their scientists put it to good use too, testing it to see how it works so they can make their own. Though without access to the hermium, which is only found on Mercury, mass production is impossible. They're stuck repurposing what they've seized. But the Geans are scavengers that way. It's the only reason they have a shot at winning battles—and why the war has dragged on for so long.

Ofiera doesn't open the doors, though. She stares at the grasshopper's livecam screen, her eyes glassy, caught on something I can't see. The docks are bustling as usual with tourists and travelers, only these people wear the dark, muted colors and natural fabrics, cottons and silks, that Geans favor instead of the bright hues and synthetic materials beloved on Venus and Mercury. And just as I suspected, security is thick. Geans in military navy patrol in groups of two or three along the docks. If our IDs don't hold up—and they might not, since the Geans are now using our tech—we won't just have trouble with the agents coming on board; there's nowhere for us to run or hide without finding more troops.

"Ofiera," I say, my heart speeding. I need her to keep it together right now, not fall into another ND fit. I take a deep breath, commanding my muscles to loosen and my pulse to slow. "Open the door, Ofiera."

She doesn't move. Doesn't speak.

Mierda.

Neural degradation. Characterized by a marked change in behavior after extended use of a neural implant. Symptoms include headaches, nausea, hallucinations, mood swings, losing chunks of time, memories bleeding into your partner . . . I could go on. They warn us all about this stuff in the Academy before we even get an implant. Ofiera should know that as well as I do.

But if she didn't report it when the symptoms first started, and none of her other partners noticed anything, no one would have pulled her from the program. No one would be checking her for it either. Most people can have the implant for fifty or sixty years before the slow rewiring of the brain's neural pathways triggers some sort of cognitive failure, and Ofiera is maybe a year or two older than me, twenty-five at the most.

But if it's not ND, then what's wrong with her?

Damn it. Our entire mission could be compromised. I can't imagine the damage she'd do if we were in the middle of a battle when she had one of her breakdowns.

Grumbling, I reach over her to the control panel and release the airlock doors. As my arm flickers into her view, she snaps to life, moving with all her natural fluidity. Back again. She doesn't apologize; she says nothing of the lapse. But that's par for the course with how things have been lately.

She joins me as we descend to the cargo hold to await the Gean agents.

Two of the Gean soldiers wait outside the exterior airlock door, standing to the side so they seem to be waiting when they're really guarding against either of us making a run for it. The third is already poking about our crates of goods, a compad in her hands that looks familiar. One of ours.

Do not react. Do not let your fear overtake you. It's easy to push the anxiety away with a simple command to my neural implant. How can Ofiera be so calm when she can't rely on hers?

"You have alcohol," the officer says. She's a tall woman, almost my height, with brown skin and hair in thick box braids. I recognize her voice as the one that hailed us over the comms. She has that slow and meandering Gean accent.

"For the Celebration," I reply, matching her accent. The alcohol is part of our rations, but I had forgotten how Geans abhor the stuff.

She sniffs pointedly. "We Geans don't drink so much."

But like a greasy trader, I flash a full-toothed smile. "Not on duty—but after, yes?" I'd offer her some as a bribe, but I know they have a law against drinking on the job—against doing anything while in service, actually. Many of them forgo romantic relationships because of how impossible it is to keep in touch with a loved one on a tour of duty. Their standard military contracts are for five years. But catch a Gean officer off duty? Well, all that bottled-up angst has got to escape somehow.

She looks at her compad instead of meeting my eyes. She's disgusted by me. *Good.* It's better than being suspicious. "IDs," she says, and once again, I fight a wave of panic with my implant. Ofiera produces her ID before I do as if it was just at her fingertips. I take time to dig through my pockets to find mine, then hand it over.

She scans them both with the compad's face away from us. The machine beeps twice, but she remains quiet as her eyes flick over the details provided.

Is she reading our manufactured backstory, or is she already sending a warning to her fellow Gean officers that there are two spies on Ceres?

"Coming from Vesta?" she asks at last, naming one of the Aster settlements as her thick eyebrows furrow.

"Originally Pallas," Ofiera answers easily, naming another. "We passed through Vesta last to pick up supplies. You know, buy some spare parts, restock on water, eat freshly grown meat for once."

I can practically hear the officer's sneer as she hands our IDs back, but I feel only relief. The asteroid belt and its planetoids are Aster territory, and the majority of humans who prefer Asters and ships to a stable life planetside are outcasts and pirates, like Dire and his smugglers. But I'd rather have her judge us on our falsified places of work than our real identities.

"Enjoy the Celebration," she says, clearly not caring whether we do or not. She tucks her compad beneath her arm. She's done here, ready to check the next ship. Thank the thousand gods.

"Gracias por su ayuda," Ofiera says in flawless Spanish.

The officer replies in a language I don't know. Swahili, maybe? Hiro was always the one with the ear for languages. They could mimic anyone and collected accents like fashion statements.

The woman passes through the airlock; then, at a wave of her hand, her two fellow officers fall into line, and all three leave the grasshopper. We wait for them to disappear behind another ship, pretending to check our own cargo after landing, before we turn to each other.

"You speak Spanish?"

Ofiera quirks a brow. "Ich spreche alles."

Most people who speak German also speak another of the main languages, so I never bothered to learn. Same with our mother's Italian, other than the basics that are close enough to Spanish. Instead I took up Japanese for Hiro and made a valiant attempt at Chinese, but I was shit with the tonal pronunciations, and Hiro was too busy laughing at my poor conversational attempts to correct me.

I ignore Ofiera's little jab and instead gesture with my thumb to the ramp. "I have a place I used to go for information. If it's still there, it'll be the place to go now."

"If." All Ofiera's playfulness disappears. "I have my own sources," she says, and somehow I don't doubt her in the least, but she is so closed off about her feelings that she is unknowable even through the implant.

Ofiera adjusts a gray scarf around her neck, pulling it up over her hair in its messy bun. "Meet back here when the dome simulates sunfall?"

She could've just said *at sunfall*, and I would've understood. "Yeah. See you then."

She sighs somewhat sadly and steps out of the ship. I watch her go before returning to the hab quarters.

I dump out the backpack and regard the few items Command allowed us: Gean coins, varying in thickness to denote value; an earpiece somewhat like the playback device Hiro left me, old by Icarii standards but still used by the Geans to send and receive vidcalls; and my mercurial blade.

When I slip the hilt of my sword into my jacket's hidden pocket near my armpit, I feel complete again. A warrior once more.

I can't fail, I think. *I won't fail. I will assassinate the Mother. I will find Hiro.*

I debate taking the playback device. I know I shouldn't; if I'm caught with it, no ID will hold up against the truth of Hiro's words. Then again, I shouldn't have brought it with me on the grasshopper in the first place.

Reasoning that it is just as dangerous left on the ship as with me— which a part of me knows isn't true—I slide the device into a hidden compartment in the heel of my boot.

With nothing left to do on board, I head down to the hold and step into the airlock. The exterior door is open, but I can't bring myself to leave. I stand there hesitating, debating what I'm feeling. The bullet wound scar on my shoulder throbs, as if it knows I've returned to Ceres.

But there is no time for fear.

I return to the place where my life fell apart.

I HAUNT THE streets I once called home. My heart aches with longing for the ghosts of my memory. I stop at a bakery that used to sell red bean buns but now stands empty, the glass windows shattered and partially covered with plastic sheets.

All of Ceres is like this. The smell of cooking in the close cobbled streets has been replaced with the metallic tang of destruction and decay. The families who used to spill out into the neighborhoods are missing. Chunks of cobbles have been blasted to pebbles, while sidewalks ripple like a tree's roots have pushed up beneath them. Once well-tended plants now brown and die on apartment balconies.

But what's most jarring for me are the streets that remain untouched. The shops look exactly the same until I walk close enough. Then I see that the clothing stores and restaurants have changed both stock and atmosphere. The Icarii are gone, and with us, everything I used to know.

Worst of all, it feels like it's *my* fault.

I sit on a bench outside of what used to be a coffee shop and close my eyes. I pretend it's a year ago, the dome projecting blue skies above me while I sip at a sweet café leche y leche—coffee with both condensed and regular milk. Next to me, Hiro, dressed in a mix of fashions, points at passersby and makes up stories about them.

"She's having an affair with her boss," they would say. "She thinks he'll leave his wife for her because they don't yet have children, but he won't." Or "He's embezzling funds. Only a little right now, because he's scared to get caught. He wants to buy his kids the newest toys, since he works so much and thinks he can buy their love."

"Why can't you ever come up with a pleasant story for these people?" I asked once.

"What about them learning a valuable life lesson isn't pleasant?" Hiro replied with a wink that would've been flirtatious if directed at anyone other than me. "They may hurt now, but afterward, they'll understand themselves so much better."

"So, pain is progress, then?" I asked.

Hiro just smiled.

I miss them so much that I wish I could use the playback device now. But I can't. Hiro can't face these streets with me. I have to walk them alone.

I stand and let my feet carry me down a familiar cobblestone path. If Cytherea is a vibrant youth, Ceres is an ancient watcher, steady in its age but dynamic in its diversity. At any point, I find myself flanked by a mesh of architecture and culture, each layer of history as distinct as the rings of a venerable tree.

Originally the Asters created this settlement on behalf of Earth, but Mars seized it during the Dead Century War. Then the Icarii struck a deal with the Asters, a trade of energy for water, and, alongside the Asters, expelled the Martians. It belonged to us up until the Fall. But it's not just the different sides of the war that created Ceres; the Geans and Icarii are made of so many various races and cultures from Earth's continents—Europe and Asia, Africa and Oceania, South and Central America, even some from North America who had survived their Second War of Secession—that everyone's art and architecture comes alive as they build. When Ceres changed hands, no one bothered to start again at the foundation, but instead embraced the old as well as the new.

I pass government halls with fluted columns and businessmen dressed in somber suits. Residences flowing with carved designs of vines and flowers with oval floor-to-ceiling windows from which the curious peer. Heritage centers with tiered pagoda roofs and onion domes, in front of which stalls sell related foods. Carved cathedrals reminiscent of the Academy, organic and dripping like melted wax, where beggars lie with outstretched hands. Rectangular hospitals with long windows, open, gasping mouths, hauntingly empty.

But everywhere I go, I spot bullet holes and bloodstains. Rubble and rubbish fill the streets instead of the laughter of children and chatter of community. Ceres's streets used to be its veins and the people its blood. Now inhabitants watch me warily and offer no greetings. The reserved Geans here seem exhausted, beaten down by circumstance as they deal with their livelihoods and repairs to the city. Or perhaps they sense the otherness in me, made obvious by some small flaw that marks me as an outsider. I try not to let paranoia overwhelm me as I slip through the alleys. Strangely, I miss the chaos of Cytherea in this moment.

As I head from the city center to the historic district, the only eyes I see are hungry ones. Dirty children rove in packs like wild dogs, and men with danger written in the set of their shoulders reach into their jackets in warning. I don't want to fight, so I pick up my pace.

When I come to my destination, a fiery red cat with eyes like molten gold darts down the dark alley. I spot the old wooden sign for the bar on its iron post, half-hidden by a stone archway. It's not a place that advertises. The people who come here already know it exists.

MITHRIDATISM, the sign reads, named after the art of regularly ingesting poisons in order to build up an immunity.

I remember standing at the mouth of this alley and watching Hiro walk ahead of me. They slipped into the dark, and I couldn't see them, only feel them with my implant. I remember thinking how life had settled into a beautiful, predictable rhythm, and what it would mean if that flow were interrupted. Fear spiked through me, inexplicable, until Hiro called back through the night, "Follow me, Lito."

Even though I haven't seen Hiro in a year, I feel as if I am walking that same path: Hiro is just ahead of me, and I am following them into the shadows.

CHAPTER 13

[28] May not their hearts be hardened with shadows, but may they speak freely to those who would listen, [29] So that when the time comes that they must pick up their swords and shields, they do not shy away from battle, [30] But instead go happily to their duty without distractions.

The Canon, Judgments 10:28–30

The red lights strobe so brightly that even asleep I see their bloody imprints against my eyelids. By the time I fully rouse myself, the *Juno* is in lockdown; the screen with the livecam view of the stars has been turned off, and the tinny voice of the CO over the intercom reaches me from the hallway. "Battle stations," I hear, muffled through my door. "Full crew to battle stations."

I dress in my gray uniform with strangely steady hands and strap my belt of oils about my waist. There is no helping the dark shadows beneath my eyes, made worse by the lockdown lighting; as we have every cycle since the first letter, Ren and I wrote together late into the night. "Talking," as she calls it. At the end of each session, she destroys my letters to assuage my fear of their discovery.

But the dread grew roots in my nightmare-tainted sleep, and now it wraps withered branches of thorns around my heart and squeezes. Though I told Aunt Marshae about writing with Ren, I have reported that the captain says nothing abnormal, nothing that would mark her as a traitor to the Gean people. But I can tell that Aunt Marshae believes me less and less each time; soon she will demand more of me. I wonder what my Auntie will make of Ren's bid for peace, when I am finally forced to reveal it.

Outside my room, uniformed soldiers swiftly rush to their assigned posts. No one takes notice of me as I join the steady flow of traffic. I follow a group of pilots onto the elevator, and together we ride past the docking bay to the munitions deck, a flat expanse as wide as the ship but filled with Ironskin rigs and retrofitted Gean cannons. In the chaos of battle, there are hundreds on this level already, and more filing in each second.

Those already strapped into their armor stand to the right of the deck in four snaking lines, while others, in navy-and-gold plugsuits, wait next to their designated Ironskins for the mechanic to give them the all-clear. As soon as the tech waves them forward, each pilot steps into the open armor, and it curls around their body like a second skin. With a hiss like steam, the Ironskin locks, and the camera on the helmet flickers to life, an orange ring that lets the pilot see in every direction at once. To those on the outside, it looks like a halo of flame or a crown set above a twisted shadow of a body, a son of the Goddess come to kill mortal men. They are awe-inspiring and fearsome and terribly dangerous.

I spot medical staff weaving through the group of pilots in their plugsuits, checking limbs and vitals; most Ironskin pilots are forced to retire because of the degradation of their joints. In the most stressful of battles, Ironskins can strain the body so that interior bleeding in the brain is not uncommon. The doctors make sure the pilots are healthy and ready for battle. Even a hint of weakness or sickness can indicate a burnout waiting to happen.

I cannot believe Ren used to do this. I truthfully cannot imagine anyone would want to do this, despite the rewards of it; those willing to risk themselves capturing Icarii ships and fighting the quicksilver warriors are cared for even after their bodies fall apart. Just look at Ren, the Hero of Ceres. Two limbs lost, but a commission worthy of a much older soldier. Unlike Matron Thorne, a mere foot soldier, who was abandoned and given a simple hook for a hand.

The new Third Sister spots me and waves me over; she looks as if she wasn't startled awake by battle, her short hair artfully arranged in twists and her dark eyes lined with ink a shade darker than her brown skin. She and Second Sister stand among a flock of gray dresses, and I rush to join them. Many of us look disheveled, but none so much as Second Sister, the red lights washing out her fiery hair and pale, freckled cheeks.

Each Sister spreads out until we are equidistant, covering the whole of the crowd. Ironskins stomp forward, the deck trembling beneath their mass, and I follow my Sisters, wordlessly withdrawing my oil that smells of rosemary with a hint of lavender. Splashing it onto my right hand and spreading it over my palm and fingers, I press my hand to the chest of the first Ironskin amidst the strips of black cloth they've taken as trophies from defeated duelists—as high as I can reach without their kneeling—and bless them with protection and strength for the battle to come. In that moment, mine is the touch of the Goddess, and the exquisite scents of natural blooms are a reminder of Her love for mankind. Whatever they do today, they will know they are a weapon in Her hand.

After the second man leaves my side, my handprint shiny over his heart, the intercom buzzes again. "First-wave Ironskins into position" echoes over the deck. "We're coming about."

Men march away from us with purpose, the techs now standing to the right wall of the ship along a series of pods. They usher a single Ironskin into a long, cylindrical tube and close the door with a latch that screeches of metal on metal. The pods gasp one after the other, the *Juno* greedily sucking air into its lungs. My heart jolts into my throat even as I force myself to look away and focus on the pilot in front of me. My handprint is a smear of shaking fingers on his chest. These cannons and their tubes were added to the *Juno* after we captured it, and though they have been used before, it never lessens my anxiety over the safety of the human within.

"First Sister!" a voice cries out, distorted through his helmet. I peer through the crowd and find a hulking Ironskin waving at me, the oily hand on his chest not mine. He stands head and shoulders above the rest. *Ringer!* I wish I could cry his name, but all I can manage is to lift my hand high and hope he sees it. Then he steps toward the ship's tubes and disappears in the press of armor.

In my more morbid moments, I wish I knew what it was like inside the tube in the dark and quiet. I wish I knew how it felt to be launched from the *Juno* like a bullet. I have pictured it a hundred times as I lay in my bed at night, what it looks like to fly through a blur of stars in the black of space, lasers from two combatant ships arcing and crashing in waves of heat and light. Most of all, I wonder at the pure silence of it, no sound of the battle around me, my only companion my breathing in the Ironskin. An overwhelming peace just before the crash.

The *Juno* shudders as it exhales, launching the Ironskins from its belly. Like missiles they rocket through the battlefield, detritus of damaged ships and stardust sliced through by the spikes on their armor. They fly like shooting stars, each with a single wish: survive.

They will crash into the enemy ship and cling with their spikes. They will smash through its shields, force entry, and take it from the inside. We Geans cannot destroy the ships outright when we need them for our own survival; the Ironskins help us take them whole.

"Second wave," the intercom calls, "stand ready." The press and march start again as another round of pilots steps into the pods.

"First Sister," someone calls. A man in formal navy places his hand on my shoulder, and it takes me a moment to recognize his summer-blue eyes and shaved head. *Jones.* I instinctively touch my white armband, but he's hardly looking at me. "You've been requested on the command deck by Captain Saito. For your protection."

My *protection?* The command deck is safely ensconced in the middle of the ship, while the munitions deck is close to the hull and often attacked due to its cannons, but even if someone were to come aboard, who would focus on a mere Sister with so many Ironskins surrounding her?

Of course, I cannot ask this question, and Jones doesn't wait for my answer. He marches toward the elevator, not checking to see if I follow.

I return the oil to my belt and clench my slippery hand into a fist. The men behind me stand patiently, not knowing I have been called away from them. I turn my back on my duty with a heavy heart. A droplet of oil falls to the deck at my feet.

JONES JABS THE button for level forty-two like it has personally offended him. "I never knew Ren to be such a fool romantic," he spits beneath his breath, waves of anger coming off him like heat. "And she has me running *errands* instead of getting in my Ironskin, as I should be." I understand his confusion and frustration; I am just as surprised as he is that Captain Saito is prioritizing me in the madness of battle.

When the lift stops and the doors open, he streaks ahead of me toward the interior elevator that will take us to Command, accessible only from certain levels, and I'm forced to hurry to keep up with his long strides.

We're not halfway down the hallway when a metallic screech stops us in our tracks.

"Hold!" Jones throws up a hand to stop me, but I've already frozen in place, trying to tamp down my worry. There is no sound in space, so we shouldn't hear anything from the battle. But there was a noise . . . so what was it?

The sound comes again, higher pitched and far closer, and Jones, his entire body stiff with wariness, reaches for the railgun over his shoulder. The thorns about my heart squeeze tighter.

He turns his head over his shoulder to speak to me, a pale half-moon of profile, but the wrenching metal sound fills the air so loudly that his voice is drowned out. I reach out to him just as a shock rumbles through the corridor, throwing me toward the ceiling. Bright lights pop like stars in my eyes as I hit something. Like a rag doll, I fall back to the floor, and my vision goes dark.

I gather myself, quite sure I didn't black out for more than a few seconds. My knees and left wrist throb and ache. When I sit, I press a hand to the top of my head where it struck the ship, but when I open my eyes, the light doesn't return. It's not my eyes, I realize; the power is out along the hallway.

I open my mouth to cry out in fear, but of course, no sound comes. I can hardly hear Jones or the tear of metal as the ship around me shakes like a dying man in winter. There is only the darkness and the buzzing in my ears, a screeching ring that feels like cotton filled with needles.

Mother, I pray that this is not how I die—voiceless, sightless, deaf. Truly, this is hell.

Finally the emergency lighting flickers on, washing me in light as red as blood. Ahead of me, a metal panel has swung down, closing off the elevator. I look behind me to find the same. I realize with slowly dawning horror that I am trapped, cut off from escape.

But escape from what? Is the hull of the ship on this level damaged, slowly leaking oxygen from our atmo? Will I die in the dark, turning blue, my tattered throat robbed of its function once again?

Jones lies limp on the ground, and as my ears adjust and the ringing dissipates, I hear a voice crackling in the quiet of the hallway. Not his, I realize, but his compad. I crawl over to him and shake him, but he doesn't wake. I press a hand to his cheek, leaving the remnants of oil on his skin, and turn his face toward me—then jerk my hand back as if burned. I hadn't noticed it in the red light at first, but he's bleeding from a gash on his forehead.

Matron Thorne's voice comes back to me after all these years. *Foot soldiers are easily forgotten.*

Another loud sound slices the air, something between a mechanized saw and the crackle of a fire. Bright sparks of white shoot into the dimly lit hallway from the metal panel covering the elevator, leaving a trail of molten orange in their wake. Someone on the other side, cutting through . . . Goddess and Mother.

I turn away and with shaking hands scrabble for Jones's compad, patting down his navy jacket and utility belt. Finally I find it in a pants pocket, small enough to fit in the palm of my hand, and yank it close to my mouth as if I could possibly answer.

"Confirm, level forty-three compromised. Confirm."

Compromised? But the Icarii don't usually board ships, and we're on level forty-two! Why would they be boarding us now? Coming up through the elevators to this level . . . they must be trying to reach Command.

But I cannot tell the XO on the compad. Cannot even cry out. I only have my hands.

I press the connect button on the side of the compad's glass screen despite the slick oil of my sweaty hand and tap it against the wall four times, pause, then tap twice more.

"Confirm, level forty-three compromised. Confirm."

But they're also here! I huff in frustration. Slam the mobile against the hull four times, then two, waiting for the person on the other end to update their announcement. At the end of the hallway, the white light completes its circle and fades to orange, then red as the cutting stops. Not a second later, the metal falls forward, and from the shadow stretches a foot.

One clad in black like the void.

Icarii.

Harder than before, I slam the compad on the floor four times, then two; four times, then two; four times, then—

Quicksilver warriors swarm out of the darkness of the elevator shaft—two by two by two, six of them in all. They rush toward me, helmets protruding from their high collars, illuminating their faces in a blue force field similar to the hermium barriers that close the hangar bays. One seizes the compad from my hand and wrenches it away; his partner backhands me. I crash to the ground, and my body pulses with pain.

"Is he alive?" a woman with the clipped, fast accent of the Icarii asks, nudging Jones with her foot.

Another steps to her side, grabbing a metal tube from his belt, and with a flick holds a glowing silver sword that was not there seconds ago. He spins the quicksilver blade in his hand like a child playing with a toy before it disappears even faster than it appeared. "Not anymore," he says, and Jones's head rolls away from his body.

I scream, but no sound comes out. I press my hands to my face, not wanting to see any more, but one of them hauls me up, hand fisted in my gray dress. I catch a glimpse of them all crowded around me, and despite the blood roaring in my ears, despite the pulsing of the bruise blossoming on my cheekbone . . . they are beautiful.

They look like pieces of art, sculptures of marble and gold and onyx, old terrestrial paintings in soft oils. Their helmets retract one by one, revealing clear, flawless skin. Bright eyes in a range of colors from the red of a supernova to the purple of a deep galaxy. Not a scar or wrinkle among them. They are elite warriors, trained for years, but they look like greenboys. They could be mere teenagers, yet I know the stories, know how the Icarii have their doctors twist helixes, making them something *other*, closer to the Asters than us true and natural Geans.

I do not struggle, do not fight. If they wanted to crack open my head, they could do so with a fist, not even needing those quicksilver blades at their sides. I feel as if I am looking into the eyes of my death, and yet . . . I am strangely calm.

"Is this one of their priestesses?" a woman asks.

"Gray dress? Seems right." The warrior holding me has a gruff voice. This close to them I can see that the deep black of their uniforms has the lightest stitching of hexagons across the bodysuit. I am caught in the hypnotic pattern, only halfway aware that I am in shock.

"Doesn't say much," the woman replies.

Do they know what I am or not? I cannot tell from the flow of their conversation. If they aim to kill me, I hope they do it quickly and painlessly; Icarii are, at least, efficient at that.

"I know how to make her talk," another male says, cockier and seemingly younger than the rest.

"No," the one holding me says. "Either she's useful, or we kill her. We're not barbarians."

The fear comes again, the thorns from my heart multiplying and digging into my stomach. My legs waver beneath me, but the warrior holding my dress keeps me upright. Mother, please let them kill me quickly . . . My eyes blur with tears before I even know I'm crying.

"Where is your captain?" the man holding me asks.

I open my mouth and close it again, over and over, like I'm gasping. But of course nothing comes out. Nothing *can*.

"Where is Saito Ren?" The man shakes me hard. "Speak!" he commands.

Something snaps inside me.

In that exact moment, I feel all the frustration from these silent years crumpling me beneath its weight. I have wanted to speak, wanted to yell, wanted to cry out, since my words were taken away from me, but at his command something withers and blackens inside me. Now I would not speak even if it could save my life.

Fuck you, I mouth.

Behind me, a sound like ripping air. The six warriors fall into a V formation, the leader dropping me to the ground. Instantly I push against the floor, scrambling away from them as glowing quicksilver blades blaze to life, as four Ironskins march past me in a solid line and descend on them like swarming buzzards.

I watch as one Ironskin's whip cracks into a warrior's face, lighting the hallway with blue sparks; as two warriors jump onto an Ironskin, blades coming from both directions to skewer their heart; as

Jones's body is kicked and stomped upon, a rag doll caught up in the feet of a brawl.

Someone's shield fails, and blood splatters my chest and dots my face, warm as a comforting blanket.

I force myself to turn away and crawl on hands and knees to the door, now gloriously open. On the other side, a regiment of foot soldiers ten-deep snatches me up and shoves me behind them, their hands rough, their eyes pointed forward instead of on me.

No one cares that I am alive.

I am replaceable.

Foot soldiers are easily forgotten. Just like Matron Thorne. Just like Jones.

Someone gasps. Steady hands grip my shoulders. I catch a glimpse of a white dress with red paneling, a medic stationed at the rear of the squadron. "You're alive!" the nurse says in ecstatic wonder. "First Sister, you're alive!"

The fact that she cares . . . surprises me.

But she is right, this fool woman who examines my swollen face. I do not think I have ever been more alive than I am in this moment.

Even as I know, deep down, that Icarii duelists boarding the *Juno* specifically to seek out Ren could only mean something terrible.

PLAY:
▶ 07

◇———◇◇———◇

You probably won't believe me, but I was going to tell you everything—about Hemlock, about the alliance between the Geans and the Asters, about the warning to stay away from Icarii headquarters on Ceres. It was during our last leave. We were staying with Luce, as usual, and I came over with a couple of presents. First, a suitcase full of unwanted clothes for Luce to pick through and use in her attempts to become a Paragon influencer. Second, and mostly for you, some sake imported directly from Earth at great expense that my father would miss one day when he bothered to go through his collection.

I breezed into the apartment without knocking; I always liked seeing the two of you in your natural habitat, like twin stars orbiting each other. There was a closeness in your family that I missed in mine. There was no equality between my siblings and me, no trust, and while there was love, it was a hard, harsh thing.

I couldn't help but laugh when I found the two of you. She was holding up one of the paintings she had done at school, and you were staring at it as if it would whisper the secrets of the universe to you.

"That's really good," I said. It was the painting of the hyperrealistic skyline of Cytherea juxtaposed with a cartoony rabbit clutching a building, its stitched paws smashing glass as it climbed.

Luce's nose curled as she pursed her lips. She has the same nose as you, but not the same expressions. "According to my professor, it's 'trite.'"

"Why? Because of the meaning?" I asked. You stared at me like I spoke a secret language. In a way, I did; it was the language of the artist.

"But it's perfect," you said, gesturing to it.

"On a technical level, maybe," Luce said. "I still think the proportions are off. But yeah, he meant the message."

"Well, what did you want it to mean?" I asked.

Luce shrugged. "I didn't want it to mean anything," she lied. Whatever it meant to her, she didn't want to tell us. She had secrets. Considering I had plenty of my own, I didn't press her.

Her eyes honed in on the clothes I had brought. "Are those for me, Hiro? Please say yes!" She was also getting good at changing the subject. Her art forgotten, she rushed to her bedroom with the bag while we went into the kitchen.

I pulled three mismatched glasses from the cabinet above the sink and poured the sake. I could imagine my father's face flushing in anger at the audacity of using cheap industrial drinkware for something as unique and exquisite as rice wine grown in genuine terrestrial conditions.

"None for Luce," you said, placing your hand over the mouth of one of the glasses.

"She's nineteen now," I replied. "If you think she hasn't already been drinking, you're fooling yourself."

You removed your hand, wincing only slightly.

Luce rushed into the room wearing a color-changing sinvaca fur jacket and holo leggings with the opacity turned down so that her legs shimmered.

I whistled. "Forget art! You should be a model!"

Luce spun in a circle so I could admire her. She was taller than me, but with a pair of boots, no one would notice how high the leggings rode.

"Fashion is art too, you know," Luce said as if to needle me. She couldn't have known fashion was my mother's art, and that she had prodded a very sore spot in my heart with her words. She wouldn't have said them otherwise.

"Yes, but you have to do the whole military thing when you're val Akira," I said, slipping past the memories of my mother with practiced ease.

"Or a scientist," you said, probably thinking of Asuka, but I thought of my father instead.

"No, definitely not that," I spat, grabbing up my glass of sake and swallowing deeply. "I never liked putting lipstick on lab rats."

I felt your curiosity on the other side of the implant. It wasn't something I wanted to get into, so I changed the subject as quickly as Luce had.

"So how about your first commission?" I gestured my thumb back to the canvas set aside in the living room. "You know what the Icarus Science Academy on Mercury looks like? Can you draw a nine-tailed fox pissing on it?"

She laughed so hard, I thought she might swallow her sake wrong.

"I'm sure your professor would love to see how . . . *trite* that is."

The night passed in laughter much like this. Luce got out her charcoals and sketched us—you in blue, like the sheen of your raven hair, and me in red, like a field of peonies the current color of my fauxhawk. We matched so well together, it made my heart hurt.

The bottle lightened until I lifted it to my lips and found nothing left. At that point Luce was sketching a fox, its nine tails spinning off the page, and cursing in colorful Italian and Spanish and terrible Japanese—I guess she had begun learning to impress me—and you were reclined on the couch, your arm stretched over your forehead and your eyes pinned to the ceiling.

"Cazzo! Puta mierda biopaper! Won't—sit still! くそ!"

"Language, Luce," you whispered, though your heart wasn't in it.

She shoved her supplies aside and finally announced her intention to go to bed, only to be halted by the fact that she had trouble standing. "I'm never—drinking again."

You moved to help her, but I gestured for you to lie still and scooped her up in my arms. "I got it," I said.

She snuggled into my chest, closing her eyes. "Why—spinning?"

"Your brother asked me the same thing the first time I got him drunk," I said, taking her into the small bedroom off the kitchen and settling her in the middle of the gel mattress piled high with pillows and stuffed animals. One was an old friend—a stuffed ねこまた, a cat with two tails I had given Luce years ago. Another was the rabbit in the painting she had been showing you when I came in.

"Hiro," Luce said, grabbing my wrist as I pulled away.

"Here, take Mr. Bunny," I said, offering it to her.

"Don't tell Lito," she said, hugging the rabbit to her chest. "I'm almost twenty—I shouldn't sleep—hic—shouldn't have toys."

"There are bigger things in the world to worry about, and anyone who gives you shit about it isn't worth your time, love," I said, and brushed her purple hair out of her face.

"It's just—" Luce cut off, her voice wobbling. Her eyes were closed—in weariness or in trying not to cry, I didn't know. "It's just *trite*."

I squatted by the bed, stroking her hair like I used to do to my little sisters when they couldn't sleep. "The painting. It symbolizes your childhood, doesn't it?"

She nodded. "I wanted—I don't know—those good memories to fight back." She let out a long, shaky breath as her face relaxed. "Fight against—well, now."

I knew she meant you. I knew she meant the war. You had gone to the Academy, leaving Luce alone with your parents, and she missed you so much that she clung to the terrible childhood the two of you had, because at least then the two of you had been together.

"It's a good subject," I whispered to her. "Your professor just wants you to express it better, that's all. You'll figure it out."

She nodded and pressed her bunny to her face. I stayed until her breathing evened out. I don't think she was asleep, but she was peaceful at least.

When I returned to the living room, your arm had slid from your forehead to your eyes. You weren't asleep yet—I could feel your mind racing on the other side of the implant—so I sat beside the couch and leaned my head against your chest.

Your body stiffened. Your thoughts stilled.

"Hiro?" you whispered.

"Let's run away together. Never go back to Ceres."

Confusion and rejection swirled within you. With my eyes closed, I could focus only on the feelings you sent through the implant. "We have to go back, Hiro. It's war."

"But if there wasn't a war?" I asked.

"Hiro . . ."

I know how stupid I sounded. Maybe I was drunker than I wanted to admit. But I think it was Luce's words that made me bold.

"I'll end the war, Lito. Even if it kills me, I'll stop it so it doesn't have to tear any more families apart." I felt my mother's ghost hovering just out of sight. I feared if I pulled away from you, if I just turned around, she would be there, and I didn't want to see her. After all this time, I still wasn't ready to face the truth.

You dropped your hand onto my head and stroked my hair. Such a small gesture, but such an immense comfort. It was also, I knew, your way of telling me to go to sleep.

"You'll feel better in the morning," you said.

But I wouldn't. Because I knew in this moment I could never tell you what was coming to Ceres and drag you farther away from Luce than you already were.

CHAPTER 14

I'm in love with this new posting. Ceres is such a weird place, like nothing really belongs and yet it does. You can see hundreds of years of culture here, and it's all sitting on top of each other, like no one bothered to wash off yesterday's makeup but just kept applying more. It's so mixed-up.

Excerpt from an email written by
Hiro val Akira, age 18, to their family

It sounds perfect for you.

Reply from Souji val Akira

◇——•——◈◈——•——◇

Mithridatism lies in a shallow pool of silver light in an otherwise black alley. In the darkness, it's easy to pretend that it hasn't been touched by the Fall.

The building's stocky construction favors the Gean Modernist style. The bottom floors curve with the elegance of florals, punctuated by jutting spurs reminiscent of bones. The walls shimmer with ceramic scales as iridescent as an insect's wings in soft pinks and blues. The double door handles taper in the middle from the swelled knots on the ends like a human femur. On the second floor, balconies protrude with the sharpness of a jawbone. The windows are bare ports, no two the same, and split as natural rock would be. Each opening is filled with grasping green plants that climb upward or dangle to the floor below.

Then the damage becomes too much to ignore. The top floors are scorched black as onyx, and the roof, once rising and falling like a breathing chest, now ends in a cluster of slanted points. Once I see that, I notice all the other little faults. Bullet holes that have shattered clusters of scales. A balcony collapsing in on itself. A window's crystalline blue glass shattered.

An unassuming bald man stands outside the entrance, looking at his fingernails with disinterest. He's most definitely checked me as I've checked him, and sure enough, as I step toward the double doors, he approaches me with a manicured hand held out at my hip. "Not for tourists," he says.

"Not a tourist," I say. "Trader."

He doesn't look impressed. "What kind of trading?"

"Alcohol."

"Keep talking."

I dig into an interior pocket in my jacket and return with a cylindrical flask. I have never cared for it myself, not even the expensive rice wine that Hiro steals from their father, but a trader selling alcohol is sure to be a drinker. Plus, carrying this stuff around works as a bribe. "Have a cup?" I ask, but before I can even unscrew the cap, the man snatches it from my hand and tips it back.

He takes a long gulp before smacking his lips and releasing a foul belch. "Tastes like fire."

I know from my time at Mithridatism that the bar procures odd liquors. "Scorpion wine."

"Doesn't taste like it." He shrugs and hands the flask back to me. After he put his mouth on it, I'm not about to . . . I screw the cap back on and put it in my jacket.

"If it's not, I'll kill the man who sold it to me." I chuckle, and he joins me, comrades in our misfortune.

"So what are you here for?" he asks at last. "And I mean *here* here, not here on Ceres."

"Traded on Ceres back in the day when the others were in charge—the Icarii—and this was an interesting place if one wanted to spend some money on a show."

He snorts and nods. The curl in his lip tells me that my hunch is correct; this building is being used the same way it always has been. "If you have money to spend, yeah."

"Any reason to think I don't?"

"Man coming to bet would certainly know how to get in."

Knowing exactly what he wants, I pull out a thick Gean coin, equal to about fifty Icarii credits, and hope this is enough. Whereas we have moved past physical money, the Geans are practically phobic of technology after the Dead Century War and the rebellious Synthetics. He must like what he sees, because he moves to open the door for me.

"Welcome back, Mr. Trader."

Mithridatism is not how I remember it. Since the roof has collapsed, all of the natural lighting is gone, leaving only the once-bright stadium lights around the gladius arena, and many of those are unlit, either damaged or old. Now the corners are dark open spaces and the center a dim affair, casting faces in long shadows. A strip of gold toward the back of the room illuminates what was once a long bar but is now a circular table full of bottles long and thin or fat and squat, all in jewel-toned glass. While a few people mill about, filling up their cups, most ignore it in favor of the area in the middle of the room, a sunken pit where two men size each other up.

A gladius dueling ring, just like it was when we held Ceres.

Unlike when we were in charge, though, the seats aren't filled with screaming onlookers. No one cheers for their champion, even if I catch credits slipping between palms, money literally changing hands as bets are placed. The men closest to the ring are dressed shabbily, more like I am, while those who stand at the top of the stairs are clothed in silk suits or dresses with airy bell sleeves. I head down the stairs to join the more eager men of my class.

"You fighting?" one asks as I approach, a man twice my width in muscle and covered in bright tattoos of pink roses. His jaw is offset to the right, his nose curving the same way; he's definitely seen his share of battles, though whether in or out of the ring remains to be seen.

"No," I say. "Watching."

"Then go back where the watchers go," he says, nodding toward the men in suits lingering in the darkness.

But before I fully turn, a flash of silver catches my eye. Without my training, I would have stumbled on the first stair, but I catch myself and spin on the balls of my feet back toward the ring.

One of the fighters holds a mercurial blade.

The fingers of his opposite hand scrabble over the hilt before he flicks his wrist and the glowing blade emerges, a crude construction, limp and thin. You don't need an implant to use the blade, but you *definitely* need one to fully control its shape. His blade, more like a whip, comes to rest curled around his boots, but with all the heat that the metal emits, it scorches the dirt of the ring black.

His opponent withdraws his own blade, and when it roars to life, it takes on a formation close to standard. I'm not sure what shocks me more—a Gean who has learned how to wield a mercurial blade, or one who has figured out how to shape it *correctly*.

There is a moment before the two men launch themselves at each other when I feel like I need to slap myself awake from this nightmare. Then the two clash, whip against sword, I find myself back at the edge of the ring, knowing what will happen before it does.

"Didn't I tell you to get lost?" the tattooed man asks.

I can't answer. My breathing is shallow in my tight chest. I even forget to prompt my implant to calm me. We've known the Geans experiment with whatever they scavenge, our mercurial blades included, and it was only a matter of time before they discovered the link between our blades and our neural implants. But we've always believed the Gean religion and its dedication to natural bodies would prevent them from implanting themselves with the technology they consider forbidden.

Perhaps that's why it's being tested in Mithridatism on men desperate for credits, and not in the military.

Either way, I know with hollow certainty what this discovery means: *the era of Icarii technological superiority is at an end.*

The two men in the ring don't take the natural stance of a duelist; they're clearly not measuring the diameter of battle. They're more like showmen, demonstrating a weapon that the men and women around the ring watch with shadowed eyes. How many Gean captains or majors are here, their minds reeling with the same possibilities that mine have reached?

I send a thought-command to my implant that snaps me back to base level—no more fear, no more anxiety. My grip on the half wall around the ring loosens, and my breathing regulates. "Those swords," I say, gesturing to the fight. "I haven't traded here since the Icarii were on Ceres, but I remember them."

The tattooed man briefly looks at me. "And?"

In my desperation, I'm not even sure what to ask. "I used to come here for sword fights, but I thought only the Icarii had those things. So who kept this going?" If my question is heavy-handed, I don't care. "Or is this some military stuff?"

"That," the tattooed man says, "is none of your fucking business."

I do my best not to let the frustration and fear overtake me. "Fair enough," I say, as if it doesn't matter, but my mind is already searching the room for other people who might know something, whom I might corner and persuade to tell me.

"I don't know how you found Mithridatism on your last visit, but we don't give nothing out for free."

I jerk my eyes back to the tattooed man. "Then I'd like to buy some information."

He sniffs through his crooked nose as if offended by the insinuation. "Go to the bar and wait, then." He points to the table filled with liquor with his thumb; no one is there to distribute the alcohol.

"Sure. Who do I talk to?"

But he doesn't answer me as the mercurial whip flies past us—far too close for comfort. A collective gasp echoes through the room, breaths held in anticipation. The whip snaps back to the wielder's side, leaving his body wide-open, a rookie mistake.

The man with the sword presses his luck, swings toward the other's neck. There's no passion behind his move—he's not fighting to kill, just to incapacitate. But without the military blacks and their built-in shields, it would be exceedingly hard to fight without wounding—and killing—an opponent.

I expect the sword to slow in its arc, but it doesn't. It goes straight for the whip wielder's neck—and then misses. The man with the whip kicks one leg out behind him in a move so like a duelist's that my heart races, his body turning sideways, and he flicks his whip up toward the sword wielder's hand.

The sword drops. The man screams. Red blooms brightly as he clutches his hand. Two of his fingers hit the dirt of the training pit beside the blade hilt, surrounded by crimson specks.

Fucking gods. They have no idea what they're dealing with.

The man with the whip throws both hands in the air, one holding the hilt and the other beckoning for the slow but steady smattering of applause that comes from the surrounding watchers. But I can only watch the bleeding man as he stumbles from the ring, clutching his hand and moaning in agony. No one picks up his fingers.

The tattooed man roars his approval, and I slip away to the bar. I consider finding calm in the alcohol surrounding me, but instead I force my implant to do its job as I assess the situation.

Then I see a familiar face.

I probably wouldn't have noticed him at all if not for Hiro's messages. The Aster is a strange one; he doesn't wear the same wraps or goggles as his kin, and his skin isn't as see-through, just a muted, washed-out purple-gray. He moves through the darkness of Mithridatism with the liquid grace of a shadow.

He used to be the bartender here. Now he leads a man in an antique tweed suit and a woman in a silk head scarf away through a door to the storage room.

I follow without a second thought. My fingers itch for my mercurial blade, but I fight that impulse. I can still pretend I am a trader, lost on his way to the bathroom, if I am caught.

Though I know the Aster can easily see me despite the dark, he is focused on the two humans he leads through the racks of supplies, cans of food and bottles of alcohol, and even stranger things, like clothes in odd cuts and familiar tech with unfamiliar modified attachments. I keep low, moving from stack to stack, until they stop in an area with low lighting for the humans' benefit.

The Aster gestures to something in a glass case. From my vantage, I can see only the hilt of a mercurial blade. "We offer the implant with the blade, of course," he is saying. "No point in one without the other."

My guts twist into knots.

"And the training?" the woman in the head scarf asks. "We cannot simply put unfamiliar tech in our soldiers and expect them to figure it out at the cost of their lives." The man in the tweed suit nods, deferring to her. She must be his superior, and they must be high-ranking military, dressed in the expensive civilian clothes that they wear.

"We'll show you everything we've figured out so far," the Aster says, and when he smiles, his sharp white teeth gleam.

"How many implants do you have?" the woman asks.

"How many do you need?" the Aster replies, unfazed.

Her hand grazes over the glass case. "Surely you cannot supply an infinite number. I know where these things come from, after all, and there are only so many dead bodies out there."

I remember the four dead duelists in front of the hangar during the Fall, the strips of military blacks on the Ironskin like mementos. My stomach seizes; I fight the urge to throw up. They're ripping the neural implants out of the duelists we left behind at the Fall.

"Leave that to me," the Aster says. "I guarantee I can get you whatever you need." After a moment of hesitation, the woman nods approvingly.

But the man, quiet until now, speaks at last. "What about the Sisterhood? They have clear laws against this."

"You'd be surprised what the Sisterhood approves of these days," the Aster says, shoving his hands into his pockets in such a gesture of humanity that it's no wonder he's the one who worked as the face of the bar—and now the face of this operation.

"I'll take a dozen at first," the woman says, reaching for the glass case, but the Aster places his flat hand over it, keeping her from taking what lies within.

"This is just a prototype. Not for sale. I can get you the twelve, though; just follow me." He walks back into the darkness, and after a moment, the woman in the head scarf follows the Aster, the man in the tweed suit at the rear.

I wait a total of thirty seconds before I sneak through the darkness and come to rest in front of the glass case. Inside is a magnifying glass placed in front of a neural implant, as clean and new as one straight out of Val Akira Labs. I'm not sure what I expected. For it to be covered in blood and brain matter left over from the duelist it had been in?

Then I look at the mercurial blade, and it is so familiar, it feels like a fist has knocked the air out of me.

I know it as well as I know my own. From the notch missing on the end of the hilt to the pink nail polish stripe painted on it the last year of Academy, I *know* it.

Hiro's mercurial blade.

I do not command my implant to neutralize the emotions lashing me. Sorrow, relief, regret, nostalgia, and curiosity batter me like a storm. My heart roars in protest, my mind racing at the possibilities.

Hiro had warned me. *I'm guilty*, they had said, but some part of me had refused to believe it until this moment. Until I saw the proof with my own eyes.

I hear a click behind me, and something hard pokes me in the kidney. Something that feels awfully like a pistol. All at once, I realize . . . I'm a fucking idiot.

"We've been waiting for you," sharp teeth whisper into my ear, "Lito sol Lucius."

Because of course, if Hiro betrayed the Icarii, they betrayed me, and I have walked right into a trap.

CHAPTER 15

Service in the Sisterhood is completely voluntary. The Sisterhood is not a gang of thieves, stealing daughters from their families and hiding their intentions. While Aunts may visit the parents or legal guardians of those being considered for the Sisterhood, those girls given to the Sisters join with parental consent. No one is held against their will.

Aunt Edith, Order of Cassiopeia

Forty-two minutes: that's how long it takes from when we first spot the Icarii *Nyx*-class spy ship NCS *Crius* on our radar until their Captain val Richard's surrender. But sixteen hours is how long it takes for us to finish what we started in those forty-two minutes.

I wonder, as I lie in the med bay, my veins singing with a pain relief concoction, how we found the *Crius*. It is not just chance that brought us upon an Icarii ship. Space is too vast, luck too inconsequential.

Then I recall the words of the quicksilver warrior as he held me tightly. *Where is your captain?* They were looking for Ren . . . I shudder as I realize that in all likelihood, *they* found *us.*

Between the black call of sleep, I hear chatter both cheerful and grave. Some in the beds beside me complain of Ren's use of the Ironskins on board instead of sending them to secure our enemy's ship.

Nurses titter about Ren's intelligence in keeping whole regiments of soldiers back, leading to a lower death count. And others still, officers visiting and asking for help in the brig, complain that the foolish young Ren kept the quicksilver warriors alive instead of beheading them and sending a message to their people.

But I know, deep down, Ren only wants peace. If she can use those quicksilver warriors as leverage in a bid for that peace, she will.

When I come to and feel human again, well rested instead of drugged, I find I have a visitor standing at my bedside. Second Sister holds out a rich clipping of green leaves from the hydroponic gardens set into a ceramic vase with a delicately painted flower. "Your readings are good, First Sister," a nurse says, but I do not even look at her. My eyes are only for Second Sister and the bouquet.

My second appears frazzled, her red hair wild, her eyes haunted by shadows. She smiles, and it is not one of her Sister smiles; her lips curve like a crescent moon, and little dimples form in her cheeks. I force a return smile, despite how weary the muscles of my jaw are.

"If you feel well enough, you are more than welcome to return to your quarters," the nurse says. "We could use the bed for more wounded." I nod my thanks to her. "I'll leave you to yourselves. Second Sister, please see me after."

When the curtain falls shut behind the leaving nurse, Second Sister offers the bouquet to me, then uses her free hands to sign. *You are well*, she says. *I am glad.*

I'm surprised to hear that. Shouldn't she be praying that someone beheads me or banishes me from the *Juno* so that she can take my place? Then again, trying to think of the day from her point of view, I realize how strange it must have been for my fellow Sisters to know that I almost died at the hands of a group of quicksilver warriors.

I touch the soft, springy leaves, reveling in their natural freshness, then run my hands over the smooth, cold vase, admiring the gentle watercolor of a sunflower. A little black gem at its center sparkles in the light.

If Second Sister is willing to offer me an olive branch, I will take it. I set the vase on my bedside table so that I may sign. *I am also glad. Did you bring me the bouquet?*

She smiles a more tentative smile, all shyness and youth. *A present from your Ren.*

I flush at her words. *My* Ren. I look at the bouquet with new eyes. The arrangement is of plain green fronds, a staple of the hydroponic gardens for generating oxygen on board. It symbolizes a wish for good health. It means the world to me that Ren thought of me and sent them.

Do you need help standing? Second Sister signs.

I push myself up to a sitting position and swing my legs over the edge of the bed. No dizziness comes after, no nausea. *No,* I tell her. *I can manage.*

Should I arrange to have someone deliver the bouquet to your room? she signs.

I smile at the vase and fronds once more. I could carry them to my room myself, but I want to go straight to Ren's side. I wish to know that she is well, hear her tale of the battle, shoulder her guilt if I must. I am, after all, her First Sister. *Yes, I would appreciate that,* I sign to Second Sister.

As she departs, she opens the partition that sections off my bed from the rest of the med bay, ensuring that if I collapse, one of the nurses will see and rush to my aid. But without trouble, I rise to my feet. My muscles ache as if I am a child again and have missed a dose of gravity medicine, but nothing seems amiss. The nurses are so busy with other soldiers that they do not even look at me as I leave.

Then a tall man standing in the hallway, lingering like a shadow, draws my attention. I take in cool air through my nose. I know that steady presence—large, looming, but as comfortable as the shade of a tree in the summer heat.

Ringer!

I throw my arms about his waist before I even meet his gaze.

"First Sister," he says into the top of my head, and his wide chest rumbles with the echo of his deep voice. The sound of him vibrates through me, makes my entire body tremble.

He's alive. Thank the Goddess he is alive.

"Little sister," he whispers, and I melt into his arms, all the tension I'd been holding in my muscles leaking out of me. He holds me upright without strain, and I feel as light on my feet as a dancer when my head spins. There is so much I wish to say to him, so much to ask him that I cannot. When I pull away, I press my hand to his chest, hoping that gesture can convey even an iota of the gratitude I feel.

I love him so much, my older brother. And it is in a way I have not loved since childhood—pure without doubt, passionate without fear. When he strokes my hair, I do not for an instant have to pretend I enjoy the caress, do not worry that he will try to take it a step further. He is my guardian, and I feel protected.

"I am not here to burden you," he says, but even when I shake my head to tell him that he is no burden of mine, he presses a sturdy hand to my shoulder. "You have done so much today, and I am well. I have fought for the Goddess's glory and feel no remorse too deep to ignore. But you seem . . ." He trails off, and my eyes soften. He sees me like no one else does, just a tired girl in a dress, not a priestess with unlimited energy. "You should rest. I only wanted to assure you that I had lived."

For that I am thankful in a way I cannot say. Being a pilot is dangerous, and despite how youthful and strong Ringer is, one day he will succumb to the Ironskin's weight. I still have Ren to visit, though, so I motion for Ringer to follow me. Even if he does not talk, I enjoy the silence with him.

But he does speak as we glide along the empty hallways, about things that are not the battle. As if he knows that all I have thought of in the med bay are the wounded and dying who were not as lucky as Ringer and me. The thought of Jones's head rolling from his body comes to mind, and I shudder.

"Do you ever look at the stars and imagine they form images, First Sister? I have seen animals long extinct, and the eyes of family members watching me from the cosmos. Once I saw the exact outline of my father's longship."

I listen to him, my mind at ease. I could drift to sleep at the sound of his voice, like thunder echoing over a windy plain. He continues to talk of the stars and of his home on Máni. I imagine myself alongside him, truly his sister, and am so at peace when we reach Ren's chamber that I hug him once again.

"Be well, First Sister," he says, and parts from me. I watch until he disappears down the hallway and pray that he told me true, that he holds no lingering guilt and thus has a dreamless and restful sleep. He deserves it after all he has done this day.

When I knock on Ren's door, no one immediately answers. I lean against the wall in my exhaustion, giving myself a small moment to close my eyes. Perhaps she is not there, or maybe she has a visitor and cannot answer . . .

But then the door at last slides open, and it is just Ren, looking as she normally does out of uniform—rugged but relaxed, handsome but approachable.

"First Sister . . ." Her voice is rough, scraped raw from all the shouted commands and barked orders of the last hours. With the strain I hear, I wonder if she has been screaming, if her decisions during the battle erupted in heated discussion afterward. Her black eyes hone in on the dark blue side of my face, the great bruise that the quicksilver warrior left me with, and I wonder if my appearance displeases her. She quickly drops her gaze and steps out of the doorway. "Sorry—come in, I'm . . ." But she doesn't finish, and I follow her into her room, letting the door close behind me.

Her quarters have become so familiar to me over the past few weeks that I've come to think of them as my second room. When she first moved in, I thought I'd never be able to see it as hers, always Arturo's. Now I have to think hard to remember what the room looked like when he inhabited the place, with his pictures of family and glass cases of early Martian weapons along the walls.

Now that Ren has had time to settle in, the walls display ink paintings of rippling water, black curves interrupting negative white space. Her desk looks disorganized to my eye with its compad, nests of charging wires, and used tea set, but Ren never fails to find exactly what she's looking for. There are a few items she fidgets with, a glass ball she flicks from hand to hand and a pen she chews on when thinking, littered among the useful items. But everything else in the room is spotless, if only because someone, a Cousin most likely, comes and cleans behind her. Otherwise I'm sure her clothes would dot the floor and her bed would remain rumpled with sleep.

"I'm surprised you came, after what happened to you," Ren says, passing by her desk, the place she usually sits when we talk. I follow her into the strongest light of the room, and she furrows her brow when she takes in what has become of me. My heart sinks; she must really hate the way I look now. "I am so, so sorry this happened to you on my watch. Do you blame me?"

Of course I don't. I shake my head vehemently.

"I should have cared for you better." Ren speaks to the air, or perhaps the past. "When I saw we were being boarded, I requested that you be brought to the command deck for your protection, but the duelists . . . They found you on your way to me. If I hadn't sent that soldier for you, you would have been safer with the Ironskins."

I wish I had the words to ask her why—why the warriors came after us, why they were looking for her. But I am, in a way, too tired to care now. It is over, and I want to forget it all ever happened. I dip my chin.

"First Sister." Ren lifts her prosthetic hand toward my cheek as if to brush it, but drops it with a jerk; her flesh hand shoots to the place where her skin meets metal and clasps it gently.

Immediately the rest of my day melts away. I forget about my brush with death and the way my face displeases her and focus only on the twitch in her eyes and the motion of her thumb rubbing at her skin that betrays her pain. I reach out for her shoulder with concern, but catch myself before I touch her. My hand hovers over hers.

"I'm aching after today," she admits. "The doctors already gave me something, but nothing too heavy. You know the rules . . . No distraction during duty."

And a captain is always on duty.

I frown and hold out both of my hands in front of me. I wiggle my fingers in a gesture I hope she reads as *massage*, an offer to help soothe the pain. "You can try," she says. It took a week or so of awkward, invented hand signals before we began to understand each other, but now she takes my meanings more easily. She releases her prosthetic shoulder, and I step beside her and grasp the place between her neck and arm with one hand.

I work my fingers and thumb into the soft flesh and knead at the hard muscle beneath. Ren tips her head back so that she faces the ceiling and lets out a moan that brings heat to my cheeks. She bites her lip against the sound. After a minute or so of standing quietly, Ren clears her throat. "Do you think . . . Do you think I could lie down for this?" she asks.

I gesture to the bed's length, and Ren takes my assent and positions herself on her stomach. I'm glad she doesn't notice or comment on the blush I can feel burning on my cheeks. I take a short moment to remove my boots, the same color as my dress, before I sit on the bed and tuck my legs beneath me. Balancing over her prone body, I use both hands and press into the muscles of her shoulder and back. With her face buried in the sheets, I hear her muffled moans as my hands dip beneath the straps of her tank top.

She flinches at times, certainly due to the pain, and in places where I find ropy scars, remnants of her past battles, she shudders against my hand. I remember the faces of the Ironskin pilots as they stepped into their armor—wan with fear, but also determined to look death in the eye. Then the memory of the quicksilver warriors hits me, their otherworldly glow, their silver blades begging for blood. Ren lost her limbs to secure the fate of Ceres against warriors just like those. How did she face them so bravely when they held the power of the stars in their hands?

Then a bothersome thought arises as my hand crests over her opposite shoulder and finds a crater of a scar, indicating missing flesh: After a thousand battles in a never-ending war, what scars does she wear beneath the surface?

"I hope you are not disgusted by me," Ren mumbles against her pillow.

But she is beautiful. I open my mouth to tell her so, though of course nothing emerges. My immediate reaction is startling, however. I know that Ren is objectively attractive, but this is the first time I've admitted to myself that *I* find her so.

My hands have paused in their work without my realizing it. She turns her face toward me, looks up at me in concern amidst the tangled sheets. I press a hand to her cheek, wishing I could simply tell her how I feel as opposed to writing it down; I do not want to retreat, do not want to pull away to gather the pen and paper from my pockets. I fear even the slightest lull in my answer might shatter the moment, that I would convince myself my admission is better left unsaid.

But despite the embarrassment from my limitations, the shortcomings I know so well, I can chase away her shadows of doubt; I can soothe the scars that linger beneath her skin.

You are beautiful, I mouth, just as I had tried to speak to the quicksilver warriors. No sound comes out, of course, but my lips form the familiar words as I try with all of my might to tell her what I think. To truly communicate with someone who is receptive to my thoughts and feelings. Who *cares* about me.

She closes her eyes. Lies very still on the bed. Her lips twist in a strange expression I do not recognize. Have I hurt her? Did she misunderstand? Or does she not care for my compliments?

She opens her eyes. Her look pins me in place. "Do you really think so, or is that a honeyed lie to make me feel better?"

I stiffen in surprise, then let her see how stung I feel by her accusation. I wish I could write to her: I thought we were past lies.

Beautiful, I say again with no voice.

"Even as twisted and ugly as I am? Even with these metal limbs that cannot feel?"

Beautiful, I say once more.

Her face smoothes as she releases her pinched expression. "Rest with me, little dove," she says, rolling over. Gently, so gently, she guides me by my waist to lie down beside her. The comfort of the plush bed surrounding me and the heat coming from Ren are so intoxicating that my eyes close without any fuss. Within seconds my breathing slows and my muscles relax, and I sag into the mattress. Despite how much I slept in the med bay, I am so weary.

"No matter what happens to me," Ren whispers as she lies very still, her arm thrown over my waist, "I will shield you."

And as I sink into sleep, I do not know whether I imagined her words or not.

PLAY:
▶ 08

◇—•—◇◇◇—•—◇

When we graduated from the Academy, no one was shocked that we were at the top of our class. And with your background, I was shielded from any claims of nepotism in my placement. But I swear to you, my father had nothing to do with our posting on Ceres. He hated that I would be so far from him and in a place like the asteroid belt, where skirmishes with the Geans over resources were so common.

When he warned me about the dangers of Ceres, I felt that, for the first time, I began to see more than just the vengeful fox behind his mask. I also saw fear. Not fear for my safety, but fear for himself—and the only thing my father cares about is his reputation. There was something about Ceres he didn't want me to know.

Of course, that meant I was determined to find out what that was.

Our first year—well, I wouldn't call it inconsequential. Despite being the youngest and greenest duelists there, we had our share of victories. We repelled Geans in the Pallas Defensive, stopped outlaw acts of piracy on our transport ships during Operation Ice Gap. But we were merely followers there, not leaders. That didn't come until later.

190

Did you ever wonder at the change, Lito? How I began drafting strategies with an almost preternatural knowledge of the Geans' location? It all started at the bottom of a bottle.

And you always told me drinking wouldn't get me anywhere. How little faith you have in me, Lito!

You know the bar: Mithridatism, our usual spot. We first went because we heard from other duelists that they had that game you used to play at your low-level Cytherean school—gladius, or whatever—and you begged me to go, and since I had also heard there would be ample opportunity to gamble with my father's money, I figured, why not?

Mithridatism was packed into one of the narrow historical district streets, its exterior shimmering with colorful ceramic leaves that looked more like clumps of dragon scales to me. It was big enough to be a hotel, but instead of a lobby, it had a gladius ring set up in the middle of stadium seating. The floors above circled like the rings of a tree, the ceiling a high glass arch that let in natural light—at least, as natural as light from a dome can be.

You remember how it was, a cacophony of sound instantly swallowing you—people clustered in the atrium shouting to be heard above the latest Cytherean banger, a few people dancing to the electric tune, and an announcer calling out gladius results. The bar was this long slip of metal in the back hidden in recessed lighting, and that's where I headed.

I grabbed a drink of candied snake venom, one of the bar's staples, and by the time I returned, you were with the booker. There were a lot of other duelists I recognized there, including a couple I never wanted to see outside of headquarters, but you were thrumming with such high energy, you probably didn't notice anything other than the ring and the two combatants, wearing the white suits that counted points scored from the electronic blades. I wondered if I'd have to drug you and drag you out at the end of the night.

You paid your entry fee. I bet against you. I remember you snorting and elbowing me. "Wow, thanks for the confidence, Hiro."

"But if you win, you'll make even more money." You never would've accepted my money—my father's money—otherwise, so this was a good solution. I could drink and watch you fight and throw money around with abandon—what was better than that?

Unlike being a duelist, gladius is a solo game. I couldn't direct you, and you couldn't reach to me for advice. Once the white suit was on and the blue shield barriers were up, it was just you and your opponent, no one else in the world. And even if I could have helped, I wouldn't have. Sports bore me. Take the threat of blood out of fighting, and there goes my interest.

You won some, and you lost some. Well, you won a lot more than you lost, and I could tell that the longer you played, the more you wanted to keep at it, as if you were shaking off the dust that had piled up on you through the years at the Academy when you had been fighting with me at your side.

But I didn't mind. I had the bar. So when you wanted to go back, I'd go with you. It wasn't every night, and sometimes we'd forget the bar for a week or two at a time, but we'd always end up back there, you in the ring, me with a drink. I'd even grown accustomed to the Aster staff, like that weird-looking bartender—you know the one, the guy who doesn't wear goggles.

But then I found him. Or he found me. My father's secret. My father's shadow.

Hemlock, the monster who lived at the bottom of the world.

CHAPTER 16

Homo sapiens asteroides are as different genetically from *Homo sapiens sapiens* as we are from our Neanderthal ancestors. The "Asters," as they are called colloquially, genetically altered themselves hundreds of years ago on Earth and thus have different needs from ours, such as a dark environment for their mutated skin and eyes. The physical labor we assign them helps their bodies adjust to our gravity.

Thomas val Kant, head researcher at Val Akira Labs

I immediately roll to the side, and then I'm up and running between the racks to the exit. The Aster's HEL gun goes off, but the laser shot flies wide, illuminating the space only long enough to leave a faint impression of it on the backs of my eyelids. When I hunker down, my back pressed against a rack full of modified Aster goggles, my shoulder aches with the memory of another bullet, a scar I still carry.

"Clear the place of civs," the Aster snaps, and I spot the tattooed man from the gladius ring at the door to the bar. So much for my exit. "Tell the others to get in here. We can't let him escape."

I reach into the hidden pocket of my jacket and withdraw the hilt of my mercurial blade. I didn't want it to come to this, but they already know who I am, and I have little choice but to fight my way out, especially if they are intent on keeping me here.

My mind runs with questions as I tiptoe from one rack to the next. Why do they want me? And was it my imagination, or did the Aster's shot go wide on purpose?

A moment later, I have my answer. "I don't want to kill you, Lito sol Lucius," the Aster calls into the dark. He sets the HEL gun aside, as if that is proof of his statement. Instead he lifts the glass casing and picks up the mercurial blade—*Hiro's* blade. "But I've always wanted to fight one of the famed Icarii duelists without holding back. See if you're everything they say you are."

I should be nervous as he starts toward my hiding place, but I'm not. The pounding of my heart roars in my ears, but I focus on his voice, telling me exactly where he is even as he steps into the darkness.

"I suppose Hemlock won't be too mad if I cut off a few pieces."

That name again. *Hemlock.* The name Saito Ren said on Ceres, the same name Hiro used in their recordings. The Aster who orchestrated the Fall. Souji val Akira's monster. Is that who's giving the orders here?

"Come out, Lito. Come out and fight me." The Aster's footsteps echo in the paths between the racks. "You don't have an unlimited amount of time here. I've called for more men. Soon this place will be overrun with Asters, and while I know you'll be more than happy to kill them all, I wonder if you'll be able to with no shield on you and a dozen guns pointed in your direction."

His talking masks the soft steps I take as I sneak through the stacks, keeping out of his range of sight.

"Right now it's just you and me, Lito." His voice is a purr, and I chafe at the familiarity of my name in his mouth. "Just one of me. Kill me, and you might have a chance at escaping."

I position myself to his left. As soon as he passes by, I'll have a clear shot at his back.

"Escape, and you won't have to find out what Hemlock plans to do with you."

I shut out everything beyond this Aster—the way he knew who I was, Hiro's blade in his hands, the order that I be taken alive. There is only my body, my mercurial blade, and my opponent. *I am Lito sol Lucius*, I tell myself. *I am one of the greatest duelists in Icarii history.*

He passes in front of me.

I jump at his back, my blade flaring to life with a thought from my implant. I swing toward him with all my strength, and—

He spins on his heel, his blade answering mine. They lock together, the energy sparking and lighting up the dark space.

"You should know," the Aster says, his pupils narrowing to slits in the bright light, "we have excellent hearing too."

I have always used my height to my advantage, but in this moment, I am at a loss; even the shortest Asters are still taller than me, and they have an extraordinary reach with their long, spindly limbs. I never considered what it would be like to duel an Aster—why would I? Where would they get the blade, or the training?—but now I am punished for my hubris. The Aster uses his greater mass—and thus superior strength—to push me back, and when I jump away, his blade comes swinging after, giving me no time to rest or reset.

I fall into a frantic defense, repelling his blade and retreating as swiftly as I can. But he's not paying attention to the diameter of battle. He's not watching his feet, isn't calculating his moves or taking into account the racks of materials around us.

He may have reach, but I have experience and training. He whips the blade diagonally at me, missing me by mere centimeters, and I slide sideways around one of the racks, out of sight and out of reach.

"Lito—" is all the Aster manages to get out before I brace my shoulder against the rack and push with all my might. It topples on him, its contents falling with meaty thumps and metallic clangs. I hear the Aster cry out in a language I don't know, and use the time to back far enough away that I'm outside his blade's reach.

I look around for anything I can use, and spot what the Aster left behind on the glass case. I reach for the HEL gun and hope it's not fingerprint locked.

Then I feel someone familiar ping on my implant.

Ofiera.

Is she here? Maybe she's keeping this Aster's promised reinforcements from reaching me. I can feel her from another room, somewhere close and growing closer.

Be careful, Ofiera, I think to her, doubtful that she'll understand due to our distance.

"Coward!" the Aster yells as the rack trembles. "*Siks!*" I don't doubt he can extricate himself; part of an Aster's genetic modifications are their adaptable muscle mass and bone density, and while every Icarii has basic genemodding as a child to keep them healthy regardless of gravity, the Asters mutated themselves to become better spacefarers than standard humans. They're strong, even if they're untrained.

The Aster flings the rack off himself. His face is flushed purple with exertion, and his long white hair is wild about his face, falling from his Aster-fashioned plait. He starts toward me, the blade still gripped in his hand, but stops short when he sees the HEL gun I point at him.

His mouth forms a thin line, but for once, he is silent.

"You're good. I'll give you that," I say.

"I know."

His confidence knocks a chuckle out of me. He seems strangely young in this moment. "Who taught you how to duel like that?"

His smirk returns, and with it, his pointed teeth. "The Hero of Ceres."

Oh, thousand gods. I know the name coming before he says it.

"Saito Ren."

Mierda.

I knew. Some part of me knew that she was alive. I sensed it in my very blood, in the scars she left on me.

I had dragged Saito Ren onto the ship thinking the Icarii could examine that new, thinner Ironskin of hers, but they must have released her. Somehow they must have saved her from the brink of death like they saved me, and then used her as political leverage and traded her back to her people. She had lost an arm and a leg, but that didn't make her any less dangerous. Maybe she wasn't in an Ironskin anymore, but her mind . . . After facing her, I was scared of her tactical brilliance.

"And Hiro?"

"Who?" the Aster asks, and despite his *eat shit* expression, I cannot tell if he is playing with me or not.

Anxiety roils in my guts, but I banish it with my implant. I'm an idiot—I shouldn't have mentioned Hiro here. Shouldn't have even gotten into this fight. I try to find Ofiera again, try to reach out to her, only for the Aster to use my distraction to his advantage.

He jumps at me. His sword flares to life. I pull the trigger, but nothing happens. The HEL gun is fingerprint locked—then it's cut in half by a blade.

I freeze. His hot breath hits my cheek.

I remember Ceres and the Aster who shot me and—

And I'm going to die—

My instinct takes over. *Inside of his reach. Middle is open.*

I tackle him, and we both fall into the racks. He grapples for my sword, still live and burning, while his has sputtered out.

Weakness. Lack of control. Cut off his hand.

I swing toward his hand, but he drops it quickly, releasing the hilt—*Hiro's hilt.*

His other hand curls into a fist. He drives it against my jaw. The adrenaline keeps me from feeling it.

Spin the blade. Slice his throat.

I flip the blade in my hand and drive it down. The Aster jerks his head at the last moment, and the blade slices through his plait instead.

Kill him.

"I yield!" he screams. His eyes are wide, and this close to him, I see the irises surrounding his large pupils are gold like an animal's. "I yield!"

The blade burns next to his throat. I could shift it a centimeter and kill him.

Kill him. Now.

"Lito!"

Ofiera's voice rattles me.

I don't look away from my opponent—he's already used my distraction to his advantage—but I do stay my hand. My breathing comes heavy. My heart beats too fast. My shoulder burns like fire.

"Lito, let him up," Ofiera says. She takes small steps toward us, I see from the corner of my eye. "Lito, don't do this."

I hear her scream for another Aster in my mind. *Don't!*

"He tried to kill me!" I say, and I am ashamed when my voice shakes.

"I know. I know, Lito. He was foolish. He was scared. He *is* scared. Lito? Lito, look."

He was just a boy!

I meet his golden eyes. His breathing is shallow beneath me. His face is so alien, but I can read something familiar there. Something I don't want to see, but that I identify with. *I don't want to die.*

I jerk away from him, taking steps back until I hit the wall. Training keeps me from dropping my blade, but the glowing metal retreats into the hilt.

The Aster says nothing as he sits up, shorn hair scattering around him like falling snow, and touches his neck. The spot I very nearly sliced.

Ofiera looks between us, her brows furrowed. "Thank you, Lito," she says, but her voice is soft and sad, and I try to feel what she is feeling through her implant but find only guilt.

Guilt. For what?

Men rush into the room, mostly Asters but a couple of humans among them, including the man with the tattoos. They all have either

HEL guns or railguns. The reinforcements the Aster promised. I raise my blade, but Ofiera shakes her head.

"Don't, Lito. Don't fight."

"Ofiera?" A prickling sensation starts in my stomach and runs through my body like liquid fire until even my fingers are thrumming. "Ofiera, what are you . . ."

But I know the truth with roaring certainty: she's working with them.

My grip tightens on my blade. Could I fight them all? Most likely, if they were not trained as the Aster was. But if he joined the fight, and Ofiera too—

She takes a step toward me and holds her hand out. "Let me have it, Lito."

This attempt to disarm me is the thing that finally ignites my anger. "Fuck you, Ofiera. You're really going to betray me to the Geans?"

"Like Hiro has?" she asks, and I fall silent.

Yes, like Hiro, a part of me whispers. My implant swallows it all: the anger, the confusion, the panic. I feel blank when I place my blade into her waiting palm.

There is nothing else I can do in this moment.

"Come, then," Ofiera says, wrapping her hand protectively around the hilt of my blade. "Hemlock wants to meet you."

CHAPTER 17

There is no greater treasure a Sister has than her fellow Sisters. There are bonds that form among them that last their entire lives.

From Inside the Sisterhood *by Dr. Merel Jäger*

❖

"What kind of toys did you play with as a kid?" Ren asks odd questions now that we have spoken of bigger things; she wants to know everything, every detail of my life, as if by knowing these things she will truly know the heart of me. Yet I cannot tell her that she already knows more about me than anyone else has ever bothered to uncover.

"If you could see any place in the galaxy, where would it be?" she asks. Or "Do you think we could ever trust Synthetics again in the future?" Questions that have nothing to do with my past, but instead focus on my beliefs, my inner thoughts.

I cannot possibly create such imaginative questions, but Ren never lacks for them. Some questions I do not know how to answer. "If you could meet one person in the universe, present or past, who would it be?" Or "Have you ever been in love?"

The last question haunts me. I have long known that I could feel attraction for both men and women, but have I actually loved anyone? I thought I cared for Arturo, perhaps even loved him, but I see now that I loved only what he could offer me. Do I love Ren? Fool that I am, I do not know. My chest warms when Ren is near. My heart speeds when I imagine us together, talking in our own way. But is that love?

Every night that Arturo and I slept in the captain's bed, wrapped in sheets and each other, he whispered promises to me. Promises that he had no intention of keeping. I swallowed his words with all of the hope that only a girl who has nothing can. *Why would he lie to me*, I thought then, *when I have given him everything he wants, a silent, obedient companion, and asked for nothing in return?*

I should have known we Sisters are no better than pets to them. We are called for when we are wanted, left alone when we aren't. They feed us, care for us, and name themselves heroes for it, never acknowledging that they are the ones who hold the chains that keep us tethered to our stations. But that is so difficult to remember with Ren.

Every night after we dine and write together, we retire to bed. She does not paw at me, does not command me to do any more than what makes me comfortable; she does not even move to kiss me, though I am not sure whether I wish she would. I offer to massage her. Sometimes she accepts, other times not. Mostly she wishes to sleep alongside me, sharing my warmth, whispering words of a world she dreams of—peace, a home, prosperous planets for the Geans and Icarii both. She does not give me promises, but hope; she tells me to dream alongside her, to imagine a world that we have changed. And slowly, I begin to.

My locked-away hopes begin to leak through: I imagine a home on Mars with her in a gravity-controlled settlement, a family of our own making, and flowers in the garden that we tend together.

During my work in the chapel taking confession, I daydream of her bed. Odd that I long for it when I had previously dreaded it, knowing that I must do my duty in order to have the future that I wished for. I had wanted freedom from the Sisterhood, a house planetside instead of a ship; now home is the captain's quarters, a bed, a young captain, our undefined future.

AUNT MARSHAE SUMMONS me every three days, demanding information. I give her lies and am shocked when I do not even feel guilt for doing so. She tells me I have disappointed her, failed the Sisterhood, will upset the Mother; nothing disturbs me enough to make me waver from my promise to continue digging, all while feeding her falsities.

This time, however, she greets me by tossing a file atop her desk.

"A message for you, niece." Aunt Marshae laces her fingers together, leans her chin against her clasped hands, and waits, watching the biopapers instead of me. I straighten my spine as I cross the room and pick up the stack; I refuse to bow and scrape to her.

But my traitor heart races when I see who it is from. *The Mother.* She's contacted me again.

Because I have not been providing Aunt Marshae with the information she asked for? Because I have grown dangerously close to Ren?

I read the letter quickly.

From: The Mother
Subject: Instruction
Body:

Dear First Sister of the Juno,

I hope this missive finds you well. Now that Ceres is back among the faithful, we may turn our attention to expanding Her work, aided by the spoils of our victory. As thanks to the Goddess, we aspire to consecrate a new temple of the Sisterhood to Her works on Ceres, so that we may focus on what more the Goddess may bring us. First, however, I must congratulate you on your success in receiving the captain's claim, evidence of Captain Saito's trust in you. I am pleased with your dedication to the task, and wish for you to know that your commitment to the Sisterhood does not go unnoticed. Second, I ask you not to let that service trouble you. Even when you write, though expressly forbidden by the Canon, the Goddess knows the truth in your heart: you are faithful, and do only as you must. Finally, I ask you to continue to make yourself invaluable at Captain Saito's side. Watch what she does. Listen to what she says. Make note of it for a later time. Report directly to me. At the Mother's Celebration, Saito Ren will be questioned for treason before the Agora, and I believe any help in this matter would prove you an apt First Sister of Ceres.

All within Her cosmos,
Mother Isabel III

Emotions war within me until my heart feels too big for my chest. Goddess, this is so much worse than I imagined it would be.

The Mother wants to expand the Sisterhood, and with it, the war. She wants to try Ren for treason against the Geans—and by the Agora, the seven Aunts who lead the seven orders of the Sisterhood. She wants to make me the First Sister of Ceres—but *only* if I inform on Ren.

A chill runs through my entire body, and I feel faint.

Isn't this what I wanted? A posting on a planet, a home with a garden where I no longer have to take soldiers into my bed?

Yes! part of me screams.

The other half whispers: *Not like this.*

"Do you have anything to tell me?" my Auntie says.

I meet her gaze and harden my eyes. Try to brace myself so that I do not swoon like a thin tree in a heavy wind.

No, I sign.

She drops her hands to the desk, fingernails scraping across the smooth metal as if she wishes she could dig those nails into my skin. "The Mother seems to think that you do."

My hands remain still.

Her lips tremble with barely restrained anger. When she finally speaks, her words are low and tempered. "What happened to 'Your success is my success'?"

The Mother says I should report directly to her. I do not need to tell her that; she has already read the letter, probably memorized its contents to use at a later time.

Another thing that lies unsaid between us: the Mother has essentially cut Aunt Marshae out of the equation, and this infuriates the middle-aged woman. Now my success is mine alone. Does she wonder if the Mother and I planned this? Does she wonder whether I have personally been in contact with the Mother, merely waiting to reveal this latest deception?

Let her wonder. She deserves to be the one toyed with, for once.

"Sleep well, First Sister," Aunt Marshae says coldly. A threat?

I do not bid her farewell as I leave.

I SIT ON the end of my bed, staring at the browning fronds in the sunflower vase, Ren's gift to me.

The Mother's words burn on the backs of my eyelids. My heart is heavy, my stomach tight with sickness. My mouth tastes bitter no matter what I drink.

I have to warn Ren.

But I *can't* tell Ren.

Does she know that she has made enemies of the entire Sisterhood? Does she know that she will be tried by all seven orders when she returns to Ceres? And what will happen if she finds out that I was instructed to spy on her from the beginning?

I briefly think of the amber-eyed girl, thrown into space from the *Juno.* Would Ren do that to me too?

I could arrive at the Celebration and tell the Mother everything that Ren has told me, everything from her upbringing to her current yearning for peace. The Mother would reward me with a posting on Ceres. *First Sister of Ceres*, I think, and I'm ashamed at how I yearn for the title. I could run the new temple, manage the Little Sisters who would grow into full members. I would never have to travel with a ship or soldiers again.

But could I take that position at the cost of Ren?

What is so wrong with wanting peace?

I withdraw the pen and paper from my pocket and allow my hand to write what it wills. When I read the finished note, I feel relief and horror simultaneously.

The Mother will try you for treason at the Celebration on Ceres, it reads.

I want to fling it away. Rip it into pieces. Burn it.

It's just a piece of paper, I convince myself, not a venomous snake.

But these words could bite me. Who else would warn Ren of the Celebration but me?

I shove the paper and pen into my pocket, but I can feel them there, heavy as a stone.

I will warn her. I feel I owe her that, if only for her soft questions and gentleness toward me. I will warn her, and it will be done. My words cannot stop the Mother from trying her. Cannot stop the Agora from coming to Ceres to speak against her. Cannot stop the Sisterhood from sending spies to watch her. But if it helps her prepare, even a little, it will be worth it.

I make my way from my room and walk quickly through the empty hallways, briefly wondering where everyone is before spotting a clock. It is midcycle on the ship, so everyone is either at their post or in the mess hall. I shouldn't be surprised to find Ren's room locked, but I am disappointed. I consider waiting for her in the hallway, only to realize that I have no idea how long it will be before she returns and that my failure to report to my chapel would not go unnoticed.

Wondering how I will survive the long, torturous hours of confession when I wish to speak with Ren now, I return to my room to prepare for my duty.

But Second Sister is there, sitting primly on my bed with her hands in her lap.

My smile drops.

What are you doing here? I ask.

She doesn't answer but instead strokes the dry brown fronds and the ceramic vase holding them. One finger caresses the black jewel in the middle of the sunflower before her other hand holds up a compad. On it, I can see myself.

I rush across the room, but she shoots upright and holds out a hand to stop me. I cannot tear my eyes away from the compad screen, where I see myself sitting on my bed, a paper and pen in my hand.

Watch, she signs, then starts the compad's video.

So I watch, as she commands. Watch as I take out the pen and paper from my pocket. Watch as I write my traitorous note to Ren warning her of what is to come. Watch as I face forward, as if peering into a mirror.

But it's not a mirror. I'm looking at the vase that Second Sister gave me in the med bay. At the sunflower, where she hid a camera.

Second Sister slips the compad into her pocket. She smiles a triumphant grin, forming dimples in her cheeks. *You have no idea what I had to do to get that camera,* she signs. *But it seems it was worth it in the end.*

This is it, then. My undoing.

Will she become First Sister, happily spying on Ren, when I am dead?

You betray our mission, she continues. I don't miss her words: *our* mission. Aunt Marshae and the Mother gave her the same assignment they gave me, only she didn't receive Ren's favor. Has Third Sister been given this mission too? Have other unranked Sisters? How far down does it go?

Bile claws up my throat, but I force myself to sign with shaky hands. *Will you enjoy watching me die like the last Second Sister?*

This Second Sister sneers, but I do not understand her expression. Not until she carefully signs, *I will not tell on one condition.*

Name it, I say, trying to look brave. But tears spring into my eyes. I am angry at her and crying in frustration and angry at myself for crying, and that makes me cry all the harder.

I am tired of what Auntie says, she signs. *I am tired of being second.*

I clench my hands into fists at my side.

You are mine, she says. *Your bed. Your food. Your service. I am First Sister, in all but name.*

I begin to understand. Once before this happened to me. On my first ship assignment, an older ranked Sister held me down on my bed with a knee to my chest and pulled my hair until I agreed to do as she wanted me to, to act as if she were my captain. I did her laundry, changed her sheets, brought her meals to the chapel, all like her personal servant. *You are mine,* she had signed, just as Second Sister does now.

With a heavy heart, my eyes bubbling with vengeful tears, I give her what she wants. There is nothing else I can do when she holds proof of my treason in her hands. Fighting the pain, I sign what she wants me to sign. *I am yours.*

And in the quarters that used to be mine, she smirks with victory.

PLAY:

▶09

◇————◈◈————◇

"**S**omeone wants to meet you," the Aster who never wore goggles told me.

"Sure, I always love meeting fans," I said, but the way he smiled was more like a wolf's snarl with his sharp canines, and it made my hair stand on end. I instantly sobered.

He told me to follow him and left the bar. Without a word, another Aster stepped into his place. None of the other patrons even noticed the switch; to them, one Aster was as good as the next, even if this one wore traditional wraps and goggles.

You were playing gladius, but for one very long minute, I considered waiting until you were finished so that you could come with me. I didn't know where that Aster was going, and for the first time in Mithridatism, I realized how very alone I was without you by my side. But this was a public bar, and I convinced myself that no matter what happened, there were people around who would witness it—whatever it was that he wanted to show me.

Now I wonder how things would have been different if you had come with me that night. Would we be where we are now, a universe apart? Or would we be traitors together?

I followed the Aster into the back room, some storage area, and wondered if he would try to kill me. That thought actually amused me. Would I fight him as you were dueling in gladius, or would I let him end me once and for all? I've always suffered from *l'appel du vide*, the call of the void, that insufferable curiosity about what death holds.

Then he opened a door, and all I could see were stairs that led down into a darkness so thick it was liquid. Stale air rushed up to meet me. There was something wrong about it, like there was no filter, that unnerved me thoroughly.

"You're not about to offer me wine in your cellar, are you? Because I'll have you know, I'm too well read to fall for that."

He kept grinning with those pointed teeth like he could smell my fear. I felt like, on some level, he was challenging me, and without fully deciding to, my feet led me down the stairs. As they say, curiosity killed the cat, but satisfaction brought it back.

Down in the basement I met my father's shadow.

Maybe you'll meet him too, so let me say this: Don't let his ugliness fool you; he is an Aster. He's both unbelievably kind and terribly bloodthirsty. And I think the first time I saw him was much like the first time I saw you: I loved him immediately.

He was what my father wanted to hide from me. He had information my father hoped I would never know written in his very skin. And he had plans, Lito, so many plans that he was willing to share with me.

He inspired something in me that my father and the military combined had never been able to give me: A purpose. Motivation. Hope that things could change.

I gave him information he could use to blackmail my father, and he gave me intel on the Geans. In fact, it's thanks to him that we won the Battle of the Belt, destroying the majority of Gean forces surrounding Ceres. The partnership was so valuable, I thought we'd always work like that together. I suppose that's why I felt so betrayed by Hemlock when the Fall came.

He had warned me to stay away from Icarii headquarters. I knew he had been working on something big with the Geans, some treaty that would give Asters more freedoms in Gean space, but I never knew exactly what. And then when the bomb went off and Geans dropped to Ceres, all I could think was that it was *my fault*.

I told you when this began, I'm as guilty as they come.

But we made it out of the Fall alive, so fuck the rest.

Does betraying the Icarii to spite my father make me evil? Or was I evil from birth, the fox inside my father a mirror to the one inside me, passing to me through our shared blood?

Who can say?

But I do know Hemlock wasn't the only monster down there.

CHAPTER 18

The Aster presses his hands to a nondescript section of wall between two racks and slides a false door aside. Wind from below batters me, cold and musty, and I shudder; it's all too reminiscent of my time in the Spire's basement, recovering from the Fall. But I know this place, if only from Hiro's descriptions. Once more, I'm chasing their shadow.

"Go," the Aster says, and I don't have to be told twice. The weapons at my back and Ofiera make sure I follow his order.

Stepping down each stair feels like I'm perpetually walking off the precipice of a cliff, and when I reach the bottom expecting another stair, a little shock runs from my guts up to my head. But Ofiera has followed me down and presses a hand to my shoulder as if to comfort me. I jerk away from her. Perhaps I'm angrier than I realize, because I don't want her touching me when she has betrayed me like this.

Down here, I catch a whiff of something damp and warm, and it turns my stomach in the way rotten meat would. But it's so faint, I lose it a moment later. Somehow that worries me even more.

Ofiera knocks on a door just in front of us, but I can see nothing in the unlit space—not until the door opens and I catch the faintest glow of deep red light. She guides me forward but stands between the doorposts, blocking the way back. I hadn't noticed it until now, but she's wearing green-tinted Aster goggles, only these have been modified with black retrofits. For human eyes in the dark, most likely, if she's having no trouble seeing down here.

I turn to the dim light and try to make out my surroundings, but the thick paper lantern covering the single candle, diffusing and dimming the flame, makes it impossible to see the entirety of the room. In the shadows I make out the Val Akira Labs logo and, stepping closer, find familiar silver boxes, exactly like the ones on the grasshopper. The medicine—it was bound for Ceres?

"What the fuck is this?" I ask, and look at Ofiera. Another piece of the puzzle slips into place. Ofiera had been determined to clear the Asters in Dire's smuggling operation, and now it seems she's working alongside them.

I catch movement in the shadows.

"Ofiera," a voice calls from a corner. A spike of fear shoots from my chest to my fingers, but I force my implant to calm me; dangerous as creatures who lurk in the dark may be, they do not speak.

"It took over a dozen men to subdue him, but here he is," Ofiera replies, as if reporting to a superior.

"And Castor?"

Ofiera huffs. "Almost got himself killed trying to *duel*."

"Stupid boy." The voice is deep but strained; the hissing whisper reminds me of the growl of a waterfall. The figure moves again, and I hear the clicking of heels against two different surfaces—one muffled by a rug, the second a sharp tap against concrete. Even when he steps into the dim light, it takes me a few moments to adjust to his features.

One word shouts at me above all my senses, a myth that belongs in a childhood horror story: *vampire.*

From what I can see of his face and hair, with no hood or goggles to hide him, he is as pale and insubstantial as a white wax candle. His eyes—large, luminous, devouring—are solid black from one corner to the other. His white hair is lanky and missing in patches from his bulbous dome of a head. But he is, in his quiet way, aristocratic. His clothes are deep purple velvet, a trimly cut suit that fits him snugly and is long enough for his spindly limbs. His white shirt, frilled in an out-dated fashion, clasps beneath his chin to hide his neck. I almost expect a show of wealth through jewelry, but he is bare of ornament.

He is no vampire. He is Aster. Yet . . . something is different about him. Something is . . . wrong. The shadows pool strangely across what skin he shows.

"Ah, Lito sol Lucius. In the flesh."

"You must be Hemlock," I say, the name intimately familiar. He is the Aster whom Saito Ren named, the one Hiro said was their father's shadow. *Unbelievably kind and terribly bloodthirsty.* He is the secret leader of Ceres, the one who made the pact with the Geans, and apparently is also involved in smuggling operations with Dire and the outlaws in the belt.

It's hard to tell where his skin ends and his lips begin, but when his mouth parts in an open smile, I catch nothing but the curve of upturned shadow dotted with crooked teeth. "Indeed I am. You've been a patron of mine for a long time, so I'm honored to finally meet you in person."

I suppose he's right; I came to Mithridatism with Hiro and played gladius almost every week, but I never spoke with any Asters. Never tried to get to know them. "Then I'd like to make amends. An apology is due."

"Oh," he purrs, "aren't you a kind soul." He steps forward, entering more of the light, and I immediately see why the shadows rippled on his face. His skin is scarred, pitted with burns and slashes. Unlike with other Asters, I can't make out the delicate blood vessels beneath his skin, but instead see only a lump of unformed clay.

Anything I wanted to say is lost, shocked away by the horror of him.

I can't tell where he's looking with eyes that do not change. As he steps toward me, those eyes glow like a cat's. "A dear friend of mine, Yarrow," Hemlock says, long fingers coming up to press against my shoulder, "shot you here."

The scar aches in memory of that wound. I keep myself from flinching. Hiro cut off Yarrow's head after that.

"If this is about your friend—"

"It is not. He was simply in the wrong place at the wrong time, as they say. And when it came to choosing sides, dear Yarrow performed . . . poorly."

My heart beats a heavy rhythm against my sternum. "Then . . ." If this is not about revenge, could it be about the Geans? Does he still work with them? Will he hand me over to them now?

"Peace, Lito sol Lucius." He clasps his hands together in that graceful way of his. "Have you ever thought of peace?"

Hiro's words echo loudly in my head. *I'll end the war, Lito. Even if it kills me.*

I keep the anger from my tone as I form my next question. "You want me to buy that, when you're selling Icarii tech to the Geans?"

His mouth parts in that shadowy smile, but this close to him, I can see that his teeth are yellow and rotting. "Peace for the Asters, then."

From what Hiro said, that seems to match up.

"Peace," I repeat, the word strange on my tongue. "Does that mean you will do me no harm?"

"Well, I certainly never said that." *Unbelievably kind and terribly bloodthirsty.* He lifts a hand, fingers curling into his palm elegantly. "That depends on you."

I let out a long, slow breath through my nose. My fingers itch for my mercurial blade, but Ofiera holds it instead of me.

"In good faith, I offer a trade, Lito sol Lucius." His left hand brushes against the soft velvet of his jacket as he pushes his long hair over his shoulder. "I will give you something of great value: knowledge. I offer freely the answer to any question at all, and I promise to give you the truth so long as it is in my power."

"And, in return, I assume you will expect the same from me?"

He laughs, and it sounds like choking. "You've bartered before, I see."

This is a game that children would play, though never with questions that could end in death.

"First of all, I am the Hemlock you've heard so much of, and I am . . . shall we say, partnered with the outlaws in the belt." He reaches past me to pick up the lantern and gestures to the Val Akira Labs crates full of medicine. His animal eyes flash in the candlelight. "I give that information as a gift, so you do not waste this opportunity on an easily answered question."

Hemlock takes the lantern back into the shadows, the room so much larger than I thought it was, and sits on a wine-colored love seat. He places the lantern on a glass side table and pats a plush pillow beside him. "Join me, Lito." With a small glance at Ofiera, I do. "I think it only fair that, because of all between us, I go first."

"Then ask your question," I urge him. Now, more than before, I want the truth from him: about the Fall of Ceres, about his involvement with Saito Ren and Hiro, about his future plans.

"Did you know that your military has killed over ten thousand Asters in the name of research?"

His soft words are a punch in the stomach and not at all what I was expecting. My head reels, and I search my mind, every memory I have, for anything that even hints that this is true.

"That's not—" I start, but then I realize . . . I actually don't know whether it's true or not.

"I assure you," Hemlock says, his fingers trailing down his ruined cheek, "that it is."

I remember Hiro's words all those years ago. *I never liked putting lipstick on lab rats.*

"Your military works hand in hand with Val Akira Labs, and we are always the first test subjects for anything they create," he goes on. "We try the most dangerous substances to ensure you *pretty humans* don't come to harm."

"I assure you, I didn't know," I say, my feelings laid bare, and I hope he hears the truth in my voice.

"You feign to care so much for us Asters when you kill us indiscriminately?" Hemlock asks. My stomach forms a hard knot of sickness as I remember the Asters at Val Nelson Mining. Even after Ofiera found proof of their innocence, I killed without conscience.

"But that is a second question, so you don't have to answer it. Wouldn't want to be accused of cheating," he says, wagging a finger in my face. "Your turn."

My mind, in its jumble, grasps for a single clear thought. I could ask him about his involvement with Saito Ren, discovering the truth behind the Fall of Ceres. Or I could ask him about the Mother's Celebration, completing the mission as given to me by Command. Yet one question floats above them all, so that I speak without fully thinking it through.

"Where's Hiro?"

There's no mistaking Hemlock's facial expression; he actually smiles at me. But I can't tell whether it is at the need in my tone or if he is making fun of me for, as he sees it, wasting my question.

I don't regret it at all.

"That depends on whether you wish to kill them."

And again, my mouth gets away from me before I think it through. "I don't," I say, realizing once the words are out how true they are. I think about Hiro's recordings, all the questions they answered and the even more numerous questions they raised. I have been in denial, believing that I could kill Hiro without first asking them what the hell they were thinking. "I've been commanded to, but . . . I want to talk to them. I want to understand them before I decide what to do."

"To do what you think is right, regardless of what your Icarii commander says." It is not a question; Hemlock's keeping to the rules of our exchange. His eyes glow with candlelight.

"Yes," I say, and I feel that I am admitting to treason.

"It's a start," Hemlock says, and crosses his legs, one long, thin limb over the other. "I cannot say where Hiro is now, but I know where they will be. Hiro has every intention of attending the Mother's Celebration."

"Does Hiro plan to complete their mission and kill the Mother?"

"That's another question, and it's not your turn."

I chew on my lip, feeling strangely like a student being chided by his teacher.

"It is apparent to you that I know Hiro val Akira," Hemlock says. He places his hands in his lap, and the oddest memory rises within me of Hiro methodically making Luce and me dinner, their graceful hands chopping potatoes to go in their homemade curry. Hemlock and Hiro are worlds apart, yet . . . there is something in one that reminds me of the other, a rawness burning beneath their surfaces, a gentleness that hides potential destruction.

My heart churns in my stomach. "Hiro's father conducted the experiments on you, didn't he?" I ask the question without thought for our game, but when Hemlock smiles, I know I'm right. "How did you escape?"

"Escape?" It disturbs me that I have already grown accustomed to Hemlock's broken laugh. "It is not so thrilling a tale, but it shows how prone to violence you are to think that." I frown, but Hemlock barrels onward. "I agreed to let him experiment on me for payment. After he no longer had use for me, I was discarded. I came here."

"But . . ." I almost ask why—why would anyone submit to torture that leaves their body like *that* for mere credits? But I'm afraid I know that answer.

Because while every Icarii has an annual salary, the Asters are not considered Icarii. They have few ways to earn enough credits to buy Icarii technology. They may have water, but we have hermium. They become our guinea pigs, a step before human trials, so that the heart of their people can survive in the asteroid belt with our domes and ships.

I never liked putting lipstick on lab rats.

I stand before I am aware of doing so. Hemlock does not react other than to cock his head. "And where do you think you are going?"

"I . . . need to find Hiro." Preferably before the Mother's Celebration. I need to talk to them about all this—the experiments, the Asters, the Fall of Ceres, Saito Ren, their blade, working alongside Hemlock . . .

"Sit down, please." Hemlock pats the spot next to him again. "We're not finished here."

But I am. I walk toward the door, toward Ofiera, daring her to raise a hand against me.

"Lito, I'm sorry, but I can't let you leave," she says, and that apology breaks the dam holding my anger at bay.

"You're *sorry?*" The rush of questions, one right after the other, overwhelms me. Everything I meant to ask Hemlock comes spilling out. "Were you working with Hemlock to orchestrate the Fall of Ceres? Was Saito Ren your contact with the Geans? Did Hiro help, or just stand aside while it happened?"

"Sit down," Ofiera commands, clearly not intending to answer a single one of my questions. Then I feel her influence on me, her neural implant overwhelming mine in an attempt to control my body as she did in the grasshopper weeks ago. I feel the urge to return to my seat, but I fight her.

I have to leave. I have to find Hiro.

I meet her eyes and imagine the tether between us. If she can control me, maybe I can control her and force her to move. I tug on the tether. The back of my head burns with the start of a headache, but I don't stop. *Focus*, I coach myself. *Focus on her, on bending her to your will.* But as my hands curl into fists, the world around me fades and shifts.

A flash of light. A world blooms, and I find myself in a glass building full of green plants, growing from floor to ceiling. A greenhouse or hydroponic garden.

A boy dances into view—an Aster boy—yet instead of disgust, I feel that he is the most beautiful boy in the galaxy. His long hair shines like silver starlight, his eyes are a luminous mix of blue and green—like the sea, something in my mind supplies—and his skin is tinted icy blue from the tracery of lacy veins beneath. The entirety of my chest burns as his long fingers grasp my smaller hand and envelop it gently. I am so small compared to him, and it is so easy for him to wrap me in his arms so that I feel protected and complete. He leans down to whisper something in my ear, and I turn my face sideways so that I catch his lips with mine. He tastes like sugar.

"You are beautiful, Ofiera fon Bain," he says.

Ofiera. Of course. This is her memory, her emotions.

The Aster releases her, and I feel my stomach—*her* stomach—pitch with wanting. We have so little time before we must part, I want to touch him every second we are together, leave no space between us so that I can pore over his details in memory. "I love you, Sorrel," I whisper between us.

A flash. The image shifts.

A wall of glass separates us. Sorrel struggles against the restraints on his chair. A man in a lab coat takes a needle the length of his forearm and positions it at the back of Sorrel's shaven head.

"What are you doing?" I ask, shaking.

The man in the lab coat presses the needle's tip to Sorrel's neck and, meeting resistance, leans into it, muscles straining. With a sickening pop, the needle punctures Sorrel's skin and slices into his spine. Sorrel's face twists in agony as he screams, the sound echoing through me and stripping skin from bone.

"Stop! What are you doing? Stop it!" I slam my fist against the glass between us.

They don't stop.

Flash.

I gasp for air as if I'm surfacing through water, and tremors rack my body. My hands seize for purchase but find only cold gel that slips through my fingers. "Welcome back, Ofiera fon Bain," a different man says, wrapping a blanket around me. It doesn't help the shivering.

Instantly I look for Sorrel. I find him to my right, and my heart launches into my throat. My unsteady legs wobble beneath me as I force myself from the table. The blanket falls from my shoulders, but I don't care about how cold I am as I trip and fall against the glass wall that, even now, separates us.

Sorrel smiles at me. Presses his hand to the glass. I place mine over his.

"You have five minutes," the man says.

Flash.

"Oh-feaaaaaaaaar-uhhhhh."

This time it is a woman in a lab coat who wakes me. Her smile is a loaded gun.

I stumble from my cryo pod. Let out a cry like a dying animal as I land against the glass and slide down, down to the floor. "Sorrel—"

His hands are bound behind his back. There is a strange discoloration beneath his skin. His nose is crooked—broken. He twitches, muscles jerking uncontrollably. Drool dribbles down his chin.

"What did I do wrong?" I cry, trembling fingers scrabbling over the glass.

"This isn't your lover," the woman says, and when I calm down enough, I spot the minute differences between them—the way he sits, his muscle mass, how his toes curl beneath his feet.

The woman speaks my fears aloud: "But it can be Sorrel, any time you decide to liberally interpret your mission parameters again."

This is what happens when I do not please them.

Flash. I surface through water and suck in a deep breath of air.

"Welcome back, Ofiera fon Bain."

Flash. I come back coughing, my lungs screaming for oxygen.

"Breathe, Ofiera, just breathe."

Flash. I bloody my fists on the glass. Five minutes are not enough.

"Give me back my husband! Give me back Sorrel!"

Flash. I gasp in my first breath and save my strength for my arms. My legs. For when they show me Sorrel. For the five minutes we have together before we are dragged apart again.

Flash. "Ofiera?" The man who wakes me floats above me, haloed by light. I strike him with the heel of my hand. Slide from my pod, kick his kneecap sideways. His screams drown out the sound of my bare feet slapping against the floor as I run for Sorrel.

I am so close when they tranquilize me. My wet fingertips leave streaks against the glass.

Flash. I refuse to breathe at all, hoping it kills me. The woman waking me slaps me across the face, and I unwillingly gasp in air, just another one of my many births.

Flash. I run my hand softly over the dome of Sorrel's cryo chamber. This is the closest we've been in years, no glass wall between us.

"One last time," a man says. I catch his reflection in the glass. But him, I recognize—this one is familiar to me.

I turn to face him when he reaches my side. "Take care of this for me, and I guarantee we'll release him," Souji val Akira tells me.

The memory crashes, one image inside another like paper folding. When the last pixel burns out, I am left in the cold and dark, and it takes me a precious few minutes to run my hands through my hair and down my face, remembering who and where I am.

"No," Ofiera snaps, her lips twisted. "Those memories are *mine*."

I hadn't meant to see that. Whatever is wrong with Ofiera's implant, whether it is ND or something else, fighting her for control led to memory bleed between us. How long have we been under? It felt like hours but couldn't have been more than a couple of minutes.

"What was that?" The Aster she loves, the torture, the waking from cryo again and again—

"Ofiera?" Hemlock asks.

She clutches her shirt just over her heart. She grinds her teeth, chewing on words that do not come.

"That's enough for now, starchild," Hemlock says. "Go on upstairs and rest. I will show our guest around."

We stare at each other, victims of her shared memory. No words come—no apology or comfort is suitable for what I saw.

"Ofiera, darling," Hemlock says, and finally her heavy breathing slows.

"If I'm not here, I can't guarantee he won't attack you," Ofiera says.

"Oh." That purr returns to Hemlock's voice. "I think he'll be a good boy now. Don't you?"

My face burns at being called a *good boy*.

Ofiera spins on her heel to leave, but just before she closes the door behind her, she slaps a pair of goggles into my hand, identical to hers. "You'll need these," she growls, anger radiating through the implant. Then she is gone, the door clicking and locking behind her.

"Unfortunately," Hemlock says, "we cannot allow you to do anything that will upset the balance of Ceres before the Mother's Celebration, or we lose the chance at everything we've planned for." I turn back to him as he speaks. He holds the lamp and gestures to another part of the room swallowed by darkness. "But I can show you what Hiro saw, and perhaps you'll understand what *all* of us are fighting for."

I look at what little of the basement I can see—bookcases against the wall, moldering carpets over the concrete floor, furniture that does not match in style or make, crates of Val Akira Labs medicine. Then I look at Hemlock, at his scarred face and black eyes that shimmer with tapetum lucidum, a feature I never knew Asters possessed.

"Is that agreeable?" he asks.

Without a word, I step toward him, intent to follow wherever he leads. Wherever Hiro leads.

"Let's go," I say.

CHAPTER 19

There is a coldness to the moons Máni and Skadi that is hard to describe—a darkness that can stay within the heart of a man all of his life.

From Outside Earth's Moons *by Magnus Starikov*

The following week is consumed with duties for Second Sister. At the end of my day, I return to my room to find her already there, curled in my bed as if it belongs to her. I sleep on the floor, waking when she kicks me and signs for something she wants—a glass of water, another blanket, a foot massage. I have not lived like this since I was unranked on my first ship assignment, and the lack of rest carves my face into a hollow thing.

One night I stay with Ren, only for Second Sister to double my chores. Each time I do not do as she asks, she signs, *I will tell Auntie*, with sharp, angry hand motions. So though I visit Ren, I leave at the end of our sessions. Ren could command me to stay, but she never does, simply watches me go with a concerned frown.

"They're overworking you," she says, and I simply nod and smile as if that is the trouble.

I wish I could tell Ren of Second Sister's blackmail, but the Mother wants to try her for treason and Aunt Marshae watches her every move. I cannot drag her into my mess or make things worse for her when she is already fighting an unseen war. No, this battle with Second Sister is mine.

Taking confession during the week is perfunctory, my mind fastened to solving the riddle of Second Sister. The soldiers notice my impersonal approach and, in fact, report on it. Aunt Marshae comes to punish me with silly tasks, scrubbing the floor of the Sisterhood dorms by hand or cooking alongside Cousins when I should be off duty and resting; I expect her to enjoy reprimanding me, but her heart is not in it.

I wish I trusted one of the other Sisters on board enough to ask for help. But I know that if anyone other than Second Sister catches wind that I wanted to warn Ren of something the Mother told me in confidence, I will be punished as harshly as the amber-eyed girl, stripped of her dress and tossed out of the *Juno*.

There is only one person I can name who might be willing to help me while holding his tongue. I only wish I knew for sure that I was not risking everything by involving him. But as Second Sister's demands grow, I cannot see that I have any other choice.

WRITING GOT ME into this, and I pray to the Goddess that writing will get me out of it. Funny, because according to the Mother, if the Goddess is watching over me now, she's frowning at my foolishness. *Treason in order to get to know a captain? Ha! The truly beautiful and talented need no pen and paper to impress themselves upon others.*

Though I like to believe the Goddess understands exactly what we Sisters go through and is far more forgiving than our Aunties tell us. At least, I force myself to believe that as I hide in a shower stall away from Second Sister's camera, take what is left of my pad of paper, and fill it with words. Words that are, for the first time, not for Ren.

When this is over, I will have to ask Ren for more paper. When this is over, perhaps I'll explain it all to her and it will be nothing more than a silly memory to laugh at.

I stuff the scribbled papers into my dress and head from my room to the lower decks of the *Juno* where the soldiers reside. Many stare at me as I pass, but not in a way that is abnormal; their eyes flutter over me just long enough for me to know they have noticed me but do not linger. They are, after all, still on duty. *As you should be*, a part of me notes.

I should be in the chapel, since it is daylight hours, and while that is enough for some officers to note that I am acting strangely, I can use my punishment from Aunt Marshae as an excuse for shirking my duties. Hopefully no one will push the issue.

I have never visited Ringer's room personally, though he has told me the number and letter of his bed assignment. But when I come to his quarters, there are several out-of-uniform soldiers milling about inside, gathered around a table and looking at something on a compad. They laugh and clap each other on the back, and while I don't know what they're doing, I curse that I had the bad luck to find them gathered like this. I'll have to come back later.

As I turn down the hallway and retrace my steps, my luck changes. Almost as if he was waiting for me, I find Ringer at the elevator, finger poised in front of the illuminated call button. His bushy eyebrows shoot up his forehead in surprise at seeing me on his level of the *Juno*, a place Sisters do not frequent. "First Sister," he says, "I was just about to visit you. What are you doing here?"

Goddess's blessing, Ringer was coming to *me*. I smile, try to fight it, and give up. Who cares if Ringer knows how happy he makes me? I pat his arm and cock my head. His thin lips slowly curve upward to match my expression. When the elevator doors part, I enter and wave him in after me. He follows like a shy boy, ruffling the back of his close-cropped blond hair.

"Are your confession hours over?" he asks, disappointment seeping into his tone.

I shake my head no.

"Are you returning to the chapel, then?"

I nod, and he smiles brighter than before. He escorts me back to the chapel in silence, and it is only once we are safely ensconced behind its doors, away from the prying eyes of cameras and listening ears of fellow soldiers, that I withdraw the carefully arranged pile of papers that I wrote for him.

"What's this?" he asks, and I push the pages toward him.

I'm sorry, Ringer. If you had something you wished to confess . . . it must take second place to this.

He hesitates for a moment, then slowly takes the papers between his callused fingers. He looks at the first page, but his eyes flick away quickly as if burned by what he saw.

Perhaps this was a mistake . . .

"Did you . . ." He gestures to the papers; he cannot bring himself to finish the question.

I swallow hard. Suddenly my heart feels too big for my chest. With this gesture, I am placing the fate of that very heart in his hands. I clench my eyes closed and nod.

I hear him move away from me, heavy footsteps against the floor, and I quickly look up. But Ringer does not go for the door, does not leave the chapel with the evidence of my treason in his hands; instead, he sits in the chair where I usually take confession, head hanging as if the weight on his shoulders is too immense, and lets his eyes rove over the first page.

I sit down at his feet as he reads the letter I wrote him. Listen to his heavy breathing as he takes it all in. And when he finishes, he brushes a hand over my head protectively.

IN THE EARLY hours of the cycle, I take the elevator down to the secondary launch bay, where the escape pods are kept. I do not have to go far; Ringer already waits for me exactly where he told me to meet him. "Remain here for her," he tells me, and rushes to hide his bulk in the shadow of the closest pod. Even though I know he is there, I can hardly make him out with the lighting of the bay turned off. No one mans this bay at night, when it's used only for emergencies. That's likely why Ringer picked it for our meeting place.

I twist my hair around my first finger in nervousness before remembering how my Aunt Delilah would smack me for fidgeting. Then I hold my hands flat at my sides and square my shoulders, forcing myself to look as unafraid as I wished I felt. After tonight, this will be over, I reassure myself; I just have to clear my mind and trust Ringer.

Second Sister arrives not long after me, and I'm proud that I don't startle when she prowls forth from the shadows. *What?* she signs. *If this is some sort of trick, I will tell Aunt Marshae about you.*

I don't back down; instead I do as Ringer told me to do. *Give me the compad with the video and swear you will not tell*, I sign. *This is your only chance.*

Her mouth opens; her shoulders shake. I think at first that some fit has come over her, but then I realize—she's laughing. Without sound, she appears to be going mad.

This is your last chance, I sign again, my hands moving more sharply.

She shakes her head, waves a hand through the air before signing, *I will tell Aunt Marshae now.* When she turns to leave the bay, another figure emerges from the darkness, a hulking figure carved straight from the shadows. The blackness pools beneath his brow so that I cannot see his eyes, and in this moment, even I fear him.

"Grab her," Ringer says, his voice echoing in the depths of the bay.

Second Sister stops short, hand held to her chest in surprise. She looks at me with a question on her face. *You can—*

But I cut her off, seizing one of Second Sister's biceps while he grabs the other. She tries to slap her hand against my bruised face, to use my wounds against me, but I am taller than her and keep her arm held so tightly that she cannot reach me. She opens her mouth to scream, but, of course, no sound comes out.

This part Ringer and I had planned: We would force Second Sister to give us the compad with the video and, once we had it, make sure she knew she could never tell anyone. *Or else.* That part remained unsaid. I suppose I should have asked how Ringer planned to make that known.

But I feel in this exact moment that the situation has slipped beyond my control. He drags her across the bay like a doll who weighs next to nothing and stops beside the glowing blue shield that seals us off from the velvet cosmos on the other side. I stumble after them, trying to keep up.

"Do you have the video of First Sister on you?" he asks.

Second Sister's face is torn with shock and fear, eyes wide and filled with tears, mouth stretched as if screaming, eyebrows crinkled together.

"Do you have it?" Ringer asks more forcefully, shaking her by her shoulders so hard that her head whips back and forth, red hair falling into her face.

I want to beg her to tell the truth, because I have never seen Ringer this way and do not know what he is capable of. But I cannot sign and hold tight to her at the same time.

This is Ringer the soldier, not Ringer my brother. This man is every part the killing machine the Geans want him to be—and all because I told him everything, from Second Sister's blackmail to the way Ren convinced me to write with her. Guilt coils low in my belly.

No no no, Second Sister emphatically signs, shaking her head all the while.

"Have you made copies of the video?"

No, I swear it, she signs with trembling hands. *It was hard to get even one camera, one compad.*

"Where is it?" he asks, and Second Sister's hand freezes beside her face, both blank slates, too frozen by fear to answer.

But Ringer doesn't care, just lowers his head so they are forehead to forehead. "Where!" His face contorts into something horrific. Even

I jolt in fear at the sight of my sweet, kind brother transformed into a monster before my eyes.

But he does not notice me, does not calm. He sees her and only her; I am no longer of consequence.

"Let me make this very clear," Ringer says, and with his left hand he reaches to the bay's unlock button. With a slap, the blue shield lightens and hums, signaling ships may come and go when ready, and I have never hated that sound more than I do now because I know what he's going to do.

Second Sister does too; her entire body shakes.

Just like the amber-eyed girl . . . We both remember her body floating in the black.

Ringer bunches his fist in her dress and hauls her backward, pushing her so that she is inches from the shield. I press my hands to my mouth, wishing *I* could scream for help. If she slips from his grasp, she is gone—out into the black of space and beyond. Gone like the amber-eyed girl, a ghost between us now.

"If you don't bring the compad back to First Sister *immediately*—and I mean *this cycle*—or if you happen to tell Aunt Marshae or any other Sister about this incident, you'll find yourself very, *very* cold and alone—do I make myself clear?" He lets her slip another inch until she is clinging to his wrists with both of her hands, pulling herself toward him by her nails, the only lifeline she has to this ship. Her feet slap uselessly against the metal floor, slipping without any purchase. Tears flow down her freckled cheeks, and my stomach churns with sickness.

Fool. I am such a fool. I believed Ringer when he said he'd take care of it—take care of *me.* I didn't think he meant *this.*

Second Sister nods so frantically her hair clings to her wet face. She makes a noise of agreement.

No, not a noise. It can't be a noise. Just a sound made from exhaling. But it's clear she's agreed.

"Good," Ringer says, pulling her back toward the ship with such force that she stumbles and falls to her hands and knees. I hear her dry heaving as he presses the shield button. Its hum fades, the wall growing to its darker blue, solid once again.

"You can handle it from here, First Sister." Ringer does not spare me a glance as he stalks back into the shadows like he belongs there. I do not stop shaking even after I lose track of him in the darkness; I feel that he is everywhere, surrounding us, every part of the Gean curse I had hoped to avoid.

Goddess and Mother . . . what have I done?

I kneel to help Second Sister to her feet, but she shoves me away violently. I can do nothing for her as she hugs her knees to her chest and noiselessly sobs into her dress. To Second Sister, I am just as bad as Ringer.

It's only when I head back to my room that I notice the scratches on both my hands and wrists. I don't recall when Second Sister gave them to me, but the sight of my blood is proof of what I've done.

SECOND SISTER BRINGS me the compad with trembling hands. I ensure the video is on it before I wave her away.

She leaves my room without meeting my eyes. She is so pale, she looks ill. Perhaps she'll seek help in the med bay, but I doubt it; we Sisters do not like to show our wounds to those who would not understand them.

The scratches on my wrists ache with cleansing medication. Cool bruises have cropped up alongside the scabs in the shape of Second Sister's hands. *But when did she give me those?* I wonder. I shove the confusion away; I have other things to think of.

First I erase the video, then I crush the compad. And though it hurts me to, I throw out the browned fronds and hide the vase with its camera in a drawer, wrapped in a dress. Did Ren even send me the bouquet, or was it all Second Sister? It doesn't matter; I'll never be able to look at the vase again without thinking of what's happened tonight.

Though my body aches with pain and my eyes burn from lack of sleep, I immediately leave for Ren's quarters, the note in my pocket.

"Little dove?" Ren seems confused by my presence when she answers the door, and that upsets me all over again. I blink away tears. Have I cared for her so little that she is surprised by me now?

"Hey, it's okay. Don't cry. It'll be okay. Come on, of course you're welcome here . . . What's happening? Dove, what's happening?" She catches my hands and looks at the bandages on my wrists. Her eyes widen in concern, but I shake my head, trying to tell her it's not what she thinks. "Did someone hurt you?" she asks instead of what she wants to ask, and again I shake my head.

I refuse to think of Ringer as I force myself to pull away from her and reach into my pocket.

She comes toward me again, but I force the paper between us like a shield.

"What's this?" she asks.

I shove it toward her hand.

For a moment, we stand still, quietly facing each other. I hold the paper, wishing I didn't have to give it, and she looks at my hand, wishing she didn't have to take it.

Finally she does.

The Mother will try you for treason at the Celebration on Ceres. I know what she reads over and over. I pace in the quiet, my nervousness overflowing at last.

What are we going to do? I sign before remembering Ren doesn't know the hand language of the Sisterhood. But something I said shocks me: Somehow Ren and I have become *we.* And *we* are in this mess together.

She crumples the paper in her fist. Shoves it deep into her own pocket. Meets me with flat black eyes that I recognize from her official duties as captain. "Let's never speak of this again," she says, and I stop my pacing in shock.

What are we supposed to do, ignore it? Does she know I was asked to spy on her? How many other Sisters were as well?

"Little dove, take a breath. Write it down."

In frustration, my movements are sharp. I jerk the empty pad and pen out of my pocket, and the pen slips from my fingers and flies across the room. For some reason, this is what breaks me. I drop the empty pad, and the tears come all at once.

Goddess, why is this happening? I pray. *Is this not Your will?*

Ren's arms surround me and hold me tightly. I lean into her chest, because she is steady and strong and I am not.

"It'll be okay," she whispers to me. "It'll be okay."

But it won't. How does she not understand that it won't?

Since I cannot inform on her—*will not* inform on her—I will remain on the *Juno* without her. She will be tried for treason and, at the very least, lose her commission of the ship. I don't want to consider what the worst punishment will be.

Remember the amber-eyed girl, a part of me whispers, and, after seeing Second Sister almost slipping from the emergency bay, it is all too real, all too close to the surface.

One way or another, Ren and I will part. I am surprised by how much this realization makes my chest ache.

I break away from her and mime writing. She understands me immediately, going to her desk and retrieving another pen and pad of paper. "See? I had it waiting for you," she says kindly.

I take the pen and paper in my hand and start writing.

I love you. I never want to leave you, I scribble in my frenzy.

Then I stop.

Love. Is it true?

Looking at the words, my cheeks burn and my stomach flutters. But is that love? Or is love the thing that makes me want to warn Ren of what is coming despite what it means for me in the Sisterhood? Is it love that drives me to protect her over myself?

And is it love that she does the same for me?

I rip the paper from the pad and slip it in my pocket. I cannot give it to her. Suddenly I feel embarrassed by the words, like I am made raw by them. Like they are every wound and every hope I have ever felt, displayed before a stranger, to destroy as they will.

"Better now?" Ren asks, not pushing to see what I've written. She lets me keep this secret that is also hers.

I release a breath that has been sitting heavily in my chest, and I do feel better. Ren knows she will be tried for treason. She will be preparing even now. I have done all I can do, warning her of what I know. I write one last thing on the paper before returning it and the pen to my pocket.

Let's face Ceres together, I tell her.

She takes the paper from me and then grasps my hand in hers. "Together," she agrees.

That is all we can promise each other when we fight the unknown.

PLAY:

▶10

◇———————◈———————◇

M y mother's name was Mariko. Her friends called her Mari. She always pretended to be surprised when I or one of my siblings told her something we'd learned, no matter how simple or childish the fact was. She taught us the value of tradition, even when our father said it was nothing more than sentimental superstition.

There is one afternoon I can picture with exact clarity, though I don't remember how old I was or whether my siblings were present. In my memory, my mother and I stand before the family altar. A picture of my recently deceased grandfather has joined the portrait of my uncle. She lights a stick of incense, the smell clinging to me even now, and rings a bell before turning to instruct me.

"Put your hands together," Mother whispers into my ear, "and speak as if Grandfather is here with you."

"But he's not," I said like a petulant child. "Father says this is pointless."

But Mother didn't grow angry or defensive. Instead, she turned to me and smiled kindly. "Your grandfather lives on, so long as you remember him in your heart. If you want to, you can look at the family altar as just a place to reflect on him and his life so that you never forget him."

I liked that explanation, and as I turned and spoke to the grandfather I missed dearly and as the burden on my heart eased, I learned something terribly important.

My father *didn't* know everything.

My mother's name was Mariko. She became a val Akira by choice. As is tradition in marriages, she took the name of the partner with more social power. But she never belonged to my father. She loved fashion and modern art and her children. She hated biting her tongue. You would think this would have kept my father from marrying her, but even my grandfather must have thought he needed someone to give him a spine, someone like Mariko.

Shinya hates talking about it, but from what I've needled out of Asuka, I know our parents did love each other. They were even happy—at least for the first few years of their marriage. My father climbed the ranks at Val Akira Labs, just as his father intended for him, and my mother made a name for herself as a Paragon influencer on Cytherea. They followed their passions, and at the end of the day, they came home to each other and their two beautiful children.

Then I was born, and something went wrong.

Oh, don't mistake me. I know it's not my fault. I was a godsdamned baby. What could I have done that fucked up their marriage *that* badly?

When I first met you—and I'm sure you remember me telling you this—I thought I was one of those reconciliation babies. You know, the ones born when two idiots try to save their marriage by popping out a kid. But I've been thinking and researching and . . . well, I think I know the truth now.

There was a man at the labs. There was an affair. My father loved him, and my mother knew it, but my father would never admit it.

His reputation, you see. There were certain ways people thought about him—a loyal husband, a devoted father, a CEO who didn't promote employees based on favoritism—and he couldn't bear the idea of that perception changing, even if it was for the truth of who he was.

But my mother never could bite her tongue. She knew there were some secrets that could never, ever be told by her, but she also knew that living only for his reputation would twist my father's spirit into shapes that would barely resemble the man she had married. So she left, placing me in Asuka's arms and bidding Shinya to care for his little siblings no matter what.

Not that I remember this, of course. And Asuka has only a fuzzy memory of it, being as young as she was.

But Mother came back. Obviously, she came back.

I haven't been able to find out if my parents ever went to therapy. Asuka doesn't know, and Shinya wouldn't tell me even if he did. But there was a time of reconciliation and happiness, and a year later, little Jun was born, round and red and screeching. I took one look at the baby my mother set in my arms, wondered what all the fuss was about, and tossed Jun aside like a stuffed animal so I could run off to do something else. Luckily my father caught her, or she would've gone sailing to the floor. I'm probably most thankful to him for this, out of anything he's ever done in my entire life.

Mother left again for a time after that, but I was so young and so accustomed to her comings and goings that it didn't bother me much. Asuka cried, Shinya comforted her, and little Jun, oblivious to the earthquake that had split her parents, played with her toys. I played with her. That was when we grew close, she and I, and I began to feel that she was my baby, more than anyone else's.

Here's what I remember from this time: my mother, quiet in her rebellion. My father, yelling and powerful. The stronger he got, the weaker she became. Instead of growing together, they grew apart. But he should never have made the mistake of thinking that he could control her, bidding her to stay home, to stop teaching us tradition, to ignore her art, because after Hanako was born, she left for good.

My mother's name was Mariko. She couldn't stand the idea of her or my father living a lie for the rest of their lives.

Sometimes I wonder if this is why I am who I am: unabashedly me. And sometimes I think of how this must remind my father of the woman who walked away from him, and wonder if that's why he hates me so much. Not for who I am, but for who I remind him of. For Mariko.

Because I also can't stand the idea of living a lie for the rest of my life.

CHAPTER 20

May the heart of the universe keep you, and may you never forget that we are all born from the same stuff as stars.

Ancient Aster proverb

Hemlock leads me, like a guide to the underworld straight from ancient myth, with the red lantern held before us. We pass mountains of refuse that seem haphazardly saved, unimportant items like old theater posters stacked high on a desk dotted with wayward paint splotches or empty glass bottles arranged according to color and size, their logos stripped away. There are books too: not the recycled biobooks we use nowadays, but actual wood-paper bound by an ancient spine. I wouldn't be surprised at all if he led me to an old wooden boat, a faintly glowing river of souls.

We stop at another door, this one at the very back of the room, something I never would have found without his guidance. He sets the lantern on a table, shoving aside ceramic dolls with dresses as fine as cobwebs to balance it atop a glass case of little plastic figures playfully posed. Every space down here is crammed with things, and none of them look worth a single credit. But there is no dust coating anything either; everything is artfully cared for, even the broken things.

"You'll need the goggles now," Hemlock says, and I dutifully put them on. "You're going to see a place few humans are allowed to see."

Panic runs up my spine, but I fight it away with my implant as he cracks open the door. It hisses slightly—or do I imagine that?—and I once again catch the whiff of warmth and rot. "Hiro came here?" I ask, but Hemlock only smiles.

He holds his hand out. "After you," he says, and I force myself forward. The pressure immediately changes and wraps me in a firm embrace. The air is dry and cold, like the bottom levels of the Spire back in Cytherea. But the goggles have been modified for human eyes and illuminate the darkness as if I were holding a torch. Even if my eyes ache at the strain of the strange lenses, I can see everything around me as we descend.

The Under is not as I imagined it. It is not narrow tunnels of gray rock, or industrial silver plating holding the interior of Ceres at bay. It is mathematically curved hallways in smooth white plastic, 3D-printed mesh holding naturally growing moss, copper running through the walls like the thick roots of an ancient tree, and hexagonal rooms clustered together. What little light there is seems to come from the moss. I push my goggles aside to check, and find it glows faintly in soft blues and greens. "Bioluminescent," I say, and catch Hemlock's cat eyes like floating orbs in the darkness.

"Come this way," he says, and I put my goggles back on.

We pass branching hallways that meander up and down, and with no marking system I can find, I fear that even if I get away from Hemlock, I'll be unable to escape this labyrinth. Everything looks the same, like an anthill or beehive. There are no doors; privacy does not seem to be a primary concern among the Asters. I curiously peer into each room we pass until I see an Aster changing their wraps, then look away in embarrassment.

Hemlock chuckles. "*Siks,*" he mutters, a word that I do not understand but have heard Asters say before.

We come to a room so much like the others we've passed that it seems unremarkable to me, but once we enter, the scent of rot assaults me, sickly sweet and cloying. It takes me a full ten seconds before I focus on something other than the stench and notice that the beds, placed against the walls following the hexagonal pattern, have occupants.

The Aster I dueled cuts off midsentence as soon as he sees me and sneers. I wonder if the reason his skin is less transluscent and he doesn't need goggles is because of Icarii experimentation, but I'm pulled from that thought when Castor snaps at Hemlock. "What's *he* doing here?"

"Nice haircut," I tell him.

He growls at me. "This is a sickroom. You know, for those who are ill, who shouldn't have to deal with *siks* like him here—"

It takes me a moment to realize he said both *sick* and *siks*, as the pronunciation is the same. I open my mouth to respond, but Hemlock waves me off and says something to Castor in the Aster tongue. Castor switches languages so I can't follow.

Then I stop listening altogether. Faces peer at me from the beds, all of them big-eyed and strange. But not strange in an Aster way; they're *wrong*, like Hemlock is wrong. What did Castor say, that this was a sickroom? Then all of these Asters must be . . .

One is hairless and red, their skin blistered with thick, moist pustules. Another holds slender, thin-boned arms to their chest, curled like bat wings stripped of skin and unable to unfurl. One's eyes are so close together so that they look almost cyclopean. Another's ears are like cauliflower beneath their ice-white hair. One has weeping open wounds on their scalp, their hair falling out in thick clumps. Another one, not more than a child, has metal threaded into their skull, sticking out at an odd angle.

On and on and on, another and another, each more horrible than the one before. I spin in a circle until my stomach seizes, and I fear I'll be sick.

I recall what I saw in Ofiera's memories, of the needle threading into Sorrel's spine, his face twisted in agony. Her words echoing in the small space as her bloody knuckles beat against the glass.

They're all experiments.

Castor cuts off speaking to Hemlock, then hastily switches to English. "So *now* it makes an impression on you, when you come face-to-face with it?"

"Hemlock—what the hell is this?" I have to fight the bile crawling up my throat to speak.

"Oh, Lito . . ." Hemlock speaks as softly as a loving parent. "You know who did this."

The same place that did this to him: Val Akira Labs. The same place they now smuggle medicine from—to heal what has been broken. Hemlock's question from before assaults me: *Did you know that your military has killed over ten thousand Asters in the name of research?*

"Command?" I ask, and my words are barely above a whisper. "They did this—they made them sick?"

A soft tremor runs through Hemlock's misshapen face. "Lito . . . they're not just sick. Whole families. Elders and children. They're dying."

Everything within me flares white. I lean over to vomit and fall to my knees. The stench is all I can smell—that rot coming from their skin—and my breathing is shallow, my throat burning—*they're dying, They're dying*—

The twisted, disfigured Asters watch me with wide, accusing eyes from their deathbeds.

"I didn't know," I gasp. I'm sweating despite the cold.

But what excuse is it that I didn't know? I never listened to anything but what I wanted to hear. I never saw anything I didn't want to see. I ran from the lower levels of Cytherea because I could, and never went back because I cared only for myself, not the others down there with me.

I never liked putting lipstick on lab rats.

I can hear Hiro at my side, *feel* them here, their breath on my ear as they whisper, *We're all Souji val Akira's trash down here.*

I spin, half expecting to find them there. But of course not. *Of course* they're not here. It's all a product of my tangled mind.

I stomp out of the room and into the hallway, and I do not stop even when I hear someone call my name behind me. I lose myself in the branching pathways, turning this way and that without care, until dizziness overwhelms me and I brace myself against the wall.

I don't know where I am. I'm lost, in all senses of the word.

Hiro . . . I wish Hiro were here.

"Lito . . ."

My hands instinctively become fists at Ofiera's voice.

"Come with me, Lito," she says, holding up one of the red lanterns. She leads me to a plain unclaimed room, out of the hallway so that we can have some semblance of privacy. I follow her, ripping off my goggles in the process. Around us the moss glows, but the light she holds is so *bright*, like the heart of a swelling planet, dim red fire flickering and churning, and after so much time straining in the goggles, I have never seen something so beautiful and natural. It *hurts* to look directly at it.

Dazzling, alluring pain. I let my eyes burn alongside the fire. It aches all the way into the back of my skull.

But instead of my words being calculating and measured, everything that slips from me is frantic. "What the fuck is this, Ofiera? How long has this been going on? How could Hiro know without telling me?" I stop at that last question. I know the answer from Hiro's messages.

Hiro didn't want me to follow them. They didn't want me to leave Luce behind. Because they knew if I saw injustice like this, I would waver . . .

How can I ignore this if I can do something about it?

"What am I supposed to do about this?" I ask Ofiera. "What do the Asters want from me?"

"For now?" she asks. How does she sound so calm when I know she has suffered their twisted research firsthand? "Kill the Mother, just as the Icarii have asked of you. Destabilizing Ceres will benefit them too."

I shake my head. "How?"

Ofiera's words come easily. "Once the Mother is dead, we hope to put another ruler in her place—one we have chosen because she speaks for peace. We will leave Ceres in the hands of Hemlock and this puppet First Sister of Ceres."

"And after?"

"I suppose you have two choices." Ofiera lifts one hand, then the other. "You could return to the Icarii and forget everything you've learned here. Or you could commit yourself to a cause bigger than you or I: justice."

The icy chill of the Under settles in my chest, rattles in my bones. This is the same choice Hiro had, and I know what they chose: they worked with Hemlock from the inside.

But just look what it cost them. They were sent on a high-risk undercover mission in Gean space, split from their partner of the past decade, and marked for death by Command. Doing anything less than fulfilling my mission will put a target on my back.

I see the strings the Icarii have tethered me with now. The mission to assassinate the Mother and kill Hiro is just a way to prove myself to Command. Hiro will never return to them, so hunting them down is *my* test. *My* proof of loyalty.

And if I don't prove I'm loyal? I can't return to Luce.

But if I do? I'll be ignoring this, and the military will continue to run its tests through Val Akira Labs, dooming countless Asters to an agonizing, slow death. That's as good as losing my soul.

How can I fight for someone who does *this*?

"I get it. I see how Hiro got involved with the Asters. But what about Saito Ren? And how did you start working with them, Ofiera? Why are you doing this?"

She doesn't answer. Her face becomes hard as a stone. I was an idiot to expect any answer to my questions, to think they were anything other than a waste of breath.

Then, as soft as a prayer, she says, "Sorrel."

My heart shatters. Or feels as if it does, because her emotions leak into mine through our connected implants. I consider sending a pulse from my implant to do away with the sorrow . . . but I linger in it.

"Who was he?" I whisper, voice matching hers. I remember the scene from her memory, the boy who held her so gently. The boy who screamed in agony as she tried to get to him. The boy she was given only five minutes with when they woke her from cryo again and again. "Who are *you*, Ofiera?"

"He is just an Aster, and I am just a child of Mercury." Her eyes glass over and look past me so that she's not seeing me at all. "I grew up at a time when the powerful on Mercury thought the Asters worthy of a say in their people's lives among us. But almost as soon as they started trading with the Asters, the power imbalance became obvious. We wanted their water, but the Asters' need for our energy was far greater. More and more Asters came to work for us at the cost of their own health. My parents were called diplomats here on Ceres, but they should have been called flesh traders, convincing Asters to agree to dangerous jobs and experiments."

My mouth opens and closes. The settlers of Mercury first started trading with the Asters during the Dead Century War, before the Icarii even seeded Venus. But that was over a hundred and fifty years ago . . . impossible.

"Ofiera . . . how old are you?" She *can't* be my age.

Ofiera smiles, and in her eyes, I see suns rise and fall. "Hasn't anyone ever told you it's rude to ask a lady's age? No, I suppose that is something from my time . . ." She shakes her head at a joke only she understands. "I have been kept in cryo for years at a time, waiting for Command to use me on missions, so I have lost track." She sighs wistfully. "I was born somewhere over two hundred ago."

Over two hundred—

"Thousand gods," I mutter. I am so astounded, I feel nothing other than the shock. The geneassist must have spun back her age to keep her youthful. Or maybe she has spent more years frozen than awake.

Should I feel betrayal that she didn't tell me? Or anger at Beron—and Command—for pairing me with her when, at her advanced age, they *had* to know about her neural degradation? But somehow that seems idiotic. Why be mad about one drop of rain in the ocean, when everything I've ever known was a prettified Icarii lie?

"They keep you because you're skilled." I speak my thoughts without filtering them first. I realize how much of a child I must seem to her.

"Sorrel and I were one of the first partnered pairs. I was the first human to receive the implant and not die in the process. My control over *any* neural implant, regardless of programming, was the effect of intensive surgery and arduous experiments on me, now deemed too dangerous to reproduce. It made me . . . too useful to give up."

"That's why Beron chose you as my partner." It's so clear to me now. "He thought you could force me to kill Hiro even if I changed my mind and stayed my hand."

Ofiera smiles, but it is hollow and sad. "I'm sorry, Lito. It's your punishment. Hiro's punishment. Even my punishment."

My heart drops into my guts. Again I fear I'm going to vomit. I put a finger between my teeth and bite down, focus on the burning sensation instead of the swarm of emotions rattling about my brain.

"I was commanded to force you to complete your mission by any means necessary. You would kill the Mother. You would kill Hiro. And you would return to Command." Her eyes gleam in the firelight, tiny points of stars so like an Aster's with their luminous black gaze. "If you chose to complete your mission of your own free will, you would be cleared of all suspicion. If you didn't . . ."

I drop the finger from my mouth. "Back to the basement." I shiver.

"Oh no, Lito, so much worse." Ofiera furrows her slender brows as if she doesn't want to tell me. "They would blame you for losing Ceres. They would tie you to the crimes of the Asters, of Hiro, even of the Gean Ironskins, just to have someone to blame in the public eye. They would call you a traitor, even if you weren't."

Would they, when I have been everything they've asked of me: a shining example of low-level scum bettering himself through hard work; a spectacular duelist for kids at the Academy to idolize and imitate; and a loyal soldier ready to sacrifice body and mind for the greater good?

Then my hand falls to my neck, bare in these tattered Gean clothes. Hiro was my partner, yet look how Command has treated them. I could be named a traitor. Hanged. Hunted down and slaughtered. Or perhaps they'd even use me as an experiment, like they did Ofiera. They're no different from me.

"Why." I whisper it, not even a question. I let the raging sorrow wash over me, ignoring the tug of my implant to wipe it all away. I *want* to feel this.

Ofiera watches me, tries to read me. Gods, she's good at it. I can feel her beneath my skin. "It was never a question for me, Lito. For as long as I've tried to build a life with Sorrel, they've stopped me. Called me a spy for 'sharing privileged Icarii information.' Called me a tool because my body, as a soldier, belongs to them. I watched as the man I loved was experimented on, suffered as *I* was experimented on, all in the name of their progress.

"Without someone strong enough to challenge it, a government can turn anyone into a villain. I have lived for hundreds of years doing as they've asked, believing I never had a choice. I have seen rebellions rise and fall, but for once, Lito, I see something worth fighting for. *Now* I have a choice, and I'm making it. I'm joining Hemlock."

"And Sorrel?" I flinch even thinking of the naked pain on his face. "What about him?"

She shakes her head slowly, sadly, closing her eyes as if she does not want to see the world without him in it. "He's still in cryo. I have been told, time and again, that once I complete my assigned mission they will release him to me. That we can live out the rest of our lives together."

"But they never have . . ."

She shakes her head. "No. And I know they never will. He is nothing but a stick to beat me into submission. A carrot to reward me when I'm good."

I try to imagine that silver hair iced in place. Those lips paler than they should be, frozen in cryo. I feel a pang of sorrow in my hollow heart akin to losing Hiro all over again, and I know I am feeling the same thing Ofiera feels.

"But if you betray them, they'll kill Sorrel."

Ofiera smiles, but it doesn't reach her eyes. "This time I will not take no for an answer. If it is my life they hope to hold ransom, I will remove myself from the equation."

She'll kill herself. For Sorrel. "No . . . No, Ofiera—"

"I am not Icarii. Not anymore. How could I continue to do the bidding of those who don't see my humanity? Those who use me and cast me aside when finished, as if I am a common tool?"

My breath shudders as I exhale, pent-up energy inside me clawing to get out. Her words find purchase in my ragged emotions. We are tools to the Icarii. Nothing more. "Ofiera, we can take him back. With help from the Asters, maybe—"

She quirks a brow. "Suddenly you want to betray the Icarii openly?" I fall silent. "Are you so ready to turn your back on them, to leave Lucinia in their hands?"

Luce. The righteousness crackles out of me, leaving me deflated. If I help Ofiera take Sorrel back from Val Akira Labs by force, if I do not complete my mission exactly as I was given it and return to Command, they'll call me a traitor . . . I will lose Lucinia, and she will lose me.

I am the only one she has.

"Why are you telling me all this?"

Ofiera comes closer to me, places a hand over my own. "I am no Icarii," she says again.

And . . . I understand. She will not force me to do what I do not choose. She is not like Beron, willing to sacrifice me as one cog in the greater machine, even though this machine is farther reaching than I ever imagined.

"What about Hiro?" There is much hope in my voice. I do not erase it.

"Only Hiro can answer for Hiro's choices," Ofiera says. "But Hemlock told you the truth—Hiro will be at the Mother's Celebration." When she removes her hand from mine, she rubs the muscles of her lower back. She seems older in that moment—weary from the years she's lived in this world.

I want to help the Asters and Ofiera, but I also want to care for my sister, the person I love most in the cosmos.

It's an impossible choice. A poisoned choice. One even Hiro didn't want me to make. One I'll have to make anyway.

To choose between what is right, and my sister.

"I'll let you think," Ofiera says, leaving the lantern in the hexagonal room with me.

Leaving me all alone in the surrounding darkness.

CHAPTER 21

Sometimes I wonder why the children of the Goddess possess such a yearning for war. I understand the tales they tell themselves: Our faithful Gean flock needs the technology that the Icarii refuse us. Why shouldn't hermium be shared for the taming of Mars, the revival of Earth? But the Icarii are unwilling to relinquish their hold on the secrets of gravity, unable to release their pride. Is that truly rational behavior? Perhaps man is a creature meant to love war by virtue of his own nature. Even within me, I feel the urge to destroy.

From the journal of Mother Isabel III

I hardly have time to worry; within three days, preparations for docking at Ceres begin. Soldiers fill the hallways with buckets of soapy water and wax, detailing the ship by hand, since the cleaning droids the Icarii had on the *Juno* have been disassembled for parts. The bay is a flurry of activity, mechanics checking carriers and podships in preparation for the crew who will go planetside. Uniforms are ironed, buttons and pins are polished to a golden shine, and scuffed boots are touched up with black dye. The *Juno* and her crew look their best.

Ren's room has been cleaned too. The neatness stands out to me, her desk bare compared to its usual mess, knickknacks placed carefully at the corners, papers filed meticulously into boxes. Paintings have been straightened on walls, and the bed has been made as if no one has slept in it. Maybe Ren hasn't; she is the only thing in the room out of place.

I'm not accustomed to seeing her in full uniform within the comfort of her quarters, but she stands like an elegant commander at the large livecam screen, watching the stars pass her by, shoulders squared in navy and gold. Her hands are clasped behind her back, one golden, the other stark white.

Ren. I mouth her name. She doesn't turn, because of course she cannot hear me—but because of her, I have almost forgotten that.

When I reach her side, her eyes float from the viewing port to my face. Dark shadows halo them, matching mine after our shared sleepless night.

Ren, I mouth again.

"It's time, little dove," she says, her voice soft like a whisper.

Let's face Ceres together. That promise, *together*, binds us tightly.

I slip my hand into my pocket, feel the rough edges of the torn paper there. I have one note left, one already written. As much as I should have, I could not force myself to discard it.

I love you. I never want to leave you.

Will we part after Ceres? I wonder. And, worse, a small voice inside me whispers: *Will Ren even survive Ceres?* This plain room, the way Ren presents herself, the message from the Mother . . . I hug Ren's arm and place my head against her shoulder. I am far more afraid than just for myself, than for my station. Let Second Sister have it if she wants it. I close my eyes and pray to the Goddess that she protects Ren, that whatever happens at the Celebration will be something good for us both.

And if not for the two of us, then let it be good for Ren.

"First Sister," she says, and I react without thinking, my lips twisting and my brows furrowing. She hasn't called me that in a long time. Why now? "Little dove," she says, quieter, extracting her arm from my grip and placing both hands, flesh and not, on my shoulders. "Do you know what I've tried for in every decision aboard the *Juno*?"

I do not think to school my expression; I allow her to see whatever I naturally feel because I trust her that much. *Peace*, I mouth.

"Peace." Her black eyes shimmer with tears. "Peace is all that matters."

No, Ren, *you* are all that matters. I reach into my pocket for the note—*I love you. I never want to leave you*—but before I can withdraw it, she hugs me to her chest, her lips hovering at my brow.

"I have always thought peace was worth dying for," she whispers into my hair. "I wish I had known that throwing away your life for peace is so much harder when you are in love."

When I look up at her, a tear rolls down my cheek. I wasn't aware I was crying, but now that one has fallen, they all fall, one right after another. Why is she talking like this? Is she afraid of facing the Agora? The Mother's words burn in my deepest nightmares.

But I don't want to betray Ren to become the First Sister of Ceres, not when I could have Ren. I want this. I want her.

I place my hands on her cheeks and pull her toward me. She does not resist, crashing against me, one hand tangling in my hair, the other on my lower back—and I lose track of which is the prosthetic and which is flesh, what is natural and what isn't—because as soon as I come close to her face, her eyes are the same view as the window, black filled with shimmering stars, and I do not know if she is the cosmos or if she is simply *my* universe.

Our lips touch. My body flares like a supernova. It is not chaste, this kiss, not patient or loving, but deep as the core of a planet and full of heat and need. We push toward each other, again and again, teeth grazing and lips swollen, as her hands fall to my hips and mine bunch in her uniform to hold her close, closer, closest.

Do not go. Do not leave me. I love you.

A knock interrupts us. When Ren parts from my lips, gasping for breath, she leaves a trail of kisses on the corner of my mouth, my cheek, my temple. "Come in," she says, and looks to the screen of stars, now filling with a shimmering gray planetoid that reflects in the darkness of her eyes. She takes one blasted step back from me, and we release each other with slow hesitation as the door opens.

"At your service, Captain Saito," Aunt Marshae says, and everything within me is scooped out so that I am hollow. "Are you ready to face the Agora?"

Ren's uniform is rumpled from my hands; she does not fix it. "Yes," she says.

That emptiness inside me grows and grows until I am losing every piece of myself except the fear.

"Please do not forget me, little dove," Ren whispers at my side. I'm not sure whether it's a question or a command; with a captain, it's always a command. But not with Ren . . .

She heads for the door, and I fumble for the message in my pocket. Before I can pull it out, thrust it toward Ren, Aunt Marshae steps between us.

Ren leaves. The door closes. Aunt Marshae's face twists, losing its mask, as her lips curl into a smirk and her blue eyes freeze like ice. She watches me the same way that she watched the amber-eyed girl stripped of her clothes and sentenced to death.

"You think you've won some game, refusing to tell me what you and your dear captain have been writing together, how you've warned her about the accusations she will face," Aunt Marshae says, and though I try with everything left within me to hide my expression, she must see it; I am trembling. Did Second Sister report on me after all? "But you will not mess this up for me. There is more riding on this than you understand, things I have spent years working toward.

"The Mother has called for you immediately. You will report to her in person. You may tell her the truth of your betrayal and face your sentence, or report on Ren. This is your last chance."

Why? I sign, though my hands shake so badly I wonder if my Auntie understands me. *Why give me a chance at all if you knew?*

"Because, niece," Aunt Marshae says, her skin stretching thin over bone when she smiles from ear to ear. "Your success is my success."

AS THE FIRST Sister of the *Juno*, I am among the first to descend to Ceres, alongside our highest-ranking soldiers. I should be filled with excitement; I have not been planetside in over a year, not since I was assigned to the *Juno*, and this departure means I can acquire new belongings if I so desire. But instead my stomach twists with dread, and I fear I will be sick as I enter the podship and strap myself into one of its dozen seats.

Ren sits toward the front of the ship, chatting with the CO. She does not look at me as I enter. Ringer is not far from her, watching me intensely. I have not sought his company since that terrible night in the bay with Second Sister. I hate to admit it, but whenever I think of him, I remember fear instead of the support he has offered me throughout my past year on the *Juno*. I do not meet his gaze.

Aunt Marshae is close to Ren but next to Second Sister, my Auntie speaking while Second Sister rests, demure, clasping her hands together in her lap. I find a seat as far away from them as I can.

"Captain Saito." The intercom clicks on, the pilot's thin voice filling the space as everyone aboard falls silent. "You will be taken to the council meeting at city hall where the Agora awaits you."

I clench my eyes closed. To hear the pilot say it makes it all too real.

"First Sister." I jump at my title. "The Mother has summoned you to the Temple. I'll take you there first."

I nod toward the ceiling and then feel foolish; the pilot is not watching me.

I remember Ren telling me that the Mother wanted to create more Sisters and intensify the war effort, and then consider the Mother's letter asking me to betray Ren to become the First Sister of Ceres. But as I settle back into my chair, clasping my hands beneath my chin in a vague gesture of prayer, I can only think of Aunt Marshae's twisted face and threatening words.

This is your last chance.

I HAVE SEEN the Mother a total of three times in my life. The first time I was not even a Sister but a child in Matron Thorne's orphanage, dreams of an apprenticeship still bright in my mind. Mother Salome II had stepped down, retired to become a Cousin as her youth and beauty faded, and the Agora confirmed her second as a worthy successor. Consecrated as Mother Isabel III, she paraded with her retinue through the greatest cities of Mars. I saw her then, hair brighter than mine, eyes that shone like emeralds.

She wore a silk dress as white as freshly fallen snow and a stole as red as blood. Patterns of flowers embroidered in thick gold lined the edges of the stole, shimmering as brightly as the rings on her fingers. Around her neck, over the high collar of her dress, was a choker of pearls, matching the beads across the slender diadem and veil on her head, but it was her necklace that held my gaze, something simple enough that I, in my childish fancy, could imagine myself owning it.

"Would you like to be someone like her?" Matron Thorne asked me, and I said yes, because I wanted to wear finery and be carried through the city on a litter and loved by everyone who saw me.

The second time I saw her, I was a Sister, my voice freshly taken and my first assignment given to me, though I had not yet left for my first ship. She had returned to the Temple of the Sisterhood on Olympus Mons, at which all Sisters are trained and turned from children into women, and the Aunties beamed as she admired their new crop of girls before bed. My Aunt Delilah was the proudest of all, for when the Mother first saw me, she ran her hand through my golden hair, the color not unlike her own, and kissed my forehead. It was in that moment I earned the hatred of all my fellow Sisters.

The third time, I was between assignments. I had been Second Sister on a transport vessel, taking soldiers from their assigned ships planetside and back, but after an Icarii shuttle found us, I was to be promoted for, in their words, "keeping a cool head in active battle." I would never understand why they put it that way; when the shuttle rocked with the Icarii's laser blasts, I had frozen in shock and floated, inert, in the lack of gravity. But apparently that was enough to be considered composed in battle.

Afterward I returned to the Temple to rest, and in that time, I was nameless, a Sister without rank. Mother Isabel III came to dine with those of us in the Order of Andromeda, and though she was still beautiful, she had been the Mother for nine years and had begun to age, as one does. There were sly smiles all around, Aunties whispering about when the Mother would choose her second, but I didn't care for gossip—not until the Mother stopped me in the hallway and stroked my cheek as I went back to my temporary room. Later, Aunt Delilah told me that the Mother had personally assigned me to the *Juno*, a recently captured Icarii ship and the newest pride of our fleet.

I wonder now if the Mother has somehow remembered me—*me*, not my rank, not my ship, but the girl who had watched her all those years ago and coveted a pearl necklace.

As the podship drops me off at a square building lined with circular columns, a government building that is nothing like the Temple on Mars, I purposefully think only of the Mother. I can sense her inside, as if her too-large presence cannot be held by four walls and a roof. When did it become that way? Despite her favor, I always thought myself far beneath her. But now . . .

Now she wants me to report on Ren. *Betray* Ren. Go against the Sisterhood's laws. Weren't our voices taken from us to prevent this?

The podship zips back into the sky, blowing my skirts and hair toward the doors, where soldiers wait in navy and gold. They open the double doors as I approach as if they too know me. But how could they, when I am just another girl in gray?

At the entrance an aide waits, a middle-aged woman with golden skin, her black hair in a severe bun. She leads me through the cold marble hallways, a style neither Gean nor Icarii but something far, far older—Earthen, maybe—and I follow with my hands forcefully held at my sides. Aunt Delilah's corrections ring true after all these years; I straighten my back, tip up my chin, and walk as if floating, my feet in their boots ghosting over the ground.

The woman leads me through an oaken door to a rather bare ante-chamber where a vase of moon lilies sits on a glass table. I wonder if the flowers are fake, or if somehow they have grown these rare beauties here. Even with worry choking me, I find myself beside the flowers, my fingers brushing the petals, soft as silk and white as starlight.

They're real. Goddess be praised. This is a miracle . . .

For a moment, I imagine myself as the First Sister of Ceres, in charge of growing things like this. But then I remember the sunflower vase Second Sister gave me, and the camera she used to spy on me . . . I take the image of myself as the First Sister of Ceres and shove it far away from me; I cannot betray Ren, even for something as miraculous as naturally grown flowers.

"Do you require anything, First Sister of the *Juno*?" the woman asks. I gently shake my head, but she places her fist over her heart—saluting *me*.

I stand with only my dread for company, wondering if I should sit on one of the settees, when I hear someone call me. The door to one of the rooms opens, and out peeks a pale face framed in golden hair.

"First Sister, come in."

Instantly I forget the flowers.

She is exactly as I remember her last.

Except she's not. Because it is from her mouth that I hear words come. Voice from a throat as scarred as mine—or one that should be.

The Mother can talk.

"Please, First Sister," the Mother says, pushing the door open wider and gesturing within. "We have much to speak about."

PLAY:
⏵11

❖———◈———❖

L
ito . . . this is hard to say.

[A few quiet seconds, filled only with the sound of breathing.]

I'm not coming back.

I *can't* come back.

Even if I complete my mission, I can't . . . I can't even face myself.

My father is thorough. This is a suicide mission. I know it. He knows it. I won't make it through this.

But just like when I went to the Academy, I'll do this mission *my* way, not his. It's the only thing I *can* do . . .

It haunts me . . . Are my siblings forced to stare at an empty place at the table set for me? Will they forget me, all pictures of the old me thoroughly scrubbed? When they visit the family shrine—*if* they visit— will they spare a thought for me?

I don't know where I'll be when you get this. I can only beg you not to follow me. Listen to this recording, and try to understand why I did this. Try to understand what it is to make an enemy of my father. And stay out of it. He's not an enemy you want to make.

[A soft laugh, punctuated by a sob.]

I am my father's child after all. I am the fox, the shape-shifter, wearing a mask.

Fuck—I'm crying . . .

I'll miss you, Lito.

Take care of yourself. Take care of your family.

I'll always love—

[A rustling sound. A knock on a door.]

Yeah? Yeah . . . I'm ready. Give me a second. Yeah.

[Sniffing.]

I'm fine. I'm good to go. Let's do this.

[End.]

CHAPTER 22

GOD is WAR

KILL THE COCKROACHES

thousand gods = thousand lies

A sampling of graffiti found on Ceres

After hours alone in the little room, I take the red lantern and walk the halls. No one stops me. I find Asters in their honeycomb rooms in various states of their day—dressing for jobs, in conversation, tending to the glowing moss. They ignore me, for the most part, and I begin to feel like a ghost, haunting a place I do not belong.

Watching Asters simply living their lives, I learn things about the them that I never knew. Their eyes aren't all black; their pupils expand and contract depending on the level of light. While they have no eye whites, their irises are brightly colored—golds and greens, blues and browns. They all have white hair, but it comes in a variety of textures. The standard family unit, from what I can tell, is much larger than ours, though I see few children. But I don't make the mistake of believing there are no kids; perhaps this just isn't the place for them, or they're being kept away from me because I am an outsider.

In the evening, an Aster leads me to a room cluttered with long tables and benches. Together we eat a calorie-intensive gray liquid served in mismatched cups and bowls. Only Castor eyes me suspiciously, while Hemlock and Ofiera look pleased and surprised by my inclusion. Afterward, I'm guided to a room full of beds and given an empty one. Even sleeping is a communal activity among the Asters, and I fall asleep to the sound of soft breathing, so much like my Academy days that I'm comforted by the steady presences around me.

The next day, I ask Hemlock to take me back to the hospice. Most of the bedridden spend their time sleeping, but I end up conversing with the little girl who has metal sticking from her head. She introduces herself as Rose, though she admits this is not her Aster name, just her "flower name" that she gives to *siks* like me. She speaks Aster and English, and I teach her some Spanish words while she teaches me some Aster.

Toz, a cup. *Zof*, furniture for sleeping—but not equal to a bed. *Rij*, a color that Asters can see but I can't, she explains, that is something like a more intense red. *Siks*, the word I've heard Castor often use, which is apparently slang for *Homo sapiens sapiens* like me.

I try not to think of how she is dying, but can't help it when she pauses in the middle of a sentence to fight tremors that shake her whole body. It reminds me of Sorrel's torture again, and I feel sick imagining grown men doing that to a child. Even sicker imagining myself returning to Cytherea as if I don't know this is happening beneath the glimmering surface.

That afternoon, Castor comes to retrieve me from the hospice and tosses something metal at my head before even greeting me.

I catch it instinctively. When I open my hand, I find the hilt of my mercurial blade.

"Get the fuck up," Castor says. "You think you have time to sit on your ass? Do something useful."

"Useful how?" I fight a wave of anger at the sight of Hiro's blade in Castor's hand.

"Get the fuck up," he repeats.

He leads me out of the room to Rose's soft farewell. "Good-bye, Lito. Goodbye, Castor. I'm telling Hemlock that you said a bad word."

Castor leads me to the largest room I've seen in the Under, an open expanse that is small by human standards but large enough to jog in circles.

"Fight me," Castor says, sliding into a rough duelist position. For a moment I'm reminded of Talon all those weeks ago at the Academy, begging to learn from me.

I look at my blade in my hand. "You could get seriously injured. I could kill you."

He barks a laugh. "You wish."

As much as my muscles yearn to be used, I hesitate. "I'm not sure I'm even supposed to have a weapon. Did you tell Hemlock about this?"

Castor rolls his eyes in his hotheaded way, and again I wonder how old he is. He could be Luce's age, all uncontrolled youth and re-bellious fire. "Hiro dueled with me."

I straighten.

Castor smirks. "I see I have your attention now."

"I thought Saito Ren taught you to duel?"

"You want me to tell you? Then beat me."

I don't even need a connection with him to know Hemlock has forbidden him from telling me shit. "Liar," I say.

He laughs, his eyes crinkling at the corners. "Fuck you."

And with a flick, Hiro's sword hums to life and he attacks.

I LOSE TIME in the Under. After breakfast, I visit Rose until Castor comes to fetch me, and then we train. Asters stop by to watch us, faces changing as the hours do and afternoon turns to evening. After four days pass, I realize that all of this training is not just my way of working through my feelings about the Icarii and Luce and the Asters—it's my subconscious forcing me to prepare, as if it knows, one way or another, that I'll attend the Mother's Celebration.

On the fifth day, Ofiera comes to our makeshift training room, sending the Asters scattering. "Castor, Hemlock wants you upstairs."

"Don't fucking lie to me. You just want me out of the way." He intentionally runs into her as he leaves.

"Castor," Ofiera says, hard as a stern mother. She holds out her hand, and, like a mopey teenager, Castor drops Hiro's mercurial blade into it before storming off.

"He's a good student," I tell Ofiera when we are alone.

"You're a good teacher."

"Better than Hiro?" Despite Castor's promise, he spoke little of Hiro. Only small things, such as how he gave them the recording device and arranged the delivery to Luce.

But Ofiera doesn't take the bait, ignoring my questions about my former partner. "If I didn't know better, I'd say the two of you have started to like each other."

"Growing respect," I say with a shrug. "He's still half a bastard."

Ofiera's lips gently curl in a smile. "He's young. Give him time."

"So he can grow into a full bastard? No thanks."

She chuckles before we fall into an uncomfortable silence. I can feel the prickling of her anxiety on the other end of the implant.

She clears her throat, and it echoes in the room. "Lito . . . I came to tell you that tomorrow is the Mother's Celebration."

"Ah . . ." So she needs to know what I will do.

These past few days, I have, like Hemlock promised, seen things few humans would. And I know, more than ever before, that I am standing at the precipice of something new: a chance to change things for the better.

I remember Ofiera's words: *I have seen rebellions rise and fall, but for once, Lito, I see something worth fighting for.* Now *I have a choice, and I'm making it.*

It's time to make my choice too. Even if I end up leaving Luce behind . . .

I remember her as I left her. *Tienes que volver a casa, Lito. You have to return home.*

This shouldn't be how this ends. This shouldn't be my war.

But it is.

I've always been a part of this war. From the moment I earned the Val Roux Scholarship to the Academy, climbing the levels of Cytherea for my family, I was nothing more than a soldier. I went for the same reasons anyone on the bottom level would—no more cramped two-bedroom apartment for four people, no more bland slop called dinner, no more poorly recycled air that left you slightly out of breath— but I became exactly what the military wanted me to be. Strong. Courageous. Loyal. I never asked questions, even when I should have.

I did it all for Luce, but now—even if I choose her, I will return home knowing far more than I ever wanted to know of the Icarii. Could I ever be that soldier they want me to be again? Or would the blood that stained my hands rot me from the inside out?

This is a war I never wanted. But does anyone ever want war?

At least, for once, I have the option to choose for which side I fight.

Congratulations, Lito. You're everything the Icarii want you to be.

I'm sorry, Lucinia. I hope you understand. I choose to fight for all of the Asters who suffer like Rose and Hemlock. For those who yearn for change like Castor. For those who have known love and loss like Ofiera and Sorrel.

And for those who saw the truth and did what was right. For Hiro.

I choose my soul. Not *them.* Not the Icarii.

"I'll kill the Mother," I say, "and then I'll join Hemlock in whatever way he needs me."

And somehow . . . I feel Luce would be proud of me in this moment.

"Then here," she says, handing me a shoulder bag. Inside is a pile of fresh clothes, white and sand-colored robes and green-glass goggles. "And, Lito, just because Castor hasn't shown you the showers doesn't mean Asters don't have them." She waves a hand under her nose. "Clean yourself up."

I'm almost stunned into silence. "Did you just make a joke?"

She smiles in a way that reaches her eyes and leaves the room without another word.

But I don't need her to say a thing. I can feel her hope radiating on the other side of the implant.

THERE ARE FIVE of us dressed in traditional Aster wraps that cover every part of us from our hair to our fingertips. Though they fit nothing like my Icarii military blacks, it's almost comforting to wear clothes like a second skin again.

Our goggles have been modified. While the Asters need them as strong as possible to see in our bright lights, ours have been treated to look like Aster goggles without actually blinding us. In the dim lighting of the bar, I could see nothing, but outside in the simulated sun, I can make out a good two meters in front of me, albeit tinted green. Ofiera seems impressed that I can see that much; she says it's likely due to my living in the dark Under for a few days.

She also instructs me not to eat or drink anything offered to me at the Celebration, otherwise we run the risk of identifying ourselves as not truly Asters. But my empty stomach doesn't protest—I couldn't eat anything even if I wanted to with the way nervousness chews on my guts.

Hiro will be at the Celebration. That is what both Ofiera and Hemlock said. I have no reason to disbelieve them—I could even sense that Ofiera was telling the truth—but the thought has yet to fully sink in. I'm not sure I'll believe Hiro is with me again even when they stand in front of me and we meet eye to eye.

When we leave the bar, the man with the rose tattoos ushers us to the door and in the same instance welcomes in other revelers, already stumbling despite the early hour of the day. We stick together as a group of Asters would, Ofiera in the middle, since she is the shortest, shuffling in our trailing robes with our heads down.

The other three members of our little party are actual Asters. One is Hemlock, another carrying a bag is Castor, and the third I believe is a woman. They lead us without fail down the street toward the heart of the Celebration and our final destination, the Senate.

At least it *was* the Senate. Now, as the throngs of people part to let us pass—cutting off their cheers of "Earth endures, Mars conquers!" and all wearing stares of hatred and revulsion—I find that Ceres's signs have changed. Between streets, red banners are hung, proclaiming in bold white that the Mother will give an address at the Temple of Ceres at 0900. Of course they turned the damned thing into a church.

The Geans' official religion preaches against idleness and distraction, which you would never catch the Icarii adhering to. While we are multifaithed, I would suspect the majority hold little more than a passing fancy for the Thousand Gods Below the Sun, keeping up their prayers and rituals more out of historical remembrance than true belief. But the Geans are so firmly entrenched in their religion that it makes up one-half of their executive government.

When we kill the Mother today, we cut off one of the Gean snake's twin heads. My mind reels as I think of the implications of our success . . . or failure.

I shove my panic down into the dust at my feet. I will not even entertain the thought of our being caught, not even think that every person here would be happy to rip our guts out and hang us from them in the Senate's lobby if they knew what we aimed to do.

No, they're too distracted. With a religion as oppressive as theirs, any time they can relax, any freedom they experience is quickly over-indulged. We cut down an alley on our way to the back of the Senate turned Temple and find people in the nude coupling in shadowed corners. A few women in dresses tight enough to show every curve and cut high enough for us to catch flashes of the shadow between their legs beckon patrons over with nothing but a look.

A boy in lace approaches us and spits at our feet. "Get lost, cockroaches."

We're more than happy to.

As we slink forward in our huddle, I can feel Ofiera's temper raging on the other end of the implant. I send her a pulse of calm, urging her to erase the anger; that emotion will not suit us here. I feel the heat in her flush away as cooling thoughts of peace replace fury. But underneath it all I feel her resolve, sharp as a mercurial blade.

We reach the back of the Senate and find the small door that leads into the basement where workers enter, unseen by government officials—or church members, now that this is some kind of chapel. Castor produces papers from his robes and hands them to the man on duty, a guard in a navy Gean military uniform trimmed with a single line of gold. Not high ranking, probably some foot soldier who drew the short straw for active duty on a day when all of his friends are getting drunk.

"Paper here says only three work permits," the man says, speaking slowly and enunciating each word. "And I count five of you." We're taller than him, we outnumber him, yet he speaks to us as if we are dim-witted and weak. "Two of you will have to get lost." He holds up two fingers to make a point.

Ofiera says something in Aster, and I'm instantly thankful to Rose for teaching me some rudimentary words. I don't catch all of it, but I understand enough to know she's telling Castor and the woman to continue with their part of the plan—planting the bag Castor carries somewhere. I have a dark suspicion what's inside.

"Stop, stop, stop," the guard says. "Three. T-H-R-E-E." Now he holds up three fingers. "Speak English if you're going to talk at all. This is Gean territory." He fails to realize the irony of his words: Ceres was originally an Aster settlement.

Castor and the woman depart the group without another word, leaving Hemlock, Ofiera, and me with the guard.

"Three," Hemlock says, holding up three fingers and pointing to his forehead, an action dangerously close to the two-fingered gesture the Icarii use as an insult. The guard grits his teeth so that his jaw flexes, but he says nothing.

He spits in our footprints after we pass, mutters something about multiplying cockroaches, and turns his attention back to the compad. Such futile gestures from the man who opened the village gates to wolves dressed as sheep.

AS WE ENTER the bottom level of the Senate, no one glances our way—or if they do, they look away again quickly, expecting us to be here for no other reason than cleaning. I realize with startling pain this was exactly how so many of the duelists were killed in the Fall of Ceres, and I'm not sure how to feel about it.

An Aster walks in with a bomb, but no one looks at them—or if they do, they look at them with revulsion. Hundreds of lives are lost because no one bothered to wonder whether the people who served us actually hated us for our treatment of them, because we were told they *enjoyed* servitude and we believed it. I'm painfully aware that Castor is most likely reenacting that exact same plan elsewhere on Ceres. A distraction for us and what we've come here to do, or something else?

Calm down. I have to calm down. One step at a time. One decision at a time. I reach out to Ofiera, feel her resolve, let it become mine.

Kill the Mother. Yes, that is a thought I can focus on. A strong edge to grasp in my mind.

The three of us ascend the stairs and emerge near a set of oaken double doors where two soldiers stand guard. Hemlock produces our work permits and holds them out with a shaking hand—an affectation or true nervousness?

The first guard takes the papers but barely glances at them before handing the pile back. "Not here," he says. "Inner sanctum isn't for you people."

Hemlock says something in Aster and holds the papers out again toward the second guard, a shorter woman. She waves them away like they would burn her. "You heard him," the woman says. "Rules are rules for a reason."

"Damn," Hemlock says in that hissing whisper of his. Both guards' eyes widen. The woman reaches for her railgun over her shoulder.

Before her fingers finish wrapping around the grip, Ofiera darts forward and jabs a hand into her ribs. Over her shoulder, the woman's face blanches white. Blood trickles from between her lips. Ofiera pulls back with a hidden dagger clutched in her fist.

The man goes for his railgun and ear at the same time—surely to call for backup—but Hemlock hits him in the head with a wild swing of his fist. "Ow!" he snaps, shaking his hand. "Lito, would you—"

The man pulls his railgun into position and points the barrel at Hemlock. I snap and fling myself onto the soldier's back, wrap my arm around his neck, and tighten until only the tips of his boots scuff the ground. A wild shot fires into the air, far too close to my ear so that all I can hear is ringing, but Ofiera disarms him before he fires a second shot. He falls limp in my arms.

I curse—but cannot hear my own voice—as I lay him out on the ground. "They'll have heard us—" I start, but Ofiera stomps a heavy boot onto his temple, crushing his head beneath her heel.

Red splatters all over me.

"*Mierda*, Ofiera!" I rip off my goggles and push back the hood of the wrap. The ringing still pierces like tiny needles in my right ear, but I can hear from my left.

She pulls her goggles down to rest around her neck and removes the hood from her head. Instead of looking at me or the man she killed, she looks at Hemlock. "It's time," she says, and not a second later, a nearby explosion roars through the corridors and the ground rumbles beneath our feet.

"Castor," I say. Neither Hemlock nor Ofiera corrects me.

"The bomb will draw soldiers to Castor's location to extract the Warlord and the members of the Agora, but that doesn't mean you won't have a fight ahead of you," Hemlock says, cradling his wrist in his opposite hand. "I can't guarantee you more than twenty minutes to get in, kill the Mother, and get out."

I want to ask what all this means—what other plan he's put in place alongside ours—but Ofiera draws her mercurial blade from beneath her wraps, and, with a flick, the sword glows to life in standard formation. "Then let's go," she says, and I prepare to follow.

CHAPTER 23

The Mother holds a special place in Gean society as both the head of the Sisterhood and the representative of the Goddess. The Ascension of the Mother is marked by a new Age, and usually occurs every ten to fifteen years under the supervision of the Agora. One can easily see the importance of the Mother when our very years are measured by her rule.

From After the Dead Century *by Jeremy Sim*

"**D**on't be shy," the Mother says, and for a moment, I am a child again and she is the Goddess walking among us in white and gold. Then the illusion breaks and I notice the small things about her that have aged her this past decade—the lines at the corners of her mouth, the white in her blond hair, the dullness of her once-emerald eyes. She gestures for me to come to her, a parent coaxing a hesitant child. "Come now."

But I do not move. Cannot, because I am stunned stupid by her voice. *She speaks.*

She huffs and drops the friendly mask. "We don't have all day, First Sister," she says, losing her soft tone.

My legs march me forward without my consent, large strides that sway my hips and leave me dizzy. I do not walk this way—

Panic claws its way from my stomach up my throat. I sit in a wing-back chair, plush yet stiff with newness. Wind assaults me from the balcony, doors flung open to the closed courtyard where the Mother will address the people later. When I cross one leg over the other in a mirror image of the Mother sitting across from me, I know I am not imagining it: someone else controls my body.

Her?

I open my mouth as if I could scream or beg for answers, but of course—*of course*—nothing comes out. Just because the Mother can speak does not mean I can.

"You do not talk?" the Mother asks, cocking her head, golden flya-ways falling into her face, and that makes her look all the more human, and in that moment, *too* human. "Has Aunt Marshae not granted you that right? Or do you keep silent out of conviction? Don't worry in these chambers, First Sister, no one will—or even can—report you." She giggles like a girl and turns to the skinny wooden table at her side, atop which rests a steaming teacup.

I am too shocked to even shake my head. How would I ever be able to speak, and what does Aunt Marshae have to do with it? They took my voice from me, they put me to sleep and altered my throat somehow, maybe even with the geneassists the Icarii love and only Gean criminals visit.

But then how can she speak freely to ask such questions?

"I see," the Mother says, saucer in one hand while the other dips a silver tea infuser into the cup, in and out, in and out. "You don't know. Aunt Marshae did not deign to tell you, even after she assured us that you were her 'greatest asset' on the *Juno*." She frowns, and I feel like a Little Sister again, my Aunt Delilah disappointed in me. I brace myself for a slap that does not come.

But this is a test; of that I am now sure.

"We are in a unique position since gaining Ceres, First Sister," the Mother continues, as if my mind is not a storm. "It wasn't Warlord Vaughn who made this possible—it was the Sisterhood. We brokered the deal with the Asters to take Ceres. The Warlord simply sent his men once the ink was dry. And now we've consecrated this building as the Temple of Ceres, where my hope is that many Sisters will be raised and taught, just as they are at Olympus Mons."

More women with their throats closed like wilting flowers.

She places the infuser on the table beside her. It leaks onto the real wood. "And soon, the Goddess will put us in charge of all Geans, even the military, and we shall lead them to victories as we did here on Ceres—but oh, listen to me, I'm getting ahead of myself."

Ren was right: the Mother wants to expand the war. And not just that. She means to control *all* of the Gean government by cutting out the Warlord.

She pulls the teacup to her lips, ignoring the cream and sugar on the side table. "Mmm," she moans through puckered lips. "I love it bitter."

My mouth is dry.

"What did you think of my offer to become the First Sister of Ceres?" She holds the teacup with both hands, an offhand gesture, but her eyes, as sharp as gemstones, are cutting and determined. There is nothing casual about her look, and while, at one time, I would have loved to be promoted like this, now there is nothing I want less. "Initially Captain Deluca asked for you to join him in his retirement, but after much prayer with the Agora, he instead put you forward as a candidate."

Arturo, haunting me even here. And the Agora—did they influence his decision to leave me behind? The Mother says it was *prayer* that changed his mind, but I suspect it was *pressure*.

"Then a need arose on the *Juno*, and Aunt Marshae assured us she had the perfect Sister in place to do the Goddess's work. She reported to us often regarding how tirelessly you worked with Captain Saito, how you *wrote* with her."

The Mother offers a disapproving frown when she mentions writing, but all I can do is wonder what Aunt Marshae said in her reports. *Your success is my success, niece.* How deep of a hole did she dig, promising her superiors that *she* was doing good work on the *Juno* by convincing me to betray Ren?

"After Aunt Marshae's last update, I told the Agora that you should be the First Sister of Ceres. I knew we'd have no trouble with you." She smiles at me softly. Sympathetically. Like I am a child. "You're exactly the type of woman we could use here."

Does the Agora know she can talk? *Of course*, a part of me snipes. *They hire the surgeons who do away with our voices.*

She scoffs at my hesitation. "Please tell me you don't hold loyalty to the *Juno*, of all places?"

No. No, not the *Juno*—but her captain . . .

"Ahhh," she says, as if reading my mind. "We come to the heart of the matter."

I try to stand but find my legs arrested beneath me. My fingernails dig into the arms of the chair until my knuckles hurt.

She takes a deep breath of the tea's steam through her nose. "You've grown quite close with Captain Saito, as I commanded you. I'm glad that you're so thorough. That's what I look for in a second."

Second? What in the Goddess is she talking about?

"You received Captain Saito's dossier, didn't you?"

I dip my chin in assent, but even this feels like a betrayal.

"Good. Then tell me everything you know about Captain Saito, anything she said that was different from her dossier, no matter how small, and I will be able to take that as proof to her trial with the Agora. Show me your loyalty in this matter, and not only will you be rewarded as First Sister of Ceres, but I will also make you my second. You could become the Mother when I retire." Her eyes crinkle in the corners. Her mouth has laugh lines. But she is young, not old enough to retire, though she has been the Mother for ten years. Which means, if I accept this, I would work alongside her as her apprentice, like some twisted creature perched on her shoulder.

Goddess . . . did I really just think of the Mother as some sort of puppet master?

Isn't she? a part of me whispers.

"Nod if you understand what I'm asking of you." She pulls the cup away from her mouth so that I can see the stern, flat shape of her lips.

I nod, and I remember Aunt Marshae's words. *This is your last chance.*

"Good," she says, and puts the teacup on the side table. Some liquid sloshes out, joining the puddle the infuser sits in. The tea washes across the table, begins to trickle over the edge. I watch it falling—*drip, drip, drip*—unable to look at her.

I see her move from the corner of my eye, and something flares like heat in my head, followed by a sharp pop. The beginning of a headache disappears just as quickly as it came on, and I realize, with detached clarity, it felt more like a cage unlocking. I slump forward in my chair, whatever held me there now released.

I suck in cold air as perspiration beads my forehead, trickles down my temples into my hair. "Ahh . . ." That noise. From my throat? "What—"

I stop. I look around the room for the source of the voice. The Mother sits watching, lips curled into a smirk. Mouth closed.

The shakes start in my hands. Travel into my chest, then down into my legs. Even my face trembles as it all overwhelms me—fear, anger, excitement, shock.

The room—the room I can hardly pay attention to despite its fine wood and bound books and shimmering glass doors and paintings of pastoral scenes—blurs until I can see only the Mother clearly in front of me.

"I . . ."

I test it. My voice.

This is what my voice sounds like.

"I am . . ."

I place my hand on my throat.

It is not cut. It is not genetically altered. It is whole.

I can talk.

I am speaking.

"It's called a neural implant," the Mother says. "The Icarii have used them in their duelists for hundreds of years."

The Icarii use such technology, but for us to do so as well is forbidden. Or should be. Is anything about the Sisterhood as I believed it to be?

"Now that you've demonstrated your zeal, now that you've earned the right to your voice, I will show you how to operate the implant, even how to command someone to do your bidding," she says. "I've turned yours off so that we can speak as equals, one woman to another."

I say nothing. I am too shocked, and perhaps too familiar with my longtime companion, silence.

Now that you've earned the right to your voice . . .

She leans forward, elbows on her knees, as if to meet me in the middle of the room. "Now," she says, "tell me everything about Saito Ren."

She did this to me. She did this to every girl in the Sisterhood. She put us to sleep. Invaded our bodies with something forbidden. Took away our ability to speak—no, not the ability, just the memory of how we did it. I can see it now, as air fills my lungs, as a scream builds inside me.

I place my hand on the back of my neck at the top of my spine. It *hurts.*

"Why?" I use my words, words through numb lips, and still the sound of my voice makes my ears ache, echoing in my skull and rooting into my brain. It is all but unrecognizable, having been gone from my life for years. It is deeper than I remember, more sonorous. But it is *mine.*

"We have some evidence that Saito Ren is not who she says she is, that she is a traitor, a double agent since her return from the Icarii. They're the ones who patched her up with that hack job on her arm and leg—I'm sure you've seen it." The Mother sneers. "But we need *more* evidence, like firsthand testimony that you can provide. If the

Sisterhood brings forth the truth of Saito Ren when Warlord Vaughn traded so much for her return, we can finally wrest control from that doddering old fool and command the whole of the Geans. We will lead them to victory and the light of the Goddess."

"No, not that," I say. I am surprised at the strength in my voice. It is harder than I remember as well. "Why did you take—" I press my hand to my throat.

The Mother leans back in her chair, back straight, so poised—I'm sure her Auntie would be proud.

I cannot help but laugh at that thought, and my voice, actual *laughter*, fills the air so that I cannot stop once I start, and I begin laughing at my laugh like a snake consuming its own tail.

I laugh until tears sting my eyes.

I laugh until they roll down my cheeks.

"First Sister." The Mother's voice is stern. Controlled. Scornful. "I understand this comes as a shock to you and that you must have many questions, but"—she clears her throat, drops her voice so that she sounds like honey, sweeter and imploring, like I'm some greenboy she wants to manipulate—"you don't want me to have to tell the Agora that you weren't willing to aid the Sisterhood, do you? Aunt Marshae assured us you would cooperate, but if you won't . . . I can always name someone else the First Sister of Ceres. It will be as easy to take the title away as it was to give it."

I say nothing, and the Mother's facade fades until her frustration shows in the lines of her face.

"Quickly, First Sister. The Agora is waiting. The Warlord too. Saito Ren will go to trial today, one way or another. I will testify, with your words or without them."

If she didn't need my words, need *me,* she wouldn't offer me such a reward as Ceres, so again I say nothing, the silence my familiar ally.

The Mother leans closer to me. "Tell me," she commands, all hardness and anger, "about Saito Ren."

The message I wrote feels heavier in my pocket.

I love you. I never want to leave you.

Ren. My captain. My love.

This is your last chance, Aunt Marshae says in my mind.

This woman took everything from me, and still she wants to take more. Take and take and take, like a ravenous black hole sucking up everything around her—light and love and my very right to *live*.

I *hate* her.

But there is someone who will protect me. Someone who would even kill for me.

"Ringer!" I cry as loud as I can—and it sounds like an explosion. The ground trembles beneath us, and I scream, so loud I cannot hear the Mother's response.

I see her mouth moving when I peek through my parted fingers.

See the door open, Ringer filling the frame.

See him dart forward with a soldier's speed and seize the Mother by her dress.

See her eyes widen in shock.

See Ringer's hand form a fist and smash into the Mother's fragile face.

See the Mother's nose spurt warm red blood.

My hand twitches. My knuckles ache. Blood splashes, dappling surroundings. Staining my dress. My hands. Cold against my hot fury.

Ringer's fist strikes her again and again.

I do not stop him. I simply watch.

CHAPTER 24

There are few things more powerful than the bond between a Rapier and Dagger. Breaking that bond requires an act of loyalty stronger even than the memory of love.

High Commander Beron val Bellator of the Icarii Special Forces

With our cover blown so quickly, we have little hope of getting out of this alive—but the adrenaline coursing through my veins and my implant singing alongside Ofiera's prevent me from feeling even the smallest twinge of fear.

I pull my mercurial blade from beneath my wraps, give it life with a thought. I feel whole again, the blade an extension of my arm and a symbol of all that I have worked for as a duelist.

I lead the way through the door. Already guards swarm the hallway, ten in all. Three break from the crowd and rush at us, railguns braced against their shoulders and aimed to kill. Without a word, I nudge Ofiera to the left, and I dart right.

I focus on a single opponent and measure the diameter of battle. The first soldier raises her railgun. I slip beneath the shot, dropping low into a squat, then coming at her middle. She's no match for me. I gut her and move on to the next.

It isn't until I have bested two other guards that I realize Hemlock has not followed us into the hallway. I send Ofiera the feeling of confusion, but she sends back calm. He's probably gone to continue Castor's work of creating a distraction for us.

Kill the Mother. That's my mission, so that's what I'll focus on. Not Hemlock, not their plan, not the world around us, or the memories of Luce—

Here. Now. Diameter of battle. Jump. Slice. Blood.

Others fall at my feet. My shoulder aches, but I ignore it.

We dart around the curve in the hallway, eight bodies lying in our wake. The remaining two guards have gotten smart after we dispatched their colleagues. They've ripped a door from a storage closet off its hinges and cower behind it as if that will stop our blades.

Without Ironskins, the Geans are like paper for us to knife through, and these men and women in navy uniforms don't have any of the tech we do, just shirts that are sliced as easily as skin.

One guard pulls something off his back and points it at us. It's larger than a railgun, and it takes me a precious three seconds to realize that it's heating up with an orange glow.

"Lito!"

I'm not sure if Ofiera cries out over the implant or with her voice, but I jump sideways and crash into the wall just as a spattering of red beams scorches the air. I cast a quick glance behind me, see that the hallway is peppered with holes.

Thousand gods, he's got an Icarii HEL cannon, and that could've been my chest.

"Ofiera!" I call her name, pushing an image into her mind. She runs toward me, and I lace my fingers together, brace my cradled hands against my stomach. Her left foot leads her, jumping into the stirrup I've created, and I push her up toward the ceiling with all my might. She takes flight like a bird, arms outstretched, mercurial blade curling like a scimitar.

The guard traces her path, pointing the HEL cannon's mouth up at the projectile coming for him. But I rush forward in a straight line and push my mercurial blade into the door, skewering him on the other side. His scream gurgles with blood. The HEL cannon falls to the ground.

With a flip, Ofiera lands on the other side of the barrier. I withdraw my blade, and the door falls flat, the dead guard on top of it. Ofiera's blade pierces the last soldier's neck as he reaches for the fallen HEL cannon. His eyes dim. He hits the floor with a thump.

She nods to the ornate double doors beside us. "Through here is the wing where they're keeping the Mother," Ofiera says, a piece of hair stuck to the corner of her lips. "We'll fight to make it to her antechamber, then bar the door against reinforcements. One of us will guard the entry point while the other locates and neutralizes the target."

Neutralize. What a wholesome word for slaughter. "I'll kill her," I say, calling a spade a spade. "That's my mission." From the Icarii and Asters both.

Ofiera's eyes harden, but she says nothing. Under her breath, she counts to three, then flings the door open and rushes forward. I have to remember that she is Command, was Hiro's Rapier, and is used to going first even if I'm unaccustomed to having anyone lead me.

The soldiers in the Mother's wing stand ready. Each of the twelve is straight-backed and strong, dressed in a white-and-gold uniform I've never seen before. A special guard for the Mother herself?

Their faces are blank slates, eyes bulging and glassy in a drug-like fervor. There is something off-putting about them, and a chill runs down my spine when, without a word to the others, half withdraw into a room at their backs, most likely moving to exfiltrate the Mother. I point them out to Ofiera. Time's ticking.

"Focus!" she snaps, and I barely have time to jerk my attention back to the lead guard before an electric whip flies past my face. I stumble into the wall and meet the white guard's stoic face—emotionless, unreadable—before finding my feet again.

"What the fuck are they?"

"Trouble," Ofiera says, stepping closer to me.

The white guards line up in a V formation across the entirety of the hallway and withdraw hilts that look suspiciously like our mercurial blades. But when each flares to life, it is a long, curling whip sparking with electricity like the weapon of an Ironskin.

"Shit." That's all I have time to say before all the whips come rushing toward us.

I successfully dodge one, only to almost fling myself into another. I can feel Ofiera on the other side of my implant—measured, but not calm—doing the same as me, trying her best to jump and spin closer to the white guards without skewering ourselves on the pattern of their attacks.

But there *is* a pattern—and it is mathematical. How are they attacking without saying a thing? How are they predicting which pattern the guards at their sides will use?

"Lito!"

Ofiera sends me the same image as before—her in the stirrup, my flinging her toward the attackers—and I cry back, "Go!"

She runs at me, whips flying after, and I boost her into the air. Two whips come at me where I stand still, and in the precious second before they hit me, I fling myself to the floor to dodge one and roll to avoid the other. The scar on my shoulder roars in pain and I hear Ofiera let out a high-pitched screech, but I'm back up on my feet half a second later, having covered some of the gap between me and the white guards.

Ofiera lands on one of the two at the point of the triangle, her blade skewering his throat. But her shoulder drips blood from a successful attack. I take the chance Ofiera has opened, and as another of the white guards turns to attack her, I rush at his back and stab my blade through his heart.

Two down . . . and Ofiera has broken their formation, even if she sacrificed her left arm to do it, so they are forced to shift themselves to a new arrangement to deal with us at close range. Of the remaining four, two turn to focus on me while the others watch Ofiera.

Again, without a word, they attack. Two men sling whips at Ofiera, but I have no time to see how she fares before the other two are on me.

Is this how an Ironskin feels, fighting two duelists at once, not knowing which way to look first?

A whip comes so close to my side, I feel its electricity shiver through my muscles.

No, I think as I push myself into a run at one of the two men, *at least an Ironskin has a shield!*

A whip comes flying at my chest, and I slam onto my knees, skidding across the ground, and aim to gut him with my blade. He steps sideways—so like a duelist—as his companion aims at me. The tip of his whip slices across my back, and I feel hot, angry blood soak into my Aster wraps.

Not deep—I can feel from the implant it's not fatal—and I am so focused on the man in front of me, on killing one of these two, that I slice at the man's ankle as I roll away.

He doesn't scream. Did I miss?

I push myself up and spin back to them, see the man lying on the ground, face unreadable, not even twitching with pain. Blood gushes from the stump of his shin, his foot not two meters from him, but his partner continues to fight without care.

What *are* these white guards?

Ofiera comes to my side, sending me a pulse of calm so I don't round and attack her. She's soaked in blood, but only the blood on her left arm is hers.

"They have neural implants," she says, holding one of the white guards' heads up by the hair, gore and bones dangling below the neck, before tossing it back to the others.

I didn't see the implant, but I believe her. My guts twist. I thought Hemlock had only been selling neural implants to the military as recently as the Fall of Ceres. Then when were these white guards created?

"Two left," I say as the remaining guards step shoulder to shoulder. Are they even now communicating through their neural implants?

"Two and a half," she says, nodding to the footless man trying desperately to push himself into a sitting position, ignoring that he's knocking on death's door. With a neural implant, he wouldn't feel even a hint of pain if he didn't want to.

Is that what's making them wordless, emotionless killers, able to slip into unspoken patterns and attack as one? *Like Icarii infantry drones*, I think with a shiver.

Ofiera produces a knife from somewhere in her wraps and, a heartbeat later, the man without a foot has a throwing dagger sticking from his neck. "Now there's two."

Standing side by side, the remaining white guards don't know how to deal with an experienced pair of duelists. We move uniformly, dancing partners who have finally learned each other's rhythms.

One, two, three—parry the whips that come flying at our torsos.

One, two, three—step sideways in a defensive stance that leaves nothing open to attack.

One, two, three—duck the whips that swing back like pendulums.

One, two, three—take the opening and go for the neck.

Mirroring each other, Ofiera and I slice sideways and part heads from bodies. The last two white guards fall dead to the ground.

"There are still six more," Ofiera says, and I know what she really means: We are wounded. We are tired. During our struggle with the first set of white guards, the remainder likely had time to seize the Mother and hide her away from us.

My shoulder aches, and I rub it halfheartedly. We have only the smallest chance to catch up with them, defeat them, and kill the Mother . . . but there is no other choice than to try.

"Let's go."

My stomach pitches with dread as Ofiera rushes for the door that leads deeper into the Mother's wing. But she stops short when she reaches the other side, and I almost run into her. Instantly I see what made her freeze up. The remaining six white guards, bleeding out on the ground, holes from a laser weapon smoking on the backs of their heads. The door to the Mother's antechamber, already flung open.

Who could have pulled this off, killing these emotionless soldiers while they were focused in the opposite direction? Only someone they trusted . . .

I rush around Ofiera and barrel into the antechamber, so I'm the one who sees the culprit first. Ofiera comes up behind me, silent as my own shadow, and gasps in surprise as she claps eyes on who awaits us.

"I didn't think you'd make it this far," Ofiera says.

But I stop hearing her. I don't even feel her on the other end of the implant anymore. It takes all my strength to keep myself upright.

"Lito," the figure begins.

Hiro's voice speaks to me out of Saito Ren's mouth.

No. It can't be. A tall, dark-haired woman with a bloodstained Gean naval uniform and a HEL gun in the palm of a stark white hand.

Saito Ren's face, but beneath it, Hiro's.

I'll always recognize you, Lucinia told me. *Even now it's like seeing your face through water.* And I understand, catching a glimpse of Ren one moment, Hiro the next.

My mercurial blade slips through my fingers, crashes to the floor.

"Hiro."

I know they are Hiro, even if they are changed. Even if the gene-assists did their work so well that Hiro's face resembles Saito Ren's starkly. For a moment I am in the park all those months ago, facing down Saito Ren's Ironskin with Hiro at my side.

But . . . this is Hiro.

I am the fox, the shape-shifter, wearing a mask, they said, and now I see it all.

They turn to me, so slowly, their brows furrowed together. They've never looked like this—*afraid*—before, like they don't want me to see them this way.

And this . . . what have Beron and the military *done* to them?

"What have they done?" I raise my hands, stumble toward them, but pull back at the last second. I can't cross that invisible line they have drawn between us.

"Lito . . ."

Hiro's arm and leg. They're gone. I cut them off Ren, but now they're missing from Hiro—

"Did they do this to you?" My eyes burn. I want to hold Hiro, but they don't move toward me even a centimeter. "Did they take your limbs—for *this*?"

I can't shove away the anguish fast enough, my implant useless against the anger that swells up inside me. And truly, I don't want to. I *want* to feel this churning ocean of grief. I want to suffer it. The way Hiro drops their eyes, I know . . . Command took their limbs, changed their face, made *them* into *she* so that they could complete this damned mission.

"What have they done to you?" I ask again. I take one more step toward Hiro, but then feel an icy chill descend over me.

Calm. Peace. Serenity.

I struggle against it; I don't want these emotions when I am so upset over Hiro.

"Stop it," I snap at Ofiera.

She frowns, but doesn't speak.

Finally, Hiro does.

"I told you not to come," Hiro says, and again I can see both Hiro and Ren in the movement of their lips.

Hiro turns their back on me to leave, but I don't let them go. My heart screaming, I stumble forward and throw my arms around their shoulders and hold them in place. They're taller now, their head brushing the bottom of my chin instead of falling on my chest, and I close my eyes and push my nose into their black hair. The color is wrong. So unlike them to be muted and plain. But the smell. Thousand gods, I breathe them in and feel like I am home for the first time in a year.

The words we said all those years ago at the Academy, the words Hiro reminded me of in their recordings, come back to me now. *I'll make sure you stay you, okay? And you make sure that I stay me.*

"If we lose ourselves," I whisper to them, "we lose ourselves together."

A shudder runs through Hiro. Their head dips. A little sob escapes them. Then they slouch, melting into my arms. Accepting that I am here with them. That we are together.

My heart races, but not with fear. I found them. *I found them.*

But the moment is over too soon, and when Hiro turns to face me, their eyes are filled with tears.

"We're almost done now, Lito. Soon it will all be over. Plenty of time for tears after all that." They wipe their face with a navy Gean sleeve, then start toward the Mother's chambers.

I do not even pick up my mercurial blade as I follow.

CHAPTER 25

I wish the truth had been revealed to me before I became what I am. Would I have been able to take on the mantle of the Mother if the Agora had shown me the darkness that awaited me? But if this is what the Goddess requires of me, She shall find me willing. The Warlord, that old buffoon, is unable to enact Her design. I am the only one strong enough to ensure that Her children will survive. The meager pickings we scavenge from the Icarii aren't enough anymore to slow down the wilting of our planets. But to bring the Icarii back to our flock, we first must annihilate their pride. We will take something that the Icarii hold dear, even if we must ally ourselves with the strayed mutants among the asteroids.

Ceres. It all comes down to Ceres.

From the journal of Mother Isabel III

◇—————◇◇◇—————◇

The door opens behind us—hadn't Ringer kicked it open?—and the Mother collapses to the ground at Ringer's feet.

At *my* feet. Ringer is gone. Vanished, as if he were never here at all.

She sucks in greedy breaths of air, blood streaking her swelling face. I am also breathing so heavily my head spins. But the person in the doorway is the last I thought I'd see.

"Ren—"

"First Sister." Pain is written in every stretched line of her face. She doesn't seem surprised to hear me speak, which makes me wonder just how much she knew about the Mother and—what did she call it, the implant?

"Ringer protected me—" But I turn around in a full circle and can't find him. When did he slip out? Where did he go?

"Ringer?" Ren repeats. She glances about and shoots me a confused look when she doesn't see anyone else.

Two more people appear, dressed in bloodied Aster wraps. The first is a small woman with dark hair and serious eyes. I can tell immediately from the way she holds herself that, despite what she wears, she is a soldier. She has a nasty cut on her arm and in her hand is the hilt of a quicksilver blade; these two are Icarii warriors, then.

The other is a tall, handsome man with sun-starved olive skin and warm, liquid brown eyes ringed by thick lashes like a girl's. He moves with the grace of a dancer but the power of a stalking wolf. Though his hair and eyes are natural colors, he is like the other Icarii I've seen, beautiful and frightening all at once.

He does not look away from Ren, his eyes like hollow pits.

Who are these people? Where did Ringer go?

"Ren," I say, because I don't know what else to say. *Ren, Ren, Ren.* I love the sound of her name now that I can form the word, the pursing of lips, tongue touching the roof of my mouth. I want to cry for help, but all I say is "Ren . . ."

"*Bitch,*" the Mother curses at me, her voice hoarse after screaming. "The Goddess will smite you!"

"How much did she tell you?" Ren asks, coming to stand just in front of the Mother.

The woman looks up, hair frizzing into a golden halo around her head, and sneers at Ren. "Traitor," she spits.

Ren ignores her.

"I can talk." I shiver and take a step closer to Ren. I wish she would hold me like she did on the *Juno*. I wish she would kiss me again and make all of this go away. "She wants me to be the First Sister of Ceres, even become her second, the next Mother after she retires. But only if I tell her everything you've said to me. I was scared, and Ringer came to save me."

"Ringer?" Ren asks again, and frowns.

"Yes, Ringer . . ."

"And what happened when the bomb went off?" Ren prompts.

I open my mouth, then close it again. When I was screaming . . . was there an explosion?

I think this is the most I've spoken in my entire life. I am used to eyes on me, but not like this—not for what I *say*. I am uncomfortable beneath everyone's gaze.

The female warrior closes the door, starts to push one of the wingback chairs against it.

"Don't bother, Ofiera," Ren says. "They'll send Ironskins as reinforcements. Chairs won't hold against them."

The soldier—Ofiera—frowns, but stops as commanded.

The Mother was right. Ren can command quicksilver warriors? She *is* an Icarii traitor.

"Kill the Mother, Lito," Ren says. "Complete your mission."

"Wait—" the Mother gasps as Ren takes a step toward her.

"Hiro—" The other quicksilver warrior, Lito, clenches his hands into fists. Ofiera offers him the hilt of a blade, but he ignores it and her.

The frustration wells up within me until my eyes are burning, but I refuse to cry now, even if it is out of anger. "Ren, what is happening?" I cross the gap that has formed between us and press my hand to her biceps. I feel the cold of her prosthetic even through her navy jacket.

Ren doesn't look at me. Lito growls as he steps to Ren's other side. "We deserve to know, Hiro."

Hiro . . . Who is Hiro?

My nails dig into Ren's jacket even though I know she can't feel it. I want to grab her cheeks and turn her face toward me so that she will finally see me. It's like she hasn't even looked at me since she walked in, and I want to yell at her as if this is all her fault.

Maybe it is. The Mother said she was working with the Icarii, and she told me true.

The words build until they overflow. "How could you betray the Geans? Why does he call you Hiro?" *And Goddess wither it, where did Ringer go?*

Ren turns to me, placing the quicksilver warriors at her back. Lito openly glares at her but doesn't leave her side, and I have the strangest feeling that he is not so much angry at Ren as protecting her. From me?

"First Sister," Ren says, and finally takes me in. Everything other than her fades away. Her dark eyes swallow me whole like the cosmos; her smoky voice drops to a whisper. "Little dove, what did the Mother tell you about the neural implant?"

My hand slides down her arm, falls to my side. "She kept me from talking. She took my voice away with that thing in my brain, forbidden technology of the Icarii."

"And Ringer?"

"Where did he go?" I look around the room. How did he disappear so quickly? "He came to save me when I called him, and he grabbed the Mother and—"

"No, little dove. Look at your hands. Really *think* about what you saw, not what you wanted to see."

Ren gently takes my wrists and pulls my hands up for me to see. They're a bloody ruin.

How?

I called for Ringer because I was scared, the door opened, and he came into the room.

But Ren opened the door when she entered.

Ringer was gone, and the last place I had seen him was the podship. My hands are bloody.

The Mother laughs one harsh, loud bark of a laugh. "You're damaged," the Mother says. "You've been damaged by the implant, and we never knew!" She dissolves into giggles, curling into her lap as her shoulders shake.

"Neural degradation," Lito says. His face shows shock. "They're using the neural implants in the priestesses just like the white guards . . ."

"What are they—"

"You were hitting the Mother when we entered the room, little dove," Ren says. Her voice is barely above a whisper, but I feel as if she is shouting at me.

"No, that's not true—"

Really think *about what you saw.*

"I . . ." What did I see?

I close my eyes. I see nothing. I feel . . . I feel the tension in my knuckles. I feel the burn of scratches across the backs of my hands and wrists. I feel the implant burning in my brain. The warmth of blood on my hands.

She's damaged.

No . . . no, no, no . . .

She's been damaged by the implant.

Neural degradation.

My head fills with fire. My legs shake, threatening to give out beneath me, but I feel a strong pair of hands gripping my shoulders, holding me up.

"Ren . . ."

I open my eyes. Lito holds me. He furrows his brows as if he too is swallowed by this tragedy.

Dark-eyed boy, what would you know about pain?

Really think *about what you saw.*

It all comes crashing down, this paper house I've built.

Ringer made me feel safe, so he appeared when I needed him,

always knowing what I wanted to say without my having to say it, never wanting to sleep with me when all other soldiers did.

"No," I say, my voice wobbling. "Hringar Grimson is a soldier. He is from the Selene settlement."

Ren stares down at the Mother, who laughs even harder. Lito's face softens with compassion.

Damn quicksilver boy! I shove him away. I don't want his pity.

Ringer stood by my side when the amber-eyed girl who was Second Sister was stripped of her rank and killed. He visited me when I was hurt. I wrote him letters begging for his help. He attacked Second Sister to stop her from blackmailing me.

Really think *about what you saw.*

It was me . . . It was always me.

I comforted myself. I threatened Second Sister with death. I hurt the Mother. *My* hands.

I tried to kill her.

Ringer is . . . me.

Was his story just that—a story I had heard, a story I had read? With the thousands of soldiers' confessions rattling about in my head, I have heard about all sorts of lives. As a child, I read everything I could get my hands on in the orphanage. Did I allow a pleasant fantasy to replace my grim reality?

And his sister—the girl I wanted to be, who was saved from the Sisterhood because of her bravery?

Not real. Not real. Not real.

Really think *about what you saw.*

My legs give out. No one catches me this time, and I collapse to the ground. The tears roll down my cheeks unbidden.

"I'm sorry, little dove," Ren says, but she doesn't help me up. "Kill the Mother, Lito, so you can go home." She touches Lito's shoulder as softly as she would touch me. "You need to go. Get out of here before the Ironskins come. Hemlock's bomb let me slip away from the Agora, but it didn't give us infinite time."

"What about you, Hiro?" Lito says.

Ren shakes her head.

"Fuck that," Lito spits with ire. "What are we supposed to do—leave you here?"

Ren doesn't answer. She meets my eyes. All I see is a shattered person, pieces glued together but run through with cracks.

We both are nothing but broken dolls now.

In the moment when no one is looking at her, the Mother jumps to her feet and rushes for the door—and she's so close—she's been moving away from us this whole time, using me as a distraction—

But Ofiera bounds after her, seizing her arm and twisting it behind her back, forcing her to kneel with a cry of agony.

"If you can't, I will, Lito," Ofiera says, holding the Mother with one hand and offering up a quicksilver blade in the other.

"If you do it, the Goddess will smite you!" the Mother yells. "I am the incarnation of the Goddess in this world! I can give you whatever you want, or curse your souls!"

Lito takes a blade from Ofiera and grips it tightly. "Dammit, I'm not doing anything until you explain, Hiro!"

Ren snatches the Mother up by her wrist. "No!" the Mother shouts.

"Relax. I'm just going to tie you up," Ren says.

Lito stiffly nods, and Ofiera comes to Ren's side, offering her strips of her wraps to tie the Mother's hands tightly behind her back and gag her so she stops speaking. *Now you know how it feels*, I think as I watch her struggling. Even if I cannot make out her words, I know she is cursing us.

I push myself to my feet, wobbling a bit. I grab the nearby table to steady myself. My hand falls into the tea the Mother spilled. It's cold now. "Please," I say. "Tell me what is going on, Ren."

Lito comes to my side, and somehow I *feel* him there, just as curious as me. I don't understand what this tether is between us as we reach out toward Ren, but we are united, him and I, in one common goal.

"All right," Ren says, and she has a little half smile on her face and mischief in her eyes like the captain I know—or thought I knew. "You've come this far. I'll tell you what I can in the time we have left."

I feel Ren reach out for me, not with her hand but mentally. I feel her mind open up like a blooming flower, connecting to me, to Lito, to Ofiera. The four of us becoming one. Seeing directly into Ren's memories, stored in the neural implant like a recording. The image of a fox dances across my vision.

Suddenly, I am seeing the truth of Hiro val Akira.

PLAY:
▶ BONUS TRACK

———◇——◈——◇———

I come to with an oxygen mask over my mouth. The lights above me flare and fade, flare and fade, as a woman in blood red wheels my bed down a hallway. I try to see more of my surroundings, but I'm bound at my wrists and ankles.

Fuck. Everything hurts. くそ.

"Lito?" My voice cracks with disuse. "Lito!"

My twisted limbs, my bloodied face, my punctured torso—every time the pain flares, I kill it. Lito might find clarity in the pain, but I don't. I'm weak, and I fucking hate it. I rage against it as much as my captivity.

"Lito!" I cry until my throat strains hoarse. "リトはどこですか?" The woman in red abandons me beneath harsh blue-tinted lighting. "Where is Lito? リト! Lito sol Lucius—" She doesn't even look at me when she closes the door between us, sealing me off from the rest of the world.

In the quiet, I scream. Not simply because I hurt, not solely because I am frustrated—though I am—but because I think the silence will fucking kill me. A dead soldier doesn't speak, and so long as I am alive, I

295

will yell, I will hurl invectives, I will rock until this damn bed tips over and spills me out and I smother to death beneath the sheets and heavy metal.

"I demand to speak to a superior officer! I demand to speak to my partner, Lito sol Lucius! Do you know who I am? I demand to speak to my father, Souji val Akira! I have rights!"

On and on, shit pouring from my lips. No one comes to stop me, though I know they're listening with their cameras and their wires. I can even imagine my father on the other side of a monitor, watching me as little pixels, straining against my bindings, reopening my wounds until my bandages are stained red, spittle flecking my lips. He'll shake his head. He'll turn away. I have always been the family embarrassment.

I cease when the door opens. A second bed is wheeled in. I have no idea how many hours it's been.

"Are you quite done?" a man in military blacks asks, but I don't even look at him.

It's the sight of Lito in the second bed that calms me, that finally slaps the words right out of my mouth. He's awake, but clearly on something that's thrown him for a loop. He's bandaged around his chest and left arm. "Hiro . . ." Lito's smile is sloppy, and he looks more like he did when we first met and he was a gangly boy and his nose was too big for his face.

But he's alive. Thousand fucking gods, he's alive, and that's all I care about. We almost died on Ceres. I had been fighting so that he, at least, would escape after the Ironskin went down. After all that Hemlock had told me and I ignored—*my fault, my fault, my fault*—I didn't give a damn if I died so long as Lito could live. But somehow, through luck or the gods, we're both here. Even if *here* is some dark basement, and we're both bedridden and bleeding.

"Lito . . ."

"Use up all of your words, Hiro?" Beron val Bellator steps between my bed and Lito's, but there's no kindness in my commander's face. We have never liked each other, Beron and I—he reminds me of how much my father watches me, while I remind him that, despite our differences in rank, I am more powerful than him, and all because of my name: val Akira. "Shame, because here I thought we'd have a lot to talk about."

Of course he's here to torment me. Asshole. "Oh, trust me, I always have spare words for you, Beron." I lean back into the bed as if I have never been more comfortable. All a show. "How about calling my father for me? I'm sure he'd be eager to know about the shitty conditions you've been holding me in."

"We've already been in touch with him." Beron's face would put even the most experienced gambler to shame. "He's aware of the situation."

"Then why am I still here? Why can't I leave?"

Beron smiles.

A chill runs down my spine.

It finally happened. I think of my mother's empty place at the table. *Father sold me out.*

"You should thank your deities of choice that Lito saved you," Beron says. "He dragged you and that Ironskin pilot onto a podship. Managed to blast off from Ceres and set a course for Icarii space. We picked you up, found the two of you almost as dead as that pilot."

"Saito Ren?" I almost choke on my words. "He brought her too—"

But he ignores me and pulls my attention back to my partner, pale as milk in the bed next to mine. "Lito has extensive nerve damage," Beron says. "It'll be a while before he's ready to return to active duty. I asked him what I could, but he's not fully coherent."

I look at my partner and listen to the steady beeping of the machines monitoring him. He's drifted off sometime during my conversation with Beron, and his face is soft with sleep. I hope it is dreamless, after all that we have seen.

"Hiro, we have some questions for you about the Fall of Ceres."

I had prepared a hundred smartass remarks for Beron, but nothing for that. "What do you mean, the 'Fall of Ceres'?"

"Ceres has fallen to the Geans." The slash of Beron's lips falls with the gravity of his words. Though he doesn't voice his anger, I see it in his eyes. Instead, reserved, he asks, "How did you and Lito survive?"

"Supply run. We weren't in the city when the bomb went off."

Beron narrows his eyes, and I wonder what he might have heard, what he might know, that makes him act like this. Is he suspicious of me?

It would be more suspicious if I groveled and acted contrite. Instead I smirk as much as I can, which isn't much with half my face bandaged and the other half swollen and bruised. "We came back to find shit had hit the fan, then retreated to an emergency evac site."

"And when did you kill the Ironskin pilot?"

"*After* shit hit the fan, but *before* I almost died on the shuttle." I make a show of yawning. "Shouldn't I be resting so I can heal?"

But Beron doesn't rise to my bait. He tamps down the anger even if he's too old for a neural implant.

"Wake me if you need me," I say, closing my eyes.

"Oh, I will, Hiro." I jump when I feel Beron's hand against my hair, stroking like I am some fucking pet of his. There's something hard in his eyes that I've never seen before when he whispers, "We have great plans for you."

"The hell is that supposed to mean?" My heart beats so heavily I have to force my implant to quell my fear.

But Beron only smiles, and it is such a believable mask that a weaker person might think there is kindness in him. "Rest up, Hiro. You'll have a new mission soon enough."

Ofiera fon Bain is a plain woman. Her arms are a little too long while her torso is squat. Her hair is shit brown, her eyes a shade lighter and flat. She suffers from a face that makes her look like a bitch, a problem with which I am intimately familiar. But she wears a rapier and dagger crossed on her shoulder, marking her as Command.

Beron likes her, which means we'll never get along.

"With Lito out of commission for the foreseeable future and a mission of utmost importance that has fallen directly into our laps, we are assigning you a new Rapier."

I open my mouth to protest, but only manage to weakly groan. "Nnnaaa . . ." I've been so numb recently, high on the medication they force into my veins, that I haven't been able to keep track of everything they've done to me. A couple of surgeries to patch up the worst of my wounds from Ceres, I guess, but I hurt so often with such an overwhelming storm of pain that even the implant can't kill it all.

"Get up, Hiro," Beron commands.

As much as I want to tell him to fuck off, I find my arms pushing back the covers, my legs flinging themselves over the side of the bed. "Ber . . ." My words are still slurred, but my movements are sharp, every bit a soldier in fighting shape. Except—

Except my limbs aren't right. The ground is farther away than normal, like I'm wearing heels. Or . . . I'm taller? "Wha . . . what . . ."

"Keep them calm," Beron says to Ofiera, and every bit of fear evaporates out of me—*poof*—like some ancient ice-pick lobotomy just scrambled my brain. I didn't tell my implant to do that, but I'm calm just the same.

I should feel horrified as I march myself to the full-length mirror on the back of the door. I should feel like throwing up at the person I see in the mirror—*not me*.

But I stand calmly. I say nothing. My eyes rove from my feet to my face.

Not my leg. Not my arm. Not my body. Not my face. *Not my* fucking *face*.

"You and Ren had a lot of similarities," Beron says. "Well, enough of them. Who knows, maybe the two of you can trace your family tree back to the same roots."

Of course he would think that, as if only one Japanese family left Earth. "ばかやろう!" I scream. "You racist—"

But the cold hand descends on me again, and my voice is stolen from me.

"Look at the facts, Hiro. You speak the same languages as Saito Ren, and you needed minimal surgery to become her." Beron's face twitches as he fights a smile, fails. "Or would you rather Lito undertake this mission? If you don't feel up to it, there's always him . . ."

Now I am silent by choice. I have no doubt that, even though they have exercised their butchery on me, they would do the same to Lito if I threw him to these wolves to save my own skin. And what would it take to re-form him? Shortening his legs, twisting his genetic profile, and even then . . . His Japanese is terrible. He's no actor. I am the Dagger, the underhanded spy, of the two of us. A sinister Lefthand, through and through.

I can't look in the mirror. My eyes meet Beron's instead, glare with every ounce of hatred I possess.

But it's not just him, I realize. I look toward the camera in the corner of the room and push my feelings into this unfamiliar face. I want it to say: *I know what you're doing to me. I know this is punishment. I know you're there, Father, you and your monster, watching me fall.*

"I'll go," I say. My voice is hard. I refuse to give them any pleasure from this.

"Good choice, Hiro. Or perhaps I should call you Commander Saito?" Beron mocks me with a loose salute. "You'll return to the Geans soon, Saito Ren, and then you'll destabilize the whole of Ceres and kill the Mother."

It takes me two months before I am stable enough to be out of my bed for more than a few minutes. The nurses release me from my restraints only to guide me through exercises with my new prosthetics that send my muscles into violent spasms. My entire body aches and burns, twisting in excruciating memory of what I've lost.

Afterward, I'm strapped back into bed, my only activity reading through Saito Ren's history and staring at the ceiling until it becomes familiar.

When Beron comes to check on me, he offers me only basic updates on Lito. "He's recovering," he answers whenever I ask. "But he'll have all the time he needs to do so, since we can count on you to be our Saito Ren."

Nightmares plague my sleep. Phantom pains scream in my missing arm and leg. But nothing is worse than when I catch a glimpse of myself in a window and see Saito Ren staring back at me.

I fear I'll go mad in the basement of the Spire. Or that I've already gone mad; the Aster cleaning my room seems familiar to me when he grins with his pointed teeth.

The first time I see him, I am with the nurses and say nothing. Later, I tell myself I merely imagined the similarities, that there is no way Castor could be on Cytherea. But I begin to see him more and more, cleaning the hallways, lurking in the background as the nurses work with me. Then a night comes when he arrives to clean my room and we are alone.

"Got a full pan of piss for you," I tell him, and he grins that Castor smile of his with the sharp canine teeth. The relief that I didn't imagine him is even greater than that of knowing Hemlock is keeping an eye on me.

But instead of answering me immediately, he starts mopping the room.

"Aren't you going to say something deep and foreboding?"

"Aren't you going to tell me to fuck off and that you don't want to hear from an Aster ever again?"

Castor has a point. Hemlock warned me to stay away from Icarii headquarters but failed to mention that being on Ceres at all would most likely get us killed by the Geans. Still, at this point, I'd have tea with my own father if it gave me someone to talk to.

"Let's skip past that," I say. "Time being precious and all."

"If anyone asks, I'll tell them you cussed me out until I cried." Castor smiles his toothy smile.

But he keeps cleaning. I suppose he has to in order for his cover as a janitor to hold up.

I clear my throat. "So say I want to listen to what Hemlock has to tell me. What exactly would that be?"

Castor pauses, pushing his goggles onto his forehead so I can see his golden eyes. "Well, if Hemlock were here, he'd say that, should you be willing to continue working with him, he would be glad to resume your partnership."

"And if I asked Hemlock why he would ever believe I'd trust him again, referring back to our previous argument that we skipped over?"

Finally Castor stops mopping. His hands tighten on the handle. "You should know from experience that the right hand doesn't always know what the left hand does, Hiro." Castor gives me a pointed look, and my heart aches for Lito. "I'll simply say this: you weren't the only one who got fucked by this deal."

"But between the two of us, I'm the one in the fucking hospital bed," I say before thinking, and all the anger that Ofiera and the drugs have been tamping down comes surging up, the dam broken and the flood roaring. "I'm not even *me* anymore. I lost my fucking arm and leg because they *cut them off*, my face is twisted into one I see in my nightmares of Ceres, and I'm in pain *all the time*, like I'm on fire from the inside out. Honestly, most days I'd rather be dead, so don't drag your sorry ass in here and tell me that you got fucked too."

"How surprising," Castor says sarcastically, rage thinly veiled. "You're mad because you're the victim of Icarii scalpels and tubes and drugs. We Asters would never understand that . . ."

I feel only the slightest twinge of shame when I remember the Asters who lie dying in the Under on Ceres.

But Castor goes on: "We've heard that the Icarii will be trading Saito Ren to the Geans in exchange for the high-ranking political prisoners they took on Ceres. Wherever you end up as Ren, I'll follow. If you want to work with Hemlock, all you have to do is find me."

"And what the fuck would Hemlock ask of me now?" The anger washes out, leaving only tears. "How much more can I give?"

"Whatever you're willing to," Castor answers softly. "But who do you hate more, Hiro—Hemlock, for siding with the Geans to help the Asters, or the Icarii, for doing *this* to you?" He gestures to all of me.

I don't look at myself, because I can't bear the sight.

When Castor leaves, I think about all that he said. But it's not even a question, and there is no debating what my heart tells me: this war *has* to stop.

Exactly four months after the event the Icarii call the Fall of Ceres, I am released from the Spire, packed onto an Icarii *Nyx*-class vessel, and brought to a place consecrated as neutral space for the exchange. I don't know where I—as Saito Ren—will be stationed, whether it will be Mars or Earth, but I do know Ofiera is meant to follow and rendezvous with me in secret. Unknown to her, Castor will be doing the same.

The trade is executed without trouble. It's not hard to act my part; I am exhausted and in pain from my prosthetics. When the Icarii prisoners are released from Gean custody, many burst into tears; walking away from the Icarii, I feel I could do the same. I am also relieved to be away from my captors—from Beron and, looming behind him, my father.

The Gean podship returns to the large cruiser, and Warlord Vaughn, an old man with wild white eyebrows and a powerful set to his shoulders despite his advanced age, greets me in the airlock. He pushes others aside just to clap me on the arm. "Good to have you home, soldier," he says.

I know from the file what Ren would say to this old man she saw as a father figure, but I am embarrassed when my voice wavers as I say it. "Thank you for coming for me, sir."

But Warlord Vaughn only rests his heavy hand on my forearm and nods, my emotional slip passed off as a soldier's relief. I have spent the last few months studying their customs and military culture. Memorizing their oaths and learning the intricacies of their strange religion. Even learning that, though Saito Ren has a mother and brother on Mars, she sees the military as her family first and foremost.

Later, as I settle into my assigned cabin, a uniformed Gean man brings me a tray of food. Warlord Vaughn enters on his heels, looking far more at ease than I saw him earlier. "I hope you don't mind if I join you."

I hoist myself into sitting position on the bed, and the Gean officer passes the tray into my flesh-and-blood hand. My prosthetic rests limply at my side, ignored. "Of course not, sir, but I can't say I have much of an appetite."

"I know from experience it will return with time." When he smiles, his eyes disappear into his wrinkles. It's hard to remember he isn't some kindly old man but one of two leaders of the Gean people—and a power-hungry warmonger at that.

I do as I did when I was upset as a child, eating a bit but mostly pushing the food around with my chopsticks. I wonder what the Warlord sees when he looks at me—a wounded soldier, a broken spirit, someone completely unfamiliar to him? I certainly hope it's not the latter.

"I've already decided that you will be given temporary leave for the next year in order to recover," the Warlord says. "But rest assured, you will always have a place among our ranks, Ren. You're far too clever for us to waste your mind on something trivial."

A whole *year*? "That's too much, sir—and I'm not just saying that because I want to get back to work."

He chuckles, his eyes crinkling at the corners.

"I mean it," I say. "I've already been practicing with the prosthetics—not much else to do where the Icarii were keeping me." To prove my point, I pick up the tray with my prosthetic. It's more difficult than I'd like to admit; I have to keep my eyes on my hand to know I've actually gripped the tray before lifting it from my lap. But when I look back at the Warlord, I see he's watching my face instead of my hand. "Please, sir."

"What would you have me do, Ren?" He calls me by Ren's given name, a sign of familiarity, and shakes his head like a disappointed grandfather. "You'll never pilot an Ironskin again, so you'll never command a unit either. And I'll never forgive myself if I throw you back into the water too quickly when you're so close to drowning."

I listen to him, my heart sinking. Certainly I wasn't turned into Saito Ren just to be retired and left to molder in a Martian settlement somewhere, only occasionally consulted for my cleverness.

The Warlord clasps his hands together in his lap. "So tell me, Hero of Ceres, what you think I should do."

The title sends a shiver through me. "Hero of Ceres?"

He lets out a little bark of laughter. "That's what they're calling you."

"The Hero of Ceres . . ." I shake my head in wonder.

And all at once, I have an idea.

"Let me return to Ceres, sir." I think of Castor's words and Hemlock's offer. There's nowhere else in Gean space that I have allies like I do on Ceres.

"Ren, I'm not sure—"

"If you'll allow me, sir?"

He doesn't seem to register that I cut him off. Instead, he nods for me to continue.

"I'm the Hero of Ceres, and Ceres is still very much in transition. If I am to rest and recover, let me do it there, where I can be a symbol of hope to our people. Even when things are hard, I can be an inspiration for them—at least until I'm recovered and ready for a new assignment."

"Hmmm." The Warlord doesn't look at me as he considers my words. Have I overstepped? Acted as Ren would not? Worry prickles in my gut until the Warlord speaks again. "We do have many of our top physicians on Ceres. And there are plenty of garrisons there to prevent any kind of local unrest. I'll allow it, but if I hear that you're not recovering as fast as I think you should be, I'll send for you to return to Mars."

I keep my face purposefully blank like a soldier should, despite the joy of victory I feel pulsing in my veins. "Yes, sir," I say.

The Warlord places his hands on his knees and pushes himself from his chair. "I'll tell the captain to set a course. Welcome back, Hero of Ceres."

I let the title buoy me along for the rest of the night. It is the closest I'll ever get to hearing my real name again.

I smile at the wordplay, and decide that I like it far more than I should. That is who I am, now that the Icarii have betrayed me: *Hiro of Ceres.*

Returning to Ceres is the easy part, but not two weeks after I get settled in I sense Ofiera through the implant. As soon as I arrived, I sent word to Hemlock through his network of Asters, and we immediately set to planning what to do with her.

By now, we are ready.

Though I've been placed in a ground-level apartment for my own comfort, I spend as much time in the historic district as I can without drawing suspicion. This is where Ofiera chooses to approach me one afternoon as I'm having tea. She sits at the table next to mine in the shop and strikes up a conversation by commenting on the ongoing repairs to Ceres.

I lean over in order to whisper to her. "Why don't you just stand up and scream, 'I'm a secret agent'?"

She straightens as if slapped, and the flush on her cheeks makes me truly laugh for the first time in months.

"Not here. Meet me at Mithridatism," I tell her before leaving the shop, my drink unfinished. A real shame, because their tea was delicious.

Predictably, she follows, making it too easy for Hemlock's men to surround her and take her hostage; she doesn't even put up a fight. At first it shocks me, then it worries me. In the Aster language, she speaks to her captors.

"Fuck" is all I can say when the Asters give her a pair of goggles and lead her into the basement to meet Hemlock.

I thought I'd never like Ofiera fon Bain, and I hate being wrong.

"Killing the Mother sounds like something that would benefit your peace," Hemlock says. In the basement of Mithridatism, I have to wear green goggles that have been attuned to the darkness so that I can see him and his surrounding junk. "So why the hesitation?"

"I'm not hesitating," I say, because I'm not. I don't hesitate, not when I've made up my mind. "I just don't see the point in killing one woman only to have another replace her. Who knows if she'll be just as bad, or even worse?" I scratch my thumbnail up and down the hilt of my mercurial blade. Ofiera brought it with her to Ceres in case I needed it, but so far I only use it to strengthen my body through practice. Unfortunately, the only person willing to practice with me is Castor.

"So kill the Mother and return to your Icarii," Hemlock says, shrugging a shoulder. "Or don't. Abandon the Icarii who have abandoned you and work toward your peace with me."

I'm certainly not going back to the Icarii when they turned me into *this*—trapped me in a body not my own, with a face I cannot look at without wanting to peel off my skin. When I was a child, I wanted to be anyone other than me. Once I finally began to love myself, they changed me into someone else. Ironic, really.

"My problems are not your problems, Hemlock," I tell him.

"But that doesn't mean our respective problems don't have a similar solution."

Ofiera shifts on the other side of the room, coming to sit with us in one of Hemlock's mismatched chairs. The little toy soldier put in her box for rainy days, brought out when someone wants to play with her. It's no wonder she shares a common goal with me. It's no wonder that, once she met Hemlock and they spent an afternoon touring the horrors of the Under, she agreed to work with us.

"The Icarii are right," Ofiera says. At first I didn't think we could trust her, but I can sense the truth of her intentions through the implant. And whatever Hemlock told her about her Aster lover, Sorrel, must have convinced her to march to Hemlock's tune. "Killing the Mother would destabilize Ceres. And while we don't know who will replace the Mother, it would be better if someone who supported peace were put in her place."

"What if," Hemlock says, "I present you with an opportunity to—oh, what is that old terrestrial expression—kill a large bird with a small stone?"

I snort but don't correct him.

"As the Hero of Ceres, you could request an excellent commission on a ship that used to belong to the Icarii."

I purse my lips. "And why would I do that?"

"After its capture, the *Juno* became the biggest ship in the Gean fleet, and one of the most prestigious, with its full assignment of Iron-skins and soldiers." Hemlock's eyes shine in the dark. "The *Juno* is now in charge of protecting the space around Ceres."

Ofiera presses a finger to her lips in thought, as if Hemlock is onto something. "It would be a good assignment to hear Gean military chatter."

"And," Hemlock adds—I fight my urge to groan, because he loves pausing and sounding overly dramatic—"I can tell you that one of the Mother's top candidates for First Sister of Ceres, a prime position to become the *next* Mother, is on the *Juno*."

"Another heinous child who lifts her skirts for power?"

"Just a girl." Hemlock's lips curve into what could be considered a smile, but he pointedly does not show his mangled teeth. "My contact aboard the *Juno* assures me that she already has the Mother's favor. All she needs now is a little push in order to be chosen as the First Sister of Ceres. With you there, you could influence her, or do away with her if necessary."

Ofiera shifts forward in her chair. "Do you think that we could convince her to support peace as an option, turn her to our side?"

"Not you, starchild," Hemlock says to Ofiera. "But a soldier worthy of a king's ransom from Warlord Vaughn himself, a woman who is to be rewarded by the military as the Hero of Ceres . . ." Both of them turn their eyes toward me.

I prickle at the gendered description of me, but I am Ren now. Thanks to Command, I don't have any other choice. I'm exactly what

Ren was—with long legs and dark hair and female presentation. くそ. "You think I should ask to become captain of the *Juno*?"

"And gain access to so much that would benefit us, yes." Hemlock's long fingers run across the back of my prosthetic hand. I don't feel it.

"It might not work out. She might not be chosen as First Sister of Ceres." I clench my flesh hand into a fist just to feel the pressure.

"This is undoubtedly true. But I have heard it said that the wise farmer sows many seeds," Hemlock says, and if he weren't my friend, I'd hit him for the stupid metaphor. "Besides, your being on the *Juno* would be a huge benefit in and of itself."

"All right, say I do become captain of the *Juno*. That's outside of my mission parameters because it doesn't bring me any closer to the Mother. And what's Ofiera going to do?" I can't keep the disbelief out of my tone. "She's supposed to make sure I kill the Mother at the Celebration, or before if I can. She can't follow me onto the *Juno*. So what happens when she goes back to the Icarii empty-handed? 'Whoops, I totally lost the deep-cover operative. Hiro's a wily one!' Can't say Beron will fall for it."

Ofiera and Hemlock smile at each other as if they know something I don't. "Leave that, my dear Hiro," Hemlock says, "to me."

The first time I see her, I'm standing in the docking bay, having just bid farewell to the retiring captain, Arturo Deluca. Those celebrating toast me with sparkling water far too bubbly for my taste, clap me on my flesh-and-blood shoulder, and avoid looking directly at my prosthetics. They're considered unsightly here among the Geans, these people who love everything natural—and suffer for it.

Except for her.

She is natural and . . . perfect.

Curves that rise and fall like a sigh. Hair like beams of sunlight made tangible. Even in that gray dress that makes most of the priestesses look flat and bland, she stands apart from everyone.

Her eyes are blue fire consuming everything in her path. Her face is that of a satisfied cat presenting me with a dead bird. All who step in her path are scorched by those brilliant wildfire eyes. And even as she realizes the truth—that she has been left behind—she holds her posture rigid as a warrior would, her gaze as sharp as steel.

It's the first time I think that maybe . . . maybe this plan of Hemlock's will work. There is something of a soldier in this girl, and if there's one thing a soldier wants, it's to finish their duty and go home. I can help her do that. I can help her find a better position on Ceres. And she can become the agent of peace we all need.

I cannot help but smirk at her as I approach and clear my throat.

"You must be the First Sister."

CHAPTER 26

Beginning in the new Age of the Horsehead under the guidance
of Mother Salome II, all Sisters assigned to combat zones are to be
trained in vital safety courses, including basic self-defense, essential weapons handling, abduction escape techniques, and war zone
emergency response. While we believe the Goddess watches over
the Sisterhood and know our soldiers will fight to protect every girl,
we also want to prevent tragedy when we can. After all, we never
want harm to come to our beloved Sisters.

Warlord Vaughn at the Ascension of
Mother Salome II, twenty-five years ago

Hiro val Akira . . .
It feels like a lifetime has passed, though it couldn't have
been more than a few minutes.

Still, a few minutes is all we have.

I have never heard the name Hiro val Akira before this. With as
little as I know of the Icarii, why would I have? *Foot soldiers are easily
forgotten.* How true Matron Thorne's words are. In no time at all, I
have forgotten pieces of Jones, the man who died to save me from
the invading quicksilver warriors aboard the *Juno*, who warned me

that Ren had changed after Ceres. His face is nothing but a blur in my mind now.

Those very quicksilver warriors stormed our ship looking for Ren. Now I know the truth of it: it wasn't just that Ren was a Gean captain; they knew who Ren really was, knew that Hiro was no longer following their mission, and wanted to eliminate her—them, I mean—before they did any damage posing as Ren.

Aunt Marshae was right. The Mother was right. Ren is a traitor to the Geans.

Because they aren't *Ren* at all.

"You lied to me." The words shock me even as I say them, but once they are out, I cannot stop the others that follow. "You *used* me."

"Little dove—"

"Do not *call* me that!" The rage pulses at my temples, sends me into a flurry of bitterness. "I am nothing to you!"

"That's not true—"

"You used me like"—I stumble over my words—"like I am some tool of your sick trade!"

"Maybe at first it was as simple as that, but then—"

"You are no different from Aunt Marshae! From the Mother!" I spiral like a dead leaf rotted from its branch, swirling down, down, down. "You are no better than the Sisterhood!"

Hiro stops as if slapped. Their face takes on that serious quality, their eyes dark as black holes. I recognize the look from when they cast the amber-eyed girl out of the *Juno*. *Do not fuck with Saito Ren.* How many other monstrous things did they do to get here?

"You want to play that game?" Their voice is soft and husky. A shudder runs down my spine, remembering that same tone while we were curled together in bed. "You were spying on me for the Sisterhood, something you neglected to mention at every turn."

My face heats, but I do not cry. I am proud of myself for that, at least. "It was an assignment. I wasn't fulfilling it."

"Still. I trusted you," Hiro says.

"Trusted I was a foolish girl, one easily manipulated thanks to her past in the Sisterhood."

Fuming, we both fall into silence. We have nothing more to say, no more accusations to fling. The thing in the room that is too big to name haunts the space between our bodies: everything changed when we fell in love.

I love you. I never want to leave you. The note in my pocket . . .

I wish I had known that throwing away your life for peace is so much harder when you are in love. The words Hiro said to me on the *Juno* before we left, perhaps the truest thing they've ever said.

"Hiro, we don't have time . . ." Lito trails off, looking toward the door. The Ironskins are on their way even now, and I am unsure if I want them to apprehend these criminals or not.

Peace. That mythical ideal. How could this moment lead to that?

"The Agora already confirmed you as the First Sister of Ceres," Hiro says, looking at the Mother, tied and slumped on the ground. "Blame her death on Ren, the Hero of Ceres, as an act of protest against war, against what the Mother stood for. I will play my part admirably. Demand peace. Then everything can change for the Geans, and maybe the Icarii too."

I tip my chin up. "And if I refuse?"

Hiro's face falls, lips curling downward, eyes shadowed. "I know," they say. "You're right. I've used you. Manipulated you. If I were you—" Their voice breaks, and they swallow hard before continuing. "If I were you, I would choose to leave me here just to spite me."

But even now, I don't want that. I have always wanted to leave the Sisterhood, wanted a home of my very own with someone I loved as much as I loved Ren. All those silly dreams of a house on Mars with a little garden and birds singing out front and Ren living with me are just that—something a child would believe in.

Saito Ren is dead. The person I love is an Icarii warrior dressed up in her skin.

But I have also been given a tremendous opportunity, if only I can ignore my wants for the greater good.

"I repeat, what will you do if I refuse?" I ask, because how am I to give my future to the Sisterhood when they have lied for so long, taking my voice and damning my mind to imagine falsehoods?

Hiro's eyes do not leave my face. "Second Sister."

All the air flees from my chest. Rage and jealousy take its place. Was Hiro grooming her the same way they groomed me?

A knock on the door makes me jolt in fear, but Ofiera opens it without a second thought, allowing in an Aster in wraps and—Goddess—Second Sister herself with her fiery red hair.

"We don't have much longer," the Aster says. "The Ironskins are finishing up at the bomb site, and infantry are already on their way here."

But I only have eyes for Second Sister, ignoring everyone from the captain I thought I knew to the Aster working alongside them. She has every right to fear and hate me, this girl who most likely reported on me to Aunt Marshae—yet in this moment, all I feel is guilt for my own actions. I was Ringer. I scared her. I hurt her. I threatened to throw her out the airlock like the amber-eyed girl. That was why I'd had bruises and nail-shaped scratches on my hands and wrists—attacks from her.

"I didn't know. I thought I was someone else—" It is so hard to explain. Tears well in my eyes. "I am *so* sorry—"

It is—

Second Sister starts signing but cuts off, realizing she has no need to sign here. Then she clears her throat and says in a voice shaky with disuse, "It is . . . what it is." She shakes her head as if fighting off the past, perhaps even struggling with her forgiveness. But that is okay. I do not deserve her forgiveness. "I thought that, when you spoke that night in the airlock bay, you were like me. That whatever they'd done to you as a child hadn't worked."

I remember the noises she'd made—they were noises after all—the sob as she watched the amber-eyed girl die, the protest when I, as Ringer, threatened her.

"The implant that takes away our words damaged me," I say, and the weight of that admission drags me down until my legs waver beneath me. "I saw someone who wasn't there. Acted as if I were some soldier . . ."

"I noticed strange things about you when I . . ." Now she flushes, speaking of her own behavior. "When I blackmailed you." She clears her throat, her voice growing steadier with its continued use. "But it wasn't until that night when you threatened to kill me that I realized something was very wrong. You spoke to me with a deep voice. You stared at me like you didn't know me. You . . . you spoke to yourself like you were of two minds." She wraps her arms around herself.

"I'm sorry—" I start again, but Second Sister cuts me off.

"I never thought I'd be standing here with you," she says. "After Paola was thrown from the *Juno*—the woman who used to be Second Sister—I didn't know what to do." A whole new wave of mourning crashes down on me now that I know the amber-eyed girl's name. If Second Sister was privy to that secret, how close were they?

She blinks her rising tears away, refusing to let them fall. "I begged her not to report on what she heard from the soldiers—I knew nothing good could come of it—but Paola refused to listen to me, told me she had to do what was right. Then Aunt Marshae discovered what she was doing and punished her for it." Her voice wavers, and my heart aches at the memory of us, standing side by side in the docking bay, watching as Paola threw her arms wide and fell through the hermium barrier. *Trapped*, she'd signed, a warning to all her fellow Sisters.

"I wish things could have gone differently for Paola," Hiro says so softly it takes me a moment to understand their words. I remember asking them why they'd punished the amber-eyed girl, remember the name they'd responded with in guilt: *Aunt Marshae*.

"I wanted to remain loyal to the Sisterhood, but after what Marshae did to Paola . . ." Second Sister shoots a furtive look at the Aster, the one called Hemlock, from Hiro's memories. "I knew what I had to do. I took up her work." She forces a watery smile, and in her eyes I see a love that transcends friendship. "It's what Paola would've wanted."

"But you . . . I couldn't trust you. I knew it would be me or you, and you were her favorite, her dedicated little pet—she already questioned my loyalty because of my closeness to Paola." She curls her hands into fists. "So I told Aunt Marshae about you, even if you would kill me for it." A flash of outrage rises within me, but I swallow it down. "I thought you were just like her—ruthless and cruel and manipulative. That was . . . wrong of me. I was wrong." Her strength wavers, and she drops her gaze to the floor. "I'm sorry."

It would be easy to let my anger consume me, to thrust her apology back in her face, to reject her even as I learn the truth about her. Why should I trust her when she has tricked me with her offer of friendship before? Let her go back to Aunt Marshae and rot in that woman's shadow.

But even as I think that, I know: this was the fault of Aunt Marshae; it wasn't Second Sister.

"We did what we had to in the Sisterhood," I say firmly. I hold my hand out to her, a peace offering. I am proud to see how steady the movement is when I feel anything but. "We don't have to act like that any longer."

She slips her hand into mine and holds it firmly. "No longer," she says, her expression bare. "My name is Eden. And yours?"

"I . . ." It is hard to admit I do not remember mine. Is it because of the brain damage from the neural implant? I simply shake my head. "I cannot recall," I say, and leave it at that before changing the subject.

Perhaps one day I will choose a name, but there are other, more important things to decide first. I gesture to the Mother, kneeling at our feet.

"What should we do?" I ask, but when I speak, my words are only for Second Sister. This is for *us* to decide.

"I want to change things," Eden says resolutely. "I want to stop the Sisterhood from doing this, make these . . . implants? Make them illegal."

I nod along with her. In a way, I do too.

But my dreams of a little home and a family?

That could never exist, a part of me whispers. My dreams were as real as my past—which is to say, not at all.

Can I be bigger than myself? Can I put away my dreams, become something greater than what I am for the good of everyone? Can I be someone who lives for peace?

I can. I can because there is something strong within me that has always been there, and perhaps I called it Ringer, but now I know it exists. Now I know I can change things.

"I am the First Sister of Ceres, so named by the Agora," I say, loud enough for all in the room to hear.

"Then that just leaves what we do with her," Hiro says, glancing at the Mother. The rest of us turn to consider her. Her eyes dart with fear for a moment, only to be replaced by fuming hatred.

I take a good, long look at the Mother. Her hair is a mess, face swollen with bruises and covered in sticky, half-dried blood. Hiro says something to Lito and pulls a Gean-reclaimed HEL gun, its fingerprint lock disabled, from the holster at their side. "Look away, little do—" They cut off, and I ignore the stutter my heart makes. They clear their throat. "Look away if you don't wish to see."

"Not yet," I say, and lean down so that I am face-to-face with the Mother. Our eyes burn with the same resentment as I pull the gag from her mouth. At first, she says nothing—and I feel a slight burning at the base of my spine—but then her eyes jump from me to Hiro's HEL gun.

"You can still remain loyal," she says softly, speaking to me despite looking at the soldiers amassed around her—all people who want to kill her. "Stop this traitor, and I will forgive you. No one will have to know what occurred in this room. You can keep your title of First

Sister of Ceres, and I will make you my second so that you may still become the Mother after me."

This is your last chance.

I ignore her offer, just as I did Aunt Marshae's, offended she would think me that weak.

Now that you've earned the right to your voice, she had said. Those words consume me.

"Why did you take our voices away?" I ask.

She jerks her gaze back to me. At first I don't think she'll answer. Then, after a huff: "The Canon states that a Sister should hold her tongue."

"But you know what it feels like, to be without a voice. Even you must have been a speechless Sister at one point. So why do to us what had been done to you? Why not change things?"

She straightens despite her position on the floor; in this moment, she speaks with all the authority of her office. "We silence the neophytes because, as a lowly Sister, you had nothing of worth to say," she says. "The Goddess chooses who is worthy, She deems who holds power in the Sisterhood." She looks me up and down, and I can see the scorn, the disappointment, burning in her gaze. "You want your voice? You have to *earn* it."

I stand, unable to help the overwhelming sense of rage that washes over me at her words. I am not sure what I expected when she sees nothing wrong with her rule. Apologies? Not from her. The entirety of my head begins to ache.

"Any last words?" Hiro asks. It is more than she deserves.

Stubborn until the end, she merely smirks up at us, lips pressed together tightly.

Something as sharp as a knife jabs into the back of my head. I feel the cage descending, and I realize all at once it is like when the Mother slipped her mind inside mine like a hand inside a puppet, controlled my body as she forced me to walk and sit. Controlled *me*, because she only knows how to control the Sisterhood, and Second Sister's implant is broken. But I shove her away in my mind with such a force that my vision blurs before me, and I fling my hands out to my sides.

"I am not yours!" I shout.

A fire flares inside me. The room spins and darkens.

A hole opens in the Mother's forehead. Blood runs down her face. Her body collapses to the ground. Her hair is stained red.

It takes me a moment to realize my arm is outstretched. The HEL gun is in my hand. I took it from Hiro. I shot the Mother.

I lower the weapon. My hand doesn't even shake.

Everyone looks at me—Hiro and Lito, Ofiera and Eden, even the silent Aster in his wraps—their eyes wide enough to drown in. Shocked, each of them. I don't know why they would be, after all I have done. After they found out who I really am.

Damaged.

I am Ringer. And so there is some part of me, even if it is broken, that is a soldier.

It is strange. I thought, when I could not talk, that I would never stop speaking if I had the chance. But now I can find no words that deserve to be said in the quiet of this room, blood and tea spilled across the cold marble floor.

"Leave," I tell the Icarii. "Leave Ceres, and never return. This place is mine now."

CHAPTER 27

Sometimes the greatest action a man can take in war is to refuse his orders and do nothing at all.

> *First Icarii president Pablo val Cárcel,*
> *address to the Venus Parliament*

———◇——◇◇——◇———

At our backs, the First Sister of Ceres bars the door to the Mother's quarters against entry. The scar on my shoulder won't stop throbbing.

"Dress quickly," Hemlock says, breaking his silence and shoving a set of Aster wraps into Hiro's arms. "We're out of time. The Ironskins will be here any second."

Hiro does as Hemlock says, dressing as we move, and Ofiera and I hastily put on our goggles and pull the wraps over our heads. But there's no helping the cuts in our robes over Ofiera's arm and my back, and with every piece of me exhausted and sore, I can only hope that no one will find our opaque skin and bloodied clothes suspicious.

Seeming to sense my fatigue, Hiro elbows me. "Ready?" they ask, and I catch their old smirk on Ren's face. I never imagined they'd be leaving Ceres with me, yet here we are together.

"With you, I am," I reply, letting their energy become mine.

"There are a few routes the Ironskins might use to secure the Mother's quarters," Hemlock says, stepping over the bodies of white guards, but instead of retracing our steps, we go the way Hiro must have come, through hallways of the dead and, once we exit the Mother's wing, into a stairwell. "There's one that we can use to avoid patrols."

"Still might need this," Ofiera says, and holds up Hiro's mercurial blade, unmistakable with its scratches and dings and pink nail polish.

"Hello, old friend," Hiro whispers, taking it into their white prosthetic hand.

Then the sound of boots comes from every direction—in the hallway behind us, on floors above us, and below us, as a unit marches up the stairs.

"Cower," Hemlock says as the Geans approach.

He curls into the corner of the stairwell with his head down, and we do the same. I make sure my back and the cut in my robes are pressed against the wall, and seconds later, Gean guards in navy and gold rush past with heavy Ironskins taking the stairs three at a time. I try not to see the black scraps of cloth tied to their armor, try not to imagine how outnumbered we are.

Then my shoulder screams like someone stabbed a hot blade through me.

"Agh—" I bite off the whimper, but it's too late.

One Ironskin stops. Hiro and Ofiera stiffen on either side of me.

The pain strikes me in waves, one right after the next. I tell my implant to be rid of it, but it's too much, too fast. My breathing quickens as I clutch my shoulder and press tightly on it—it feels like I'm bleeding—

The golden halo makes it so that the Ironskin doesn't need to turn its helmet in our direction in order to watch us. "You," it says, pointing at me. "What are you doing here?"

"Cleaning," Hemlock says.

"I didn't ask you." The Ironskin once more emphatically points directly at me. "What are you doing here?"

The words rush up my throat before I know what I'm saying. "*Rij zof toz siks*," I say, every single Aster word I know crammed into a nonsense sentence of *color furniture cup sapiens.*

The Ironskin doesn't even twitch. Time feels frozen. If this Gean knows Aster, we are dead.

"*Rij zof toz siks*," I repeat, trembling against the pain.

The Ironskin's accusing hand falls to its side. "Get out of here," it says, then continues up the stairs.

All of us release a heavy breath when it is out of range.

Hemlock stands before the rest of us. I stumble to my feet behind him, and Hiro catches me when my knees threaten to give out. I can feel the concern radiating off them despite the covering wraps and goggles, just like on Ceres a year ago when I reassured them my shield wasn't down. But we can't stop here; we don't have time to waste on my weakness.

I release my shoulder, force myself to ignore it. "Let's go," I urge them, but they follow me closely, not reassured in the least.

Hemlock leads us down the stairs, ornate wood giving way to rough concrete. We emerge in an underground service tunnel, though the cold does little to fight the fire of my scar.

I can immediately see why this isn't the way they would use to extract the Mother: a portion of the tunnel has collapsed, and water has pooled in spots, fetid and still. Damage left over from the Fall of Ceres.

"We can pass if we know how," Hemlock says, jogging the twenty meters to the rubble. Ofiera guides him carefully around the larger boulders, while Hiro stays with me, footsteps soft despite the pebbles littering the floor. "Castor appointed a crew weeks ago to clear portions of it. They should be waiting for us just over this."

One by one, we climb close to the ceiling over the debris, doing our best not to kick up dust in the cramped space. Hemlock slips through first, and Ofiera follows closely after. But as I work my way over the rubble, something rakes claws along the edge of my consciousness: Ofiera shouting through the implant.

I hurry through the thin opening and jump down, landing beside Hemlock and Ofiera on the other side. Hemlock lets out a pained sob, and I stop short, balanced on the balls of my feet. Standing over the bodies of three Asters is a newer-model Ironskin—thinner and faster and even more deadly. Trapping us between it and the way we came.

Its halo flickers as it assesses us, come to meet these rebellious Asters in a secret tunnel. Measuring Ofiera's lack of height for an Aster. Looking at the blood splattered on all of our robes. There is no question: We shouldn't be here. And that makes us enemies.

The Ironskin summons its electric whip. "You're not going anywhere," it says, voice box crackling.

My shoulder roars, waves of pain threatening to drown me, and then I am back in the park in Ceres a year ago, and I am looking at Saito Ren for the first time.

My body screams. Blood runs down my useless left arm. My heart races frantically. I gasp in breaths that feel too thin, *too thin*, and my implant is useless to fight it—

Kill them, kill them, kill them—

I can't move.

The Ironskin takes one step toward us, and Ofiera rushes alone to meet it. Hemlock withdraws a HEL gun from his robes. Such a temporary solution. If I can't fight, we'll all die—

—kill them kill them killthemkillthem KILL KILL KILL!

"Lito, I'm right here." Hiro's voice is a soft whisper beside me. When did they make it through the rubble? "Deep breaths." Their hand, so warm, touches my shoulder, grounds me. I need pain—I need to focus—the implant isn't working—why won't it take this all away—this fear—

It all collapses, one memory atop the other, this house of sand so precariously built, until I see the truth spread out before me. The darkness birthed something in me on Ceres, something that grew and grew until it didn't just taint my dreams, it walked with my legs, spoke with my lips. I caught glimpses of it here and there—fighting Talon, killing the Aster boy, during the bleed with Ofiera, dueling Castor—but now I realize I'm looking in a mirror.

It's me. The monster inside me is me.

My eyes burn. "Something is wrong with me," I say, and feel a snap within me.

I fall. Hiro kneels beside me, gripping me tightly. I fight to focus on them, their solidity, instead of the past dragging me down into a deep-blue sea of nothingness. The ocean's waves, what once brought me clarity, are no longer peaceful; they are raging.

"There's no shame in being afraid," Hiro says.

And in my futile struggle against the far stronger tide, I know this is what I needed to hear: there's no shame in *feeling*.

So I let it come. For the first time I stop fighting it, stop swimming, just let the waves batter me, let the current suck me down and the ocean crash above my head. Let the sea take me where it will.

And as I focus on my breathing . . . I find that the currents take me down to a place that is tranquil and soft. A place where I can look at my fear, my weakness, accept it as part of me, but also let it go. Because it is part of me, but I don't have to carry it with me all the time.

The past fades away. My heart slows. My breathing becomes even. And when the storm has passed, I can swim up, my head breaking through the waves, and leave the sea behind me.

"I'm out!" Hemlock shouts, his HEL gun faintly glowing. "Please do something now!"

Ofiera struggles against the much more powerful Ironskin, and without a partner, she is forced to think defensively, constantly wary of its whip. Though Hemlock's bullets have taxed the Ironskin's shield, nothing has penetrated, and Ofiera has yet to find room to attack. Soon she will tire, and that is when the Ironskin will strike—and kill.

Hiro squeezes my shoulder one last time and stands, face turned toward the Ironskin, ready to join Ofiera, but I grab their wrist.

"No," I say, and their face snaps back toward me, eyes wide in surprise. "Together."

Hiro doesn't hesitate. Just nods and helps me to my feet. "Together."

The two of us summon our mercurial blades.

We're with you, I send to Ofiera, and with one last jump over the Ironskin's whip, she retreats to join us.

Her arms tremble. Her breaths come quickly. The wound on her arm has reopened. But she reassures me through the implant as she comes to my side: *I'm with you too.*

"Thank you," I tell her and Hiro. I can feel them both through the implant, know that they understand this wordless thing I have faced. It is not defeated; it may never be. But for now, it is at rest, and that is enough.

"Let's fuck this guy a new face hole," Hiro says, pointing the tip of their blade at the Ironskin in a clear challenge.

"So crass," Ofiera mutters. Louder she asks, "Lito, care to lead?"

The Ironskin boosts toward us, and we jump aside or roll in different directions. Through our shared connection, I guide us to surround it, calculating the diameter of battle and finding that, no matter which way the Ironskin goes, we can pin it.

"Ofiera!" I push her through the implant, and she darts forward, all speed and icy rage, mercurial blade rebuffed by the Ironskin's shield again and again. It flings its whip after her, but Hiro comes at it from behind, parrying it, and it has no time to correct its course. Just as its shield flickers out, Hiro cuts through the Ironskin's elbow and the whip goes flying overhead.

Then I am shooting forward, the Ironskin swinging around to smash into Hiro, and my blade comes up toward its neck.

I have only one moment to hesitate, but I don't. I take the opening. I slice the Ironskin's head from its shoulders.

Its body crashes to the floor.

I look down at the pilot, not knowing a thing about them. A thought aches in my bones: *How many Saito Rens are we creating?*

It's Hemlock who finally breaks the silence. "I believe I'm taking a page from our dear Hiro's book when I say . . ." He uses shaking hands to point to the dark tunnel before us. "Let's get the fuck out of here."

Hiro barks a laugh, so free and familiar that my heart aches at their nearness. We press together, shoulder to shoulder, just as it always should have been.

AFTER WALKING THE two-kilometer tunnel, we enter a basement much like the first, take the stairs upward, and emerge in what had been a fresh garden restaurant but is now shuttered. We startle pigeons into flight as we crack open a door that had been nailed shut.

Outside, we find a frantic crowd. Many are still celebrating, unaware of what has occurred, while others are openly screeching, "Something is wrong! Something is wrong at the Temple!" I have never been happier to be ignored as we return to Mithridatism.

In the Under, Hemlock leads us three humans to a room with a handful of lanterns, making it much easier for us to see. His white hair is slipping through his wraps as he mock-bows to us and says, "You'll forgive me if I rest before setting up transport for you all."

"No," Hiro jokes, "get to work now."

"I believe this is the correct gesture to that," Hemlock says, placing his first two fingers in a V shape to his forehead in Icarii insult, and I flop down onto a cot, aching with laughter.

"Have you taught him anything that *isn't* awful?" I ask.

Hiro hefts a shoulder. "Nope."

We all laugh, giddy that we are alive. My face muscles ache from smiling.

"I need to take care of this," Ofiera says, motioning to the cut on her left arm, but I can sense her true intention from the other side of the implant: she wants to give Hiro and me some time alone. "Find me later so we can patch your back, Lito." I catch her smiling as she leaves the room, and I smile back.

Gratitude, I send through our connection.

When we are finally alone, just the two of us in a darkened room, I shift on the uncomfortably thin bed. "Remind you of anything?"

They snort and flop onto the cot beside me. "Academy, of course."

We look at each other in the candlelight. The silence is not un-comfortable. Hiro is the one who finally breaks it. "I know I'm not who you remember—"

"You are," I say.

"I'm not," they reply more insistently, their prosthetic hand clutch-ing the sheets tightly beneath them. "I know what shit you're going to say about me being the same on the inside, but even that's not fucking true, Lito. This past year . . . I wear more scars than just the ones you can see."

They close their eyes, and I do not fight them. Even if we are not bound by our implants, I can sense the shifts of their moods all the same.

"What you showed us in the Temple . . ."

Hiro meets my gaze with eyes that have not changed. Their eyes are all that remain of the old them. Of who they were. Sorrow ties my guts into knots knowing that Hiro never had a choice in what they became—trapped into presenting as female, their very limbs stolen from them. And it may as well have been my fault.

"Lito." Hiro's hand slips across the cot, takes mine into theirs. "I never meant to get you involved."

"So you said on the recordings. But Beron involved me anyway, and then I made my own choice."

"And what choice is that?" Hiro's expression is earnest in the candlelight.

"I'm supposed to kill you." I don't know how my voice is so steady when I am anything but.

"You could," they say, and do not pull away from me. "I know even if you want to help the Asters from inside the Icarii, you can't return without fulfilling *that* part of your mission."

I know it's all wishful thinking, even as I whisper, "Why can't we return together, report that we completed the mission, become partners again?"

"Lito . . ." A flicker of pain crosses their face before it is replaced with a resolved determination. "I am never going back. Not to the Icarii. Not to my father. Not to anyone who would use me like they did. They cut off my limbs. They changed me into our enemy. I don't even recognize myself in the mirror. I can't look at myself naked. I . . ."

They stop. Swallow hard. Clear their throat. My heart aches alongside theirs. "I won't go back to a people who will never accept me as I am. To a government that uses my body however it sees fit. To a society that experiments on people different from them without feeling a single stitch of guilt. How could you?"

I don't hesitate. "You're right. I'm not their soldier either," I say. "Not anymore. I made my choice before I ever left the Under. I'll fight for the Asters, *with* the Asters, however I can."

Hiro's voice is barely above a whisper. "And Luce?"

Though my heart bleeds at her name, I have faith in her. I believe she can make something of her life, even without me. "I think she'd be proud of me."

Hiro smiles in a way that lights up their eyes. "I know she would."

I push a lock of Hiro's black hair behind their ear so I can see their face. The new face that I fight to memorize as *theirs*.

"You should know Hemlock and I already have a plan as to where I'm going next," Hiro says.

"I'll come with you."

Even if Hiro sighs in what sounds like frustration, there is a relief to the set of their face, the slouch of their shoulders. "No," they say, "you can't."

My stomach tightens at the swift rejection. I shrug as if it doesn't hurt.

Hiro smirks like they know exactly what I'm feeling even without our implants connected; they probably do. "There's still more to be done, Lito. This is just the beginning. You walk your path, and I'll keep following mine. Ask Hemlock what you can do if you're willing to help."

"I have an idea," I say, and think of Ofiera and Sorrel. After two hundred years, it's past time someone put her first.

"You're really going to do this, Lito?" Hiro asks. In their sparkling eyes, I see a plan. I see resolve. I see rebellion like a coming storm. "There is no going back. You have to at least ask yourself what you'll be fighting for, no?"

I answer them with a mischievous smirk of my own. "For peace," I say, and I think of our words from long ago. *If we lose ourselves, we lose ourselves together.* "You make sure that I stay me."

Hiro moves forward and presses their forehead against mine. "And you make sure that I stay me."

I squeeze their hand. Even if our paths separate now, I have faith that peace will bring us back together in the end.

CHAPTER 28

I knew there was something wrong as soon as they opened the gates
and let us into the courtyard. It was just so quiet, when moments ago
everything had been shouting and laughter. We all stumbled over
each other as we moved forward, because we didn't look at where
we put our feet. We could only look at that body, hanging from the
balcony by her neck.

Anonymous witness at the Mother's Celebration

The sky is gray, programmed to make the entirety of Ceres as
somber as the Mother's funeral procession. She lies in a glass
coffin like a sleeping woman from myth, waiting for a true
love's kiss that will never come. She has been made beautiful again,
the blood washed from her golden hair, her skin patched in the places
that I destroyed. Her neck is covered by a high collar and a string of
pearls; I like to believe it is because, impossibly, they could not ade-
quately cover the rope burns on her skin.

It had been my idea, and Second Sister—Eden, I mean—helped me.
We hung her from the balcony, her body a banner to the rebellion
of Saito Ren. Afterward, we tore our dresses and slapped our cheeks
and banged our fists against the wall. It was so easy to shed tears in

that moment, when I had been fighting them since I left the *Juno*. The Ironskins came with Gean officers and found two women weeping without sound, nothing more than a set of victims who had witnessed the Mother's gruesome assassination.

Saito Ren, we confirmed when an Auntie had been sent for. *Yes, it was Saito Ren who did this. She left with two Icarii. She is a traitor.*

Ironic, really, that the Agora got me to testify against Saito Ren after all.

No words passed between Eden and me, but after years of shared silence, we needed no speech; we enjoyed what we did, the display we left over the Temple courtyard so that those who revered the Mother as an infallible incarnation of the Goddess could see her as the broken leader she truly was. Perhaps they did not yet know that fruit had rotted on the vine, but they will. We will see to it that the Sisterhood is pruned.

The Mother's body was sent to medical examiners who confirmed she had been beaten, shot, and hung from the neck. But I was surprised when the head doctor produced a small silver grain no bigger than a gnat and placed it into the palm of my hand. "Her neural implant," he said, as if I had not just learned of this thing's existence. Apparently it fell under the purview of the First Sister of Ceres to decide what to do with the thing. I put it in my pocket alongside the note I would never give to Ren. *I love you. I never want to leave you.*

All bad memories now. Things to be buried. Just like the Mother.

Eden and I walk before the waiting crowd at the Mother's designated grave site in the heart of a Ceres park. Aunt Marshae and another Sister stand beside the massive gravestone, more monument than marker. The Sister is short and slight, with choppy bangs and large doe eyes. She had been the Mother's second until the Geans took Ceres, then she spoke in favor of me. There is a story there, but I do not know it. The girl—for that's what she is—looks hardly more than a child, but already I see that Aunt Marshae leans close to her, whispering in her ear. Eden pinches my elbow, and I meet her gaze; they're plotting against us, I know.

Aunt Edith, the ancient head of the Order of Cassiopeia, shuffles to a waiting voice amplifier in front of a wreath of real flowers. Her steps are small and pained; she puts all her weight on a cane. She has been the head of the Order that leads the Sisterhood and trains Aunts for longer than I've been alive, and she's been one of the seven Aunts of the Agora since I was a child. Long has the Sisterhood waited for her to name a successor, and it is with a heart of stone that I watch her hold out a hand for someone to join her on the stage.

Aunt Marshae steps forward and takes Aunt Edith's hand. The buzzing in my ears turns into a torrential roar as she speaks. I hear nothing she says. But when she meets my eyes, I see the stark brutality lurking inside her.

Your success is my success, niece.

Does she know what I've done? Perhaps she even knows that the Mother died by my hand. But my becoming the First Sister of Ceres made her head of the Order of Cassiopeia, and she seems willing to let me have an inch of freedom so that she can take a mile.

I take Eden's hand in mine and squeeze as the funeral goes on. I feel her concern on the edge of my awareness, but I can do nothing to reassure her. I am afraid of what is to come when already Aunt Marshae has been two steps ahead of me at every turn. All I can do is hope the two of us are enough to work against her.

As the funeral comes to a close, I realize it is not Eden I want as solace. But the captain I thought I loved is long gone from Ceres now, and there is no comfort to be found elsewhere.

I VISIT AUNT Marshae in her new office in the Temple of Ceres. She admits me without even looking at me, just like she did on the *Juno*, then immediately dismisses the girl with the choppy bangs. "Wait outside, Lily," she says, and the girl leaves.

She has a name, this girl. And that means she can introduce herself; that means she can speak.

But now I can speak too.

"Her name is Lily," I say.

Aunt Marshae stops her work at my voice. She drops her pen to the desktop—real wood, now that she is someone—and looks up to meet my eyes. I feel that she is finally seeing me, *really* seeing me, for the first time.

"The Mother," I say, touching my throat.

"Of course," Aunt Marshae replies, then gestures to the chair that Lily just vacated. "Sit."

I don't. Instead, I take the small metallic grain of rice that came from the Mother's head and place it between us.

"I know," I say.

She doesn't have to ask what it is I know. *Everything* is the answer.

"And what do you intend to do about it?" Aunt Marshae asks, nails raking into the fine wooden grain, already ruining her expensive antique desk.

I do not show that I noticed her tell, the action that betrays her nervousness. Good. She should be nervous.

"I will put myself forward to the Agora to become the next Mother," I tell her. "Change is coming to the Sisterhood."

Her lips lift in a smirk as she clasps her hands together, her dagger-tipped fingers lacing together tightly until her knuckles are stark white. "You're right about that, niece."

I keep my face flat and expressionless.

"If there's one thing I've learned from my time with you," she says, "it's that there are not harsh enough measures in the Sisterhood."

I sneer at her. My time with Ren has left me brutally honest, and I let her see the hatred I hold for her. I remember the shiver of exaltation when I pulled the trigger and the Mother fell dead at my feet, but I push that thought away.

"Well, Auntie," I say, forcing a smile. I repeat the words we shared at each other's expense long ago on the *Juno*. "May you bloom in Her Garden as She commands."

The slight is a promise, just as Aunt Marshae said: *It's only forbidden if I say it's forbidden.* We will go to war with each other, and whoever falls will be forgotten, while whoever remains may interpret the Goddess's will.

I take the Mother's neural implant with me. Lest I ever forget what I did to get it.

CHAPTER 29

What is a soldier who does not follow orders? A deserter. A traitor. A rebel. A stain on society who will be hunted and killed.

High Commander Beron val Bellator of the Icarii Special Forces

"Lito." Ofiera's frantic energy snaps my attention away from the compad screen where a blank page waits, only the first line filled.

Dear Lucinia,

"What's wrong?" I ask. Her worry latches onto me, her fear becoming mine. Ever since leaving Ceres, she's been different. Almost like she lost something in the darkness of the Under. But I know that's not true; she's been raw as an exposed nerve since I proposed my plan to her.

"Beron's sent a reply. He wants to speak with us."

I push myself from my narrow bunk and tuck the compad beneath my arm. Nervousness chews at my edges. Time to perform like I've never performed before. Luce may be the creative one of us, but I can act when I need to. And right now, I need to with all of my power . . .

Because it's not just my life on the line.

I enter the command deck, Ofiera on my heels. "How do I—"

"Here." She points to a button to establish communication. "Due to our location, we'll be on a two-minute delay."

It's as live as we're going to get out here. I steel myself and push the button, and a moment later, a face appears on all command deck screens. It's not the face I'm expecting, and bile burns its way up my throat.

Souji val Akira.

Instantly Hiro's warning comes back to me: *He's not an enemy you want to make.*

Too late. He's my enemy now. Only . . . he can't know that yet.

"Lito sol Lucius. Ofiera fon Bain." Souji val Akira's voice is rhythmic and deep. It brings to mind ancient stone wells and cool, fresh water. "Your commander, Beron val Bellator, has reported on your mission to me."

The hair on the back of my neck stands up. Why is Beron reporting to him? *He acts like he hates politics, but he's got all of Cytherea's politicians in his pocket.* Because he's in control, of course, regardless of his title. He commands all of Cytherea. This is the proof of it staring me in the face. *He's so skilled at telling stories that no one but me, it seems, has realized that his entire life is a story.*

"I'd like to speak with you about the success and failure of that mission," he continues.

Success, in that we killed the Mother. *Failure*, in that we reported to Beron that Hiro val Akira was nowhere to be found during the Celebration. *They must have completely abandoned their mission and be hiding among the Geans*, we sent. A bold lie when the Geans are reporting it was Saito Ren who killed the Mother, but one we had to tell. What else were we to say—that Hiro was there and we let them walk away?

"I also want to personally extend my thanks to you both. While the Icarii people may never know what you have done for them, I do, and I honor you for it." I can't tell from Souji's expressionless face whether he is relieved that Hiro is still alive out there, or whether he's disappointed. Certainly a father only wants his wayward child to return to him, not to suffer the death of a traitor . . . but after hearing the story of Hiro's mother, Mariko, I can't be sure of that.

"As Beron has commanded, return to Cytherea as quickly as possible. I have come from Mercury to personally offer you commendation and a new mission regarding stolen goods from Val Akira Labs."

The message ends there. I clear my throat, look to the command deck screen as if I am meeting Souji's eyes, and prepare my response. Ofiera is all anxiety at my side, sharp as a mountain peak, but I cool myself and square my shoulders. *Let them see the Icarii warrior they want to see.*

"Souji val Akira, it is an honor to hear from you directly. As we told High Commander val Bellator, we did everything within our power to complete the mission as given to us by Command, but still, we regret the failure of being unable to find and assassinate the traitor Hiro val Akira." I believe I do a passable job of presenting myself as sorrowful, allowing my shoulders to dip and my expression to waver. "We are on our way back to Cytherea as I send this message."

The message completed, I send it back to Command. It will take two minutes for them to receive it, and then they must listen to it and create a response; once they send theirs, we'll receive it approximately two minutes later.

In the time that follows, Ofiera and I turn off the recording instruments and speak. "He wants to personally hear our report," she says.

"Don't worry. There's no way he knows what we're planning."

She chews on her lip, but says nothing.

"He can't know, Ofiera. No one will know until Mercury sends word that we've appeared in Spero. And by then—"

"By then we'll have Sorrel."

"We will." That's the mission: Report to Beron that we're returning to Cytherea. Instead go to Spero. Pull Sorrel out of cryo. Save him so that the Icarii can no longer use him to control Ofiera.

That's why she's been such a bundle of nerves: she's sorely afraid something will happen to the love of her life now that we're no longer walking the path they gave us. I understand how she feels; I have only a vague idea of what will happen to Lucinia once they realize I'm also a traitor.

We wait the rest of the time in silence, our anxiety mounting with each minute.

Finally, a light on the command console blinks, a sign that we've received a message. "Eleven minutes," Ofiera says. It's not just my imagination, then; it's a quick reply.

Souji val Akira greets us again, but this time Beron lurks in the background, his face pinched. I can read only anger from him—his usual emotion—but Souji is a puzzle. *A man in a mask.*

"Lito sol Lucius, keep your apologies," Souji says. "We have discovered an opportunity in the belt that will more than make up for your failure." My stomach churns at his words; I wonder what that opportunity is, whether it involves Dire and the Asters and their medicine, though I suspect we'll never find out, since we aren't actually returning to Cytherea.

"We'll speak more soon. Until then, know that I've kept watch over your sister. She recently accepted a job at Val Akira Labs." Souji smirks, and his smile is nothing like Hiro's. A chill runs down my spine. I think I see it, the monster that Hiro says lurks within their father. "She's a smart girl, Lito sol Lucius. I cannot wait for you to see what we have in store for her."

The message ends. Souji's smirking face is burned onto the backs of my eyelids, and I am shaking so hard, my legs threaten to give out from beneath me.

"Luce . . ."

Ofiera's hand tightens on my shoulder. "He won't hurt her," she says, but I don't believe her. Val Akira Labs leashed Ofiera for hundreds of years by keeping Sorrel in cryo; what will Souji do to Luce in order to control me?

I want to run home to my sister, just like I promised I would. But

I can't. While she's working for Val Akira Labs, she'll be under Souji's thumb, at his mercy, her every move watched.

She's a smart girl. In that, Souji is right. He doesn't even know how smart she is, and that underestimation will be his undoing. I hope, anyway.

When I close my eyes, I picture us in the park, sitting on our hill, eyes turned to the dome's repetitive clouds. My words come easily then, as they did every time we were together. In my imagination, Luce understands me, is even glad I've come to some sort of inner peace about my decision.

I grab the compad where the empty letter for Luce awaits. I type quickly.

Luce,

I'm sorry. I love you. I found our old friend the nine-tailed fox, and heard a thousand stories that are truer than myths. I don't know what they will tell you, so I want you to hear it from me: I chose this, because it is what I believe is right. I can no longer ignore what is happening every day in Cytherea and Spero, on the planets of Earth and Mars. Please be cautious in your new job for Val Akira Labs. Souji val Akira will do whatever he can to control you and, by extension, me. If you can, run. If you can't . . . or you don't want to . . . disavow me. Tell them everything you know, even show them this message if you have to. And be careful.

One day when there is peace, I hope our paths cross again.

All my love,
Lito

I release a breath that takes away the tightness in my chest. I send the message to Hemlock, who will be able to get it to Luce through his back channels.

When I step back to the command console, I am steady again. I am Lito sol Lucius. I am a duelist. A warrior.

And now, a rebel.

"Copy, Souji val Akira." I smile at the screen. Let him wonder what my look means. "I look forward to seeing you face-to-face. Lito sol Lucius, out."

I send the message and turn to Ofiera, not a shadow of doubt within me. I know this is my path; I know this is what I was meant to do.

We'll change everything, those of us who fight for what is right.

"Let's go save Sorrel."

PLAY:

▶ TO SOUJI VAL AKIRA

I s this fucking thing working? Castor, make this—

[Static ripples across the screen, followed by the image of Saito Ren's face wearing Hiro val Akira's trademark smirk.]

There we go.

[Hiro leans back in a chair as an Aster walks out of frame. They are wearing a tank top, and they purposefully place their prosthetic hand on the desk to be seen.]

Hello, Father. Long time no talk. I know how that brain of yours works, so you're probably wondering how I'm sending this to you. I'll save you some trouble: I'm somewhere outside of Icarii reach where the technology is utter shit. I mean, look at this recording. It was hard enough capturing my voice, much less this stunning visual.

But that's the thing I want you to see, Father. I want you to look at me as you listen to what I have to tell you. I want you to meet my eyes, see what you've made of my body, and face your choices. I wish I could do this in person, but hey, you know what they say, broken beggars can't be pick-and-choosers, am I right?

[Hiro clears their throat as their face falls. They run their flesh hand over the prosthetic.]

I know what you did to Mother. Something like what you did to me, right, making me disappear? Only she didn't live, while I'm still here, a thorn in your ass.

The Gean Mother is dead. I'm alive. And I'm coming for you, Father. That's what I want you to know.

I'm going to knock you right off your throne.

So take a good look. The next time you see me, you won't recognize me. I wonder what it's like not to recognize your own child. Perhaps you'll tell me, afterward.

I've made a lot of good friends out here, Father. Many who think the same way I do about you. And I plan on making many more. After all . . .

[Hiro's smile returns, and they lean close to the camera and wink.]

It's a big universe out there.

[End.]

ACKNOWLEDGMENTS

Some authors say their books are their babies, but this novel was more like a loud roommate who wouldn't shut up. Thanks to everyone who helped me get this out into the world so it can talk to other people.

Alexandra Machinist, agent of my dreams, I believe in myself because you believe in me. Every day I feel blessed to have you, Ruth Landry, and everyone at ICM Partners on my side. Mike Braff, I've always wanted an editor to give me an enthusiastic "Hell yes" to making my story even more queer. You, Kate Caudill, and the whole Skybound team have not only given my book a home but also made it better. Laura Cherkas, copy editor extraordinaire, you caught things I never thought about and made me sound smarter in the process. Sam Bradbury and the Hodder team, thanks for bringing my work to the UK.

Jeanne Cavelos, you're the Gandalf of my tale. I wouldn't be here without you spreading light into the dark spots of my writing and teaching me everything you know. My fellow Odyssey class of 2016, my Fellowship, I know I can always count on your bows, axes, and pens. Meagan Spooner, your elf eyes saw something in me that I couldn't see in myself; your words of encouragement found me exactly when I needed them. And my Tomatoes—Joshua Johnson, Rebecca Kuang, Farah Naz Rishi, Jeremy Sim, and Richard Errington—may not be able to carry my story, but they can carry me when I fall down.

Special thanks to all my beta and sensitivity readers, among them Enrique Esturillo Cano; Pablo Ramírez Moreta, PhD (who helped with my science); Mike and Lora Howard; Krista Merle Anderson; Dean Kelly; and Jamie Lee. Antoinette Castro, thank you for capturing me at my best in my author photo.

All my heart to my friends who have supported me along the very, very long path of publishing, especially the Cold Ones—Laura, Colleen, Nick, and Hillary; my mom and dad, even if you might not understand what's going on in my head; and my brother Connor, who should've been born the elder child. I know what love is because of all of you.

Finally, to Pablo Valcárcel Castro, my Ranger, my Dúnadan: Gracias, mi amor. This book, and my life, would be a pale shadow without you.

Turn the page for a sneak peek at
Book Two in The First Sister trilogy,

THE SECOND
REBEL

Coming soon from Skybound and Gallery Books!

It is with my abundant thanks that I receive your offer, Aunt Margaret. My affirmation on Olympus Mons cannot be postponed. However, if you are to oversee the Temple of Ceres and its Sisters, let me be clear: Because of the tragic passing of Mother Isabel III—may the Goddess welcome her into the Eternal Garden—no one has imparted the proper conduct to our dear First Sister of Ceres. She needs your guidance—your *stern* guidance, and a watchful eye.

Message excerpt from Aunt Marshae,
head of the Order of Cassiopeia

◇——◆◆——◇

G olden light falls through the greenhouse windows, tumbling through the leaves of tall trees and climbing ivy. Below, kneeling amidst the roots and stems, I am bathed in a calming green glow and wrapped in the loamy scent of wet earth. The morning broadcast, coming from a compad I left near the entrance, softly filters through the foliage and fills the air with swaying orchestral music. I am, in this place, in this moment, perfectly happy.

Of course, all things must end, and as the melody comes to a close, it is replaced by the dulcet tones of an Aunt. "Today, let us consider the Meditations," a woman I instantly recognize as Aunt Margaret says. The daily broadcast from Mars must be an old recording, since Aunt Margaret is here on Ceres. "Specifically, chapter 1, verse 12." She speaks clearly and with force for the recording; in person, she talks with a Gean clip, putting the onus of understanding squarely on the listener's shoulders. Still, she is a welcome change to Aunt

Marshae. By comparison to the Auntie in charge of me on the *Juno*, Aunt Margaret is as gentle as the Marian's Fire roses I tend, with their gentle yellow centers and orangey red exteriors.

The recording catches the sound of turning pages. Aunt Margaret must be preparing to read from the Canon, as opposed to quoting from memory. But I know Meditations 1:12 by heart, and while I used to solely consider the scriptures in my head, now, with my voice, I join in as she reads. "'Nature may be bent by mankind,'" I quote alongside Aunt Margaret, "'but never broken.'"

While Aunt Margaret closes the Canon with a thump and goes on to speak of tenacity and faith, the usual things associated with the verse, I continue to Meditations 1:13. "'What is plucked may yet bloom. What is burned may yet nourish. What lies fallow may yet grow.'" They are words that have come to mean much more to me on Ceres as the months have passed. As trials, one after the other, have set themselves before me.

This is what the people know: Four months ago, Mother Isabel III was slain by Saito Ren, the captain of the *Juno* gone rogue, in a protest of the Annexation of Ceres. This was a shock to everyone, but particularly the Sisterhood. Before her death, the Mother named me the First Sister of Ceres because of my valiant attempt to unmask the traitor Ren with help from Aunt Marshae.

Those are all lies from the Agora, the seven Aunts who lead the Sisterhood. This is the truth: The Sisterhood suspected something traitorous about Saito Ren from the beginning and hoped to embarrass Warlord Vaughn, who had traded highly valuable political prisoners to the Icarii for her release, by proving it. Aunt Marshae and the Mother assigned me to spy on Saito Ren, but I never gave them the information they wanted. Undeterred, Aunt Marshae lied to her superiors to make herself look good and made me desirable as a side effect. She was named Aunt Edith's replacement as the leader of the Order of Cassiopeia, and I became the First Sister of Ceres. She is, even now, I'm sure, working to undo my appointment as part of the Agora on Mars.

Perhaps the most startling facts are the ones that only I know. The person called Saito Ren was actually Hiro val Akira, an Icarii gene-assisted into Ren. They had come not only to assassinate Mother Isabel III, but to influence someone who might rise to the status of Mother who aimed for peace between the Icarii and Geans. Someone like me.

Only Hiro did not kill the Mother. They failed in that task. The Mother was murdered by my hand.

After she revealed the illegal usage of Icarii neural implants within the Sisterhood to take away our voices—well. To say I reacted poorly would be an understatement.

My hands slip from the soil to the pocket of my dress. I feel the outline of the ring box there, a shape and weight that brings instant relief. After the Mother's implant was turned over to me as First Sister of Ceres, I feared losing it, as small as it is, so I decided to keep it in something larger. But now I fear to leave the box anywhere, knowing that, even now, secrets are hard to keep.

The door to the greenhouse opens with a whoosh, releasing both pressure and heat. Whoever she is, as only Sisters are allowed here, she lets the stresses of the world in as well, and I am reminded of everything I must do. Everything I must be. She turns the compad's volume down until I can no longer hear the morning broadcast, but it is not until the visitor says my name that the tension releases from my shoulders.

"Astrid." My secret name. The name I have chosen, since I cannot remember the one I was born with.

"Good morning, Eden." The Second Sister of Ceres, who was also my Second on the *Juno*, moves until her shadow falls over me. At one time we were enemies, but fate—disguised as the actions of Hiro val Akira—brought us together. Then we realized who our real enemies were.

"It's afternoon, Astrid, not morning." When I look up at her, I see she's diplomatically keeping her face pleasantly blank. She is beautiful, my Second, as are most who advance in the Sisterhood, but her fiery red hair and emerald green eyes are particularly noteworthy on Ceres, where few look like her. "You're due at the dedication ceremony in less than an hour . . . and you're wrist-deep in dirt." Ah, *there's* the judgment in her tone I know so well.

I gently pat the earth over the newly planted rose seeds and clap my hands to rid them of excess soil. My fingernails are ragged though; there is no hiding that. Eden glares at my dirt-stained fingers and the dark half-moons beneath my nails. "I can wear gloves," I say with a shrug. Eden sighs, so I add, "Tending a garden is an important part of my worship."

"I've been meaning to talk to you," Eden begins, playing with a pair of gardening gloves I abandoned, "but it's hard to get you alone lately."

She has no idea. "About what? Caring for my hands?"

"No, no." Eden tosses the gloves aside. "About the communications tower. I want to earmark some funding for the tower so we can improve the transmission speed between Mars and Ceres." I keep quiet while I pretend to think about it. "Then perhaps you'd get your morning broadcasts in the morning instead of the afternoon."

I cannot help but laugh at that. I have lost track of time in the greenhouse, and the broadcast didn't help. "I'm sorry, Eden, but next month's budget has already been approved."

Eden jerks upright. "For what?"

I take in a deep breath before I speak again. "I promised Lily that she could build the shelter for Asters displaced during the Annexation of Ceres."

I expect Eden's scoff, so I am not hurt by it. "Her again."

I level a hard look at Eden. We have had this conversation many times, and I refuse to have it again. Aunt Marshae may have left for Mars to be trained and confirmed as Aunt Edith's replacement, but that does not mean she didn't leave eyes on Ceres. Keeping Lily happy with her pet projects ensures that, if she is reporting to Aunt Marshae, she will be more favorable toward me. Placating an asset is the first way of turning them. I learned that directly from Hiro.

"I should get ready," I tell Eden as I brush by her, not inviting her to follow but not barring her either. After a moment, she falls into step beside me, and we walk companionably out of the greenhouse situated in the inner courtyard and across what we have renamed the cloisters, filled with tilled rows of vegetables and skinny-trunked fruit trees. Eden plucks an apple, pink as her lips, as we pass through the miniature orchard and into the high-ceilinged stone hallways of the Temple of Ceres.

The Temple, once an Icarii courthouse, is the center of Gean worship on Ceres and the seat of my power. Perhaps that is why I feel kinship with it. Or perhaps it is that I aim to build myself in its image: to appear as one thing, but be another.

Eden takes a bite out of her apple, juice dripping down her chin, and tosses the rest to me with a playful smile.

THE PILOT WHO navigates our podcar through the streets of Ceres is unnecessary when the programming of the vehicle does all of the work, requiring him to simply watch the screens in silence, but we Geans adhere to one of the oldest Sisterhood laws: *May no machine be set above a human.* At least, openly we do. My right hand finds the cube shape in my pocket, and even through my gloves, the feeling of the box is pleasing.

Step by step, I work toward becoming the next Mother. Step by step, I will make these neural implants illegal. I will change the Sisterhood, and the Geans, for the better.

Already, I have left my mark. Ceres is much improved from when I took power four months ago. The streets are no longer rubble-strewn, the buildings no longer pockmarked from Gean bombs. Shelters have been opened for those displaced in the Annexation. Unemployment is lower than on both Earth and Mars; I wasted no time getting the people to work rebuilding their communities. And with Aunt Margaret assigned as my Auntie, she brought Sisters to the city and helped me start the Green Garden Initiative. Even now, passing through rows of commercial buildings, I see the fruits of our labors: metal trellises in strips of green, covered in reaching tomato and cucumber plants. The GGI works on multiple levels, but, at its most basic, it ensures that Ceres produces its own food and no one goes hungry.

The months have not been without troubles, of course. The destruction of the Icarii warship *Leander* had many on Ceres fearing life in the asteroid belt. But if the Gean military knows what happened to the ship, they have not felt the need to share it with the Sisterhood, and so I focused on increasing patrols around Ceres as opposed to panicking about the unknown *something* out there that destroyed the *Leander*. For all we know, it was an accident. Now, the *Leander* Incident is a memory.

Still, I believe my greatest achievement was my first. When I was the First Sister of the *Juno*, six Icarii quicksilver warriors boarded the ship looking for Saito Ren. After the battle was over and the Geans stood victorious, Ren decided to cage the warriors as opposed to killing them—the Warlord's preferred method for dealing with prisoners. But then the Mother was assassinated, and the six Icarii were forgotten.

Except I didn't forget. As soon as I had the power to do so, I released them with a podship and sent them back to the Icarii bearing a message of peace. With one gesture, I opened a dialogue of friendship between us, ending in the current ceasefire as our heads of state debate terms for a peace treaty.

Perhaps their release is the reason broken chains have become synonymous with my rule of Ceres. As our podcar slows to a halt at our destination, I spot the symbol woven throughout the gathered crowd on flags and handmade posters: two manacles connected by a circle of chains, broken. Snapped in two. Fragmented, and thus useless. A symbol of freedom.

The pilot gets out to open the door for us. In our brief moment alone, Eden nudges me and gestures to the banner hanging from a lamppost, the chains a dark gray against the white background. "I'm sure that'll thrill Aunt Margaret," she says wryly.

I have no chance to respond—that it is not Aunt Margaret I am worried about—before the pilot opens the door and the noise of the crowd assaults us. As I step out, the cheers turn wild. Packed shoulder to shoulder, the people are barely restrained behind stanchions and thick velvet ropes. It is only the presence of soldiers that keeps them in their place, though a select few residents reach across the line, hands desperately grasping for me as if power flows from a mere touch. I gesture at my bristling soldiers to leave them be.

Eden and I walk single file on the packed-earth path beneath a wrought-iron gate, away from the chaos of the crowd. Around us, the stretches of green hills are dotted with leafy chestnuts and almond trees, while the trail is lined with cypresses, offering both shade and shelter. Above, the projected sky is bright blue and calm, a perfect day to dedicate a new park.

Before I have even found peace in the nature surrounding us, we break from the tree line into a stretch of field where a wide stage has been set. More stanchions guarded by soldiers keep the attendees on one side, while Eden and I approach from the other. I can hear a ripple pass through the crowd as a few people spot us, but it is little more than low chatter from this distance. They are excited, and that is a good thing; it will not be hard to whip them into a frenzy.

It is at the back of the stage that Aunt Margaret waits for us. Now that Aunt Edith has retired, Aunt Margaret is the eldest member of the Agora. With her short gray hair like the coat of a sheep and wrinkled, rosy cheeks, it would be easy to think of her as a grand-mother figure and nothing more, but I know firsthand it would be foolish to mistake her old age for softness. She has ruled the Order of Pyxis for the past twenty years, like steel thorns beneath silken petals. The golden medallion she wears around her neck, one of only seven, is evidence of her office: she is a member of the Agora.

Aunt Margaret gestures for the soldiers to leave us alone. They back away, but not far enough for me to speak openly; while Aunt Margaret knows I have been released from the oppression of my neural implant, its very use in the Sisterhood is still a secret to most. "Did you see them waving that symbol of yours, shouting, 'Unchained! Unchained!' like a bunch of idiots?"

Eden's elbow digs into my side as if to say *I told you so.*

I lift my hands and flex my fingers. *I had nothing to do with that,* I sign. It is strange talking with the hand language of the Sisterhood now, but sometimes I must.

"Well, letting them get away with it isn't doing you any favors on Mars," she says.

I have heard what they whisper on Mars, that the symbol of the broken manacles is meant as a reprisal to the Order of Andromeda's chain-wrapped stone. Being that I am from that Order, it is almost as likely as the idea that freeing the quicksilver warriors gave me the symbol. But truthfully, though I do not know where the symbol came from, I like it, and so I cannot bring myself to do away with it.

What would you advise me to do? I ask instead.

"Bah," Aunt Margaret spits. "It doesn't matter now. After all this is over, we have more important things to focus on." She pats my arm with a soft smile, once more calling forth the image of a doting grandmother—or what I would imagine one were like, had I not been an orphan. "Afterward, we'll talk. All of us."

All of us, like her, Eden, and me? But no, as she steps toward the stairs leading onto the stage, I spot the small Sister lingering in her shadow.

I shoot a look at Lily—short, plain Lily, with her brown hair cut in a childish bob at her chin. Of all the people here, Lily is the *only* one who looks unhappy. Because Aunt Marshae is displeased, or because of the news Aunt Margaret wishes to share?

I do not have time to think about it. Aunt Margaret gestures for me to follow her up onto the stage. "Pull your head out of your ass, girl," she says before offering me an arm to take. Onstage, she'll affect an elderly shuffle, allowing me to brace her, to really pull at the crowd's heart. It is a song and dance we have done before, and one I am sure we will do again.

We have been planning this dedication ceremony for the past month, and today it comes to fruition. Everything goes smoothly, for once.

After Aunt Margaret says a few words and leads the crowd in prayer, we each take our place on either side of a silk-covered figure and grab hold of the golden ropes that hang beside the statue. Aunt Margaret nods at me, and we pull together without a word.

The sheet falls, revealing a statue with the likeness of our late Mother Isabel III. The crowd applauds politely, a few cheering in fervor for the Sisterhood.

And, with a beautiful smile on my face, I stare into the stone eyes of the woman I killed, knowing I would do it again if given half a chance.

BACK IN MY chambers at the Temple of Ceres, my ears ring with the thrum of the crowd, but better that than the overwhelming memories of the past. Though I have done my utmost to make the space mine, pulling down priceless icons and paintings and hanging plants in their place, this is the very room where the Mother greeted me four months ago and taught me that I could speak. The stark, hard leather chairs have been exchanged for comfortable divans and sprawling couches, but this was the sitting room where she forced her will upon mine and controlled my body.

The space does bring comfort at times, with its shelves of books in a variety of languages, its private bedroom with a spacious bed and bathroom with a sprawling tub, its office with its real wooden desk and glass doors that open onto the courtyard. But while the blood has been washed away, the memories remain.

Just there, I shot the Mother. Over there, Eden and I wrapped sheets around her neck to hang her body from the balcony. And there . . .

That is the place I stood as I discovered Ringer was not real.

There is no point in thinking about him, I chide myself. Hringar Grimson, the specter soldier, was created thanks to the neural damage from the Icarii implant the Sisterhood put inside my brain. But there is no need to consider his ghost, no need to ruin a good day such as this with thoughts of the harm done to me by the Agora.

I close my eyes and try to recall the overwhelming peace and happiness from the greenhouse this morning, but there is no chance of finding it when the day is far from over. Eden and I still have to meet with Aunt Margaret to hear whatever news she bears. My head begins to spin when Eden sits at my side and tosses something into my lap. When I look down, it is her bare feet on my skirt. She wiggles her toes. "Rub them," she says.

I snort a laugh. "Eden!"

"Pleeeeease."

Still, she has coaxed a smile from me. "Only if you rub mine."

"Deal," she says, gesturing for me to offer her my feet, "but I want you to rub my feet like you hate them."

The two of us are giggling when the knock on the door comes. We sober at once, and Eden jerks upright as Aunt Margaret enters escorted by Lily. Guards are stationed farther down the hallway, but none of them would dare stop an Auntie from going where she pleases. "Oh, stuff your formality," Aunt Margaret says. "Sit down and relax."

Still, when Eden settles at my side, she's much stiffer than before. I fight the urge to reach for the little box in my pocket, to rub it in my anxiousness. "Can I offer you something to drink?" I ask. "I can call for some tea or lemon water."

"Bah, at my age, if I drink anything, I'll have to piss two minutes later." Aunt Margaret sits on the sofa facing mine and Eden's.

Lily settles beside her, straightening her skirt over her legs with fingers covered in itchy-looking pale patches. When she sees me noticing the scalelike clusters, she shoves her hands beneath her thighs.

"Let's get to business," Aunt Margaret says, pulling my attention from Lily. "I've called you all together—First Sister, Second, and Third—because I have news about the future of Ceres."

I rarely think of Lily as the Third Sister of Ceres, though she is. "Go on, Aunt Margaret," I coax, as Lily turns her big doe eyes on me.

"The Agora has sent word that it will convene to consider the matter of choosing the next Mother." I lean forward, unable to help myself. "Which means, as one of the sitting members of the Agora and leader of the Order of Pyxis, I must go."

With the way Aunt Margaret's green eyes sparkle with a mischief that belongs to a woman half her age, I know she is not here merely to inform us that she is leaving Ceres. Anyone with sense can see that I aim to become the next Mother, and Aunt Margaret is a clever woman who has worked alongside me for the past four months.

"What advice would you give those who wish to put forward their name before the Agora for consideration?" I ask, keeping my tone light.

"Usually succession is a straightforward matter." Aunt Margaret adopts the same inflection, a teacher explaining to her students. "The Mother chooses her successor and trains her for a period of years. Her Second shadows her, gets to know the Agora, and learns how to rule. Of course, this time, with the tragic way Mother Isabel III passed, we have no successor."

"Things," Lily chimes in, her voice airy, "will not be straightforward this time."

Aunt Margaret continues as if Lily did not speak. "Now for the Agora to consider someone, their name will need to be brought forward by an Aunt."

Eden straightens until we sit shoulder to shoulder. Her warmth is a comfort to me. "*Any* Aunt, or an Aunt of the Agora?"

Aunt Margaret smiles as if pleased by the question. "Any Aunt may make a suggestion, but recommendation from an Aunt of the Agora will carry a certain weight to it."

"It makes them a stronger candidate," Lily says.

"Or a target," Eden whispers.

Lily turns her swallowing gaze to Eden. "Yes, there are rivalries among Aunts of the Agora. One Aunt's choice may automatically be dismissed by another, simply because of bad blood between them—"

"Politics," Eden scoffs, cutting her off.

"However," Lily continues, louder than before, "it still stands that a recommendation from an Aunt of the Agora draws attention, and one needs that to make a good impression. It requires at least four votes of yes from the Agora for a Sister to become the next Mother."

There is no chance that Aunt Marshae would ever recommend me for the position of Mother. Aunt Delilah, my Auntie from when I was a Little Sister, would not either. But if Aunt Margaret is taking the time to explain this to me, it must be for a reason.

I sit up straight, tilting my head to feign curiosity and smiling to encourage her to speak the truth. "Who do you favor for the position, Aunt Margaret?"

"That depends," Aunt Margaret says, "on what the candidate could offer me."

Ah, yes. *Politics.* I look between Aunt Margaret and Lily. Surely Aunt Margaret would not back her over someone like me when I both outrank her and have successes to my name. No, this is just a negotiation dressed up as a discussion.

"What is it that you want, Aunt Margaret?" My curiosity is gone; now there is only the shrewdness that she has perhaps come to associate with me.

Aunt Margaret chuckles. "I admire your tact even when there's no need for it. We stand at a river's edge, and the only way to cross is with each other. So let's be blunt." She points a withered finger at me. "You want to be the next Mother?"

I do not hesitate in my answer. "Yes."

She points at Eden. "And you?"

Eden looks between me and Aunt Margaret. There are things she could never tell—that she wishes to avenge Paola, the girl she loved on the *Juno*, and that she wants to make the neural implants illegal like I do—so instead, she focuses on what an Aunt would understand: power. "I want to be her Second." After a moment, she rephrases. "The Mother's Second."

"And Lily wants to be the First Sister of Ceres," Aunt Margaret says as she leans back into the sofa.

That is news to me. I do my best to keep the surprise from my face.

As if Lily is not sitting right beside her, Aunt Margaret goes on. "Lily was, at one time, Mother Isabel III's Second. It was Lily, through her outreach missions, who put the Mother into contact with the Asters of Ceres, and it was Lily who oversaw the negotiations that led to the Annexation."

Now I *know* my face betrays my surprise. I had heard rumors but had never given any heed to them. Lily is awkward at best, no grace to her at all; I could not imagine what the Mother saw in her. Knowing that it was not her, that it was what she offered, helps me to understand. "But she was not the Mother's Second when Isabel passed," I say.

"Suffice it to say they no longer saw things eye to eye after Ceres was annexed," Aunt Margaret surmises, but Lily clears her throat to get our collective attention.

"The Mother went back on her promises to the Asters," Lily explains. "It was a point of contention. And I was assigned to . . . other duties."

So goes absolute authority. Still, she could have supporters in the Agora who knew of her and would make her the Mother now. But, no . . . Aunt Margaret specifically said that Lily wants to be the First Sister of Ceres. Well, whatever her reason, I am fine with that.

"If I were the Mother, naming Lily the First Sister of Ceres would be easy to arrange." I let my gaze flow from Lily to Aunt Margaret. "But I have yet to hear what *you* want, Auntie."

Again, Aunt Margaret chuckles. "I've seen your work these past four months: The Green Garden Initiative. The Mother Isabel III Memorial Park. You think like one of the Order of Pyxis." I hold my tongue, knowing that she will go on, if only I am patient. "I want a guarantee that you will increase our budget. I want to bring the same hope to Mars that you have given to Ceres."

Eden stiffens at my side, but the request is a simple one for me. The Order of Pyxis, in charge of establishing gardens, farms, and parks, is one that I favor regardless of Aunt Margaret's influence. I know I cannot guarantee what Aunt Margaret will do with the budget increase right now, but with careful wording in the future as the Mother, I might.

"It will be done, Auntie," I say with a smile.

Like a businesswoman of old, Aunt Margaret holds out a hand. I take it, and, palm to palm like equals, we shake. "Pack your bags then, First Sister of Ceres. We're going to Mars."

ABOUT THE AUTHOR

LINDEN A. LEWIS is a queer writer and world wanderer currently living in Madrid with a couple of American cats who have little kitty passports. Tall and tattooed, and the author of *The First Sister*, Linden exists only because society has stopped burning witches.